"Born story-teller Ian Whates takes us on a gripping, terrifying trip-of-a-lifetime, through the heights and depths of the exotically grim city of Thaiburley, in this excellent fantasy thriller."
  Tanith Lee

"Adventures in a nightmare citadel – a story that hits the ground running and doesn't let up."
  Liz Williams

"Brilliantly inventive."
  SFX

"It is his characters who live through the story and make the reader need to know just how it's all going to pan out, human characters who may seem familiar but then there's that one thing, that shifted alteration that changes the world and changes the reader too."
  Michael Cobley

DREAMS & NIGHTMARE

ALSO BY IAN WHATES

The Gift of Joy
(stories)

IAN WHATES

City of Dreams & Nightmare

THE CITY OF A HUNDRED ROWS
VOL. I

ANGRY ROBOT

ANGRY ROBOT

A division of HarperCollins*Publishers*
77-85 Fulham Palace Road
London W6 8JB UK

www.angryrobotbooks.com
Going down

An Angry Robot paperback original 2010
1

A catalogue record for this book is available
from the British Library

ISBN-13: 978 0 00 734524 3

Set in Meridien by Argh! Nottingham

Printed and bound in Great Britain by
Clays Ltd, St Ives plc

To Helen.
For everything.

ONE

Only men of the right sort were eligible to join the Kite Guard. Only those with families of sufficient standing and the proper pedigree were even permitted to apply. Tylus qualified. Just.

From an early age his parents had groomed him for the part, sculpting his soul with philosophy, channelling his mind with geometry, anemonautics and alchemy, broadening his intellect with semantics and linguistics and honing his physique with fencing, swimming and pugilism. It seemed his whole life had been spent in preparation for the day he would apply to join the Kite Guard.

The day the Guard actually accepted him was the proudest of his parents' lives. At the lavish party to celebrate, his father, a functionary of minor significance within the mechanism of senior government, puffed and preened to such an extent that any there would have been forgiven for assuming that it was *he* who had achieved something commendable rather than his son. His mother became the focus of the local coffee circle for many months on the back of his success – no event was considered complete without her.

Yet in all the joy of that day and in all the years of toil and dedication that had led up to it, nobody ever stopped to ask Tylus whether this was what he wanted. Not even Tylus himself. Not until it was too late.

He wondered afterwards whether this played a part in the events of that night. Could it have been a simple, straightforward arrest had he been more diligent and more enthusiastic in his duties? Might all that was to follow have been avoided had he been the guard his parents always intended him to be?

These were questions that would haunt him often in the days that followed.

Tom was unnerved, far more so than he cared to admit. Not scared, no – he would never confess to that – just a little unsettled. No doubt this was due in part to being so close to his goal, a goal which, in his heart of hearts, he had never believed achievable. Yet as the Rows fell away one after another, and he climbed unseen into the city's highest reaches, where both custom and law forbade him to go, he began to hope and, eventually, to believe.

This was Thaiburley: the City of a Hundred Rows, known by many as the City of Dreams and by those who dwelt beneath it as the City of Nightmare.

Tom was born to the nightmare but now, for the first time in his young life, he had caught a glimpse of the dream.

Presently he was crouching in the shadows on yet another Row, willing himself invisible as he hid beneath a wrought iron staircase, his heart pounding and blood racing. He refused to dwell on where he was, on the impossibility of it all. If he did, he would likely lose his nerve altogether and bolt straight back down again.

His feet were sore from all the climbing, all the walking and occasionally running. It felt as if the sole of his
left shoe was wearing through again, but there was
nothing handy to patch it with and, besides, he had
lived with worse things. At least it wasn't as cold up
here as he had half-expected it might be.

The staircase that hid him rose from a broad, stone
walkway, walled on one side with the familiar yellow-
brown stone that predominated throughout the city.
The wall's surface contained an apparently endless row
of evenly spaced doors, all of them closed. He assumed
that behind these doors were quarters or dwellings of
some sort. The other side of the walkway stood open
to the outside world, with just a calf-high sculpted
guardrail separating passers-by from a headlong plunge
into a veritable abyss.

Having looked over that rail once, Tom had no intention of venturing anywhere near it again. This was
the other reason he was so unnerved; he had again
fallen victim to his insatiable curiosity and peered over
the edge, even when a tiny voice at the back of his
mind whispered that it would be a mistake to do so.
Below him, the walls of the city had dropped away,
dimly visible where torches and lanterns burned, before disappearing into the darkness completely. In their
place there was nothing: a vast, gaping space. Raised
in the crowded slums of the City Below, Tom had never
seen so much emptiness. It horrified him but at the
same time pulled at him. His head spun, he couldn't
breathe and felt himself breaking out in a sweat. For a
moment he had lost all sense of where he was, uncertain even of which direction was up or down.

This all occurred within a handful of seconds, though to Tom it seemed far longer before he was able to stagger back from the edge, wondering for a panicked heartbeat whether in doing so he was actually surrendering to the void, so uncertain was he of his own judgment. Then he felt the solid stone beneath his feet and perspective was restored, leaving him safe to scrabble to the nearby stairway and to haul his trembling body beneath it. There he was determined to remain, until his legs felt more stable and his heart ceased pounding quite so quickly.

Never having experienced anything like this before, Tom had no name for the awful sensation, though anyone who actually lived at these levels would have nodded knowingly and informed him that he had just suffered an attack of 'vertigo', before slapping him on the back with a jovial smile and telling him not to worry, that it would soon pass. Lacking such sage advice, Tom could only wait and hope that it would.

He knew that when he did move, he was going to hug the wall as closely as possible; anything to avoid approaching that drop again. The wind up here was ill-tempered and unpredictable. It huffed and puffed with erratic bluster, and he was afraid that going too far away from the wall would leave him vulnerable to a particularly strong gust picking him up and tipping him over the balustrade.

Slowly his thoughts cleared and his breathing returned to normal. His legs still felt as if somebody had used the bones as moulds, pouring jelly into them before removing the bone and leaving just the jelly behind, but he knew that time was pressing. Night was not about to linger for his sake; it had a nasty habit of turning into day when you least wanted it to, and he intended to be long gone before dawn arrived and Thaiburley started to stir. His legs would just have to cope.

The rest of the gang would be amazed when he returned and told them of his exploits, and none would dare call him a liar, not when Lyle was there to back him up. His status was assured. All of them would want to be seen with him, to associate with him, even Barton, who boasted so often and so loudly of his own exploits but who had never ventured beyond the Shopping Rows. Tom had left those behind long ago. Then there was Jezmina. How could she fail to be impressed when he returned a conquering hero from the furthest reaches of the City Above?

Of course, before he could do that, there was the small matter of completing this unlikely task, the task Lyle had set him, which he had accepted in a rush of blood, dazzled by the wide-eyed smile of a certain girl who'd been looking on. Yes, all he had to do was achieve the impossible and then retrace his steps – all of them, without being caught, through a city that would be stirring with the onset of morning.

That was all.

He was feeling progressively better and knew that it was time to move on, though he wished he'd kept a better check on the Rows. The truth was that Tom had no idea precisely how high he had come, how much further remained to go.

At first he'd kept count, reciting the lines of the levels-verse which every citizen, Below or Above, learnt almost as soon as they could speak, but there were so many of them; and so many other things to worry about as well: not being seen, for example. Despite his determination not to, Tom had quickly lost count. He knew this must be somewhere close to the top, but had no idea how close.

The first lines of the nursery rhyme ran through his mind again.

From the Streets Below to the Market Row,
From taverns and stalls to the Shopping Halls…

The early stanzas were easy enough: they dealt with the known world, the Rows near to home, the ones that were permitted and accessible. But the higher he went, the more difficult it became to remember the right sequence as he ventured into areas of the city he had never imagined visiting in his wildest dreams.

From trinkets so cheap to exclusive boutique…

It was no good; he might as well face the fact. His memory of the verse faltered and everything became a muddle long before he reached this far in the rhyme's verbal record of Thaiburley's bewildering Rows.

His musings were interrupted as two figures emerged from one of the many doors along the walkway. Two men, chatting amiably. They wore the deep blue tunics of higher arkademics. Tom felt a surge of triumph and relief. Higher arkademics were to be found in the residences – he remembered that much – which meant there were only the Tiers of the Masters between him and his goal, the Upper Heights, the very crown of the city – the roof of the world.

Where the Demons lived.

The arkademics strolled towards him: two tall, fit men, looking far healthier than any who were to be found in the City Below, even Lyle, who was one of the best-fed people Tom knew. He tried to hunker down a little lower and thought invisible thoughts, willing them not to see him.

As they drew nearer, he became conscious of their words, and also of how loud his own breathing sounded. He did his best to take shallower, quieter breaths.

"I would never allow something like that, surely you must realise as much." The man currently talking was the older of the two and spoke earnestly, as if it were vitally important that his companion should believe him.

The other, who was nearest the edge and so furthest away from Tom, walked with his head bowed, as if his thoughts weighed heavily.

"Magnus, you know I want to believe you, but Syrena says that…"

The older man made a disdainful noise and stopped walking. "And you would truly take her side against *me*?"

The younger man also stopped and the two faced each other. They were now just a few paces away from Tom, who remained statue-still, hardly daring to breathe. In his mind he kept repeating his own private litany: *you can't see me, you can't see me, I'm invisible, there's nobody here, nobody here*, over and over, desperate to stay hidden.

The younger man's face was clearly illuminated by the lanterns lining the walls as he looked up. Strong, handsome features dominated by piercing eyes. It was the eyes that concerned Tom. If he were to glance beyond his friend's shoulder and slightly to the left, the man would be looking straight at Tom's hiding place. Fortunately, his eyes never wavered from the other man, the man he had addressed as Magnus.

"There's no question of taking sides, but even you have to admit that her arguments *are* compelling. It's because I respect you so much that I've agreed to this meeting at such a late hour, so that we can talk frankly, away from curious ears. I'm not accusing you, Magnus, I'm simply asking for an explanation. Don't I deserve at least that much?"

The older man sighed dramatically, and rested a hand on the other's shoulder. "Thomas, Thomas..."

The boy froze in his hiding place, thinking himself undone, believing that he had somehow been discovered by some arcane, sorcerous means, but the man continued talking and it was clear that the words were not directed at him but at the other, younger arkademic. The boy remembered to breathe and stared at the pair with renewed interest. Here was another Thomas. If they shared a name, what else might they have in common?

"Have things between us really come to this?" the older man continued.

"That rather depends on what you have to tell me." There was steel in the young arkademic's voice; a determination not to be fobbed off.

Without warning, everything changed. One second the two figures were involved in apparently relaxed conversation; the next, Magnus was anything but relaxed, moving so rapidly that at first Tom wasn't sure of what he was seeing. He had to replay the sequence in his mind to be certain. Yes, there could be no doubt; the older man had drawn a knife from his belt and plunged it into his companion's chest in one fluid, serpent-swift motion.

The other Thomas staggered backwards – three faltering steps that brought him closer to the edge, almost against the balustrade. He stared down at the blade that still protruded from his torso, as if unable to comprehend what was happening. His hands clasped weakly and ineffectually at the knife's handle.

Then his gaze rose from the weapon to the face of its wielder. "Why, Magnus? Why?"

Magnus had followed his victim's stuttering retreat, stepping forward like some stalking predator as the other moved back. When he spoke, it was in the same measured tones he had used throughout, his voice betraying no hint of regret.

"Questions, Thomas. You always did have too many questions."

With that he lifted both his hands, again in a rapid, assured movement, and pushed the other firmly in the chest, sending Thomas staggering backwards, so that he teetered on the very edge. Just a low stone barrier stood between the wounded man and that long, fatal drop. For an instant he hung there and the watching boy hoped irrationally that he was not about to fall after all, but then the man's body seemed to sag, his legs buckled and he toppled over, vanishing into the night without another sound.

Tom could picture that fall all too easily: the long plummet past Row after Row, past terraces and balconies and stretches of featureless city wall – the city that he had spent the best part of the night climbing through – with the murdered man's body gaining speed the whole way, until eventually it struck ground. The Market Row, Thaiburley's ground floor, had long since spread beyond the walls and any faller from this height stood a good chance of killing someone or destroying a hut or other structure with the force of its impact. Such things were not unknown. Sky-bounty the lower citizens called the fallen dead. Whatever remained of the body would be picked at and fought over, at first for whatever might be valuable – a shattered limb or surviving organ could raise a good price, as could the ring on a soon-severed finger, a finely wrought knife still in its scabbard, a piece of quality silk or linen clean enough to merit salvaging and reusing. Then, once the human scavengers had claimed their prizes, the dogs and rats, the heart beetles and the spill dragons would move in to feed on what remained; those scraps that had been overlooked or had simply not been worth carting off to the dog master or any of the other darker practitioners who paid well for fresh human meat.

All of this flashed through Tom's mind in an instant, while his eyes were fixed on the back of the murderer, Magnus. His hand unconsciously reached for the dagger concealed within his clothing. He clutched the hilt so tightly that it dug into his palm.

Bizarrely, what he had just witnessed chilled Tom to the core. Not because he was a stranger to either violence or death – he had seen plenty of both in his time – but because it was so unexpected here, in one of the highest Rows of the city. In the ghettos Below, fighting, intimidation and murder were a way of life, but things should be different here. People were supposed to aspire to greater things. To have witnessed such an act of ruthless treachery in such an elevated Row disturbed him more than anything he had ever encountered before.

Suddenly, the arkademic's head came up and his back stiffened, as if disturbed by an unexpected sound, though Tom's ears reported nothing beyond the gusting of the wind and he was certain that he hadn't moved or made a noise himself. Yet even as he watched, Magnus turned around and looked directly towards him. Dark, piercing eyes that stripped away any hope of anonymity.

How? Tom knew he'd remained silent. He started his litany again, furiously repeating the lines, but it was too late, Magnus was already striding towards him.

"Come out!" The words rang through the night in that same calm voice the man had used throughout.

Tom had heard about arkademics and the powers at their command. He very much doubted either his knife or the phial of treasured demon dust that Lyle had given him would be of much use now. The dust was the only other item he carried that could be considered a weapon, but the fine, glittering powder was intended for a very specific purpose and Tom had no idea what effect it was likely to have on a man, if any. So he resorted to the only other choice left open to him.

He ran.

But he was not quite quick enough.

The arkademic moved with deceptive speed and even as Tom bolted from his hiding place Magnus was there, lunging for him. Tom felt his arm gripped. He jerked it away, but the man hung on, grasping his shirt. Tom pulled and the arkademic clung. Something had to give. Fortunately, it was his shirt. The sleeve tore away and Tom was free. All thoughts of tiredness, of aching feet and jellied legs were forgotten, as he sprinted for all he was worth, racing for the stairs that had brought him to this Row.

The back of his neck tingled and shivers spread down his spine. He drove his legs harder, expecting with every step to be struck down by a knife or something worse. If he could just make it to the stairs. Surely they weren't far.

"Stop!"

The single word rang through the air with the clarity of a bell. Spoken, not shouted, yet the force of it struck home like a dart. The voice was one that expected to be obeyed, that would not be denied.

Incredibly, Tom felt his legs faltering and he started to slow, to stutter towards a halt. Panic welled up inside him. He still wanted to run and was just as desperate to get away, but try as he might, his body refused to respond.

He knew that if he stopped, he would die. This realisation became the focus of his thoughts, the centre of his rebellion against the compulsion of that awful, irresistible voice.

Tom had to resist, somehow. He concentrated on his legs, demanding that they move faster, and they finally started to react, sluggishly at first, as if struggling to run through water, but he never quite came to a halt and after a few desperately difficult steps he was gaining a little speed and then a bit more, until suddenly he could move freely again, the voice's power evidently broken.

The stairs were before him. He threw himself at them, leaping the first section in a single, flailing bound. This stairway was not made of iron like the one he had crouched beneath but of solid, unyielding stone, carved from the same stuff as the city itself. His momentum carried him recklessly forward. Legs pumping furiously to keep him upright, to prevent him from falling, he tore down the stairs. He almost over-balanced again and again, but somehow managed to keep everything together until he reached the bottom. The steps passed in a blur and the next Row seemed to rush towards him. His feet met the level ground with jarring force. Three punishing strides later his legs finally buckled and he slammed painfully to the floor, barely raising his arms in time to protect his face. He skidded, rolled, grazing the skin from his knees and forearm, but still managed to scramble to his feet and run on, refusing to acknowledge the bumps, the bruises, the nagging ache in his left knee. He couldn't afford to feel them. Not until he was safe.

A gaping archway opened to his right and he considered diving through it, to lose himself within the inner city, but quickly rejected the idea. He was a long way from anywhere he knew and trying to hide nearby would probably be exactly what his pursuer wanted. The arkademic was bound to have some knowledge of the area, far more than Tom at any rate. To linger here would be stupid. Tom had made his ascent by clinging to the city's skin, by walking the terraces and corridors built in and around its outer walls and going up any available stairway that promised to take him to the next Row. Instinct told him to use the same approach now, that this would be the quickest way of escaping to the safety of his own levels – the familiar warrens of the City Below.

He risked a glance over his shoulder and saw no signs of anyone chasing him but refused to relax. This still felt like enemy territory and he had no idea what other powers the arkademic might possess, so he kept running for all he was worth.

Another flight of steps led to another Row. He ran through an enclosed corridor here, one built on the inside of the city walls rather than on its outer surface. This environment was a far more familiar one than the high terraces above. Narrow windows to his left looked out upon darkness. The noise of the wind had abruptly cut off as he entered the corridor and every pounding footfall sounded intrusively loud to his own ears as his feet slapped the stone floor in the enclosed tube of space. Surely anyone asleep behind the locked doors would be woken by such a cacophony and so mark his passing.

Instinctively he slowed a little, treading more lightly. He was breathing hard, the energy that fear had lent his body fast evaporating. The night's exertions were catching up with him and he began to feel his aching knee, the raw sting of his grazed forearm and the tiredness of protesting muscles.

Tom knew that he was far from safe, but the absence of any obvious pursuit robbed the threat of its immediacy. By the time he finished the descent to the next Row his lungs were fit to burst and all the aches and pains of his exertions and the earlier fall were catching up with him. He slowed to a brisk walk, needing to catch his breath. This Row boasted another terrace, which heralded the return of a wind that seemed to have gained in strength, buffeting him with renewed ferocity as he stepped out into the open once more.

The wall here was interrupted by a series of arched openings, each of which led through to a small chamber, with no other entrance or window. On the way up he had snatched a brief moment to explore one of them, discovering a featureless room, devoid of any furniture or decoration. Now, on his return, on edge as he was, he found the darkened openings unsettling – a row of enormous mouths gaping wide as if to swallow him as he passed.

His breathing became less ragged as his body absorbed much-needed oxygen and he felt able to break into a jog again, anxious to be past these ominous archways. So intent was he on the openings that it took him a while to register the new arrival. In the distance there was a figure walking with measured steps but coming closer with each one. Instantly Tom feared the worst, suspecting this could only be the arkademic Magnus or one of his agents.

Then he spotted the stairwell to the next floor. It lay between him and the stranger. Tom broke into a sprint once more, desperate to make the stairs ahead of whoever the newcomer might be.

The figure quickened pace. Dark clothes, but that could mean anything.

"Hey, you, lad, stop where you are!"

The voice carried a familiar air of assumed authority but lacked the command that Magnus had possessed and Tom knew the tone well: a razzer – one of the City Watch. Razzer or Magnus, it was all the same to him; he had no wish to be caught by either. Head down, he ran for all he was worth. The razzer started to run as well, but Tom made it to the stairs well ahead of him and charged down, laughing.

Razzers he was used to. They lacked the dark, sinister menace of murderous arkademics. Running from them, outwitting them, was something he had been doing all his life. He reached the next Row with the other nowhere in sight.

The floor of this terrace was inlaid with mosaic tiles, depicting a series of regally arranged profiles, predominantly those of men. Tom remembered them from the upward journey, when he had wondered precisely whose face he was in the process of walking over.

Some of the fear started to leave him. He was almost enjoying himself now, relieved to be dealing with the familiar. Until, that is, he caught movement in the corner of his eye – a large form swooping past the balcony to his left, beyond the city's walls. At first he thought it an enormous bird or, more terrifying, one of the fabled demons descending from the city's Upper Heights.

But then he saw that it was, in fact, a man.

The razzer sailed towards the terrace, arms outstretched, cloak spread between his four limbs, catching the wind and gliding smoothly towards a landing ahead of Tom, blocking his way to the next set of stairs.

A kitecape; Tom stood and gawped, having heard of such a thing but never imagining he would ever actually see one.

For a precious second he could do little more than stare, seduced by the sheer majesty of this man so at home in the air. He came to his senses as the seriousness of the situation sank in. He looked around frantically, assessing his options: flee back the way he had come and hope he didn't run straight into Magnus, try to keep going towards the lower levels he knew – which meant somehow getting past the razzer – or risk leaving the walls entirely to take his chances in the unknown jungle of the city's innards.

None of them sounded appealing, but he had to choose quickly and act decisively or all would be lost and the razzer would have him. The razzer, clearly one of the famed Kite Guards, was almost at the balcony. He swooped in, tilting his body upward, closing his arms slightly and lifting his legs, causing himself to virtually stall in mid-air, preparatory to landing.

Tom knew that the decision could not wait, had already been delayed overlong, but he couldn't help himself – he had to watch. Suddenly the Kite Guard seemed far more of a threat than the razzers he was used to, too formidable to try and slip past. It was going to have to be the inner city.

Yet at the very instant he reached that unpalatable conclusion, the guard faltered and appeared to lose control. One second the dark form was moving with graceful precision, the next he was floundering. It was as if the capricious wind had chosen to desert him at the last moment, leaving his cloak suddenly limp and useless. The arms which seconds before had been outstretched, supporting him so majestically, now reached in desperation for the balustrade.

He almost made it too, but not quite. With a startled yelp, the razzer dropped from sight.

Hardly daring to believe his luck, Tom rushed to the edge to stare down, completely forgetting his earlier fear of the drop. He watched the unfortunate guard tumble away, staying until the figure was swallowed by the darkness. The sense of disorientation threatened to return once he stopped focusing on the falling man, so he moved away hastily but couldn't resist a grin of mingled relief and joy.

He trotted on towards the next flight of stairs, growing in confidence all the while. There was no one else in sight; still no sign of pursuit from Magnus and nobody other than him to have witnessed the guard's fall. He wondered how long it would be before the man was missed and his smile broadened as he pictured the other razzers trying to work out what had happened to their colleague.

As Tom continued, he became increasingly aware of a sound; a bass thrumming that spoke of industry, a noise that seemed to surround him, reverberating, as if transmitted not only through the air but through the very stone of the city itself.

To his right, a gap opened in the solid expanse of wall. Not an archway such as had peppered the stonework in the floor above, but a dark, oblong, passageway. It reminded him of the alleys and runs that criss-crossed the City Below.

The sound grew ever louder, and a flickering glow of light fell wanly from the mouth of the passageway. He came to a halt, curious but wary, wanting to look into the opening but a little afraid to do so. Had it been this noisy on the way up? Had this light been so apparent? Surely not, or he would have remembered. He glanced quickly around, concerned that he might have somehow come a different way, but reassured himself that it would have been all but impossible to do so.

Finally he drew in a deep breath and peered around the corner. There was disappointingly little to see. The passageway took a left turn after a short distance and he found himself staring at a blank wall which pulsed with reflected shadow and light. It was a pulse that suggested the pumping of blood, like the steady beat of a gigantic heart. He realised for the first time that there was subtle variation to the sound as well, an almost imperceptible rhythm that seemed in synch with the ebb and flow of light washing along the wall.

Tom knew he ought to ignore this, intriguing though it was, and continue on his way, but curiosity got the better of him and, without even consciously deciding to, he slipped into the passage. With every step the air grew warmer and the sound grew louder. He became convinced that he was moving towards some sort of harnessed fire. Mixed in with the deep rumble that had first caught his attention, another sound became apparent: a rattling sigh, as if some giant were restless in his sleep.

Having taken a sharp turn to the left, the passage then executed another dog-leg, this time to the right. Tom followed, to find himself standing at the edge of a vast room. Ahead of him, dominating the whole space, was a machine, an engine of incredible size and complexity. A mass of pipes and wires, cylinders and tubes erupted from its surface. Yet was it truly a machine? For the thing seemed almost alive. Between the myriad metallic paraphernalia membranes could be seen, flexible, near-translucent sheets which resembled living skin. The whole suggested to Tom the internal organ of some impossibly huge beast, encased in pistons and tubes.

The thing was in perpetual motion, rattling and humming, never still for a second, and then, with a repeat of the great sighing sound he had heard from the passageway, it contracted; a slow implosion that produced a blast of heat and light and sound as it shrank to a fraction of its former size. Almost immediately the contraption expanded again, the membranes that held it together glowing as if from some internal fire.

Tom could only stare at this latest wonder of the City Above, overawed both by the nature and the size of the apparition. He was standing in some sort of viewing gallery, with the mouth of the passage behind him. The machine, if such it truly was, rested on a floor that was perhaps two Rows beneath him, with the chamber extending a similar distance above. When fully contracted, the thing sank until its crown was a little lower than Tom's line of sight. As a result, he was able to glimpse the tangled mess of components that formed the apparition's top, only to see that mass rise upward and the sides roll towards him as the thing expanded once more. A single huge pipe of grey metal extended from the very centre of the engine, which is what he assumed he was watching, before disappearing into the ceiling above. He couldn't decide whether this pipe moved up and down as the thing expanded and contracted, or whether it remained fixed and the moving mass slid up and down the pipe.

Whatever the truth, something about what he was watching – this strange composite of machine and the organic – struck Tom as inherently wrong, almost obscene. He shivered, despite the heat.

The engine was so overwhelming, so impossible to ignore that at first Tom had eyes only for this remarkable object and was oblivious to all else. It took him a while to realise that the chamber housing the thing was not entirely deserted.

Looking up at him from the floor and to his left was the most bizarre creature Tom had ever seen. Naked to the waist, the figure was clearly humanoid and bulged with muscles, its skin glistening with perspiration. There were two things that made this figure so remarkable. Although dwarfed by the mechanism he was evidently tending, the creature was obviously huge; Tom reckoned him to be at least twice the height of a full-grown man.

Then there was the creature's head: completely bald, with the face dominated by a single Cyclopean eye. The eye was opaque, a uniform milky white. The creature was evidently blind, yet its head had tilted upward and seemed to be staring directly at Tom.

Tom instinctively drew back and in doing so, remembered himself, remembered that he had just witnessed a murder and should be fleeing as swiftly as possible back to the streets he knew.

He had already dallied too long. Cursing his curiosity and hoping that the delay would not prove costly, he ran through the tunnel's twists and out into the open air once more. The comparative cold of the exposed night came as welcome relief after the claustrophobic heat of the engine chamber. He breathed deeply, glad to be away from the unfathomable machine and its unsettling attendant.

After a quick glance around to confirm that the terrace was still empty, he set off again. Yet he remained preoccupied, part of his mind lingering in that vast chamber with its bizarre occupants – the like of which he hoped never to see again.

Tom was distracted by his own thoughts and failed to notice the shadow that passed over him from behind. He was taken completely by surprise when something struck him in the centre of the back. It hit with enough force to wind him and he instantly lost his footing and went sprawling to the ground. A little dazed, he sat up; tasting blood, knowing that he must have bitten his lip, and wincing at the sharp, burning pain between his shoulder blades. He looked around to see what had floored him.

The figure of a razzer, the same razzer, loomed large, puncheon in hand. That must have been what hit him – the puncheon. No wonder he had been bowled over. He glowered at the evil club, which looked so innocent now that it was safely retracted into its housing.

"What? How?" Tom began, staring at the guard whom he had seen tumbling towards what seemed inevitable death mere moments before.

"I'm a Kite Guard, kid," the man said, almost growling the words. "You didn't seriously think you were going to get rid of me that easily, did you?"

The guard reached down, grasped a handful of shirt and hauled Tom to his feet.

"Now, what's a grubber like you doing up here in the Heights? No good, I'll warrant."

Tom almost blurted out that he was currently running for his life and that he had witnessed a murder only a short while ago but a lifetime of guarding his words stopped him. The chain of thought that came chasing after this instinctive reticence reaffirmed the decision. He suddenly saw the future had he spoken. His presence gave Magnus the perfect get-out. The man would be a fool not to pin the murder on Tom, who was in a place where no street-nick had a right to be and so obviously up to no good. It would be his word against that of a senior arkademic. Who was going to believe a lowly street-nick from the City Below in circumstances like that?

No one; that was who.

He had even run from a Kite Guard when challenged: proof positive of his guilt, if any more were
needed.

The guard still held Tom by his shirt and he now
lifted him off his feet, so that the two were staring eyeball to eyeball, with Tom's toes dangling just above the
floor. The man's eyes simmered with rage and Tom
wondered exactly who he was angry with – himself for
losing control of his cape and falling so embarrassingly,
or the lad who had caused him to fly in the first place.

"Well?"

The man did not really seem to expect a response
and certainly didn't wait for one, setting Tom down
and frog-marching him along the terrace, keeping a
firm grip on his collar from behind.

Tom wasn't scared of the guard. The worst the guard
could do was beat him and he had survived beatings
from men a lot tougher than this. It was what would
likely come after that concerned him. Once banged up
he would be at the mercy of the system and those
within it; senior arkademics, for example. Tom knew
that if he wanted to survive beyond this night, escape
was not simply an option, it was a necessity.

Despite his angry words the guard was surprisingly
casual in the way he handled Tom, not even bothering
to search him for weapons yet. None of the razzers
Tom was used to would have made such a basic mistake when rousting a street-nick. The kids on this Row
must all be soft, he concluded.

Tom knew that the guard's relaxed attitude offered
him a chance, perhaps his only chance. As the man
urged him forward, he let his feet drag and then
pretended to stumble.

"Hey, watch it!" The razzer's grip slipped a little but didn't let go, his determination not to do so causing him to stumble into a hurried series of shortened, pigeon-like steps as he almost tripped over his charge.

Tom used this apparent mishap to mask the movement of a hand which darted into his clothing and emerged with the dagger. Quickly then, he twisted around, slashing with the blade. Slight resistance as it ripped through the guard's cape and a deal more as it cut into the man's arm.

With a yelp of mingled surprise and pain the razzer let go. Tom was free and instantly running. Yet he had barely begun to gather speed before he heard the familiar snick that warned of a puncheon being fired. His would-be captor had reacted far more quickly than expected.

Tom tried to dodge, veering to the left, but too late.

The missile slammed into him, instantly knocking him off balance. He was falling. Only then did he realise that his attempt to dodge had carried him nearer the edge and it was towards the edge that he now fell. He tried to stop, to twist, to hold himself, but momentum carried him on. His leg struck the balustrade and, before he could do anything, he was over.

"Help me!" he screamed into the wind as the city's wall gathered pace and started to speed past. He clung on to the hope that the Kite Guard would react instantly and swoop to his rescue.

Then he remembered the knife in his hand as it slashed through the razzer's cloak before biting into his arm, and it suddenly dawned on him that with his cape torn the Kite Guard could no longer fly. Ice cold fear gripped his innards, as he realised that however hard he screamed, there was nobody left to save him.

TWO

As Tylus watched the street-nick disappear into the darkness, the small form tumbling as it fell, all the doubts that had plagued him throughout his brief career came flooding back. He felt sick and he felt angry. For several minutes, until long after the boy had vanished from sight, he simply stood and stared, replaying events in his mind's eye and wondering whether there was anything he might have done differently.

The truth was, Tylus considered himself to be something of a fraud. He didn't really think that he was cut out to be a Kite Guard – a fact he would never have admitted to anyone, least of all to his parents. Yet Sergeant Goss knew. Somehow, the duty sergeant saw right through him and recognised exactly how useless he was, even when everyone else appeared to be taken in.

Quiet rage continued to simmer, fuelled by the futility of it all; an inchoate anger, directed at anyone and everyone. He found himself resenting the boy for throwing away his young life so fruitlessly, while at the same time berating himself for not being quicker and preventing the lad's fall; then there was the ever-hated Sergeant Goss, who had assigned him to night patrol yet again. He even spared a little anger for the gods, who had seen fit to put him in this particular spot at this particular time, and for the citizens of these Rows, whose need for protection required him to be here in the first place, while still more ire was flung impotently at the Swarbs – those dour denizens of a lower level who had witnessed his embarrassing loss of control over the kitecape and had even come close to catching him in their cursed nets. Being returned for a reward would have ensured the scorn of his colleagues in the department forever after, and the reaction of his parents did not bear thinking about. Their humiliation would naturally have been transferred to his own shoulders, becoming one more burden for him to carry on their behalf. Thank goodness he'd regained command of the cape at the last instant and avoided the Swarbs' nets.

Then his anger turned full circle and came back to the boy once more, for slashing said cape, which would doubtless earn him a dressing-down from a superior who needed little excuse to do so.

His arm started to throb, where the lad's knife had cut him; the pain making itself known as the rush of adrenaline deserted his veins. Tylus reached into his cape and pulled out a patch, slapping it onto the troubled arm. The flesh-coloured symbiote instantly spread, covering and sealing the wound.

He made a half-hearted effort to wipe away the blood that had run down his arm and hand, but knew it would have to wait until he returned to the station to be dealt with properly.

Already the anaesthetic qualities of the patch's secretions were calming the wound and dulling the pain.

He trudged up the flight of steps that led back to his patrol area, debating whether or not to cut this duty short and head for the station immediately to report the incident, but he decided against the idea, remembering the last time he had done so without an actual prisoner to take in. He had been bawled out by Sergeant Goss and told that in future, anything short of an actual invasion or the city burning down could wait until the end of shift before being reported.

It seemed only a handful of minutes later that he heard footsteps hurrying towards him.

"Tylus, wait," called a breathless voice.

Turning, he saw another uniformed figure striding purposefully his way and recognised Paulos, a colleague and almost-friend. It was clear that the man had been running, and Paulos would never have contemplated such undignified haste unless something important was up.

"Goss wants to see you, right away."

"What is it," Tylus wondered, "invasion or fire?"

"What?"

"Doesn't matter."

At some point during the brisk walk that followed, the patch must have withered and dropped off, its work done, because by the time they reached the station, Tylus's arm was marred only by a ridge of pink and puckered skin, a seam of newly-healed flesh that itched insufferably. He rubbed at it in distracted fashion while sitting outside the sergeant's office waiting to be summoned. He glanced across at the solemn, dark framed portrait that dominated the opposite wall: Commander Raymond, inventor of the kitecape and founder of the Kite Guard. Tylus considered how much simpler his life could have been had the man never been born.

Paulos had given little away during the walk back, either unwilling or unable to explain why Goss wanted to see him so urgently.

Not that Tylus had to wait long to find out.

"What happened to your cape, officer?" the eagle-eyed Goss asked the instant the young Kite Guard stepped into the room.

Tylus took a deep breath in preparation for a lengthy explanation.

"Well?" Goss snapped before he had a chance to speak.

Flustered, he blurted out quickly instead, "A knife, sir; while apprehending a suspect. I'll hand it in for repair and get a replacement soonest, sir."

"That you will. But the replacement will be a *plain* cape." Goss must have seen the dismay on Tylus's face. In effect, this meant the young Kite Guard was grounded. "Kitecapes don't grow on trees, you know. You can claim yours back once it has been repaired and fully renewed." A process that would take weeks. "Until then: a plain cloak. Perhaps this will teach you to take better care of your equipment in future. Though I doubt it."

"Sir!" The prospect of patrolling without his cape filled Tylus with dread. A Kite Guard without his cape was a walking statement that the officer had fallen short in some regard and was out of favour with his commander. Like some wounded predator, a hawk with a broken wing, such a figure was robbed of all mystique and authority; those who had formerly respected him and perhaps even feared him a little no longer had cause to do so. He could already picture the smirks and knowing looks that would accompany his next patrol. The children would be the worst. Their disrespect would be more open – pointing fingers and laughter. 'Kitties'; that was what they called a grounded Kite Guard.

This struck him as an ignominious and heavy-handed punishment for a cape that had, after all, been torn in the line of duty, but Goss was within his rights and there was nothing Tylus could do about it.

"Now, this suspect," the sergeant continued, "where is he, then?"

"Fell from the wall, sir. In the struggle."

The sergeant sat back, jaw locked and eyes burning. "So, to summarise, your night's exertions have resulted in no suspect, and a torn kitecape. Is that correct?"

"Yes, sir!" Tylus could feel his cheeks colouring from a combination of embarrassment and suppressed anger.

For long seconds Goss simply shook his head, as if in disbelief, while Tylus did his best to remain still and not to squirm. Then the sergeant sat forward again.

"I don't know what to do with you, Tylus, really I don't. Fortunately, it seems that such responsibility may soon be taken out of my hands. You're to report to Senior Arkademic Magnus in his chambers; immediately."

Tylus was astonished and for a second wondered if he'd misheard. He knew of Magnus of course, everyone did, but he never expected to actually meet the man. Why would such an elevated individual want to see him?

"Me, sir?"

"That's what I said, isn't it? Do you see anyone else here I could be addressing?"

"No, sir."

"Apparently your infamy is spreading, even to the rarefied levels of the higher arkademics. Even there they have noted your unique qualities, the way you stand out in such singular fashion."

The sergeant's sarcasm and insincere tone washed over the young Kite Guard. Behind his own blank expression he was trying to make sense of this latest development and completely failing to do so.

"I am informed there was a murder earlier tonight," Goss continued. "Up in the Residences. Fortunately, the act was witnessed – by Senior Arkademic Magnus himself as it happens. Do you have any idea who the perpetrator was?"

"No, sir," Tylus replied, although he was beginning to have a horrible suspicion.

"A street-nick; a piece of scum risen from the City Below. Can you imagine that – a kid from the sewers daring to venture as far as these Rows? But of course you can; how silly of me. After all, you caught just such a lad earlier tonight, didn't you, *and then you let him go!*"

Goss shot to his feet, slamming palms onto the desktop and bellowing these last words. He leaned forward, straining towards Tylus as if it were all he could do not to leap over the furniture and assault the younger officer.

For his part, Tylus stared straight ahead, wishing he were somewhere else, determined not to focus on the contorted face that was so close to his own. He could feel the man's breath against his cheek and smell the unmistakeable tang of strong liquor that accompanied it. One more revelation in what was turning out to be an eventful night: he had no idea that Goss drank, especially not while on duty.

After long seconds the face withdrew and Goss sat down again, composing himself with exaggerated care.

"Should I arrange an escort, perhaps?" There was a swagger to the man's voice and in the way his head bobbed from side to side. "Or can you find your own way to the appropriate address?"

"I can find my way, sir!"

"Then what are you still standing there for?!"

Tylus retreated from the office as rapidly as he could, his thoughts in turmoil. A few of his fellow officers were already at their desks in preparation for the day shift. None of them would meet his eye; all suddenly found urgent things to do, such as paperwork which clearly required their undivided attention.

With a sigh, Tylus set out to find the dwelling of Senior Arkademic Magnus. Every step seemed a weighty one, as if it carried him a little closer to his doom.

Though it suffered from the low ceilings that were all but inevitable in Thaiburley, irrespective of status, there was no denying the impressive nature of the high arkademic's home.

False half-columns emerged from the stonework either side of a recessed wooden door, as if the city's walls were somehow birthing them, thrusting the columns out into the world, but the process had frozen part-way. The door itself was embellished with ornate brass fittings and studwork – testament of the occupier's wealth if not his taste. Tylus tugged twice on the ostentatious bell pull and stepped back. The servant who answered had about him an unassuming air yet still made the Kite Guard feel uneasy, though he couldn't explain precisely why. The man was certainly polite enough. Something in the eyes, possibly: too sharp, too knowing; as if their owner saw things and knew things that passed his betters by.

The servant led Tylus through a broad and dimly-lit corridor. Illumination came courtesy of a brace of electric wall-lights, dimmed to modest output – an economy the Kite Guard noted and approved of. Providing power to such a vast metropolis was a constant headache, electricity a privilege enjoyed by comparatively few. He was glad to find one of those few not being profligate with such a precious resource.

The corridor led to another wooden door – polished this time and lacking any superfluous brass adornments. The servant held the door open and ushered the visitor within, closing it once Tylus had entered without himself following.

Instantly, Tylus was aware of a sharp rise in temperature. He stood just within the threshold and gazed upon a room dominated by books. He had never seen so many books. The far wall was entirely hidden behind row upon row of cloth and leather spines, arranged upon uniform dark wooden shelving that stretched across its full length. More such were evident to his right. Yet the young officer's attention was drawn reluctantly from the wall of books by the fire that burned contentedly in the hearth to his left.

A real fire, which doubtless explained the heat. He could already feel the tickle of sweat forming on his scalp and wished the servant had thought to take his cape before showing him into the room. Homes built close to the city walls were often blessed with fires and chimneys and were much coveted as a result, but this dwelling was some way from the walls and Tylus wondered where the apparent chimney led to. Did it stretch straight up through the Rows above this to the upper Heights? Did some convoluted system of pipes and brickwork carry the smoke to the walls and the open sky beyond? Or were the fire's fumes disposed of in some arcane fashion known only to higher arkademics?

"Kite Guard Tylus, I presume."

The moderately spoken words made Tylus jump. So absorbed had he been by the books and the fire that he failed to notice the figure reclining in the upholstered armchair. True, the man was sitting sideways to him and so only partially visible behind the wings of the chair (unless sitting forward, as he now chose to do), but Tylus was a Kite Guard, trained to be observant. He should have seen him.

"Sir!" He came to attention, the click of his heels clearly audible over the popping of the fire. "Reporting as instructed."

So this was Senior Arkademic Magnus; not entirely what he'd expected. Younger than the man's reputation and notoriety had led him to picture, although such things were difficult to judge in the fire's deceptive light. A trickle of sweat chose that moment to run down behind Tylus's left ear and he wondered if it would be impolite to take off his cape.

"Relax, officer. You're not on parade now. Have a seat."

Magnus gestured towards a second chair, the twin of his own, which was angled towards the first seat with just a low table of polished wood separating them.

Tylus hesitated, surprised by the invite and uncertain how to respond.

"It won't bite, officer, and I have no intention of craning my neck in order to talk to you."

Taking a deep breath, Tylus complied, feeling uncomfortable despite the seat's deep upholstery, and not only because of the heat. He wondered fleetingly if this gesture was meant kindly, an attempt to put him at his ease, or whether it was deliberately calculated to discomfort him. He was so flummoxed by the arkademic's informal manner and the invitation to be seated that he hadn't even thought to remove his cape before sitting down.

Magnus was speaking again. "I want to show you something." He gestured, and the air above the table-top shimmered. An image began to form within the shimmering, a solid-looking something which resolved itself into a section of the city walls in miniature. "Don't worry, Kite Guard, this isn't dangerous. It's merely a recording, an echo, if you will, of events that have already transpired." Under any other circumstances Tylus would have bridled at the patronising tone, but he was so fascinated by this wonderful apparition that he barely noticed. A figure stood atop a terrace and Tylus recognised first the uniform of a Kite Guard and then...

"That's me," he gasped, unable to believe what he was seeing.

"Indeed."

Just as it dawned on Tylus where and when this was, the perspective changed, zooming in and moving swiftly past the figure of the Kite Guard, speeding down the walls and focusing on a second figure, one that was falling in an uncontrolled tumble.

The boy.

Even screaming became impossible as the air was wrenched from his lungs. At this moment of greatest mortality Tom's thoughts turned to Jezmina. He regretted never having tried to kiss her and his heart ached for all the things they would never share.

Then something touched him, hit him, enveloped him.

Netting; a swathe of thick cords that initially rushed past even as the walls had, then slowed and gained definition. Spongy cables that caught him and now bit into his body, burning his arms and legs and back. Still he dropped, but, impossibly, the net *was* slowing his fall, though surely not by enough. Nascent hope was stifled before it could properly form, to be replaced by horror as the net stretched and continued to give beneath him and he was still heading downward, albeit in slow motion compared to previously. He knew that this webbing was going to fail and rip apart at any minute, knew that he was destined to continue straight through, tumbling to his death despite the false promise of a reprieve.

Yet somehow the net held, and bit by bit its stretchable material leached the momentum from his body. Almost without realising, he was moving in the opposite direction, the elastic material pulling itself taut once more, tossing him unceremoniously up into the air, all flailing arms and legs, until he came down again, fully entangled this time, caught like a fish in a trawler man's drag.

Only then did he become aware of voices – gruff, male voices, jeering and laughing, which caused him to wonder what manner of men these unlooked-for saviours might be and why they had chosen to pluck him out of the sky. Rough hands gripped his limbs, pulling him towards the city walls. He was picked up and dropped, still entangled, to land painfully on the ground – more bruises to add to those already accumulated that night.

"It's only a scrawny lad," one voice said in disgust.

"Street-nick by the look of him."

Tom was only half-listening. His stomach still seemed to be falling and it was all he could do not to throw up.

"What's the likes of him doing up in the Heights?"

"Who cares? Toss him back!"

This last was greeted by a chorus of approval and Tom realised that fate was cruelly toying with him, that he had been saved only to be slung over the wall again. A host of hulking forms loomed over him.

"No, wait," he yelled desperately. "I know things!"

That earned him a barrage of laughter.

"'Course you do, lad. Street-nicks are famous for what they know."

"Arkademics and seers, the lot of them," another voice chipped in.

"Really, I do." He started to thrash in desperation, fighting the hands that continued to free him from the netting, unheeding of his resistance. One huge fist closed around his upper arm with a vice-like grip and started to haul him upwards. Somebody else took hold of his feet, before he even thought to kick out in earnest, and he was lifted physically into the air amid howls of laughter, to be dumped on the ground once more, beside the pile of netting.

His own thrashing probably decided matters. His stomach had been through enough. Tom hurriedly rolled to his knees and started to vomit.

The wall of onlookers drew back instinctively.

"Thaissing good-for-nothing grubber!"

"I'm not clearing that up."

"He's no thaissing Kite Guard," another voice said impatiently. "Why are we wasting our time? There'll be no reward for returning the likes of him. Throw 'im back over!"

Tom wiped his mouth and swallowed, tasting sourness. He wondered if he could make a run for it, but there was no way through the seemingly solid mass of legs and bodies. He was trapped.

"Enough!" With that one word, the newcomer quieted the hubbub. "We're not murderers."

"We were only fooling around, Red," a rather subdued voice muttered defensively.

The encircling wall of shapes parted and a single figure stepped forward, the first to become readily distinguishable from the dark mass of shifting forms that surrounded Tom. Hands reached towards him. Instinctively, he shrank away but the hands grasped him with unhurried assurance and pulled him to his feet. Tom found himself staring into a be-whiskered face.

"Hoy!" A sudden shout drew his attention outward once more. He looked up in time to see a long-barrelled weapon discharged. The gun pointed towards what looked to be a pair of ethereal eyes hovering in the air; though Tom only caught a glimpse, so perhaps he was mistaken. Whatever it had been, it immediately distorted into something unrecognisable and was limned with dancing green fire which contracted before vanishing altogether, leaving the night empty and Tom blinking away emerald stars.

Somebody near Tom hawked and spat. "Snooping little sky breckers!"

"Come on." Tom felt a hand on his back, urging him within the city; the man who had helped him to his feet evidently keen to get away from the walls. Others were already making their way inside.

"What was that?" Tom wanted to know.

"Somebody from the Heights spying on us. They won't follow once we're off the walls."

Tom found himself wondering exactly who was being spied upon: these people or him.

"Who are you?"

"Individually, I'm Red; collectively we're the Swarbs."

"Swarbs?"

"The word originally stood for Sanitation Workers and Refuse Burners, work that some of us still do, though now it just stands for us," the figure replied proudly. Not that Tom was paying that much attention. Memories of the city's levels verse stirred in the back of his mind.

Through a parkland row where deer still roam,
To the solid streets that the Swarbs call home…

If unreliable recollection served him right, the Swarbs lived on a Row somewhere below the middle of the city, which meant that his stomach-churning fall had carried him more than halfway home.

"We harvest the sky. It's amazing what folk from the upper Rows just toss over the walls as junk. Might be useless to them, but some of it's breckin' good stuff. Occasionally, we even catch people, like you. Well, no, that's not true; we've never landed anyone quite like you in the nets before. So what is a street-nick doing up in the Heights, in any case?"

Tom said nothing.

The big man grunted. "Fair enough. A man's entitled to his secrets."

Tom liked that – being called a man; especially by someone who so obviously was. He remained under no illusion though: he might not be in chains but neither had the Swarbs let him go. What was he then, some sort of trophy? A pet? Whatever they saw in him, he knew that he would have to find a way of escaping from this Red and his cronies sooner rather than later.

Tylus watched the small figure of the boy fall, though it seemed to grow no nearer the polished wood of the tabletop. He saw the scavenging Swarbs and their array of nets which girdled this section of the walls like a skirt of webbing, saw the plummeting figure strike one of the nets and keep going. The brawny Swarbs strained with arms locked and muscles bulging, attempting to keep hold of the net and the prize within as the cane framework supporting that particular net shattered and gave way. Tylus realised that he was waiting for them to fail or for the netting to break. It seemed impossible their efforts could succeed, such was the force with which the boy hit. Yet somehow the net held. Before his eyes it began to rebound, until the boy was tossed up into the air again, just a little, to come back down for a far gentler landing.

"He's alive!" Tylus gasped.

"So it would seem."

The arkademic continued talking. "The nets are elasticated, clearly. They somehow managed to absorb all that momentum, breaking the fall gently, causing no discernable damage and only imparting enough energy back to the faller to make them bob a little in the net rather than shooting them up high again. Quite remarkable material. One day, I really must find the time to discover how the Swarbs developed it."

Distracted, Tylus paid the words only cursory attention. The revelation of the boy's survival lifted his spirits immeasurably and proved far more of a relief than he would ever have expected.

All he could think was *the boy is alive*.

His attention returned to the scene being played out in the air before him, too fascinated to question any longer how he was seeing this.

A heated debate appeared to be going on among the Swarbs, and Tylus regretted the lack of sound. He could make a reasonable guess at what was being said, though: "Throw him back; it's only a worthless streetnick."

And maybe, "We can't do that, he's just a boy. Besides, think of all the effort we put into catching him."

Eventually those arguing for compassion must have won out, because the net was hauled in rather than being turned out while still beyond the walls.

After being dumped unceremoniously on the ground, the boy, freed of the netting, was promptly sick, much to the evident disgust of many there. The

Swarbs started to collect the discarded net. One of them, to the very right of the scene, looked up and seemed to stare straight at Tylus, as if suddenly aware that their actions were being observed. He tugged urgently at the sleeve of the man beside him, a figure only half visible – an arm and part of a torso that appeared to be unattached to anything else due to the limited field of view.

A face and neck then came into view, as the half-seen individual followed the first man's pointed finger, before just as quickly vanishing.

An instant later, a sharp green light swelled into view, blanketing the scene and causing Tylus to wince at the dazzling brightness.

Even that started to fade and the image disappeared altogether. Once more he could see clear across the tabletop to where Magnus sat calmly watching him.

Tylus was desperate to know what had happened to the street-nick, but he was also acutely aware of the status of the man sitting opposite him, so bit his tongue and waited to be addressed.

"You've been told of the heinous crime committed earlier tonight?"

"Yes, sir."

"Good. As you see, the murderer has succeeded in escaping both yourself and justice in general. That is not a situation that can be allowed to continue."

"No, sir."

The arkademic sighed and shook his head. "The victim was a great man and a dear friend of mine; someone who will be sadly missed by the city and its people. The individual responsible has to be caught and brought to justice. I'm charging you, Kite Officer Tylus, with seeing that this happens. You are relieved of your normal duties with immediate effect and will hunt this murderer down wherever the path may take you."

Tylus was stunned yet knew this was a task he couldn't refuse and, besides, it was his fault the lad had escaped. Almost without realising, he was on his feet and standing to attention again, inflamed by a right-eous need to see justice done.

"Certainly, sir; you can count on me. I'll begin by talking to the Swarbs…"

The arkademic was shaking his head. "A noble sen-timent, officer, but we both know how well the Swarbs react to representatives of the law, especially Kite Guards. Besides, the lad won't be there anymore. He's of no value to them and, although a capricious and contrary lot by nature, the Swarbs are not known to be heartless. They will almost certainly have let him go. I expect by now the lad is safely back in the City Below.

"Here." He leant forward and held out a folded sheet of paper. "This is my warrant, requiring that any official should place all and any resources you reasonably re-quire at your disposal. I'll send word ahead to the relevant authorities but, should you encounter any re-luctance, show this warrant and none will gainsay you anything you need."

Tylus took the document, barely able to believe that an instrument of such power should rest in his hand. "Thank you, sir."

"Now, I believe that concludes our business. Doubt-less you've had a long and busy night. Rest for what remains of it and in the morning set about your task. Don't let me down."

Tylus recognised a dismissal when he heard one. "I won't, sir!" He saluted, turned smartly around and proceeded to march out.

"Oh, one more thing, Kite Guard Tylus..."

He paused, in the process of opening the door, and looked back. "Sir?"

"That cape; see it's replaced before you set out. We can't have you going to the City Below with a torn uniform – sets a bad example."

"Yes, sir, of course, sir." Tylus turned and left, hiding a smirk and grateful to have worn the cape after all. It was more than worth a little discomfort. Let Sergeant Goss try and deny him a new kitecape now.

Magnus waited, staring at the play of resurgent flame as the fire found a fresh piece of wood to devour. He listened to the front door close, which would signal Dewar showing the Kite Guard out. Seconds later, the door to the study opened and Dewar stepped inside. So much more than a servant, this was Magnus's factotum, his man-for-all-tasks. Before Magnus employed him, Dewar had been a simple and very effective assassin, albeit one with a penchant for the sadistic.

The arkademic continued to stare at the fire. "You heard all that?"

"Of course," the other responded. "That idiot stands as much chance of finding your street-nick as I do of gaining admittance to the Chapel of the Sacred Virgins."

"Less, I would think, given your various talents."

"He won't last five minutes in the City Below."

"Oh, I think he might; after all, you're going to be there to ensure that he does."

"Am I?"

"Quietly, of course."

"And why would I want to do that?"

Magnus turned to face his companion for the first time. He resisted the answer that sprang instantly to mind – *because I told you to* – and instead responded, "Because while that buffoon is blundering around drawing everyone's attention, no one will notice the real hunter skulking in the shadows."

Now the other smiled, an act that saw his bland features take on a darkly sinister animation.

"Ahh, that would be me, I take it."

"Precisely. Find me that boy. Bring him to me."

"I don't get it. Why is this runt so important to you? So what if he saw you knife Thomas? You're up here and he's down there. What harm can he possibly do?"

"No loose ends!" Magnus snapped; then, as if relenting, added, "My elevation to the ranks of the Masters is so close, Dewar, I can almost taste it. The culmination of everything I've been working towards – I won't let anything threaten that." All of which was true, though it was only part of the answer. "He resisted me, Dewar," Magnus added quietly. "Can you imagine that? First he hid within metres of me and I never knew he was there – which is something very few people could manage – and then he broke my command to halt. Even fewer are capable of that. And yet this kid, this grubber, this nobody from the City Below, managed it; he defied my will. I need to see this boy, to talk to him, to find out how that's possible."

The man called Dewar inclined his head, accepting the information. "Very well. I still think you should have let me take care of Thomas in the first place."

Magnus shook his head. "I had to be sure. Thomas was far too valuable as a potential ally to simply be killed out of hand. Besides, he was no fool, and I knew that he would let his guard down with me, would allow me to get close enough. It would all have gone perfectly if not for that wretched street-nick, but no matter. This one I will leave in your capable hands." The arkademic gazed back to the embers of the fire. After a handful of silent seconds, he signalled the conversation was over with a dismissive wave.

Dewar started to turn away, but paused and asked, as if it were an afterthought, "What about the Kite Guard?"

"Once he has served his purpose, do with him as you will. The City Below is, after all, such a dangerous place to be."

If the earlier smile had caused the man's face to seem sinister, this one made it look positively evil.

"Oh, and Dewar, just so there is no misunderstanding; if you should fetch the boy back alive, I would be delighted. Dead would be acceptable. Returning without him would not."

The factotum raised his eyebrows in apparent surprise. "I took that much for granted."

THREE

Before starting the final descent, Tom paused for a moment to gaze upon the City Below. At first he did this with simple and heart-felt relief, but then more practical considerations came to the fore, as he took stock of exactly where he was and searched for familiar reference points.

His grazed arm had been throbbing for some while and the sole of his left shoe had worn through completely, but Tom didn't care. This was home.

His fears regarding the Swarbs and their intentions towards him had proven to be unfounded. Red took him through a bewildering sequence of dimly-lit corridors, chatting garrulously along the way. Tom walked beside him in sullen silence, making few attempts to respond. It was a reticence he subsequently regretted.

He was so preoccupied with his own misfortune that he remembered little of that march other than the lingering impression that this was a dour and unwelcoming part of the city. Finally, after travelling for some while and going through more twists and turns than the street-nick could follow, the big man stopped. Tom had no idea how far they had come, but guessed that it was a considerable distance into the metropolis and away from the wall.

"Here you are, lad," Red exclaimed, standing to one side and gesturing.

They had arrived at a gallery, an open shaft which descended through the heart of the city; though it was impossible to judge how far it went in the gloom. Directly in front of them was the most peculiar looking set of steps Tom had ever seen – they were of dark wood and appeared to be grooved and simply looked wrong. However, they were still stairs and they still led downward. Was the Swarb letting him go? He looked at the big man uncertainly. Encouraged by a broad smile and a further impatient gesture, he stepped forward towards the stairs. As he did so, there came a soft whirring sound and the stairs started to move.

Tom jumped back in alarm, at which Red roared with laughter. Recovering from his initial shock, Tom peered forward at this latest revelation. The steps seemed to emerge flat from the ground in endless procession, steadily evolving a uniform, step-like configuration as they marched relentlessly towards the drop, before vanishing downwards between matching solid rails whose black cushioned tops were moving in apparent unison with the stairs. There was something bizarre and fascinating about the military precision with which the stairway emerged, evolved and descended. Tom could have watched this process for hours.

"It's called an escalator," Red explained. "Much nearer than any of the clockwork lifts and far more trustworthy, if you ask me. Doesn't go all the way down to the City Below, mind, but it'll take you a fair way – through some fifteen Rows. Don't be tempted to jump off as you pass the different platforms, not unless you fancy a bit of an explore, but be warned if you do: the escalator won't stop for you to get back on, only stops at all when it's unused for a while. Then it goes dormant, like it was just now. Stepping back on from one of the side platforms takes some practice. You're liable to come a cropper first time out and end up travelling the rest of the way down on your arse.

"Well, good luck, lad. Reckon this is the best I can do for you."

Tom gulped, stared at the escalator and wondered whether he could find the courage to trust the thing.

"Go on, it won't hurt you."

He gave Red a weak smile and thanked him, then stepped boldly onto the moving stairway.

After a slight wobble, he clutched one of the handrails and managed to keep upright. This was easier than he'd expected.

From behind, he could hear Red's laughter. "Well done! That's the hardest part over with. Now just be ready to step off natural-like at the bottom."

The wonders and surprises that awaited him as he descended through the city's heart were many and varied, far more than he was able to fully take in, but few equalled the thrill of drifting serenely downward on the escalator.

Aware that the night was growing ever shorter, Tom was anxious to return to the City Below as swiftly as possible. In assisting him, Red had brought him deep within the city and the boy made no effort to reorientate himself, but instead simply sought the swiftest way down in the same arbitrary fashion that had taken him so far up the city's walls.

Now, as he stood at the top of the stairway and gazed out at last across the City Below, it was time to get his bearings. He was high above the floor of the vast cavern which housed Thaiburley's lowest level. The sun globes were beginning to warm up, granting this basement world its semblance of dawn. Far to the left, at the very edge of his view, Tom could just make out the start of the scrapland that was the Stain, where the detritus of generations had been dumped and left to rot.

In the middle distance he was able to see the black ribbon of the Thair, the deep dark river that provided the city with much of its power and water. The Thair which ran through the Stain was very different from the one that entered the city not so many miles upstream. Sluggish, depleted, and carrying with it the biological and industrial effluent of a city of millions, these were the waters that fed the most diseased and shunned corner in all of Thaiburley.

Things lived in the Stain; creatures that nobody cared to talk about or even think about.

With a shiver, Tom turned his attention elsewhere. To his right, the Thair's banks were bordered by beetle-like installations that leached both substance and energy from the river. A little further along, he could make out the viaduct supporting the grand conveyor; the elevated moving road that carried goods to and from the Whitleson factories. With its series of tall archways, the viaduct resembled some multi-limbed creature stalking the streets. At its far end, towards the wall, stood the docks, where great barges and vessels were berthed, loading and unloading the foodstuffs

and trade goods that were the city's life-blood. Clustered around the docks were the Runs – an infamous
shantytown of hovels where dock-workers, sailors,
beggars, thieves and whores laid down to sleep, or otherwise in the case of the whores and their marks. At
the far edge of the Runs, close to the Thair, was an area
of the city claimed by the Blue Claw, one of the many
street gangs that proliferated in the City Below. Only
once Tom reached their territory would he truly be
home; although how warm a welcome he could expect
from Lyle and the rest of the Claw was debatable, since
he would be returning empty-handed.

Having fixed the layout in his mind, Tom began the
descent, making his way down a winding stairway that
wrapped around what appeared to be a wide brick
chimney. He guessed this was a delivery shaft, similar
to those he was accustomed to seeing near the docks.
It was through such links between the City Below and
the rest of Thaiburley that commerce flowed; although
what this particular one might carry, so far from the
Thair and the trade vessels that plied it, he had no idea.
Of more immediate concern was who might be waiting
at the bottom.

Routes to the City Above were a lucrative source of
business and sufficiently rare that they were coveted
and often fought over. Somebody would be claiming
this as their own and would demand tribute from anyone passing up or down. Tom had nothing to pay with.
His ascent and descent had already been negotiated
and paid for, but only through a very specific access,
set into the city walls and close to his home turf. The
one belonging to the Scorpions. This route would be
claimed by a completely different gang and he didn't

doubt there was going to be a reception committee waiting below.

The only thing that offered any hope was the timing of his arrival. He had no idea what hours this particular gang might keep, whether they worked in shifts, were entirely nocturnal or whatever, but anyone who'd been active through the night would be thinking of bed right now, while anyone who worked a dayshift was likely to be still asleep, which meant a skeleton crew below, whose backup would be sluggish to respond; he hoped. If so, all he had to do was get past them and lose himself in the streets. He might just get away with it.

Tom's spirits lifted as he made his way down the broad stairway. The tiredness that had dogged every footfall just a short time ago evaporated. Yes, these would be unfamiliar streets, and yes, there was almost certainly going to be a scrap, but he had finally made it back to where he belonged and after all that had happened, reaching anywhere in the under-City was a cause for celebration.

There were two of them waiting below, which was about what Tom would have expected. As he descended he studied them, when the corkscrew stairwell would allow. He'd already decided on the area to make a beeline for if it came to a chase. A small street market was beginning to take shape a short distance away; a few people were already stopping to barter, which increased the chances of confusion and escape.

The two street-nicks were sitting on the bottom step, playing a game of 'flip' to pass the time. They were shaking and then tossing what he assumed to be the traditional flat pebbles onto the ground before them.

Not that Tom paid the game much attention; he was more interested in the boys themselves. They would be armed, of course, but not necessarily quick to draw blades when they saw it was just little old him coming down. One looked to be considerably larger than the other.

Ideally, a quiet approach was called for, perhaps vaulting off the stairwell early to head away unnoticed, but it was impossible to descend an iron stairway without making at least some noise. The pair were on their feet, waiting, by the time he made the final turn, their game abandoned. As he'd thought, one was short, a fair bit smaller than Tom, while the other was impressively large.

Tom put on his most disarming smile and tried to look relaxed, to saunter down the remaining steps. Their response was a suspicious scowl.

"First of the day," the shorter of the pair said.

"Lucky me!" Still he offered the open, unthreatening smile.

"Stayed overnight in the market, didja? There's passage fee to pay."

"'Course. Who's collecting?"

"The Blood Herons."

Tom nodded as if that meant something to him, which it didn't.

They stood either side as he came towards the bottom, both close enough to grab him should he try and run. The taller of the pair had yet to speak. No difficulty in guessing who was the brains and who the brawn here, and Tom knew which he considered the more dangerous. Instead of walking the final few steps, he threw himself at the smaller boy, swinging a punch to the stomach as he did so. Despite their apparent alertness, this sudden explosion of violence seemed to catch the boys flat-footed. Tom's assault carried the smaller boy over and they landed with Tom on top. He knew that he had to finish this one quickly, that the taller Blood Heron was only a few paces away, so head-butted his opponent and was relieved to feel him go limp.

Tom rolled, away from the stairs and away from the larger boy. As he did so, he clawed up a handful of dust and earth. Despite being quick, he was barely on his feet before the big Blood Heron reached him. Tom flung the earth at the other's face. Hands that had been stretched towards him changed direction as the boy yelled out and instinctively went to rub his stinging eyes. It gave Tom all the opening he needed. Instead of wasting time with a punch, he kicked out as hard as he could, landing his foot squarely in the boy's groin.

The Blood Heron let out a howl of agony and collapsed. Tom had no intention of waiting around to see any further reaction; he was off, running flat out towards the street market he had spied from the stairs.

Despite the senior arkademic's urgings and despite having worked through the night, Tylus found sleep elusive. Eventually he did manage to snag hold of the concept and wrestle it down long enough to gain an hour or so of blissful oblivion, but was all too soon awake again.

He dressed swiftly, a man with a mission; washed down a few snatched mouthfuls of dry and unsatisfying breakfast cake with a draught of bitterly dark ale, then set out. Initially the way was unlit, but it was only a short walk along a route he knew well, and the immediate approach to the station was blessed with electric lighting. Ceiling-mounted tubes of florescent gas flickered to life at his approach. He knew they were activated by sensors, another wonder of the modern age, but could never entirely shake the childhood image of invisible spirits flying before him and triggering the lights specifically for his benefit.

Armed with the senior arkademic's warrant, Tylus entered the station with a confidence unknown since his very first days with the force. Brandishing the document, he gained access to the department's most precious resource: the Screen. These wondrous devices provided access to a wealth of information about the city and its inhabitants. As far as Tylus was aware, the Kite Guard were the only arm of the civil defence or watch to be equipped with them, and even they had only one per station. All officers were trained in their use but only the chosen few were permitted access. Thanks to the warrant, Tylus now shared that privilege – temporarily, at least.

He worked quickly, anxious to be done before anyone had the wit to question his authority too closely. If one of his colleagues should muster the courage to contact Magnus, Tylus could find himself in trouble before the mission had properly begun.

He knew full well that the warrant was intended for use in the City Below, not to secure the resources of his own department. However, whoever drafted the document had been careless, failing to restrict its authority to the under-City, which enabled Tylus to push his luck. Not that he did so without misgivings. He imagined Magnus would take a very dim view of such wilful misuse of his authority, but the young Kite Guard reckoned it to be worth the risk.

He was finally exercising skills in which he had trained but had never previously been allowed to utilise: those of detection.

Summoning up the city's schematics, which appeared on the screen in stark relief, he quickly found the section of wall where his encounter with the street-nick had taken place the previous night. Deft manipulation brought a different, flatter view of the city. A tracery of stairwells developed, highlighted in red as they flowed from the relevant section downward, a network penetrating the Rows like capillaries flowing through a body. Tylus set to work immediately. The boy had been descending the city's walls, so it seemed reasonable to assume this was also how he ascended. A large proportion of the red traceries vanished, as the Kite Guard eliminated all the internal stairwells. The lad would almost certainly have chosen the quickest and most direct route he could find. More red lines disappeared. Only a few now remained and Tylus pursued these relentlessly downward, rejecting the least likely branches as they appeared. Once he came to the city's lowest areas, the options dwindled dramatically: access to the City Below was limited, deliberately so, and eventually there were just two likely candidates for the stairwell the boy might have used to exit that basement world.

The Kite Guard felt inordinately pleased with himself. With inspired forethought, he had managed to narrow the field of search from near-impossible vastness to a manageable area. Instead of blundering blindly into an unknown and notoriously perilous part of the city, he now had a reasonable starting point.

After sorting out a few further details, he set about closing the screen down, only to have his self-congratulatory mood swept away by a voice that bellowed across the squad room, silencing everyone there. "Tylus! What in Thaiss's name do you think you're up to?"

For an instant Tylus froze, dread washing through him, causing him to feel like a small child caught doing something forbidden.

Goss, his face a contorted mask, eyes bulging and cheeks flushed purple with fury, stalked across the room. Had the man no home to go to? "I'll have your cape for this, officer, permanently!"

Recovering from the shock, Tylus determined to hold his nerve. He stood and came to attention. "Sir, I'm accessing the Screen in order to perform duties assigned to me by Senior Arkademic Magnus, sir!"

That brought the sergeant up short, though he looked no less furious. "Duties?" The word spat out like something unpalatable.

"Yes, sir. On special assignment, sir!"

The sergeant glanced across to the duty officer, who gave a quick nod of confirmation, much to Tylus's relief. Magnus had obviously acted promptly in contacting the department.

"I was told to produce this in the event of challenge, sir." He handed the warrant to Goss.

The sergeant read it, his nostrils flaring as he did so, before slapping it back into the young Kite Guard's hand without saying a word. After a final hate-filled glare, he managed, "Carry on," before turning to stalk away.

A quick glance around the room showed a few ill-concealed smirks on some of his colleagues' faces, and it occurred to Tylus that he wasn't the only one who despised the sergeant. In fact, this little melodrama had probably done his status among the other officers no harm at all.

Would Goss contact Magnus? Probably not, and even if he did so, it seemed unlikely that he would dare to question specifics such as accessing the Screen.

Tylus resisted the temptation to dance an impromptu jig and instead, with as much dignity as his impatient feet would allow, strolled towards supply, to exchange his torn kitecape for a fresh one.

Hawkers and stallholders paused in the process of setting up their wares to stare at Tom as he raced past; this was the last thing he needed. Presumably he was in Blood Heron territory and the gang members were likely to know these market men and women, any one of whom could point them in the direction of a fleeing fugitive.

He slowed, forcing himself to be patient, to walk rather than run.

In doing so, he paid more attention to the market itself. Immediately in front of him was a veritable curtain of dead fowl. River ducks, by the look of them. Row after row of the things suspended by their feet from horizontal poles arranged one above the other, so that each line of downward-pointing beaks ended a fraction above the next pole. Tom counted five such poles in all and he wondered who would bother to buy ducks when they could just as easily go to the river and catch their own. A man and a woman, conservatively dressed, were busy hanging the final few birds from the bottom-most pole, tying their feet and attaching hooks to each and every one.

A sign stood beside them, written in bold hand with large, untidy script. Not that it meant anything to Tom, who couldn't read. At that moment the man noticed him and looked up, smiling, before helpfully reciting a set patter which Tom suspected might mirror the sign's message.

"Fresh off the river, caught in the early hours o' this morning. We'll even pluck 'em for you if you want."

"Don't be daft," his wife said beside him. "That's a street-nick; see the way he's dressed? Only thing he'll ever 'ave from a stall like ours is what 'e can pinch."

Tom bowed his head and shuffled past, cursing his curiosity. He'd managed to draw attention to himself even without running.

He continued down the street, eyes fixed on the ground, refusing to look up, allowing his mantra to loop through his thoughts as he willed people not to notice him.

A little further on, when he judged enough of the market lay between him and the stairwell, he ducked down an alley to his left, between buildings that seemed taller and sturdier than those he was used to. The alley led to another avenue, which he stepped into without hesitation. He was conscious of figures in the street around him but paid them little attention, still concentrating on going unnoticed.

Then something in their gait, their posture, penetrated his awareness. He looked up, and found himself staring at a Jeradine. In fact, all the "people" in sight were members of that tall bipedal, reptilian race. Tom froze, his thoughts racing. If even half the rumours were true, a flathead was more likely to eat him than anything else. He'd seen the occasional one or two before, at a distance, but never this many and never this close. They kept themselves to themselves as a rule, rarely leaving their enclave, which he vaguely thought of as being somewhere over the far side of the city. Here, apparently.

How had he stumbled into Jeradine territory without even realising? There was a human street just the other side of that alley. He would have expected fences, barbed wire and a gate, but this was all so casual, so unsecured. It was as if the short passageway had somehow transported him to another world.

Tom backed slowly towards the alley in question, his eyes never leaving the disturbing, green-scaled visage of the nearest Jeradine, with its bulbous eyes, broad mouth and its oddly featureless face which ran from the crown of the head, between the eyes, all the way to the tip of the snout in a straight, unbroken line. Flathead.

None of the Jeradine reacted to him, but he drew little comfort from that, knowing nothing of their habits or customs and so unable to gauge whether this was in any way an ominous sign or a good one.

Finally he was able to escape into the alley and scamper back to the market street. He hesitated on the point of stepping out, peering around the corner to ensure the way was clear. Several youths were gathered in front of the stall that sold fowl, talking with the owner, who was pointing up the street in Tom's direction.

He ducked back hurriedly out of sight.

Now what? They were Blood Herons for sure. If he stepped out into the market he seemed guaranteed a beating, and after the way he had left two of their members, the Blood Herons would be out for revenge and so were bound to make it a nasty one. Turn the other way and he was entering the unknown, taking his chances with something intrinsically 'other'. But at least it was a chance, whereas the street-nicks would offer him none. Drawing a deep breath, he hurried back down the alley and walked straight out into the street, turning right, wanting to put as much distance between himself and the Blood Herons as possible. Again the Jeradine in view ignored him, though whether by design or indifference was impossible to tell. From what he had heard, the flatheads were unable to shape human speech so there seemed little point in asking; though perhaps he was wrong on that last point, because coming towards him at that very moment were a pair, one of each species, clearly engrossed in conversation. What particularly caught Tom's eye was the fact that this man, the first human he had seen on the flathead street, wore the brown and orange uniform of the City Watch; a razzer.

Suddenly the night's events came piling in on top of him and he remembered the murder, the encounter with the Kite Guard and his own terrifying fall. Had word spread already? Had every razzer in every Row of the city been alerted and told to keep an eye out for him? Either way, the last thing in the world he wanted was another encounter with an officer of the watch, whatever the uniform.

Jeradine buildings differed from those of humans in a very specific manner, Tom realised as he frantically looked about: no windows. Did they prefer the dark? He was used to seeing shacks and hovels that were too crude to include windows, but these were proper buildings and still they had none. Tom shied away from squatting in one of the doorways, imaging a green-scaled hand emerging to drag him within, so instead took refuge in a gap between two of the buildings, sinking to his haunches and bringing his mantra into focus: *You cannot see me...*

The odd pair drew closer and their conversation became audible. The actual words passed Tom by as he concentrated on not being seen, but the tone of the flat-head's voice snagged his attention anyway. There was a flat, unnatural quality to it; every syllable stretched and stilted. Tom stared at the Jeradine despite himself, and saw that in addition to the loose, smock-like tunic the flatheads seemed to favour, this one sported a particularly ugly form of jewellery: a large grey crystalline ornament, an angular, sculpted box which pressed against its throat, held there by a neck band.

Then he realised that the creature's mouth was not actually opening as it spoke. Rather, the voice seemed to emerge from the peculiar neckwear.

Even as Tom stared at the Jeradine, the creature turned its head and stared at him. Not through him, as Tom was used to when reciting his mantra, but directly at him. This was the second time in recent hours that his litany had let him down. Had it stopped working? He refused to entertain that possibility and concentrated on reciting all the harder.

You can't see me...

The pair moved on. Perhaps he'd imagined it; perhaps the flathead hadn't seen him at all and it was only tiredness and nerves that made him think otherwise. He was just beginning to convince himself of this when a shadow fell across the mouth of the alley.

He looked up, to see the Jeradine with the neck-box staring down at him.

"Don't worry, the guardsman has left. I didn't alert him to your presence," that cold, flat voice said. "Assuming it was the watchman from whom you were hiding." There was something unnatural about a voice speaking without a mouth opening to utter it.

Tom looked around frantically, but there was a solid wall behind him. The creature stood blocking his only escape route.

"Nor should you fear that your fascinating ability to hide has deserted you. It still works, just not on Jeradine. We see differently from you humans."

Despite his fear, that piece of information reassured Tom and was certainly worth remembering.

"I won't harm you, boy. Haven't I proved that by not handing you in to the guardsman when I had the chance?"

Despite his lingering fear, Tom's curiosity came to the fore again. "You can speak… that box?"

"A translator, yes. A useful gadget, although it requires considerable skill to operate. They work by interpreting movement of the throat rather than by responding to actual sound. Most of my people don't bother mastering them, but then most have no need to communicate with humans."

"But you do."

"Obviously. My name is Ty-gen. You humans fascinate me, so I interact with your species often. You look tired, and hungry."

Tom was both.

"I can help. Come."

The flathead extended a surprisingly human-looking

hand – once you saw past the pale green pallor and the subtle hint of scales.

Tom stared at the hand, uncertain. Some instinct was telling him to trust this strange, talking flathead, yet he couldn't think of a logical reason why he should. After the briefest hesitation, he gripped the proffered hand, which was cool but not as rough as he'd feared, and allowed the Jeradine to help him to his feet.

A series of elevators – the clockwork lifts – took Tylus most of the way down to the City Below but after the third such device he'd had enough. He was deeply suspicious of the elevators, ever since a cousin who was fascinated by all things mechanical had insisted on showing him the inner workings of one. All Tylus had seen was a vast array of chains and huge inter-connecting cogs. He had no idea how it all came together to actually do something constructive, nor any desire to find out. His lasting impression of the experience was that anything that complicated was bound to break down now and again. Knowing his luck, it would do so when he was on-board.

He wouldn't have minded if the wretched things were even comfortable. The elevator system was convenient, yes, but certainly not ideal. His greatest misgivings lay in the cramped nature of the compartments, which seemed to grow subtly smaller and more confining as the journey progressed. Then there were the changeovers. Due to the city's vast scale, no single elevator was capable of taking you from top to bottom in one unbroken journey. At least, no public one; it was rumoured that the Masters had such a conveyance, but that was only a rumour.

Mind you, perhaps the changeovers were Tylus's own private little irritation, since so few people ever had cause to travel the entire length of the city. Any who did were forced to travel in stages, changing from one clockwork box to another. In theory, the elevators were supposed to connect, so that you stepped out of one, crossed over a corridor and instantly entered the next, ready to continue your journey. Reality rarely seemed to live up to this theory and, in Tylus's experience, transition was never that seamless.

The clockwork lifts were dispersed throughout the city, but few of the systems went all the way down to the City Below due to lack of demand, or so it was claimed. Tylus had needed to walk some distance before reaching a system that did. In the event, he needn't have bothered, since the final anticipated changeover proved one too many. Not only was the connecting elevator completely out of synch and still several minutes away, but there was a sizeable queue already waiting for it. So sizeable that Tylus doubted whether there would even be room for him on this next one, which meant waiting for the car to complete its descent to the bottom so that its tandemmed twin could return to the changeover platform. The lift system worked that way, with two cars working opposite each other – one going down as its partner rose, each stopping at every intervening Row whether anyone wanted them to or not. This made journeys frustratingly slow, as Tylus was coming to realise.

He looked at the queue, considered invoking the authority of his uniform to force a way to the front, and decided that he really could not be bothered. Why earn the resentment of everyone there only to be crammed cheek-by-jowl with them on a descent into hell? Better to walk.

Decision made, he headed for the nearest stairwell. A young girl, no more than three or four, stared at him as he passed and pulled at her mother's arm.

"Look, Mum, funny guardsman."

Her mother quickly clasped her by the arm and said, "Shush, dear," before offering Tylus an embarrassed smile. "Sorry, she's never seen a Kite Guard before."

After that, Tylus walked with chin a little higher and back a little straighter, reminded that even this far from his own districts the reputation of the Kite Guard preceded him. At least no one had yet asked why an officer of the Kite Guard was bothering with the lifts at all instead of simply flying down the outside of the city to wherever he wished to go. Explaining the treacherous nature of wind currents as they met and swirled around the walls to the uninitiated was not a prospect he relished. Any thoughts he might have entertained of attempting something as reckless as that had been well and truly dismissed following his embarrassment the previous night.

He took his time descending through the city's lower levels, falling into the steady, unhurried gait he used when walking the beat, dallying a while in the Shopping Rows – it was an age since he had ventured this far into the city's lower reaches – but otherwise simply enjoying the unfamiliar surroundings.

Immediately beneath the Shopping Rows lay the market, which was the wellspring for much of Thaiburley's food trade. Here fresh produce of every sort was bartered and sold, to be distributed throughout the Rows, where it would be cleaned, peeled, diced and sliced, processed, prepared, cooked, stored, combined and consumed in a thousand different fashions.

This was a new experience for Tylus, who had never ventured beneath the Shopping Rows before. Against his expectations, he found the place invigorating and exciting, with its constant hustle and bustle. Everywhere was movement, as broad carts laden with pallets of vegetables and others stacked precariously with cages of clucking fowl muscled their way through the streets, while trays of ice were rushed into the fish halls and lumbering oxen pulled heavier carts still. Prospective buyers were everywhere, wanting to peer beneath every cloth and into every container. A cacophony of sound surrounded him, as yells of "Mind yer backs!" and "Comin' through!" mingled with those of the traders hawking their wares.

And the smells; oh, the smells. The richness of freshly roasted coffee assailed his nostrils one moment, the pungency of exotic spices the next. There was the ripe smell of animal dung to one side, the sweetness of ripened fruit to the other, as he strolled beside barrows laden with melons and brightly coloured citrus. He took time to wander through one of the fish halls, its oddly tilted floor damp with melted ice – tilted so that melt-water, blood, gore and scales could be readily washed away at the day's end. The tang of the sea and of fish flesh was everywhere.

He remained vigilant, however, despite the distracting environment; conscious of how close he was to the City Below, which now lay immediately beneath his feet. Recent experience had shown him all too clearly what to expect from those who lived there.

Having sated his curiosity, Tylus eventually made his way to the designated stairwell. The market represented, in effect, the ground level of Thaiburley, flowing out beyond its walls and spreading into the meadow beyond; although even this was a deceptively simplistic assertion, since the city was built against and indeed into a great buttress of rock, a veritable mountain that both supported and helped shape the City of Dreams. The stairwell that Tylus now took was accessed via an arched doorway on the inside of the city's walls. As he approached, a mother emerged, shooing two scrawny children before her. There seemed a furtiveness about them, though perhaps not. Perhaps the young Kite Guard's perceptions were merely coloured by his knowledge of where they had come from and where he was about to go.

The stairs began immediately beyond the archway, descending in a long curve, the way lit by a series of flickering torches. Almost at once there was a noticeable change in the texture of the passageway, as the stairs carried him beneath the city walls and into the very rock they were built upon. He passed nobody else on the descent and, used to stepping from one floor to another within the city itself, was unprepared for the experience of an enclosed passageway. It felt as if he was making his lonely way into the depths of some mythical hell.

Was it his imagination, or could he smell something unpleasant as well? Was this what hell smelt like?

His relief when the tunnel ended was considerable. It had only lasted for a couple of minutes, but discomfort had made it seem far longer. The stairs now clung to a rock face in order to reach the floor of a vast cavern, and he caught the first view of his destination. A panorama of human habitation stretched before him – far more than he had ever envisaged. In its way, the view was quite awe-inspiring. One thing, unfortunately, had not changed with his emergence from the passageway: the smell. With growing horror, Tylus realised that the City Below stank.

He knew the way to the nearest Watch station, having checked the route before setting out. Nevertheless, Tylus soon discovered that seeing something on a schematic and being physically in the place were two entirely different things. He half hoped the relevant duty officer might have arranged an escort to guide him, since he'd contacted them about his arrival and wasn't that much later than anticipated, but apparently not. The only people immediately by the stairway were a group of street-nicks who eyed him with smirks on their faces and whispered comments behind shielding hands.

He did his best to look assured and imposing as he strode past them.

Now, if memory served him right, the quickest way to the station was straight ahead, and then to turn right. He just hoped he could remember where to turn. A broad avenue led away from the steps. To his left stretched a long, low building, empty pallets stacked casually outside half-open doors; a warehouse by the look of it. A scrawny dog stretched out beside the pallets, watching him without raising its head. Beyond was a seemingly endless mess of cobbled-together shacks, apparently built out of whatever people could lay their hands on – scraps of wood, corrugated metal sheeting, boxes, cloth, wire, rope and goodness knew what else. As buildings went, these were sorry excuses. None of them looked capable of standing up to a strong sneeze.

A small girl ran up to him, as if to beg, but was called back by a barked command from a stoop-shouldered woman who presumably was her mother. She offered the Kite Guard a quick apology and then dragged the child back behind a curtain that masked the doorway she'd emerged from, scolding her all the way.

"What have I told you 'bout razzers?" he heard as they disappeared from sight.

Tylus was so distracted by this cameo that he failed to notice the street-nicks until they were all around him. Were these the same ones who had been hanging around the stairwell? Two of them were, certainly – he recognised them – but he thought that they had also been joined by others.

One bumped into his left shoulder in passing; apparently an accident, as if he had been pushed by one of his fellows, but Tylus doubted it. Alert for some trick, he wasn't at all surprised to feel a feather-light touch on the right side of his belt, but even so was too slow. By the time he spun around, the offending hand was gone, taking his puncheon with it.

The youth skipped a few backward steps, now in front of the Kite Guard and flanked by the rest of the small gang, five in all.

"Give that back to me."

"Come and take it, razzer."

Boxing lessons may have been abandoned with the other accoutrements of youth, but Tylus still made a point of sparring regularly. Confronted with a situation like this, he immediately braced himself and raised his fists in familiar boxer's stance, rising onto the balls of his feet in the process.

The youth holding the puncheon threw his head back and laughed, which was the signal for the whole group to snigger and jeer. Then, after tucking the club into his belt, the street-nick raised his fists in mockery of the Kite Guard's posture. But it was just a mockery and no real defence at all.

Tylus danced forward, two quick steps, much to the further mirth of the onlookers. But it brought him within reach of his tormentor. He led with his left: one, two quick jabs to the face and then a third, which became the opening blow in a left-right combination. It was the right that packed the real punch. The Kite Guard doubted whether any of these grubbers had seen a real boxer before. Certainly the lad he was facing had no idea how to defend himself against one.

The street-nick collapsed backwards, to sit on the ground with blood streaming from his nose and a bewildered look on his face.

Tylus was still determined to reclaim the puncheon and knew he had to press his advantage before the rest of the gang recovered enough wit to attack him. Besides, he couldn't resist – the lad's chin was just too inviting. A quick step to readjust his balance and the Kite Guard lashed out with his foot, feeling satisfaction as the blow connected, knocking the street-nick onto his back, where he lay unmoving.

This might not have been in any boxing manual, but the kick had certainly proved effective enough.

The puncheon rolled loose. As Tylus bent down to pick it up, the largest of the street-nicks let out a bellow of rage and charged him. He swivelled and fired the puncheon. The club shot out, smashing into the lad's forehead. At such close range and with the attacker's own momentum adding to the force, the effect was devastating. The street-nick keeled over like a felled tree.

The puncheon snapped back into its casing and Tylus held it before him, brandishing it in the direction of first one of the two remaining street-nicks and then the other. Two…? He could have sworn there were five in the original group, but no matter; perhaps one had already seen enough and run off.

"Which of you grubbers is next?" he asked with practiced menace.

The pair looked quickly at each other and then back at him. He sensed it was in the balance, that they were undecided whether to attack or run. He took a step forward to help them make up their minds, thrusting the puncheon towards the nearest with renewed intent. That settled it. They both turned and fled.

Tylus felt elated. His first encounter with the dreaded street gangs of the City Below and he had survived. No, more than survived, he had triumphed!

He twirled his puncheon and holstered it with a flourish before sauntering off down the road.

The Kite Guard never saw the bowman. He had dismissed the fifth member of the gang far too readily. Fortunately for him, there were other eyes watching the confrontation; eyes that noted the point where one of the gang slipped away into the shadows.

The youth lifted his crossbow and took aim at the razzer's back. From this range, he couldn't miss.

Then came a tap on his shoulder, causing him to jerk around.

"Sorry, but I can't let you do that," Dewar said quietly.

He knew full well how he must appear to the streetnick – an unremarkable, slightly balding man of average height, no more threatening than any clerk or shopkeeper. He could almost see the shock at being disturbed drain from the youth's eyes, an unconscious relaxing on seeing the unassuming source of this disturbance. Other emotions would soon follow, with anger the most likely. At that instant of maximum relaxation, before the kid could regroup, Dewar struck; both hands moved with lightning quickness, one to the back of the shoulder, the other to the opposite side of the face. Then he pulled them towards each other, like some staggered clap with palms that were never destined to meet. The street-nick was already looking around, over his shoulder. All Dewar did was turn head and neck even further that way – far further than nature had ever intended.

With an audible crack, the boy's neck snapped.

He probably never even had the time to realise what was happening.

Dewar caught the bow as the body fell, wondering if it might prove of some use, but quick examination showed it to be crude and poorly made. He dropped the thing to the ground, where it snapped beneath his heels as easily as the lad's neck had between his hands.

The assassin looked out to where Tylus's retreating back could still clearly be seen. Word travelled quickly in the City Below. With a bit of luck, this incident would gain the cocky young Kite Guard enough respect to keep the street-nicks at bay for a while. Dewar certainly hoped so. He had enough on his plate without having to waste precious time playing nursemaid to an incompetent buffoon.

FOUR

Tom awoke to the sound of voices. If he suffered any disorientation it was fleeting; the memory of where he was and what had happened the previous night came flooding back almost at once. The Jeradine, Ty-gen, had proved true to his word, feeding Tom and finding him somewhere to sleep, even giving him some salve for his grazed arm, which was now feeling considerably better as a result.

Food had come in the form of a hot broth, which looked and smelt delicious. At first Tom hesitated, wondering what sort of food the flatheads ate and whether it might be unpleasant or even harmful to him.

Ty-gen evidently guessed the reason for his hesitation and offered reassurance, saying, "Don't worry, I am used to human visitors. I could not eat this. You can."

Tom's doubts faded and hesitation crumbled in the face of the aromas that continued to engulf him, and he soon tucked in. The soup was piping hot, scalding his mouth at the first few mouthfuls, but that barely slowed him. Chunks of tender meat and vegetables and a lightly spiced broth proved just as enjoyable as the aromas had promised, and he wolfed it down as quickly as he could. The Jeradine sat and watched; not prying, not interfering, not saying anything, simply observing.

Tom hadn't realised how hungry he was until the soup's vapours tempted his nostrils, nor had he realised how tired he was until he lay down on the pallet in the back room which the flathead directed him to. A pallet that was cushioned with the softest bedding the young street-nick had ever encountered. He fell asleep at once.

Now, as he woke, he remembered Ty-gen's perceptiveness in knowing why he hesitated before eating the broth, and he reflected on a great deal else – the little things the flathead had said and the questions he refrained from asking where another might have. Tom had never thought of them as intelligent – the Jeradine – never thought much about them at all, truth be told, but he was already developing a growing respect for this particular flathead.

His shoes were beside the pallet. Had he taken them off before falling asleep? He couldn't remember. An insole had been placed inside the left, effectively plugging the hole that had developed during the night's excursions. As Tom slipped the shoe on, wriggling his foot and getting used to this new sole, his suspicions returned. He wondered exactly what the Jeradine's angle might be. One thing life on the streets taught you beyond any doubt was that nobody did anything for nothing and, so far, Ty-gen was simply too good to be true. What was the flathead after?

The voices claimed his attention. There were two of them. One was unmistakably the not-quite human monotone of Ty-gen's box, the other definitely human; that of a girl. He rose and headed towards the sound, brushing aside the curtain that had been drawn across the doorway to lend the backroom a semblance of darkness. The Jeradine seemed fond of curtains, at least to judge by the front room's walls, which were festooned with a variety of such, large and small.

The girl had been speaking but stopped in mid-sentence and stared at Tom as he entered.

She looked a little older than him, though not by much, and was clearly a street-nick through and through. The clothes said that much about her; in fact, they almost said it too loudly and Tom immediately began to doubt his initial impression. The clothing looked too good – too well made and too expensive for any real street-nick, even a gang leader. Was she some up-City kid playing at being a grubber? Yet something in her posture said otherwise and, while dressed to impress, the clothing was practical – the sort a street-nick would wear if they could afford to – and if they were tough enough to hang on to it.

She was dressed from head to toe in black – boots, tight fitting trousers and a light, sleeveless top which, tucked in, showed an athletic but definitely female figure. Tom instantly focused elsewhere. Every item she wore looked clean, new even, including the black leather belt with its silver studs, though the handles of twin knives that hung from it did not; they were well worn and had obviously seen use. Street-nick, he felt certain, if quite unlike any he was used to.

The girl had also been appraising him, though her own inspection was far swifter. Tom felt he had failed in some way and was already dismissed from her thoughts.

"Ah, Tom. You slept well I trust?" Ty-gen greeted him. "This is Kat."

Girl and boy exchanged perfunctory nods of acknowledgement. Her eyes were dark, he noticed; perhaps appearing more so due to their being set against her spiky black hair and choice of clothes. Not as dark as his own, but even so...

Then he noticed the object on the table in front of the Jeradine.

"What's that?"

Without thinking, he snatched it up. Smooth beneath his fingers and oddly textured. Almost like glass, yet not quite.

The girl moved as he moved, either to stop him or to take it back, but she was restrained by a gesture from Ty-gen, and instead contented herself with a snapped, "Careful with that. It's valuable."

Tom barely heard her, caught as he was by the small statuette in his hand. It was a depiction of a leaping fish, sculpted from a clear crystalline substance, the like of which Tom had never seen before. Holding the figure carefully by its base – a stylised wave – he turned it around so that it caught the light, glittering and winking at him.

"It's beautiful," he said.

"Thank you," the Jeradine said. "I made it; quite literally."

Tom looked at him for an explanation.

"We Jeradine are dissimilar from your people in many ways. Our bodies work differently to start with.

We cannot metabolise certain elements of the food that is vital to us, and we excrete those elements as a crystalline gel."

"He means they shit the stuff," Kat cut in.

"Not exactly, but it's true that the khybul," here the translator produced a guttural sound that was almost unintelligible, "is a by-product that we have to regularly purge from our systems."

"And this icky-gel stuff hardens into crystal," Kat explained, evidently growing impatient with the wordy explanation and choosing to talk to him in a far friendlier manner than Tom would have expected, given her initial disdain. Perhaps she wasn't so different after all.

"Indeed," the Jeradine confirmed. "But before it completely solidifies there is a brief period when it is malleable. Khybul-sculpting has long been a tradition among my people. Apparently, there are those who value our little efforts."

"Too right. People up-City can't get enough of the stuff, especially what's turned out by the very best khybul-artists like Ty-gen here." Kat produced a fair approximation of the guttural 'khybul' sound. She then laughed; a brief bark of glee. "Course, I doubt if anyone tells them exactly where it comes from. Can you imagine it – the rich and the mighty paying a fortune for Jeradine shit?"

In truth, looking at the crystal fish, Tom could well believe it. "And you fence these for the... Jeradine?" He'd so nearly said "flatheads".

"For Ty-gen and a few of his friends, yes."

"For a cut?" His initial awe at the girl's apparent persona was fast evaporating. She was just another street-nick on the make after all.

"Of course."

It was a neat set-up. Tom was jealous of this Kat, he realised. Why had such a simple, hazard-free way of making a living never landed in his lap? He eyed her speculatively, trying to see something special in her, anything that might explain why she enjoyed so much good fortune when he didn't.

The girl's hand drifted casually towards the knives at her belt. "Don't go getting any funny ideas, street-nick. This is my pitch, you keep your grubby hands off."

"Kat, keep a civil tongue," the Jeradine admonished. "I'm sure the lad entertains no such thoughts, do you, Tom?"

"Course not," Tom replied, guiltily.

The girl watched him through narrowed eyes, clearly unconvinced.

"I need you to do something for me, Kat," the Jeradine said, "but first there's something I want to show you."

He turned to one of the curtains that adorned the walls and pulled it aside. Behind was an alcove and sitting on the shelf within was the most beautiful object Tom had ever seen.

"Thaiss!" Kat exclaimed, echoing Tom's thoughts precisely.

They stared at a khybul sculpture, but one as far beyond the leaping fish as that was from some stick figure drawn in the dust. It stood perhaps four times the height of the fish – still not particularly large, but infinitely more intricate and detailed. It was a castle, a city: layer upon layer of walls topped with an array of miniature turrets and towers.

Tom didn't need to be told what it was. "Thaiburley," he exclaimed, his voice barely above a whisper.

"A representation of the city, yes," the Jeradine confirmed.

"I never knew you could do anything this complicated," Kat said.

"Oh, you'd be surprised what we can do with the khybul when we put our minds to it."

"You've been holding out on me."

None of them had reached out to touch the figure, not even Tom, who feared that this crystal city might prove too fragile and would break beneath his clumsy fingers.

"You want me to sell this for you?" Kat asked. "It'll fetch a fortune."

"No, not for me. It's yours, to sell or keep as you choose."

"What? You're breckin' kidding me! Why would you simply give me something like this?"

"In return for a favour, an errand completed," Tygen told her calmly.

"Go on." She was suspicious now; Tom saw that much in the narrowing of her eyes, the tilt of her head. She was no doubt wondering what task could be worth such a prize. So was he, for that matter.

"Tom here has some distance to travel and I would like you to escort him back to his own part of the city."

"I don't need minding," Tom snapped, appalled at the suggestion. The words *Especially not by a girl* rattled around his head but fortunately did not escape his lips. At the same time, he didn't want to seem so helpless, not to her.

Kat just stared at him, her lips pursed into a thin line.

"I don't doubt you are capable, Tom, but this is not an area of the city you're familiar with. Kat here knows the gang territories, who is to be trusted and who avoided, and she can guide you away from the other dangers that lurk in the shadows, things which the unwary traveller might never even know were there until it was too late. Then, when you get closer to your own home, you can do the same for her, helping Kat avoid the pitfalls specifically associated with your part of the city. Together, you are stronger."

Tom thought of the traffickers, the needlers, the dog master and the web wife, and he wondered what their equivalents were in this part of town. The fact was that he simply didn't know, which meant that the Jeradine might have a point.

"And if I babysit him home, you'll give this to me, no strings?" She nodded towards the sculpture.

"That is correct."

She shook her head. "I still don't get it, this is beautiful, but..." Her attention returned to Tom, looking him over critically. "Do you run with anybody?"

He nodded. "The Blue Claw."

"The Blue Claw? Their territory's on the far side of the Runs, isn't it?"

Again, he nodded.

"Thaiss, you're a long way from home, kid."

"That much I know." He bridled at being called kid but bit his tongue and didn't complain. Despite the knee-jerk indignation he'd originally felt, he was swiftly coming around to Ty-gen's way of thinking. This strange girl might just offer him his best chance of getting all the way home and the last thing he wanted to do was antagonise her before she'd even agreed to do so.

Kat turned back towards the Jeradine. "What makes you think I won't just take him halfway home and then dump him?"

"Because I trust you. And because I would know if you did. I'd see it in your eyes."

For a second, the pair locked gazes. It was the girl who looked away. She gave a wry smile. "True."

She rubbed her chin thoughtfully; an action that seemed far too old for this wild, intimidating girl. "You know there's not another being in the whole of the city I'd do something like this for without taking payment up front, don't you?"

"But what would be the point?" Somehow, the flat voice of the translator conveyed a genuine sense of surprise, or perhaps that was simply Tom reading too much into things. "You could not take the crystal with you and it is imperative you leave immediately."

"The point?" She laughed. "We really are different species, your people and mine, aren't we?"

"Undeniably."

She shook her head, as if not entirely comfortable with a decision already made. "I must be mad." She glanced again at the crystal sculpture before letting out a long sigh. "Very well, I'll do it."

"Thank you, Katarina." This time there could be no mistaking the affection in the synthesized words.

"Kat," she said sharply. "Nobody calls me Katarina."

The flat, alien head bowed in apology. "Kat," he corrected himself.

Tom watched this final exchange with interest, his curiosity piqued. There was a story hidden in those words somewhere, he felt certain.

"Come on then, kid. The sooner we set out the sooner I can be back."

"First let the lad have a drink of something, Kat. He has had nothing since rising." Tom was grateful for the

Jeradine's delay; in truth he was parched. The girl merely scowled, as if this were the most unreasonable request in the world, and then fidgeted impatiently while he gulped down some fruit juice and followed it with a glass of chill water.

"Ready?" she asked as Tom tipped back his head and drained the last drops.

He thanked the Jeradine in parting, words that had to be spoken hurriedly, so impatient was the girl to be on her way.

"Shouldn't take us more than three hours or so," Kat said, almost to herself. "With a bit of luck I can still be back and under cover before it's fully dark."

"One thing," Tom said quickly. "The Blood Herons..."

"What about them?"

"Probably best if we steer clear of their territory."

The girl stopped and scrutinised him, before giving a barked, bitten-off laugh. "Ha! I heard they had some trouble this morning by the steps. That was you, was it?"

Tom nodded glumly, not certain how she was likely to react – the Blood Herons might be her allies for all he knew. Instead, he thought he detected a hint of approval in her gaze; perhaps, for the first time, even a little respect.

"So, it'll mean a detour, but I suppose I can always find somewhere to hole-up for the night if need be." Nobody sane wandered the streets alone after dark if they could help it. "So we go around the Blood Herons."

She was about to head off again when he stopped her. "Wait a moment."

"Now what?"

Only at this point, when they were already some distance down the road, did it occur to him to wonder about the Jeradine's apparent knowledge. "How did he know? Ty-gen, I mean. He said that I had some distance to travel, but I never told him who I was or what part of the city I was from."

"You must have done."

"No, no I didn't."

She sighed. "Look, the Jeradine are a funny lot, and Ty-gen's stranger than most. They're not like us." A fact Tom was coming to appreciate all too well. "Get used to it."

Ty-gen watched the pair disappear. The adaptability of human youth never ceased to amaze him. Earlier that very morning the boy Tom had exhibited mistrust and fear of all Jeradine, yet now he walked down a street in the Jeradine quarter without any apparent concern at all.

Confident that Kat and the boy were truly on their way, he crossed to the back wall of his main room, pulling aside one of the curtains that dominated the place; a particularly large one. Behind it lay an apparently unremarkable section of wall; simple blank stone.

Ty-gen then turned his attention to a small, high alcove beside the large curtain, checking the power levels of the battery it contained. They were adequate and would not need topping-up for a while yet. He flicked a switch and the blank area of wall started to change, seeming to grow smoother and gradually losing its sense of solidity, until it resembled glass rather than stone. The wall's opaqueness rapidly faded, as if all the colour were being leached out of it, until what remained was foggily transparent. The subterfuge was a simple one, but he felt confident that Kat would have had a good root around the room at some point and this afforded adequate protection from prying eyes. There was no reason for the girl to associate the odd contraption in an alcove with the expanse of blank wall.

Through the screen that had been revealed an array of crystals could be seen. They were built into the wall and were sufficiently elaborate to put even the depiction of Thaiburley to shame. Kat would have been truly astonished had she seen this. As Ty-gen had assured her, she had no idea what the Jeradine were capable of once they put their minds to it. Few humans did.

He waited patiently for the image of one of those few to appear, and after a handful of minutes, it did. The face of an elderly man swam into focus, masking the crystals behind.

Ty-gen appraised the image with no small amount of concern. "You're looking tired, my friend."

"Just getting old."

The Jeradine had been associating with humans long enough to know the sort of response that was expected of him. "You're not old; you will never be old."

The figure on the screen raised an eyebrow. "Age has a habit of creeping up on all of us, Ty-gen, and nothing that behaves in such a fashion is ever likely to have our best interests at heart."

Uncertain of how else to respond, the Jeradine nodded sagely, and reflected that he still had much to learn about the nuances of human communication.

"I presume you didn't call me up merely to comment on my appearance?"

"No, of course not. He was here – the boy you're so interested in."

"Ah, good. You're sure it was him? Yes, of course you are, or you wouldn't be troubling me." The man immediately answered his own question. "Sorry. As I said, tiredness."

"It was him," the Jeradine said. "Unless, that is, there are two boys running around the City Below who are able to hide effectively in plain sight."

The man smiled, "Unlikely, at least so I hope. And where is the boy now?"

"On his way home. I sent him in the company of someone I trust."

"This would be the girl; your trading contact?"

"Indeed." Mentally, Ty-gen berated himself. He should never have been lulled by the apparently frail image on the screen, should always remember that behind this weary exterior lurked one of the keenest minds he had ever encountered, certainly in a human.

"Good. Then we have done all we can for the moment." The figure on the screen gave a sigh. "The pieces are in play. Now all we can do is hope that they fall in our favour. Thank you for your help, Ty-gen; in this and in everything else."

The Jeradine bowed his head, a brief bob of acknowledgement. "I am, as ever, your servant."

"You are, as ever, my friend," the human corrected. Then he moved a hand, reaching forward to the controls on his side and the screen went blank. From Ty-gen's perspective, the crystal array built into the wall became visible once more. He stared at the familiar construct for an unfocused second before turning the power off. He wished that he could feel as loyal and as certain as his words suggested, but instead felt that he had just thrown a youth to the wolves, with no guarantee of survival. Then there was Kat, whom he had come to know and grown genuinely fond of.

He hoped fervently that the girl returned to claim his sculpture of the city but found he had no great confidence that she ever would. If either of the two young humans failed to live through the next few days it would be one further death on his conscience, a conscience already heavily burdened with too much loss and guilt.

FIVE

Dewar sat and waited. For company he had a small cup of scalding hot coffee, as strong and dark as anyone could wish for. He'd forgotten how much he missed this place, and the coffee. It was as if he had never been away. Haruk's stall still stood on its familiar pitch and the brew produced here was just as fresh and satisfying as ever. He thought he saw a flicker of recognition in the tall man's eyes, which was hardly a surprise; Dewar generally made a point of stopping off here at least once on his infrequent returns to the City Below. In fact, his instruction of "No syrup, just a twist of lemon" as the coffee was served had probably been unnecessary – Haruk had an excellent memory for customers' preferences – but he said it anyway.

He sipped, sampling the bitter hit of the tar-dark brew on his palate and savouring the heat as it slid down his throat.

Dewar could still remember when the coffee seller first arrived in Thaiburley, perhaps taking a particular interest because Haruk was, like himself, so obviously a foreigner. The man's tanned and weathered skin would have marked him instantly as such against the sallow complexions of the City Below natives even had he not possessed a pair of tribal scars beneath his left eye. This stranger, this outsider, had the audacity to try and set up business on the fringe of the market, much to the chagrin of the established stallholders.

That first day had ended in a beating, with Haruk chased from the market square. But the next morning he was back, setting up a little off-market this time, in one of the broader streets leading to the square. People stopped to drink on their way through and evidently liked what they drank. That day too had ended with a beating and the stall kicked down, its candy-striped awning ripped and trampled.

Surely this would have been enough for most men, but the coffee seller was nothing if not persistent, and the next morning found him in the same spot, the stall rebuilt and its awning cleaned, stitched together and defiantly back in place. Those who enjoyed his brew the previous morning did so again, and they were joined by others.

Dewar appreciated the man's resolute single-mindedness. He never seemed willing to accept defeat, always bouncing back no matter how frequent and forceful the discouragement. The assassin could not help but admire such determination, and he watched events unfold with relish and a growing respect. Not least, of course, because Haruk did happen to brew the best coffee around. Steadily, this stubborn outsider established his presence, initially earning tolerance and eventually grudging acceptance.

Now, years later, Haruk's stall was an accepted part of the scenery. He was doubtless paying his dues to the

local street-nicks and doing all the things that any resident of the streets was required to do. He had even
branched out, providing at first crisp, dark biscuits and
then adding small honeyed pastries as tempting accom-
paniment to the coffee. The area around his pitch had
also gained a few rickety chairs and uneven tables
along the way, an invitation for customers to rest their
weary feet and their drinks, perhaps even to linger and
enjoy a further cup or two. The furniture was arranged
haphazardly in front of the stall, spreading into the
street beyond like a pool of spilt milk.

Dewar took another sip, aware that Martha was now
late, but that didn't bother him. It was deliberate no
doubt; her way of making a statement, of showing that
she was still her own woman. Such minor rebellion
was irrelevant. She would arrive soon enough and that
was all that mattered.

Martha was not Dewar's only contact here. He had
been busy since returning to the streets, tapping old
sources, not all of whom seemed overly pleased to see
him. Doubtless some had assumed that his ascension
to the City Above meant they were rid of him; if so,
this morning must have come as something of a disappointment to them. One or two were reluctant to talk
to him at all, but a modicum of gentle persuasion soon
convinced these bashful souls that soft living had done
little to change him and that reticence was not in the
best interests of their health.

Much of what he learnt as a result proved far more
interesting than anticipated, if incomplete and tantalising. No one seemed sure of what was going on,
though a few were willing to share their pet theories
which Dewar dismissed as unfounded, unlikely and

distracting. It was all whispers, isolated fact, overheard rumour and half-baked conjecture, but once all these elusive threads were pulled together, what emerged was distinctly disturbing, crackpot theories aside. It left Dewar in no doubt that there were things going on in the City Below that neither Magnus nor, he felt certain, anyone else in the Heights suspected. This seemed far more than the usual petty squabbles and spats; something fundamental was changing. It bubbled just under the surface, a pressure which simmered and steadily built. However, none of this was his prime concern. Dewar hoped to be finished and well away before whatever was brewing came to a head. The boy was his prime concern and, to date, no one appeared to know anything on that score.

No, Martha was not his only source of information but she remained his most reliable one.

He frowned down at the small cup, which was virtually drained – he always preferred to enjoy the drink as piping hot as possible. Should he get a refill now or leave it for a minute, wait for the girl to appear?

Prompted by habit he looked around, checking his surroundings, making sure that everything was as it should be and nothing was out of place. All seemed to be in order. People continued to drift past in both directions, mostly with the casual, unhurried gait that spoke of routine rather than purpose. The curled-up figure two doorways down on the opposite side of the street still hadn't moved and Dewar still couldn't decide whether the man was dead or simply passed out, though he tended to favour the former. A scrawny black and tan dog trotted by, pausing to look up at the assassin, hoping for scraps, but not lingering. The mutt moved with a fluid grace that suggested a wholly natural origin rather than one owing any debt to the dog master's tinkering.

Dewar's attention was drawn back to the immobile man. He could have sworn he'd caught movement in the corner of his eye, though the body seemed to be in exactly the same foetal curl as before. The man was lying in front of a dilapidated and evidently unused building, a carcass of a dwelling; perhaps that fact influenced Dewar's assumption that he was already dead.

A crippled girl approached him. She was hunched on a small, low wooden platform, a miniature cart made mobile by a quartet of oversized wheels, one per corner. She powered the cart with synchronised pushes from her two arms, reaching forward and hauling against the ground like an oarsman digging into the water to pull a rowboat forward. One leg was thrust out before her; a stump that ended at the knee, the truncated limb wrapped in a swathe of material which may once have been vivid green before it became so grimy. It was impossible to tell whether the other leg was whole or not, since it was folded beneath her as she sat. The girl, no more than ten or eleven, might have been pretty were it not for a scar which crossed her forehead diagonally above the left eye, ending at her ear. The ear was mangled and half torn off. It was clearly an old wound. She wore her hair pulled back, so that the scar was fully visible, displayed as if it were some sort of trophy. The conspicuous blemish made a vivid counterpoint to the girl's amputated leg.

Dewar watched her approach with a mixture of amusement, fascination and surprise. Beggars were few in the City Below these days, had been since the Ten Years War which had ended generations before. He knew his history and was aware that tourism had flourished here before the conflict, but while the trade had re-established itself and even grown in other parts of Thaiburley, it had never really done so here, resulting in few pickings for the professional beggar, which this girl clearly was. Before the war, beggars had apparently been plentiful, organised into gangs in much the same manner as the street-nicks. In those days, it was not uncommon for mutilations such as the girl's to be self-inflicted, or inflicted by the men behind the beggars at any rate. Surely no one still went to such extremes?

The girl reached him and came to a halt. "Please, sir, my mother's sick, can you spare a few coins for–"

She was interrupted by Haruk, who rushed from behind his counter, shouting at the girl and gesticulating for her to be gone. His stick-thin frame looked almost menacing as raised arms caused his robes to billow out, increasing the coffee seller's apparent size.

The girl turned away reluctantly, pushing herself towards the market with surprising speed once she built up momentum, and leaving an insult trailing in her wake as thanks: "Brekkin' foreigner, why don't you go back where you came from?"

Hardly original; it was an over-used barb which had become blunted and ineffectual a long while ago. After a mumbled apology in Dewar's direction, Haruk returned to the counter, muttering in a language Dewar didn't recognise. The incident did cause him to reflect, though, on how times had changed. The girl had clearly singled him out. He was now an outsider here and that fact was obvious to all.

There! Movement again from the curled figure, torso and arm; there was no mistaking it this time, though it had only been a twitch. Then a reptilian head appeared from the body's far side and a spill dragon clambered up to sit on top of the man, its snout glistening with fresh blood. The scavenger repositioned itself so that only hind legs and tail were visible as it went back to feeding.

Dewar snorted; so much for movement.

People continued to pass the dead man without sparing him a second glance: there was nothing unusual here. Somebody would alert the razzers at some point and the body boys would appear, to carry the corpse away and dispose of it in the usual fashion, depending on who was paying the most for human parts at present.

One woman did pause, to give the body a cursory once-over, but she then continued on her way without attempting a closer examination. Presumably the street-nicks had already relieved it of anything remotely valuable.

He glanced back towards the market square and spotted Martha at last, though he almost failed to recognise her. Dewar thought he had seen the girl in all her moods, but he had never seen her looking like this. She was hunched over, with a shawl clutched tightly about her, as if to provide protection from the cold, though the temperature was anything but. Gone was the familiar provocative strut, instead she moved with a careful deliberation which suggested that each step was an invitation to pain. There were bags under her eyes and a ripe bruise on one cheek, though she had attempted to hide it with makeup.

All in all she looked worn out and used up, a mere shadow of the haughty, long-legged beauty he remembered.

She dropped into the seat opposite him, clearly glad to do so.

"You look like shit," he told her.

"Thanks. You always did know how to turn a girl's head."

"What happened?" His eyes focused on her bruised cheek.

She shrugged. "Some of the sailors can get a bit rough once the liquor's inside 'em."

Dewar knew from experience that Martha had no problem with things getting a bit rough. In fact she positively enjoyed it, which was one of the things that first attracted him to her. This particular episode must have been a good deal more than that.

"Are you all right?"

She seemed momentarily taken aback, as if such a question was the very last thing she expected from him, but then nodded. "Comes with the territory."

Which was true enough, he supposed; a working girl always ran the risk of violence every time she went with a new punter. Those like Martha who operated without a pimp relied on experience, instinct and luck to avoid the occasional dangerous customer. Sometimes, that simply was not enough.

"This was last night, I take it?"

"Yeah."

"Does he have a name, this sailor?"

"What's with all the questions?"

"Oh, nothing. I was just thinking that I might have a use for a man who's handy with his fists; especially one who'll be sailing out of the city in a day or two and so out of reach of the razzers."

The girl snorted. "That's the Dewar I know and love. See a woman beaten black and blue and all you think to do is admire the thug's handiwork. For a moment there I thought you might have grown yourself a heart since movin' up-City."

He favoured her with a tight smile. "You should know me better than that."

"True."

He bought her a coffee and a pair of honeyed pastries, refreshing his own now empty cup at the same time.

"So, to what do we owe this honour, then?" She licked her fingers, having wolfed down one of the sticky pastries in the blink of an eye. "You leavin' the luxury of the Heights and comin' back to this cesspit? Can't be here for your 'ealth, that's for sure, so what are you after?"

He couldn't help but smile. With a mere mouthful of food and a few sips of hot drink inside her, the girl was already showing signs of regaining her customary spirit and fight. They grew them tough in the City Below.

"I need some information."

"You don't say."

"A boy, a street-nick, found his way up to the Heights last night and involved himself in matters that don't concern him."

"Brecking Thaiss, you're joking!" The girl laughed. "How?"

"It seems this lad has a particular knack of hiding."

Her eyes narrowed. "Really?" He could see that her mind was already working on the problem. "Don't suppose you've any idea which gang?"

"No, but it must have been one more or less local to here. He went up the wall."

"Only two stairs he could've used then, which means he must've made a deal with one of the gangs holding 'em." The second pastry vanished. "Important is it, all this?"

"No, of course not, I came all the way down here on a whim."

She grinned. "That's what I thought. You'll be paying well, then."

"Assuming the information merits it, yes."

"Have I ever let you down?"

"Not yet, and now would not be a good time to start."

"I'll see what I can find out."

"Good."

"Might take a while, mind."

"No it won't," he assured her.

"These are difficult times. There's a lot of unrest – rumours of gang wars and worse. Street-nicks keep turnin' up dead, so many of 'em that even the razzers have started to fidget on their fat arses and take notice."

That was an interesting little titbit. While it confirmed much of what he'd already heard, this was hardly going to change anything. "And this should concern me because...?"

"I'm just sayin' that it mightn't be as easy to find things out. People are wary and I'll have to tread carefully, that's all."

"Tread as carefully as you like, just so long as you tread swiftly." With that, he sat back and stretched; a deliberately dramatic gesture. "Time we went to your place now, I think." The girl wasn't the only one who could make a statement. "I could do with a little relaxation."

She nodded. There was no resentment in her eyes, no bitterness, just acceptance.

Tom was conscious that there were far more Jeradine about than there had been in the early morning, though most appeared to be doing little of anything. Some were sprawled on benches, others sitting on seats, all generally loitering with no apparent purpose. It made him uneasy. Their faces were raised towards the cavern roof as often as not, which he couldn't understand.

"They're warming up," Kat explained, evidently noting his interest. "Soaking up the heat and energy from the sun globes. Ty-gen says it's essential, that they all have to do it."

This reminded him uncomfortably of spill dragons. You could often find larger specimens of the carrion lizards hauled out on some rock or other by the Thair, basking in similar fashion. This comparison to the opportunistic reptiles troubled him; he didn't want to think of Ty-gen, who had been so kind, in such terms, but he couldn't help it.

All the flatheads they passed, whether lounging or mobile, seemed as oblivious as ever to the two humans in their midst.

"Can't they see us?" Tom wondered aloud at last.

"Course they can. We're just beneath their notice," the girl replied.

Never once did he see any two of the Jeradine talking, which made him wonder how they communicated. "Don't they ever talk to each other?"

"Not so's I've noticed."

"Aren't you curious about that?"

"No, why should I be? I ignore them and they ignore me. Ty-gen's the only one I'm bothered about and he talks to me just fine. The rest can go swing. Now shut up with the questions, will you? Or I might just decide to dump you and forget about that crystal city after all."

"Go ahead. I'll manage."

"Course you will."

Despite his anger he kept pace with the girl, and kept quiet. Not for the first time, Tom found himself puzzled by the attitude of others. How could she not be curious? If he lived constantly with a mystery like this he wouldn't be able to let it rest, he'd have to find out. The boy regretted not raising the question of Jeradine communication with Ty-gen when he had the chance.

The area they were moving through deteriorated rapidly as they left the Jeradine quarter. This was still a step up from the Runs, but not by much. They walked down avenues of dilapidated buildings with broken windows and crumbling walls. The few people they passed possessed a desperate, furtive look which Tom was all-too familiar with.

He caught movement in the corner of his eye, against the wall of one of the abandoned buildings to his right. He looked closely, and saw one of the strangest creatures he had ever seen. His first impression was that it was all legs and eye. Long, slender and hairy limbs reached out above, beside and below the thing; three of them with a fourth vanishing around the corner of the building. Each limb ended in a clawed foot which had dug into the crumbling mortar of the house and fastened to it. At the centre, where the four limbs met, was a single large eye which dominated the small body supporting it. The whole thing was flush to the wall, splatted there as if someone had flung the creature at the building and it had stuck there in the flattened, splayed position it landed.

Suddenly a stone shot over Tom's head to strike the wall a fraction away from the eye. The creature scurried around the corner and out of sight.

"Brekkin' freak!" Kat called out.

"What was that?"

"One of the Maker's creatures."

Tom thought he understood. "We've got the dog master," he said. "Gets a dog and opens it up, then adds to it, using bits of other dogs, dead or alive, and mechanical oddments too, building something strange along the way. Looks a bit like a dog perhaps but isn't really, not any more. It's his creature. They say he sometimes includes bits of humans too."

Kat nodded. "Yeah, you've got it. Sounds like the Maker but he doesn't just stop at dogs: any creature you can think of plus a few he makes up along the way. Those spidery things seem to be his favourite at the moment, they're all over the place."

"Was that one spying on us, do you reckon?"

"Could have been, hard to say. The Maker likes to keep an eye on things and his creatures get everywhere."

Tom laughed at her choice of the word 'eye', but the girl didn't join in.

"It's nothing to laugh at. The Maker's a weird one and dangerous with it; not to be messed with, and his creatures are vile."

They carried on as before, but the girl seemed more watchful, more alert.

"So where are we now?" Tom asked at length.

"More questions?" but her retort lacked any real venom and she answered him readily enough. "This is Thunderhead territory. We're actually heading in the wrong direction at the moment, but it's the quickest way to get to where you want to go without crossing Blood Herons' turf. The Blood Herons and Thunderheads hate each other, a feud that goes back years."

"Thunderheads? What kind of name for a gang is that?"

The girl shrugged. "The nick who originally led them claimed he was caught out in a storm outside the walls on a visit to the Market Row one day."

That was possible, Tom supposed, though hardly probable. The average street-nick rarely went outside the walls, even during the occasional trip upstairs to the Market. More likely the kid had been told a story which featured a thunder storm and his imagination had taken it from there.

"We can head left here," she said as they approached a junction, "and start swinging round so that we're actually going in the right direction for a change."

Kat moved forward with confidence, but then he had yet to see her move in any other way. Until, that is, she strode round that corner.

The girl froze, holding out a restraining hand to stop him.

"Shit!"

He looked to see what the problem was. A group of street-nicks stood a little way along the street, four or five of them, one leaning with his back against a wall, the others in a crude semi-circle around him. Were they what had alarmed her? He couldn't see anything else that could have done. The nicks were deep in conversation and didn't appear to have spotted them as yet. Then he felt himself tugged back around the corner.

"What is it?"

"Trouble." She risked another quick peek. "You eyeballed the one leaning against the wall – big fella with sandy hair?"

"Sure."

"They call him Sharky; nasty bit of work. He's a Thunderhead, so are the two furthest from us, but the other two…" She shook her head, as if unwilling to accept what she'd seen.

"Go on."

"They're Blood Herons."

"So much for them being enemies."

"They are," she said hotly. "Or at least they were. I don't understand."

Tom failed to see what the problem was. "Alliances change quickly," he told her. "Feuds come and go."

She shook her head. "Not this one. It's legendary. Blood Herons and Thunderheads have been at each other's throats for years, ever since the Herons took the stairs from the Thunders, but that was just the start of it. Too much blood has flowed and too many nicks have fallen on both sides for those two to ever sheath knives – Stace, for one. That memory's still fresh, still burns. She was real popular with the Blood Herons, a mean bitch in a fight, but she had all the right moves and was built in a way that made even grown men sit up and take notice, and she knew it."

Kat was visibly upset. "Blood Herons and Thunderheads make up? Never!"

"So how do you explain those nicks being together then?"

"I can't. But I do know it's wrong. Something's happened, something big."

Tom was dismayed by the vehemence of the girl's reaction. It was a reminder of just how little he knew about this companion whom he was relying on as a guide. He guessed there was more going on here than met the eye, that these two gangs and the girl had a history, which was all well and good, but would it distract her now? Could he still trust her?

"What do we do then?" he asked, hoping to focus her attention on matters at hand.

"Keep heading the way we've been going," she replied. "Cut left a bit further along and hope we don't bump into any nicks."

"And if we do?"

"Brazen it out. If they are on the lookout for you, they'll be expecting to see a boy on his own, not one travelling with me."

"So why don't we just stroll past this group here then?"

"Cos they know me as a renegade, a loner. No point in raising questions unless we have to, right? Anything else you want to know, or can we get going?"

With that, they were off again, much to his relief. The girl strode forward with renewed purpose, forcing Tom into hurrying to keep up. She was muttering as she walked. "It's not natural. Must have been some killings at the top. Those two would never trust each other, couldn't be any peace while they were still in charge."

Tom stayed quiet, realising that none of this was meant for him, that the words were a reflection of some inner debate. He might as well not have been there at all, until, that is, the girl turned and addressed him directly. "You're not from around here, kid, so you don't realise how unreal this all is but, trust me, it's weird."

He felt the familiar stirrings of curiosity, wondering why this turn of events caused her so much concern, but sensed this was not the right time to question her any further and, for once, managed to resist the temptation to do so immediately.

The tight-packed buildings made way on their right for a temple, one instantly recognisable as dedicated to the goddess Thaiss, indistinguishable from any other such with its squat, domed roof. An ornamental waterfall trickled down out front, before snaking its way down a short channel to a small pool. The waterfall was ceremonial, said to represent the goddess's home at the source of the Thair. Tom had no time for this or any of the other religions that proliferated in the under-City. By his reckoning, life was too grim to be by anyone's design. On the other hand, he knew people, fellow street-nicks among them, whose faith was unshakable.

A grey-robed acolyte swept the steps in front of the temple with a crude broom. She paused to watch them pass, neither smiling nor scowling but simply staring. Tom stared back, turning his neck to continue doing so until she dropped her eyes and returned to her cleaning.

Past the temple, they came to the narrow entrance of what was an alleyway rather than a street, a simple gap between buildings. The entrance had been blocked with a section of old wooden fencing, squeezed in at a slant, as if somebody had wedged it there in a half-hearted attempt to keep people out without really believing that anyone would want to go down there in any case.

Kat kicked down the flimsy barrier. "Come on, this should help us avoid that group at least."

He followed her down a narrow passageway that smelt of dampness, decay and urine. The walls on either side were coated in moist green slime and Tom did his best not to brush against them. He had touched worse in his time, but not by choice. Matters were made all the more awkward by constant obstacles; things that had apparently been abandoned here to clutter the floor, all of which they were forced to step over or around – half a broken crate, an old chair, remnants of broken pottery.

He concentrated on following the girl without touching anything and reassured himself that each step brought him a little closer to the alley's end. It was with a huge sense of relief that he finally stepped out from between the buildings into a broader street. Kat didn't pause, not even to make sure he was still with her, but instead turned right and continued to stride onward, leaving him to keep up as best he could. Tom realised that she was still heading away from the avenue where they had seen the street-nicks, even though the passageway must have brought them some distance past where the group had been standing.

She took the next left turn, only to bump headlong into a quintet of street-nicks coming the other way; four boys and one girl. Tom stopped dead in his tracks,

looking to Kat for guidance. This was unknown territory and he had no idea whether it was best to simply
nod hello and keep walking, to run for it, or even to
stop and fight – though, given the odds, he presumed
not the latter. Kat's body language suggested she was
fairly relaxed so he did his best to act the same.

There were a few guarded greetings but no obvious
tension. Only the girl eyed Kat with any hint of hostility,
and it was she who said, "Got yourself a boyfriend, Kat?"

One of her companions sniggered. "Boy is the word.
He's only a kid."

"Who'd have thought it, the renegade with a boy?"

"Wasn't even sure she was into boys."

Tom felt certain this was leading up to a fight, but
Kat still seemed unperturbed. She smiled at him. "Take
no notice. It's the gang mentality. Once one of them
starts yapping they all have to join in, like a pack of
dogs."

With that, she took hold of his hand, too swiftly and
firmly for him to resist, and led him through the knot
of youths, who gave way, all except one, a tall, mean-
looking kid who stood his ground and glowered. Kat
didn't say a thing. She just stared at him. After a few
seconds he curled his lip and snorted dismissively, before stepping aside to let them pass.

Tom wasn't sure how he felt about the handholding
at first, but then decided that maybe he could get used
to it. Then he thought of Jezmina, and realised guiltily
that it was a while since he had last done so.

"Keep walking, don't look back – and don't let go of
my hand," Kat said quietly.

Tom was more than happy to oblige.

• • •

The further Tylus moved from the wall the more the quality of his surroundings improved, if not their smell. He turned right at what seemed the only viable point to do so, assuming his recollection of the maps held true, and walked into a street bordered by single storey brick-built buildings. The bricks were crude and looked improperly baked, but at least they were bricks.

An elderly man, gaunt and dressed in faded clothes which seemed overlarge on his emaciated frame, sat on the doorstep of the first such. He stared at Tylus with stony-faced indifference. The Kite Guard nodded and smiled in greeting and was about to ask if this was the right road for the guard station, when the man responded by opening his mouth in what might have been either a snarl or a grin – it was impossible to tell – revealing toothless gums in the process. Tylus kept quiet and hurried past.

The guard station proved easy enough to find in any case. It even had a sign over the door. Taking a deep breath, Tylus pushed said door open and stepped inside. He wasn't sure what sort of a reception to expect, but even so, the one he got surprised him. This was much smaller than any guard station he was used to, though it seemed to contain at least as many people. Compared with the Kite Guard's more ordered, restrained squad room, this was a scene of frenetic chaos, with people dashing everywhere, sheets of paper pinned to walls and huddles of guardsmen scrutinising objects of unfathomable purpose. It seemed he had arrived at a bad time, although perhaps this was normal and there would never have been a good one. The first officer he addressed barely glanced in his direction and clearly couldn't spare the time to actually talk, but instead directed him to the duty sergeant with a distracted wave of the hand. The sergeant occupied a large desk which dominated the back wall, not even having a separate office by the look of it.

The man was older than Goss and had a little more hair, but he seemed no more welcoming, at least to judge by the scowl with which he greeted Tylus.

"So, have the Kite Guard come to bail us out in our hour of need?"

"Erm, not exactly, sir, no. I'm…"

"Yes, yes, I know." The sergeant held up a restraining hand. "Had a message about you; I've got it here somewhere." He started rummaging around in a haphazard pile of papers and pulled out a creased sheet.

"Here it is." He smoothed the sheet out, held it up and peered at it. "Kite Guard Tylus, come to find some street-nick or other."

"Yes, sir!"

"Shouldn't be difficult, we've loads of the scrawny breckers running around down here. Take whichever you want. I wish you luck with your search, officer."

"Thank you, sir." Tylus felt a familiar sinking feeling, realising the sergeant had no intention of adding anything further. This was not going as he had hoped, but then what ever did? He continued to stand where he was, trying to find the right words.

"Was there something else?"

"Yes, sir. That is, I'm afraid I'll be needing some help from you and your department."

The sergeant gave a dry, mirthless guffaw. "Help? You need our help? Not a chance, son."

Tylus reached into his tunic. "I've a warrant here, signed by Senior Arkademic–"

"You think that matters to me?" the sergeant interrupted. "You're not in the Heights now, lad. This is the real world. We're in the middle of some major gang action down here, with killings every day and not enough men to even begin investigating them all, particularly since some genius up-City insisted on having a crack-down on 'corruption' in the force and made me discharge a quarter of my officers a little while back. Corruption? This is the City Below for Thaiss's sake, the whole place runs on corruption! So I don't care if you've got a warrant signed by every breckin' member of the Council of Masters and a minor deity or two besides, I can't help you!"

Tylus's stomach dropped a little further. This was definitely not going to plan. For the first time since his interview with Magnus, he began to wonder whether being handed this mission was such a stroke of good fortune after all.

The squad room door burst open and a figure came charging in. He wore the typical brown and orange, mud and clay, uniform of the city watch.

"There's been two more," he called out across a room suddenly stilled.

"Whereabouts?" the sergeant called back.

"Near the canning plant. Two Sand Dragons, both older lads, lieutenants by the look of 'em."

The sergeant muttered something under his breath and then surged to his feet. "All right, show me exactly where."

"What about my assignment?" Tylus asked in desperation. "Senior Arkademic Magnus insists you help me."

"What's he gonna do? Fire me? Fire us all?" the sergeant snapped back. "It's chaos down here, where do you think they'd find anyone to replace us? Nobody else would be crazy enough to do this job."

Despite the words, he seemed to relent, casting his gaze around the room until it came to rest on a particularly young and sickly looking officer. "Richardson, get your arse over here, now!"

The lad scampered to obey.

"Right," the sergeant told him, "you're to put aside whatever you're currently working on and help Mr Kite Guard here, got it?"

Tylus saw the young officer's eyes widen in alarm. "But, Sergeant, I've got–"

"That wasn't a request, officer, that was an order. You'll just have to fit in your existing case load around whatever Officer Tylus here needs you to do. Clear?"

"Yes, sir." The lad's face now showed the sort of weary resignation that Tylus imagined his own must display in the presence of Sergeant Goss.

The sergeant turned back to the Kite Guard. "There. I know this is not what you were expecting but it's all I can spare you – more than I can spare in truth – so make the most of it, get busy and keep out of my way. Understood?"

"Sir!"

With that, the sergeant hurried towards the door and out of the squad room. Tylus supposed he should feel grateful. After all, one officer's help was more than he thought he was going to get just a few minutes beforehand. However, he strongly suspected that this Richardson was the runt of the department, the officer the sergeant could most afford to spare. A bit like himself. Still, whatever his shortcomings, the lad was bound to have some local knowledge, which was what he needed the most. Two runts together; the pair of them against the world.

Tylus turned to his new assistant, trying to look confident and in command. "Come on then, Richardson, we've got a boy to find."

SIX

When Magnus first told him of this assignment to the City Below, Dewar had felt supremely confident. After all, this was territory he knew well, the place he had first made a name for himself. What could be simpler than bamboozling a wet-behind-the-ears Kite Guard while tracking down a street-nick who had managed to infiltrate the Heights, word of which was bound to have spread like wildfire through the streets?

Yet things were not going entirely to plan.

To start with the boy appeared to have vanished and there was not even a whisper about any daring raid on the Heights. Then there was the alarming deficiency in his old network of contacts, which had been painstakingly built up over a number of years through the judicious application of blackmail, bribery, intimidation, cajoling and violence. True, it was still largely intact, even though one or two individuals may have been a little reluctant to renew acquaintance, but their reluctance was not the real problem; it was more the one significant hole in his former network which was giving him grief. Vital links had been cut away, leaving a yawning chasm where he needed information the most. Dewar seemed to be left with no viable source within the city watch. This was frustrating in the extreme, because the watch tended to be aware of most everything that was going on, if only because they knew what they had been paid to turn a blind eye to.

In the past, Dewar had operated four different informants within the local guard units. One he knew for certain to be dead, a second he could find no trace of whatsoever and the other two had apparently both been dismissed following a crackdown on corruption within the force. This last struck Dewar as hilarious, and he wondered how they had chosen which officers to kick out and which to retain. Perhaps the tossing of a coin was involved, it being the most appropriate method that sprang to mind.

Of course, given a little time he could soon cultivate new resources, he was an expert at such things. All he had to do was single out a suitable candidate, stand beside the man in a favoured tavern for a few off-duty evenings, chat to him, befriend him, buy a few drinks – and then casually raise the subject of money. Dewar knew how the game was played, knew the steps to that particular dance by heart, but he also knew that it took time and, while he himself could be patient when circumstances required, Magnus was anything but. The arkademic would doubtless expect to see results sooner rather than later. Which meant that Dewar had a problem. Fortunately, he was rarely at a loss in such situations. After all, that was what he did best: resolve problems.

The alleyway he now walked down was a particularly wretched one, at the back of the docks and just a spit and a hop away from the Runs. Even the hovels and detritus of that shantytown were a step up from this place, which had been abandoned to the rats and spill dragons years ago. Dewar descended a flight of crumbling steps to a still-sound basement beneath the imploded shell of a building. He pulled aside rotting boards and the tangled remnants of what had once been a fishing net – things he had dragged across the entrance when leaving – and pushed open the door beyond.

Yes, patience and bribery had their place but, under the circumstances, he had decided to forego such subtleties in favour of a more direct approach.

The smell that assailed his nostrils as the door opened suggested the room's only human occupant might have made his own contribution to his uniform's colour: brown and orange. Mud and clay the watch liked to call it, proud at the association with good solid and honest earth. Shit and shit was how Dewar had always thought of it, and he never did understand how anyone could take pride in their uniform while at the same time surreptitiously pocketing handouts for dishonouring it.

The guardsman was where he had left him, still gagged and bound to the solitary chair in the centre of an otherwise bare room. Dewar had expected no less but even so felt mildly disappointed. He was forever seeking a challenge and opponents invariably failed to deliver one. Light filtered into the room via a single window – a horizontal slit of grime and filth set high in the wall, immediately below the ceiling, at a height which coincided with street level outside. That any light at all penetrated an opening made near opaque through so much accumulated muck struck Dewar as a minor miracle and bore testament to the persistence of nature's energies. Enough did so to glisten dully from the hide of the room's other occupant: a spill dragon, about the same length from tip to tail as a man was tall. Not the largest Dewar had ever seen but impressive enough. He had found the thing skulking around the ruins above and herded it down here, locking the lizard in before going in search of the city watch.

There was nothing special about this particular guardsman, he was just unlucky: in the wrong place at the right time. Dewar had knocked him out and carried him back here, to be bound, gagged and woken, in that order. The assassin had then administered a light beating; nothing permanent, nothing too serious, but painful – just enough to make it clear that he knew what he was doing. All the while he made sure that the man was conscious of the spill dragon which lurked in the shadows, hugging the wall, unsettled by all the commotion.

As he worked, Dewar asked questions, initially about the boy, about the Kite Guard and about the disquiet on the streets. After a few minutes of this he paused, as if suddenly remembering himself. "But of course, you can't answer me, can you? Not with that gag in place. And you do want to answer me, don't you?"

The man nodded vigorously, his eyes wide with fear and now, perhaps, also hope.

As soon as the gag was removed words poured from the razzer in a veritable torrent, though much of it was of little or no value, as Dewar had expected. That wasn't the point. It was what the man might come to know that most interested the assassin.

Not that he was about to admit any of this to his captive, not yet. So he feigned disappointment, gave the man a single cuff around the ear and replaced the gag, ignoring the protests and pleas.

Like the guardsman, the rat was freshly caught, though unlike the guardsman it no longer breathed. After tossing the rodent to the spill dragon, Dewar dragged his captive's chair around so that it faced directly towards the lizard, which had already begun to examine the newly presented titbit. The assassin crouched behind the chair, hands resting on its back, his face close to the guardsman's ear, and he resumed speaking, in a casual, relaxed manner, as if chatting to a friend.

"Have you ever seen a spill dragon attack a corpse? Of course you have – must see that all the time in your line of work. Fearsome sight, isn't it? The way those jaws wrench off chunks of meat."

As if on cue, the lizard placed one clawed foot on the dead rodent, took the exposed head and forequarters in its mouth and then twisted and jerked. In truth, spill dragons' teeth were nothing special. Dewar had made a study of such things when he first arrived in the City Below. Their real strength lay in powerful neck and shoulder muscles and the ability to grip firmly. Spill dragons didn't so much bite bits from a corpse as tear chunks off, which was exactly what this one now proceeded to do. The rat tore apart somewhere around its middle, bloodied entrails hanging from the lizard's mouth until it tossed its head back and pulled the grizzly snack fully into its gullet.

"They'd get through to a man's innards in no time," Dewar continued. "Of course, as we all know, spill dragons like their meat fresh – always first to a kill, aren't they? I reckon this one would go for your leg first, or maybe your foot." He stopped, shifted forward and made a show of studying the man's legs where they were tied to the chair. Then he came back behind him again. "Yes, the foot, I think. Can you imagine what short work it will make of your toes? Probably take the entire foot clean off at the ankle with the first bite." He gave a dramatic shudder. "Brrr! A horrible way to go."

Judging by the look in his captive's eyes, the man agreed with him.

The dragon lifted its leg ponderously to reveal the bloodied remnants of the rat's hind quarters, entrails and internal organs starkly visible, before lowering its head and snapping them up. The snack had been devoured in two mouthfuls, leaving behind just a smear of blood on the floor.

There was a great deal of superstition surrounding spill dragons. The level of ignorance, even among the inhabitants of the City Below who lived beside them, was alarming. Superstition inevitably led to misunderstanding, and Dewar had always found misunderstanding and ignorance to be useful tools. He needed the razzer's spirit broken but couldn't spare the time to see to it himself, so determined to let the man's own imagination do the job for him.

He stood up, stepped a little away from the chair, and took out a small phial of oil, the contents of which he set about sprinkling in a tight circle around the captive, drop by drop. While he did so, he spoke in the same relaxed, off-hand manner as before.

"Might be an idea if you jiggle about a bit while I'm not here, just to let this one know you're still alive. Mind you, once it realises you aren't going anywhere, that you can't go anywhere, I'm not certain how much good jiggling will do, but we live in hope, eh?

"Oh, and I wouldn't go jiggling about too much if I were you. Otherwise you're likely to shuffle the chair and yourself outside this ring of scent I've laid down. Dragons hate the stuff, so as long as you remain inside this circle you should be all right; until the scent fades of course, but that ought to be a good few hours away. I should be back before then. Lots to do, mind you, so it all depends on how long things take."

The scent ring completed, he paused to survey the room and decided that everything was as he wanted. The razzer sat statue-still, clearly choosing for the moment at least to avoid jiggling entirely and rely on the circle of scent.

Dewar then left to meet up with Martha and attend to other business, nodding to his captive on the way out and saying, "I'll see you on my return… hopefully."

Now, a good few hours later, the pungent smell of excrement suggested that the man was sufficiently unnerved. Dewar had no idea what action on the spill dragon's part might have caused such terror, but he did know that any perceived threat would have existed only in the razzer's mind. Spill dragons, despite their formidable appearance and the impressive size they could sometimes reach, really did feed exclusively on dead meat. Fortunately for the assassin's purposes there were plenty of whispered tales that insisted otherwise.

The lizard made a ponderous beeline for the door as soon as it opened, but Dewar closed it promptly, barring the way. The reptile's presence would help to keep the unfortunate guard's mind focused. The thing hissed at him and proceeded to dig at the door's base. He ignored it and stepped into the room.

"Good. Still with us, I see."

The razzer's bulging eyes and indecipherable but clearly desperate attempts to speak past the gag confirmed what Dewar's nose had already reported: the man was ripe to agree to anything. He loosened the gag and took out the wad of cloth from the captive's mouth.

"Please, I've got a young daughter," the man croaked.

"And you're suggesting I take her in your place? What sort of a father are you?"

"No, no... I didn't mean that."

"What then?"

"It's just... she needs her father."

Dewar brought his face close in to the petrified razzer's, "And I need information. Understood?"

"Yes, of course, anything."

They soon came to an arrangement. The last thing Dewar said to the man before rendering him unconscious again was, "Remember, if you do let me down, it won't be you I bring back here next time but your daughter."

He then rapped his newly recruited informant on the head, before untying him and lifting him up onto a shoulder, ready for dumping back where he had been caught. How the man explained the missing hours to his commander and colleagues was his problem, not Dewar's. He left the cellar door open as he went, allowing the frustrated lizard to escape and roam where it would. He had what he wanted from the creature and the place, and had now finished with both.

One informant within the Watch was hardly blanket coverage, but it was a start.

"Are they still following us?"

"Yeah," the girl said, without looking round. She had let go of his hand as soon as it became obvious the ruse wasn't going to work. At one level Tom was glad to have his hand free again, but at another he felt vaguely disappointed.

"Any idea why?"

"A couple of ideas, none of them pleasant." She gave a sigh. "I've had enough of this."

With that she spun on her heel and strode back the way they had come, towards the following knot of street-nicks. Or, rather, she bounced towards them, all challenge and attitude.

"Hey! You got nothing better to do than follow us like a pack o' snivelling hounds?"

Unprepared for her abrupt stand, Tom could only watch, impressed despite himself. If he were one of those street-nicks, he would have been startled by such a display of confident aggression.

"No harm, Kat," one of the nicks responded, raising empty hands defensively, "we were just driftin' this way is all."

"Then breckin' well drift some other way."

"It's just a little strange," one of the others said, "you travelling with company, 'specially some lad that none of us 'ave seen before."

"What with us being on the lookout for a stranger, a nick who gave a couple of Herons a dustin' by the stairs this mornin'," the first nick added.

Tom came up to stand by Kat's shoulder. Tempted though he was to join in, he reckoned Kat had a better idea of how to handle these nicks than he did, so kept quiet.

"Since when have the Thunders cared what happens to a couple of Herons? Thought you'd all be cheering to see 'em get a pasting."

"Times change."

"Not that quickly. What's goin' on?"

"Funny you should ask. Come with us and we'll explain everything."

The girl shook her head. "Can't, I got business. Catch me on the way back, maybe."

"That's a shame," the first nick said. "You see, we got business too. That kid you're with looks an awful lot like the nick we're lookin' out for and there's things we need to show the both o' you. So your business will just have to wait."

The group of nicks were already edging apart, nothing obvious, just little movements and shuffles that saw them start to fan out, their haphazard knot unravelling into a line.

Kat snorted. "So not only do the Thunderheads care about the Blood Herons these days, they run errands for 'em as well now, do they?" Her hand rested casually on her hip, close to one of her knives.

"It's not like that."

"How is it then?" The aggression was back in her voice, the challenge in her posture plain. "You explain it to me."

The nicks at each end were easing forward, so that the line started to curve towards a crescent. Tom's hand drifted to the grip of his own knife as Kat adjusted her balance, taking half a step back and in the process coming level with Tom.

"Don't come any closer," she warned, "or this'll turn ugly."

"Ugly for you, maybe. It's five against two."

She stared at the speaker, the nick in the centre, then swept her gaze across all of them. "You know me. Some of you've seen me fight. Do you really want to do this?"

The nick at the far end of the line, the girl, clearly didn't. Her gaze flicked nervously towards her friends, presumably hoping for signs of a climb-down. Perhaps she had seen Kat fight before. Tom hadn't, and could only hope that his companion was as formidable as she seemed to think she was.

With as swift and smooth a movement as he had ever seen, Kat drew her twin blades. Long, much longer than the knives he was used to, almost small swords. Kat now looked more warrior than street-nick, an image her next words did nothing to dispel.

"I fought in the Pits and lived. You know that. Why are you facing me?" The words were spoken calmly and seemed to carry more concern for the other nicks' lives than her own.

The Pits? Was Kat telling the truth, or playing on some popular myth? If true, how old must she have been? Tom had heard rumour of bouts in which children were armed and then child was thrown in against child or against slavering dogs and other creatures, but he hadn't entirely believed them. Until now. Before this, such tales were merely a threat to instil obedience: "Do as I say or it'll be the Pits for you."

Looking at Kat, as she brandished the two blades before her and started to twirl them, expertly twisting them around each other in a blur of dancing steel, he believed her.

Somewhat belatedly he pulled out his own knife, almost embarrassed to do so. It seemed totally inadequate, little more than a toy in the present circumstances. None of the Thunderheads had drawn steel yet, but they hadn't retreated either. Tom sensed that this was the key moment and guessed that the fight or flight question was currently crossing each of their minds. In their position, he knew which he would have gone for.

On impulse, he spoke, hoping to find the right words to tip the balance. "Maybe the five of you can take us if you want it enough, but what will that cost you? And who's going to be first? Cos there's no way the first one's going to walk away from this."

On cue, Kat smiled, emphasising the point. She was suddenly all menace, flash and steel personified.

"Oh look, he speaks," the nick at the centre said.

There was a single snigger from the boy beside him but the girl at the end wasn't the only one who looked nervous now. Glances flicked up and down the short line. What was holding them? Why hadn't they backed down yet? A sneer, a token insult or two and then a cocky saunter in the opposite direction was what Tom would have expected, yet the nicks continued to hold their ground.

Suddenly, all that changed. The nick standing one in from the left, next to the girl, took a shuffling step backwards. The lad at the opposite end said, "Breck," before he turned and ran, and then all five of them were in retreat, not sauntering as Tom had pictured, but running for all they were worth.

Kat laughed, a triumphant cackle. "Go on, you breckers, run!" She sheathed her knives with dramatic flourish. "That showed 'em!"

Tom wasn't so certain. There had been a look of terror on the face of the first nick to turn and flee, one that appeared all of a sudden and, now that he came to think of it, he wasn't at all sure that the nick in question had actually been looking at either him or Kat as he did so.

These thoughts percolated through Tom's mind as he watched the five Thunderheads stampede away. These same thoughts were punctuated by a woman's scream, just as Tom reached the conclusion that the nicks were not in fact running from him and Kat at all, but from something behind them.

He whipped around, to find himself confronted by an apparition out of nightmare. A great beast was pacing towards them – still some distance away, but coming closer. A dog, at least in appearance, but on a gigantic scale. Oxen were far from common in the City Below but Tom had seen a few in his time, even stroked one once, and this dog was as big as the tallest ox he'd ever seen. Sandy-brown in colour, its fur looked coarse and wiry, while it had long legs and a body that tapered to a slender stomach, and a thin tail which was currently held out rod-stiff behind, but it was the front end which truly impressed: all barrel chest, compact neck, thick muscle, and broad mouth bristling with teeth.

Tom was vaguely aware of people hurrying away beyond it, though one woman, presumably the source of the scream, huddled against a wall sobbing. By the look of things she need not have worried. The creature ignored her. Its gaze was fixed firmly on Tom.

"Oh, Thaiss!" Kat exclaimed from beside him.

"What the breck is it?" Tom hissed.

"A demon hound, from out the Stain; they raid into the city from time to time, but I've never known them to come this far."

Tom started to back away, "It's as mean as it looks, I suppose?"

"Worse. They're vicious as demons and twice as hard to kill."

"Seems to me those Thunderheads had the right idea."

"Yeah, I was thinkin' the same. Come on!"

With that they were both running, following in the wake of the now vanished Thunderheads.

Tom could hear the hound behind him and risked a glance back, only to be horrified at how quickly the beast was catching them. It had broken into a gallop, long strides eating up the ground. Then it barked; a sound that rolled forth like the tolling of a giant bell, deep and dark and more chilling than any sound Tom had ever heard before.

"It's coming!" he called out, shouting the obvious in his panic.

"We need to get off the street. Can't outrun it," the girl yelled back. "There!"

She darted to the right, choosing an alleyway between two buildings. On impulse, Tom went in the opposite direction, running into the alley's counterpart on the left-hand side, reasoning that if they split up at least one of them might get away.

He dared to hope that they both would, that the dog would keep going, that it had not been chasing them at all and they were simply unfortunate enough to be running in the same direction.

No such luck.

He charged forward and was just registering the fact that this was a dead end, that there was a solid wall directly ahead, when he heard the hound follow him, its breath and the click of claws on the hard ground sounding louder and closer in the confined space of the alley. He ran on, desperately looking for a way out – a doorway, something to climb – but there was nothing.

The wall was coming up fast, the demon hound even faster. Why hadn't he followed Kat? At least then there would have been someone with him and he wouldn't have been alone when he died.

He turned to face the hound before quite reaching the wall, determined not to be run down and killed without knowing precisely when the death-stroke was descending. The beast had slowed, perhaps realising that its prey was trapped. It padded forward steadily, confidently, head lowered, the hackles on the back of its neck standing proud, mouth curled in a snarl and eyes glinting with the promise of death. A long strand of viscous drool hung from the monster's mouth, stretching down towards the ground, and steam rose from its hide, giving the impression that the beast was newly emerged from some fiery realm of hell.

Tom still clutched his knife – he hadn't had a chance to put it away since the confrontation with the Thunderheads. He now thrust it out before him. Little more than a gesture of defiance, the blade might perhaps be useful for picking lodged food from between the demon hound's teeth, but he doubted it would achieve much else. Still, the knife was all he had, and he might as well give as good an account of himself as he could. Perhaps he might even get in a good blow or two and cause this brecking dog some minor hurt before it tore him apart.

He crouched, knife held in his right hand, left arm slightly raised, ready to provide balance. A rumbling growl started to gather somewhere deep within the hound, a crescendo building towards the inevitable bark which, when it came, was so loud and fierce that it startled Tom even though he was expecting it, causing him to miss what might have been his best or possibly even his only chance, as the dog raised its head to release the sound. For a split second the beast's throat was exposed, but before Tom could think to react the head came down again and the opportunity had passed, with him still rooted to the spot.

He couldn't afford to dwell on that though, he had to concentrate. The hound gathered itself in preparation to charge or pounce and Tom realised his time had run out. He decided to go low, in the hope that he could somehow slip beneath the hound's attack and strike at its underbelly or perhaps throat, if he got the chance.

Suddenly the dog's growling changed to a yelp of pain and the beast leapt into the air, twisting as it did so, its back legs coming down alarmingly close to Tom, who instinctively shied away, pressing up against the wall. The hound landed awkwardly, one back leg buckling beneath it, and Tom saw that the beast was injured, fresh blood streaming from a deep wound in the suspect leg. At the same time, he realised there was somebody else on the opposite side of the beast.

"Kat!"

So intent had he been on the monster and his own imminent demise that he hadn't even noticed her approach. Nor, apparently, had the dog, though it certainly had now. The hound turned its attention to the girl, ignoring Tom, presumably concluding she represented the greater threat. It might be injured, but the demon hound was by no means beaten. It attacked the girl – a lunge hampered by its unsound leg. Teeth snapped on empty air as the girl danced back, twin blades flashing towards the dog's face but missing in turn.

"Come on, kid, hurry up and get out of there!"

Easy enough for her to say. She didn't have an injured and riled demon hound between her and the only way out.

Tom edged forward, debating whether he could slip past the beast, but its bulk still blocked most of the alley. He looked left then skipped across and looked right, but there simply wasn't room. Whichever way he went, he would be all but touching the hound. It would only need the beast to turn its head as he passed – one snap of those jaws and he was a dead man.

"Come on!"

"I'm trying!"

At the sound of his voice the hound looked around, as if remembering him again. Kat took her chance and leapt in, but the hound's head whipped back towards her and Tom heard the girl cry out, though he was unable to see what was happening, how badly she had been hurt, since his view was blocked by the hound itself. He had to do something.

So thinking, he reversed his grip on the knife and flung himself onto the monster's back, smelling damp fur and feeling warmth and muscle and coarse hair beneath his arms and thighs. The hair he clung to, while he stabbed down with his knife again and again.

The hound toppled, not through any blow he had struck but because its leg buckled, the boy's weight evidently too much for an animal already coping with an injury. It didn't fall sedately like some severed post, but instead writhed and thrashed and snarled and snapped. Tom was thrown off, barely pulling his arm away in time to avoid it being caught and most likely pinned or even broken beneath the wounded beast. And still it fought. Feet kicked at him, claws like great blades that could surely have disembowelled him narrowly missing his head as he ducked and cowered and shrank against the wall. Kat was there, screaming as her twin knives rose and fell, blood trailing from their blades. A string of ruby droplets arced towards Tom, spattering his face and hair.

He wiped the warm moisture away with one hand while, with the other, frantically searching for his knife, which had been dropped during the stomach-lurching confusion of the hound's fall. At the same time he kept one eye on the back leg nearest him, the uninjured one, with its fistful of razors that were flailing unpredictably as the beast struggled to regain its feet. Not that the hound was paying any attention to him at the time. The fight was now all about Kat; but if those claws were to catch him by accident as the foot thrashed, he'd be just as dead as if the attack had been deliberate.

Finally his fingers closed around the familiar hilt. Back pressed against the wall, he scrambled to his feet, ready to rejoin the fight, but it was already over. The great hound lay dead, and Kat peered at him over the corpse.

In fact, she glared at him. "Its shoulders? Was that the best you could do? You leap on its back and try to stab it in the breckin' shoulder? Have you any idea how much fur and skin and muscle a demon hound has there? It probably didn't even feel your knife."

"Well I had to try something!"

"Fine, but you go for the underbelly, the throat, the eyes, or the sinews in the leg like I did to start with – they're the only soft spots a demon hound has. You don't go for its frissing shoulder!"

"Well it's a lot of breckin' good your telling me that now! We haven't all had the advantage of learning stuff like that in the Pits, you know."

The girl snorted. "Advantage? I've never heard it called that before."

Then he noticed her arm: the blood, not all of it the hound's, and the long gash. "You're hurt."

She frowned, following his gaze and glancing down at the wound as if noticing it for the first time. "Yeah, happens I am. Need to sort that out, but first things first, let's put some distance between us and this over-grown dog."

He grinned. "Why? It's not going to be troubling us anymore."

"This one won't, but I've never seen a demon hound on its own before. They hunt in packs."

"Oh." That wiped the smile from his face.

He stepped gingerly around the huge carcass, half-fearing one final twitch of a back leg and doing his best not to tread in the pool of blood which oozed from beneath the still form.

"Thank you," he said to the girl.

"What for?"

"Coming back for me. You could have got clean away."

She shrugged, a little self consciously. "Yeah well, didn't want to let ol' Ty-gen down, did I? And I've still got that sculpture of his to go back and claim...

"Oh, breck!"

The final comment mirrored Tom's feelings exactly. A huge form had materialised in the mouth of the alley, blocking their way out. A demon hound, an apparent mirror image of the one that lay dead behind them. This time Kat was trapped with him, and it seemed unlikely that anyone else was going to come to their rescue by crippling the hound from behind.

The two knives, sheathed after the fight, appeared in the girl's hands once more and Tom reached for his own recovered weapon, then paused, struck by a sudden thought. *Demon* hounds? He remembered the precious dust which he had been guarding so carefully, both because it was costly and because it was said to be a rare weapon that could actually affect the Demons of the Upper Heights.

Would demon dust work on a demon hound? There was only one way to find out. Instead of his knife, Tom fumbled for the pouch holding the dust, forgotten until that moment.

The hound snarled at the two of them before throwing back its head and voicing a long, mournful howl. Then it charged.

"Hold your breath," he yelled to Kat, loosening the chord at the mouth of the pouch and reaching inside to grasp a fistful of the coarse, gritty dust.

"What?"

"Don't breathe!"

That was all he had the time to say. Teeth flashed towards him, a brawny shoulder struck him and he staggered backwards. Kat's knives were there but the hound ignored her, seemingly intent on Tom. Drawing a ragged breath and heeding his own advice by holding it, Tom flung the dust towards the face, the eyes, and that impossibly gaping maw.

The passage of his hand was marked by a puff of smoke, a grey trail shot through with sparkling silver motes that blossomed into a twinkling cloud before sinking around the demon hound's head.

The results were startling and immediate; the beast hesitated, breaking off its attack. It snorted, sneezed, and then began to tremble. Initially, a slight tremor ran down its body, which soon developed into continuous shaking. Tom and Kat both edged back, waiting to see what happened.

The trembling became convulsions. The hound staggered a few paces and then its front legs gave way, folding up beneath it so that the barrel-like chest thudded to the ground. The back legs followed almost at once and the hound collapsed, to roll onto its side, pushed that way by erratically convulsing limbs. It lay there twitching, movements that became slighter and less frequent.

"What did you do?" Kat asked. "What is that stuff?"

"Demon dust."

"Why didn't you use it on the first hound?"

"I forgot about it."

"You forgot?"

"Hadn't we better get out of here?" Tom asked, keen to change the subject.

"Yeah, let's." They hurried out of the alley, both sparing a glance back at the still-twitching hound. "What the hell is demon dust?"

"No idea. Something I was given. Your arm…" The cut was deeper than he'd realised; blood now bathed the girl's forearm.

"I know. Need to get something on it."

"If we were near the Thair I'd cut you some larl reeds and wrap the wound in them," he said helpfully.

The girl grunted. "No river near here, kid, but there is an 'erbalist I know around the corner, in Ink Lane. She'll have something."

The houses in Ink Lane were single storey and neither the worst nor the best Tom had seen. Proper buildings rather than shanty huts but they had a tired, slightly wilted look, as if they had known better days. Kat went up confidently to a door that looked no different from the rest and knocked.

The elderly woman who answered greeted them sourly, as if customers were the very last thing she wanted to see. However, she led them into her front room, which was dingy and had the oddest smell of anywhere Tom could remember. She caught him wrinkling his nose and the scowl deepened. Bunches of plant stalks and withered leaves hung at intervals from the ceiling; some dried and brittle, others well on the way to becoming so. They dangled from strings that looped across the room, causing Tom to duck as he entered. The woman moved around without the need to do so, presumably through familiarity. Rows of glass and earthenware jars were racked on wooden shelving around the walls and the room even boasted a hearth, where a pot of something bubbled and steamed over an open fire. This seemed the most likely culprit for the unpleasant smell.

A younger woman emerged from a back room, presumably the herbalist's daughter or apprentice, or both; there were no introductions.

The old woman tutted when she saw Kat's arm, as if it were negligent of the girl to receive such a wound. She then brought them some water, using it to wash the arm while Tom cleaned the residual blood from his face and hands.

Without any direction, the daughter or apprentice selected two jars from different shelves, the second of which was dusty from disuse, and carried them to the herbalist. The first contained a powder, which looked golden orange in the dim light. The old woman sprinkled some over the wound before scooping a large dollop of white ointment from the second container and smearing it liberally on top. She then wrapped a bandage around the arm and they were done. Coins changed hands and the pair were ushered hurriedly from the house. The whole process took a mere handful of minutes.

Tom blinked, wondering whether the incident felt as unreal to Kat as it did to him.

He drew a breath, preparing to ask that very question, except that as he did so a mournful howl forestalled him. It was a sound impossible to mistake: the howl of a demon hound. And it was answered almost immediately by a second, similar call.

Tom stared at Kat. She stared at him. Neither said a word, they simply turned and ran.

SEVEN

"In here, quickly!"

The baying of the hounds pursued them relentlessly, drawing ever closer. Tom had no idea how many of the brutes were hunting them, but knew for certain that they were being hunted and that there was more than one demon hound on their trail.

How could they lose them? "Running water's the only thing," Kat supplied, "but we're a long way from the Thair."

So they ran, which was not a solution at all but only a means of delaying the inevitable. And now the howls sounded very close indeed and Tom knew they didn't have much longer, so he decided to take a gamble, to try something before it was too late. The only problem being that his idea was a desperate one and if it failed there would be little opportunity to try anything else.

He grabbed the girl by the wrist and started to haul her into a narrow alley.

"What in Thaiss's name? You're going to get us both killed!"

She struggled but he clung on and pulled her after him, surprised by his own strength, fuelled as it was by fear and desperation.

"Trust me!" he hissed, turning to glare at her, trying to convey in that look all the confidence he didn't feel.

Her struggles ceased and she glared back. "What choice do I have? We've lost so much time they'll catch us for sure unless you can come up with a miracle."

Could he? He remembered Ty-gen looking straight at him and then saying that his ability didn't work on Jeradine. What if it only worked on humans? He thrust the memory to one side, refusing to be distracted.

"All right, then. Crouch down like this and get as close to me as you can."

"Frissin' pervert."

"Quickly," he repeated, desperation in his voice.

"You'd better know what you're doing, or I'll kill you myself when this is all over." With that, she did as instructed, hunkering down so that her knees pressed into his legs. Tom began his familiar mantra, reaching out to hug her at the same time.

She shrugged his arms off irritably and hissed, "Watch your hands, kid."

"Shut up!" The conviction in his voice startled even him. "Do you want to survive this or not?"

Her eyes widened but she suffered him to reach around and hug her; the only reaction this time being a long, deep breath.

We're not here; you can't see us, you can't smell us or hear us, Tom began again, adapting the mantra for the occasion.

"What are you doing?"

"For pity's sake, shush. Let me concentrate."

We're not here; you can't see us, smell us or hear us.

Would it work? This was something new in more ways than one. Tom thought his ability worked on dogs – had noticed their apparent indifference to him when he was hiding and reciting the mantra – but he'd never deliberately set out to conceal himself from dogs before, and the incident with Ty-gen had shaken his confidence. Then there was the additional concern that he had never attempted to hide anyone else this way before. Could he conceal Kat as well as himself? He had to. Banishing any doubts, Tom concentrated on the all-important mantra.

A muttered repeat of, "You'd better know what you're doin'," impinged on the periphery of his awareness, but he ignored it.

Seconds later he could hear the pack approach, could hear their snorting, snuffling breaths. A dark shape loped across the mouth of their refuge, to be followed by another. Then everything grew abruptly darker as something loomed in the mouth of the alley. One of the hounds stood there, its vast form completely blocking the entrance. The beast sniffed the air querulously, as if it almost scented something but was not entirely sure.

It took one slow step towards them and then another, testing the air the whole while.

Tom squeezed his eyes to tight slits, hardly daring to look at the creature but not able to look away. He recited faster and faster, fiercer and fiercer, repeating the mantra for all he was worth.

Still the hound came closer, until it stood no more than a pace from the huddled pair, its muzzle looming above them. A sticky strand of glutinous saliva dripped down upon Tom's shoulder and it was all he could do not to flinch away. Kat now clung to him as desperately as he held her, and Tom could feel the rise and fall of her shoulders beneath his arms, her small breasts pressing against his side. He knew that she was close to panic and prayed that she did nothing to give them away. He feared too that if she didn't, he might.

If the hound were to take just one more step it would bump against them. Surely the thing must sense the pair of them at any second. Its fetid breath washed over them and Tom squeezed his eyes shut, determined not to let his concentration waver.

Just as he thought he could take no more, that his nerve was going to break, that he couldn't recite the protective mantra for as much as another second, there came a familiar mournful baying from the street beyond the alleyway. Instantly, the hound stiffened, its head whipping around. Then it turned, not without difficulty in the narrow space, and trotted off, presumably to see what its fellow hounds had discovered.

Tom remembered to breathe again.

Kat still clung to him. He felt her trembling, was conscious of her warmth, and continued to hug her as tightly as ever. They remained like that for a further minute, maybe more, her head buried in his shoulder, neither of them daring to move until the sounds of the pack receded and ceased.

Tom stayed motionless for as long as he could, but this was hardly the most comfortable of positions and his leg muscles were protesting like mad. Finally he shifted, only a fraction but it was enough to break the spell. Kat pulled away from him and hastily jumped to her feet, as if embarrassed.

"Gods, boy, how did you do that? What did you do?" Her voice was shaking. She prowled around to the mouth of the alley like a caged beast, all jumpy, nervous energy, peering out as if to make certain the hounds really had gone.

"I don't know," he replied, straightening up and flexing his legs, all the while staring at her, trying to decide what had passed between them during the brief minutes they had hugged each other, or whether indeed anything had at all. "It's just something I can do."

"Well, that's a neat trick my little street-nick, and no mistake." The girl was fully in control once more, her voice having steadied and regained its conviction. She stopped pacing long enough to stare at him, as if seeing him anew. "There's more to you than meets the eye, isn't there? No wonder old Ty-gen thought you were special."

Then she was moving again, grabbing him by the wrist and hauling him out of the alley. "Come on. The hounds aren't about to give up. They'll be back."

This was the second time Kat had touched him willingly. The first time, in front of the Thunderheads, had been awkward, an unnatural moment for both of them, but this time she had done so without a second thought. Something had changed, but Tom didn't have time to stop and ponder what. He stumbled after her, trying to think what more they could do to evade the hounds, but he was out of ideas. His mantra and its cloak of invisibility had always been enough before.

"Where are we going?"

"Back-track," she explained. "When they can't find us, they'll come back to the last definite scent and try to work out where we went. If we go back on ourselves, they might not catch on for a while – buys us some time."

"Maybe, but then what?"

"I'm thinking, kid, I'm thinking."

That was one time too many. He stopped in his tracks, wrenching his hand from her grasp. "I'm not a kid!"

She looked startled, as if it had never occurred to her that he might actually object to being called kid. "Right." Her smile was sardonic, but she resisted any temptation to respond further.

"You're barely older than I am."

"It's not all about the number of years, but you made your point." The recollection that this girl had survived the Pits flashed through Tom's mind. "Now come on!" That last was virtually a snarl and Tom was suddenly afraid that he had pushed her too far and that, despite everything, the girl might decide he was more trouble than he was worth and so abandon him in order to concentrate on saving her own skin.

They ran back through streets which had already passed in a blur once that day. People, who were beginning to emerge from their homes now that the hounds had gone, stared at them with suspicion: dozens of pairs of hostile eyes whose gaze followed them as they shot past.

They reached a more affluent quarter, where the homes were noticeably more solid and better built, and the girl slowed.

"Merchants homes," she explained. "No skimping in these houses. Now, if I can just find… there!"

She jogged across to one of the properties. It was large by the standards of the City Below, though still single storey as were most of the buildings down here, and built of solid-looking stone.

"Give me a leg-up."

Tom cupped his hands and braced himself, as Kat placed one foot into the stirrup made by his fingers, then transferred all of her weight onto that foot, with Tom straining to lift her higher as she reached for the wall's top. She made it, and nimbly lifted her body onto the roof, before reaching down to offer Tom a hand as he leapt and scrambled to follow her.

He too made it, though not as elegantly or as easily.

"Gods, kid, you're heavier than you look!" Kat complained in the middle of it all. He was too preoccupied at the time to object to being called kid again.

Once they were both safely up, she led the way across the roof with delicate steps. "Tread carefully," she warned over her shoulder. "No matter how sturdily these things are built, they weren't meant to support anythin' as heavy as us."

Tom followed as best he could, with Kat's warning ringing through his thoughts. He willed the roof to continue supporting him with every step.

They soon crossed to the back of the house. There was only a narrow gap between this building and the next, which Kat leapt with ease, while Tom was simply relieved to reach the other roof at all.

And so they went on.

He didn't ask her why they'd adopted this elevated route. He had no intention of giving her a further excuse to make him feel inadequate and in any case, the answer was pretty obvious. As far as he could tell, the hounds couldn't climb, and if the beasts did catch on to the back-tracking trick and follow them to that first building, they would have no way of telling which direction their quarry had taken from there.

Which was all well and good, just so long as they didn't run out of accessible rooftops. The moment they encountered a gap too wide to leap or a roof too high to reach and were forced to return to street-level, however briefly, was the moment they became vulnerable again. He knew all about dogs' sense of smell and didn't doubt that the keen nostrils of quartering hounds would detect the faintest of spoor once they chanced upon it.

Tom tried not to think about that and instead concentrated on the figure of Kat ahead of him. There was no denying the litheness of her movements, the way she seemed to flow from one step to the next, making him feel like a stumbling fool in comparison. Subconsciously, he started to mimic her gait, the rhythm of her footfalls. She also made the leaps from building to building look easy, where as he was finding them anything but. The vertigo that had assailed him in the city's upper Rows gathered at the fringes of his awareness, waiting to pounce, but he resolutely ignored it. After all he had been through of late, the drop to the ground here was nothing.

Kat made each jump without breaking stride, stretching out with her lead leg and soaring through the air like a bird, whereas he had to pause, focus, and then run flat out, hurling himself across the intervening gap.

"Careful!" she snapped after one particularly heavy landing. "Carry on like that and you're bound to go through at some point."

Angry protestations from within and the knocking of what could only have been a stick or broom handle against the ceiling beneath him helped to emphasise the warning. Tom expected Kat to use this as an excuse to berate him again, but instead she simply laughed and he found himself laughing with her.

"Come on," the girl said with a good-natured grin, and his spirits lifted.

She set off once more, dancing across the roofs of the City Below while he did his best to follow, though his own efforts were more akin to a blundering assault or reckless charge than any dance.

The cramped, crowded nature of these streets worked in their favour, with the buildings huddled so closely together that the pair had little trouble in leaping from the top of one to another and would be fine so long as they avoided any major thoroughfares.

They managed to do so for a further dozen or so leaps. Eventually, as they approached the lip of yet another roof, Kat came to a halt. So abrupt was this stop that Tom, who had been focusing on each individual step and not on his wider surroundings, was taken by surprise and barely avoided bumping into Kat and knocking her off the roof.

Her graceful movements had all but mesmerised him. The further they travelled together the more he began to see her as something other than a prickly and irritating guide. He had never met anyone quite like her before. This new appreciation was confusing and he felt embarrassed as she looked back and raised an eyebrow, worried that his face might betray his thoughts in some way.

"Well, looks as if it's the streets again from here on in," was all she said.

He stepped up beside her and they crouched at the edge of the roof, looking down at what was clearly a major street, far too wide to even think about leaping. A peddler pushed a barrow of dubious looking knick-knacks along immediately below them, the top of his head not far beneath their toes. One of the barrow's wheels squeaked annoyingly with each revolution. The man's every movement was laboured and spoke of intolerable effort and weariness.

A young boy scampered along in the opposite direction, presumably on some errand or other. A street-nick in the making, or was he one of the privileged few, apprenticed to some tradesman? Whichever, his hurried passage set the peddler's dog to barking. Tom had not even noticed the dog until then, so closely did it shadow its master's cart. A small and scruffy thing, little more than a tatty streak of brown fur, this was a very distant cousin to the beasts that hunted them. The dog looked set to chase the boy, but scampered back to heel at a gruff command from its master.

Kat hesitated, as if listening. All Tom could hear apart from the cart's squeaking wheel was the nearby calling of a street hawker and the rhythmic clanging of a blacksmith's hammer somewhere in the near distance. He hadn't heard the demon dogs' howls for some time, not since they'd given the beasts the slip. He dared to hope the hounds hadn't rediscovered their trail.

Evidently satisfied, the girl looked at him, briefly raising her eyebrows. "Ready?"

He nodded. "Is this far enough, do you think?"

"It'll have to be," she responded, turning around.

Kat let herself down backwards, clinging to the edge of the roof with both hands so that her feet almost reached the ground and then dropping the short distance that remained. Tom copied her. Two well-dressed women hurried past, eyeing them with obvious distaste, while the gaze of the drunk slumped in the doorway opposite was less accusing.

"This way," and Kat was off again.

As far as Tylus could make out, there was nothing much wrong with Richardson. A little quiet, it had to be said, but he put that down to the lad being bullied by his fellow officers or singled out by the sergeant. Comments made by others in the squad room – jokes at the young officer's expense – seemed to confirm his assumptions regarding the lad's status, but Tylus suspected that he was merely lacking encouragement and a bit of self-confidence.

Certainly Richardson had quickly proved his worth in the Kite Guard's eyes. From his new assistant he had already learned the names of the three major gangs whose territories overlapped the patrol area of this particular station: the Scorpions, the River Snakes and the Blue Claw. The first two he could understand, but had to ask about the Blue Claw. Apparently they took their name from a type of giant crab which lurked in the deepest parts of the Thair and was rarely seen. Reputedly as large as a house and famed for their ill-temper if disturbed, the meat of these formidable crustaceans was considered a great delicacy, but obtaining it was hazardous in the extreme, since the crabs were said to be capable of cutting a man in two with a single snap of their oversized front claw, which, of course, was blue.

Leaving out many of the details, including the embarrassing ones such as his own part in the street-nick's escape, Tylus summarised events for Richardson's benefit and explained the nature of his mission to the City Below. The guardsman thought the most likely starting point for any street-nick's ascent via the walls would have been the very stairway by which Tylus first arrived in the under-City. He further explained that this particular stairway was controlled by the Scorpions, and anyone wanting to use it would have to come to an arrangement with them first, paying a sort of toll known as passage fee, which would be made in the form of either coin or bartered service.

This information lifted Tylus's spirits considerably. He had barely arrived in the City Below and already his investigation was progressing with admirable speed. He could see the whole process unfolding neatly before him. The Scorpions would tell him exactly who had paid them to use the stairway, thus identifying the relevant gang and the guilty street-nick. Richardson, with his local knowledge, would show him where to find the boy and he would then make the arrest, taking greater care this time around, before escorting the lad up-City. Simple and effective; a resounding endorsement of investigative procedures properly applied. Even Sergeant Goss could not fail to be impressed by such alacrity and efficiency. There might even be a promotion in this. How that would stick in Goss's craw.

The relationship between the street-nick gangs and the guardsmen of the Watch struck Tylus as an odd one. From the outside they appeared to be natural enemies and yet the two groups co-existed and even co-operated with each other on occasion. He struggled to fully grasp the dynamics of the situation and, en-route to the arranged meeting with the Scorpions, quizzed Richardson in the hope of gaining some insight.

"But it amounts to extortion, surely."

"If you say so," Richardson said, a little defensively, "but it works. Every stall holder and shop keeper pays the local street-nick gang a small tithe for protection and they get no trouble as a result. Keeps the peace." Removed from the environment of the guard station, Richardson seemed to relax, and spoke far more freely than at any time before.

"But if all the traders in a given street were to band together and look out for each other, they could do the same thing, surely, cutting the street-nicks out and saving themselves the tithe."

"That's been tried, more than once. Most recently a year or so ago. Not on our patch, thank Thaiss, but we were among those roped in to bring the resultant fire under control. It was a nightmare – burned out three whole streets."

"You're saying the street-nicks set the fire? Surely not. Those other streets must have been on their turf too. The fire would have cost them dear."

"Better that than let a rebellious bunch of traders get away with not paying their tithes. Others'd get the same idea and that would cost the gangs dearer still."

Tylus mulled it over. "And if the watch comes across a group of shopkeepers or stallholders banding together to resist the gangs, they support them, I presume."

"Nah. We have a quiet word in their ears and tell them to pay up like good little boys. Best not to rock the system."

"What?" Tylus stopped dead in his tracks and stared at his colleague, appalled by what he was hearing. "The watch actually endorses these criminal activities?"

"Look, I don't know how it works up-City, but down here our main concern is with keeping the peace, and you don't do that by upsetting the street gangs and taking away their income. Now the way we go about things might not appear in any rule book, but then none of them rule books were written by anyone who ever had to try and survive down here. Maybe someday they'll come up with a set of rules writ especially for the City Below, but until then we have to improvise our own."

Tylus was impressed. This was the longest speech he had yet heard Richardson make. No question, the lad was coming out of himself now that he'd found somebody who was actually willing to listen to him. And what he said made a lot of sense, albeit in a twisted way. Tylus determined not to judge the officers of the watch too harshly; after all, he was the outsider here and didn't have to live as they did. Even so, he was singularly unimpressed by what he had heard and was finding it hard not to condemn the whole ethos of law enforcement here in the basement world.

The young Kite Guard did have a more immediate worry, a matter he was shying away from thinking about. It occurred to him that the street-nicks they were on their way to meet were likely to be the very same youths he encountered on first arriving here – the ones he had handed out a beating to – or at least their fellow gang members. He neglected to mention the incident to Richardson, fearing that the guardsman might be less inclined to arrange a meeting if he knew about it. The bottom line was that Tylus had no idea what sort of a reception to expect from the Scorpions should they recognise him, which meant that, as yet, he wasn't sure how to approach the upcoming meeting. However, so buoyed was he by the day's successes that not even this concerned him unduly. He felt sure that things would go his way, even if he did have to wing it.

His confidence wavered almost at once. A trio of street-nicks waited ahead of them and in the centre stood the lad who had lifted his puncheon earlier that day, the one he had knocked over with his fists. He managed to stifle the smile that tugged at the corner of his mouth on seeing the boy's bruised cheek, not to mention his red and swollen nose, but was completely unprepared for the look of horror that spread across the street-nick's face at sight of him.

"It's the frissin' cloud scraper," the boy yelled. Tylus had never been called that before but knew the expression: common street slang for anyone living in the Heights. "The one who topped Des," the lad went on. "Run!"

With that, the trio of boys scattered, all disappearing down different alleyways.

"Go after the kid who spoke," Tylus told Richardson, pointing as the boy disappeared around a corner. "I'll try to cut him off."

Richardson sprinted forward obediently in pursuit of the boy, while Tylus darted to the right, down a broader avenue which promised to parallel the alley they had taken. As he ran, he drew a deep breath and held his arms out stiffly and slightly behind himself.

Those who knew nothing about kitecapes tended to assume that they relied entirely on wind currents. They were wrong. The wind had nothing to do with a kitecape's buoyancy or motive power but everything to do with deflection, misdirection and obstruction. A Kite Guard did not need the wind in order to fly, but did have to be well versed in the likely effects of its strength and direction or risk being dumped unceremoniously from the air, just as Tylus had been the previous night. To fly a cape you needed to know as much about running with the wind and tacking against it as any sailor; but, of course, all that applied only when there was a wind worth talking about.

In the confined environment of the City Below, just as in the corridors of the Heights, air movement tended to be slight and predictable. Tylus had heard that, given the right conditions, gales could sometimes sweep down the length of the Thair and through the cavernous underworld, but not today.

The only problem with flying in the Heights was the lack of opportunity to really let loose. Low ceilings and narrow corridors predominated, but there were no such strictures in the City Below.

Tylus spread his arms as he ran, and then leapt. Instantly the cape took hold, slicing through the air and lifting him upwards. He was aware of people staring and one child even cheered, causing him to smile. The low rooftops fell away immediately and the under-City spread out before him. The view was impressive, he had to admit; even more so from this close a range than it had been from the stairs when he first arrived. Not beautiful, perhaps, but certainly impressive.

He was surprised to realise that the stench of the place no longer bothered him. In fact, he barely noticed it – filtered out by familiarity as his senses came to terms with the environment. The gods knew what they were doing when they put together the human body; it was a truly remarkable piece of engineering, as indeed was the kitecape.

He dipped a shoulder, banking gently to the left only to straighten almost immediately as he caught sight of Richardson first and then the smaller boy fleeing in front of him. The guardsman didn't appear to be have made much progress in catching the lad.

His view was abruptly obscured as a woman opened an upper storey window and prepared to empty a slop bucket, only to catch sight of him, presumably in the corner of her eye, after which she stared upward, open-mouthed. In the process she dropped the tin bucket, which clattered to the ground, much to the consternation of the well-dressed man it narrowly missed as he passed in the street below. He raised a fist in protest, caught sight of Tylus and promptly joined the woman in open-mouthed Kite Guard-watching.

Tylus was past them, overtaking Richardson as he closed on the boy.

The lad zigged to the left and zagged to the right, darting down even narrower alleyways. Tylus tensed his shoulders and rotated his arms a fraction. The cape responded by taking him higher, enabling him to keep track as the street-nick weaved his way through the backstreets. He hoped that Richardson could keep up, but didn't want to call out for fear of alerting the boy to his presence.

During initial training, Tylus had listened attentively as the science behind the kitecapes was explained: the alignment of microscopic components within the cape's unique structure, the redistribution of weight, lift gained by scything through the air, energy created by a Kite Guard's own movement, all were said to play a part. Tylus hadn't believed a word of it then and he didn't now. Pseudo-science, used to baffle the gullible and mask the fact that something extraordinary was involved.

Why else would it take weeks to renew a damaged cape and make it airworthy again?

Tylus had soon reached his own conclusions. He had seen some of the things arkademics could do, knew they were privy to learning far beyond the reach of most people, and was convinced that something of the sort was invested in the kitecapes. Call it magic, call it hidden art or secrets, call it whatever you liked, Tylus didn't care. All that mattered to him was that the capes worked.

The street-nick was changing direction so often in what was increasingly becoming a warren of alleys, that Tylus overshot him more than once. Finally the boy burst out into a broader avenue and the Kite Guard knew this was his chance.

Remarkably, Richardson had managed to follow the lad's every twist and turn; either that or he'd lost the trail completely and blind luck saw him blunder out into the street close on the boy's heels. Whatever the truth, the nick knew he was there and kept looking back over his shoulder, paying as much attention to what was going on behind him as to what lay in front.

Tylus swooped, coming down to street level ahead of the boy and flying straight at him. Just before the inevitable impact he braked, bleeding momentum, and lifted his arms slightly, bringing his body forward and underneath, raising his legs, ready to kick out so that his feet would hit the boy, bringing him down.

At the last instant the boy saw him and threw himself to the ground. Tylus sailed over the prone street-nick towards a collision with a very startled-looking Richardson. The Kite Guard fought desperately for elevation, the cape reacting with sufficient swiftness that, despite the brief intervening distance, Tylus only clipped the guardsman's shoulder with a trailing foot. Even that he turned to his advantage, pushing off from Richardson's shoulder and twisting around in the process, so that he was once more facing the fast-disappearing street-nick.

Again the Kite Guard set out in pursuit, but this time he was determined not to take any chances. He climbed rapidly, making sure to keep the boy in sight. Taking anything out of his belt while in the air was a hazardous business, since it meant folding half the cape and so losing the ability to fly, but he hadn't wanted to waste time by landing, so, once he was high enough, he angled towards the boy before closing both arms, reaching for his belt and unclipping the netgun.

Although there was no wind here worth the name, it would have been easy to believe otherwise as he plunged downward, displaced air streaming past him, caressing and even pulling at hair, face and shoulders. He had the weapon drawn in plenty of time to redeploy his cape, converting an undirected plummet into a controlled stoop, which brought him directly behind the fleeing street-nick.

The only thing trickier than taking something out of your belt while flying was discharging a weapon on the wing. Recoil could be a nightmare and more than one Guard, Tylus included, had been sent into an uncontrollable spin during training. Tylus had been one of the lucky ones, managing to escape without any broken bones. Even so, the lesson had been a painfully bruising one. A few of his colleagues had been less fortunate and one had even broken a collarbone, which prevented him from ever flying again despite the best attentions of expert healers.

This was the first time Tylus had attempted such a manoeuvre in anger, but he didn't hesitate, firing the gun as soon as he was in a suitable position. Recoil jarred his shoulder and elbow as compressed air squirted the net outward, but he was ready for it and held his glide.

The net shot out, the weighted front corners easily overtaking the boy as the net deployed before falling to the ground, bringing the street-nick down in the process.

Tylus landed and approached the entangled boy, who tried to pull away with obvious desperation, almost dragging the net with him.

"Please, don't kill me," the boy pleaded.

"Kill you? Why would I want to do that?"

Richardson arrived, gasping for breath and face flushed.

"Dunno, but you killed Des."

"I never killed anyone," Tylus assured him.

"Well someone sure did."

"Not me. I may have bloodied your nose and knocked your big friend down, but that was all." Richardson was staring at him querulously, but he shook his head, hoping the young officer would correctly interpret this as "not now". "If I was here to kill you I'd have done so by now rather than going to all the trouble of bringing you down alive, wouldn't I?"

"Suppose so," the lad said, a little grudgingly. He still eyed the Kite Guard with open suspicion. "What do you want, then?"

Having recovered his breath, Richardson now stepped in, which had been the plan before they arrived. "My friend 'ere wants some information, which we think you can 'elp with." The guardsman's accent slipped dramatically when he addressed the nick, matching the boy's, and Tylus wondered fleetingly whether this was deliberate or a subconscious reversion.

"Information? That's all?" The fear drained from his eyes as the Kite Guard watched, to be replaced by a sly, calculating look. "You sure about that?"

"I'm sure."

"Get me out of this net, then, and maybe we can talk business."

Tylus nodded to Richardson and said to the nick, "All right, but remember, if you try to make a run for it, I'll simply hunt you down again."

They helped disentangle the street-nick from the net. He stood up, brushed himself down and faced Tylus, Richardson hovering behind the skittish boy to block any attempt to escape.

"I'm listenin'," the lad told them. Tylus had to suppress a smile. Moments before this kid had been a quivering wreck, now he was all cock and strut.

"Street-nick went up-City late yesterday, either a Scorpion or with passage arranged through you lot," Richardson said. "We want to know who it was and where we can find 'im."

Tylus watched the lad's face; the eyes gave him away. He knew something, the Kite Guard was sure of it.

The nick shrugged and addressed the Kite Guard, evidently realising who was in charge here. "I might know somethin' about that."

"Either you do or you don't. Which is it?" Richardson snapped.

"He knows all right," Tylus said.

"Like I say, I might be able to tell you what you want to know but if I can, it'll come at a price."

Expecting as much, Tylus had brought a full purse of coin, carried with him from the City Above. He just hoped that the senior arkademic would endorse his expense claim once this was all over.

"How much?"

"I don't want your breckin' money, cloud scraper!"

"Then what do you want?" Tylus asked, feeling suddenly tired and frustrated and wondering what in the world else he could possibly offer the nick.

The lad looked at him, as if searching his face for something. Then, decision evidently made, he lifted finger and thumb to his mouth and produced a piercing whistle. Within seconds, the other two street-nicks who had been with the boy when they first arrived stepped out of the shadows and came to stand with their friend. How these two had kept up with the chase, Tylus could only guess: perhaps the lad's flight had not been as random as it seemed. The three exchanged glances, before the one they'd caught said, "We want you to take us in."

"What?" Tylus looked at Richardson, wondering whether this was some code he wasn't a party to, but the guardsman looked as dismayed by the request as he was.

"You 'eard me. We want to be thrown in the clink, all three of us. That's the price for your information. Take it or leave it."

The body of a man had washed up on the silt which bordered a kink in the Thair's course. It lay prone and was slightly bloated by days spent in the water. The face was visible in profile, head half buried in the mud. The eyeball had been eaten. A pair of blood herons had discovered the corpse, their black and aubergine plumage rippling in the late afternoon light like a film of oil on water. They moved around with dainty fussiness on stilt-like legs, though there was nothing subtle or fastidious in the wounds their darting beaks made in the body's flesh. The deep slashes left by their probing bills as they tore off strips of meat joined the lesser bite marks and nips where small fish and crabs had already taken their share. Something moved beneath the mud, causing one of the herons to spread its wings and use them to half flap, half hop into the air. The bird came down astride the corpse, where it bent its head and continued to feed.

Close to the man's body stood one of the many pumping substations that littered the banks of the Thair; giant sutures stitching the water to the land. Resembling stretched bubbles built of layered metal, these structures squatted at intervals along the river's edge in both directions as far as the eye could see. "Water fleas" the locals called them, both because of their appearance and because of the manner in which they leached substance from the river. Though in truth their layered form was more akin to that of a woodlouse than any flea.

Inside this particular bubble, and so hidden from prying eyes, something stirred; something which had no right to be there. The something had a designated name: Insint; neither man nor machine, but considerably more than both and less than either.

Insint had no liking for this place, but needs must. Accessing the substation had been easy, slipping in from the depths of the river. Of course, doing so had meant disrupting the station's normal functions, but his own systems were now patched into the station's, masking the damage. The city would not even be aware that this facility had gone offline until long after Insint was gone.

There could be no doubt now that the boy had failed, returning to the under-City empty handed. Insint would have known were it otherwise.

The Stain had been Insint's home ever since he slunk there at the end of the Ten Year War. From that polluted wasteland he had watched and waited, biding his time and only moving when the circumstances were right. The boy, with his burgeoning abilities, had been the stimulus, the thing he had been waiting for. Yet with this apparent failure priorities shifted. The boy could be a valuable tool, to Insint and to others. As such, he was far too dangerous to let live.

Demon hounds were formidable beasts but stubborn; it had taken years to subvert a pack to his will. Six in total he had claimed. Yet two were now dead; the work of years undone in moments. Still he risked the remaining four in pursuit of the boy, but they too had failed. He felt the moment when the boy used his power, doubtless to fool the hounds, and now the pack had lost the scent.

The authorities tended to keep their heads down when demon hounds were on the prowl, knowing they wouldn't stay long, but if the dogs hung around residential areas for too long, even the guards would feel obliged to react. Formidable though the demon hounds were, the watch had the means to capture or harm them once they were sufficiently galvanised to deploy such resources. He didn't want to risk losing any more of the pack. So, reluctantly, Insint recalled his hounds, sending them back to their home in the Stain.

The demon hounds' failure was a blow, but he had other resources. Part organic, part machine, Insint's body was encased within a metal exoskeleton, his back protected by an ovoid, beetle-like shell. This carapace boasted a series of small bulges, arranged in three neat lines along its length. Here and there a bulge was missing, a shallow oval depression marking where one may once have been. With a thought, a dozen of these bulges detached themselves, leaving behind more depressions. The detached drones floated away from his shell like rising bubbles and proceeded to circle around the cramped interior of the substation. After the few seconds needed to orientate themselves, they exited via a ventilation grill and were gone.

Insint was content. He sat, and waited. He was good at waiting.

EIGHT

When they started seeing lamplighters patrolling the streets and going about their allotted task, even Kat had to acknowledge that it was getting late and they would never reach Blue Claw territory before nightfall.

She looked at him quizzically: "Do you want to go on?"

Tom was tempted to act braver than he actually felt and give some nonchalant, affirmative reply like, "Of course," but instead asked, "How much further?"

The girl chewed her bottom lip and grimaced briefly in concentration. She wasn't pretty, Tom thought, not in any conventional sense – her nose was too big for a start and her chin a little too sharp – but even so, there was something about her.

"Well, we had to detour to avoid the Blood Herons, and then went even further off course getting away from the demon hounds, so I reckon…" The grimace slid gently into a coy grin. "I reckon we're just about as far away as when we set out."

Tom snorted with laughter, her grin widened and suddenly they were both laughing.

"Some guide you've turned out to be."

"Hey, we're still alive, aren't we?"

Which was a fair point; and she hadn't called him *kid* in hours. He drew a deep breath, the laughter subsiding. "Do you know somewhere around here we could hole up for the night?"

"I think so. If that's Brewers Lane up ahead, then yes."

Apparently it was, though there were no signs to declare it as such. But Kat seemed confident enough.

She led him down the street, nodding a greeting to a pair of lamplighters who were busy with their cart and their oil and their long tapers, the obvious glow from the latter's lit ends providing clear evidence that the sunglobes were dimming. A woman of indeterminate age hurried past, clutching her shawl, without giving them a second glance. Her focused determination was symptomatic of the time of day, as people hurried to complete their respective tasks and get off the streets. Darkness would not stop the taverns or the whores or the street-nicks from plying a lucrative trade, but people would hesitate about venturing out alone. Those who did were either brave or foolish. At least, those whose intentions were even remotely innocent.

Kat turned to the right, heading down a side street and then left down a narrower one. They crossed a small square with a stone fountain in the middle: a long spindle skirted by a shallow bowl with a pool of water beneath. The water was stagnant and the fountain looked as if it hadn't worked in ages. A pair of dun-brown songbirds had been drinking from the pool but flew off at the pair's approach, twittering their disapproval. Birds were not common in the City Below but a few inevitably found their way in along the course of the Thair and stayed. These two had done well to avoid the cook pot and the skewer.

Kat moved on, crossing the cracked pavement of the small square and into the tired-looking streets beyond. The fountain was barely out of sight before the girl indicated they had arrived. This was not the Runs, not a collection of rag-tag hovels tossed together like so much flotsam herded by the tide, but nor was it the sort of area that anyone in their right mind would opt to live in, given a choice.

The place she took him to was a small boarded-up room. The second floor of a two-storey house that barely qualified as having one. It stank of damp and mould, but at least it meant they were off the streets for the night.

To reach it, they took to the roofs again, Kat leading the way via a lower building – a single-storey tenement, a compartmented block of box-standard living spaces. That building was connected to this one. She used her knife to prise some of the boards away from the entrance. They lifted easily, suggesting to Tom that this was a bolthole that had been used often, by Kat and presumably others. He was surprised to see that the boards were cosmetic, that a door stood behind them, and one in considerably better condition than might have been expected. Kat reached up through the gap she'd made and unlatched the door, pushing it open. They both then squeezed through, leaving most of the boards in position.

"What is this place?" Tom wondered aloud.

"It's a safe house."

"Who's it safe for?"

"Us, I hope, for tonight at least."

The very words "safe house" suggested to Tom secrets shared. He felt an irrational rush of pleasure, gratified that Kat had brought him here, as if in doing so she were granting him a privileged glimpse into her personal world, though in truth he very much doubted she saw it in quite those terms.

The room boasted a single window which, like the door, was boarded over. The bats which roosted around the roof of the cavern housing the City Below would become active soon and nobody willingly left them easy access to sleeping areas. The bats included bloodsuckers. For now though, while it was still light, Kat kept the door open.

Tom felt physically exhausted but, conversely, not tired, his mind still buzzing after all he had been through in the past day or so.

As they sat on the bare boards of the room's floor, he asked idly, "How do you think it works, up-City?"

"How does what work?"

"Well, you know. Think about the levels verse."

The girl snorted. "That thing? I barely remember it."

"Fair enough, but even so, you know how each Row has its own name, its own type of people – Tanners' Row, Bakers' Row, that sort of thing."

"I suppose."

"Well, down here it's as if we've got the whole city rolled into one. You want a loaf of bread you go to Baker Street, you want some new shoes you go to Cobblers Yard. How does it work up there with only one type of person in each Row?"

"Don't suppose it does."

"How do you mean?"

"I don't suppose there is only one type of person on each Row. How could there be? What a Row's called is probably what it's best known for, what most of the people there do, but I reckon each Row must have its own Baker Street and Cobblers Yard. After all, you don't have to be a tanner to live in Tanners Lane, that's just what most folk there do."

The idea came as something of a revelation for Tom. He had never considered such a possibility before. Of course the girl was right. How else could the city function, how else could people live?

"Anyway, doesn't really matter much. We'll never get up there to find out."

"You reckon? I already have," Tom said. The words were out before he could stop to consider the wisdom of voicing them.

"You have what?"

"Been up there."

"Yeah, of course you have." The girl chuckled, but stopped when Tom failed to join in. "You are kiddin' me, right?"

"No, no I'm not." He was committed now.

"When?"

"Last night. I went up the walls, all the way to the Heights, to the Residences, nearly to the roof." And with that he proceeded to tell her. Once he started it all came tumbling out: Lyle, witnessing the murder, being caught by the Kite Guard, his fall from the walls, being saved by the Swarbs, everything. As he spoke he felt an enormous sense of relief to finally be talking about it. Somehow, putting what had happened into words made it more real, gave it a substance that mere memory alone had lacked. One corner of his mind heard his own words, listened to the tale and marvelled at it. That part of him felt strangely detached, as if these things had happened to somebody else and he was no more than an observer. He wondered how all these marvellous things could possibly involve him, a simple street-nick.

Finally the words ran out, the story told, and Tom felt emptied, not relieved as he had expected to be. Kat sat silent throughout, though whenever he glanced at her she was clearly caught up in the tale. What did she make of it, how would she react? For the most part he had stared at the crack of night peeking through the boarded window as he spoke, and now found himself afraid to look at the girl, until he heard her exhale a pent-up breath and say, "Breck. You really do mean all of that, don't you." It wasn't a question. "It sounds so incredible. Don't see how anyone could have made that up. Thaiss!"

He sat there awkwardly, not knowing what more to say.

"Do you reckon this arkademic will come after you? I mean, you did see him knife someone."

"Doubt it. Why bother? I'm nobody."

"You're probably right. I was just thinking…"

"What?"

"Well, they do say these arkademics can do some pretty strange things, and those demon hounds, they seemed to be after you; only got interested in me when I stuck a knife in one of them."

That observation sat uncomfortably with Tom, since it mirrored a thought that had flickered through his own mind but which he preferred not to dwell on.

"One thing, though…" the girl went on.

"Yes?" He was so relieved by her apparent acceptance of the story that he would have told her just about anything.

"You didn't say what it was you were sent up there to get. So come on, don't hold out on me now, what were you supposed to bring back?"

"A demon's egg." He said it quietly; the thing he had been told not to admit to anyone.

"No breckin' way. A demon's egg? Why?"

"I don't know." It wasn't a question he had stopped to ask or to wonder about

"And you went all the way up there for the sake of this girl, Jezmina?"

"No. Yes. Sort of. But…" But it wasn't as simple as that, and she made it sound so ridiculous. Why had he ever mentioned Jezmina in the first place? He knew the answer, of course: an attempt to impress her in some way, to show that he wasn't simply a kid. Why, what was she to him, this maverick street-nick? The next morning he'd be back home and she would vanish from his life entirely.

Yet it did matter.

"Hmm…"

"Mostly I went because I wanted to. If I refused, then someone else would have gone instead, and I didn't want anyone else seeing what was up there before I did."

"And you were asked first because of the way you can hide, right?"

"Yes."

"So everyone knows about that."

"No, not really, not in the way you mean." He wanted her to understand how much it had meant, revealing his secret to her. "I'm good at not being found – by the other lads, by the razzers, by everybody – that's all they know. I've never shown anyone why before."

"What, not even Jezmina?"

"No!" He said it hotly, defensively, then realised she was teasing him and repeated in a quieter voice, "Nobody."

Hal tipped back both his flagon and his head, swallowing another mouthful of ale. It was a quick, deep quaff and his gaze returned instantly to the man sitting opposite him: a bland-faced fellow with short brown hair – receding slightly, but still a long way from being bald. Very ordinary to look at, yet he seemed to have done all the things that Hal had dreamed of doing but doubtless never would. At first the bargeman hadn't known whether to believe the fellow or not, but the more the man talked, the more credible he sounded. Hal didn't want to miss a word of this.

Hal had been raised on tales of Thaiburley and ensnared by the mystique that surrounded the City of Dreams from an early age. As a boy he determined to journey there when he grew up, imagining himself a great explorer, crossing mountains with pack and sword strapped across his back and staff in hand, facing death a dozen times before finally cresting the peak of a high hill to gaze in wonder on the towering edifice that was Thaiburley, its highest reaches wreathed in cloud. As he matured, life dumped the baggage of responsibility at his feet. The reality of providing for his mother and four younger siblings after his father was killed reduced the dream to wistful yearning. His father took an arrow fighting off a raid on the village live-stock. The wound became infected and Hal watched this strong man, the rock of his young life, wither away before his eyes. He knew then that life had trapped him, had deliberately cheated him.

Yet throughout those terrible days he never com-pletely forgot his dreams, and when the opportunity arose to work on one of the great river barges Hal leapt at the chance, knowing that this was one of the multi-tude of vessels which supplied distant Thaiburley.

Within days of his gaining a berth, they set out for the city of his dreams. He would never forget that first clear view of Thaiburley as they rounded a bend and cleared a stand of trees. The towering city walls were just as magnificent and awe-inspiring as imag-ination had painted them. The closer the city grew, the more its sheer scale became apparent, with Hal's joy and amazement growing apace. He couldn't be-lieve that very soon he would be passing beneath the walls of the city that had been the focus of his child-hood desires.

Hal's anticipation during that ponderous approach was matched only by his disappointment at what he actually found within Thaiburley itself. The squalor, the stench and the sheer meanness of life in the City Below was overwhelming. It hit home the moment the barge cleared the walls and he caught his first glimpse, and smell, of fabled Thaiburley's underbelly. And when he discovered how unlikely it was that he would ever be permitted to see elsewhere in the great city, the anti-climax was complete. He felt deflated and cheated. Yet again life had tantalised him with dreams only to snatch them away.

Hal took out his frustration and anger on a whore he picked up at a bar that first night, punishing her for this latest – this greatest – disappointment; the sting of his palms and sharp pain of his fists as they struck her flesh brought short-lived relief. He felt ashamed and horrified afterwards as he hurriedly pulled on his clothes and left the sobbing girl, who refused to look at him and held a blanket around herself for the illusion of protection it provided, but he was also strangely exhilarated. As time passed, the horror faded and the memory of the exhilaration remained. On his second visit to Thaiburley he did much the same, though with a different girl from a different bar. This time, the resultant shame was a mere ghost of regret, easily buried beneath the rush of arousal and excitement, the sense of power the beating lent him.

Now, on the second night of his third visit, he was finally able to few a little of his dreams, if only by proxy. This new-found friend claimed to be well travelled throughout the city and had already described enough wonders to keep Hal hanging on his every word. The bargeman was more than happy to stand the fellow a drink or two in exchange for hearing such things.

"Built against the wall at Musicians Row is the wind park," the man was saying. Hal had forgotten the fellow's name and didn't want to look stupid by asking again. Somewhere during the evening they'd separated from Hal's crewmates and it was now just the two of them huddled over their ales. "This is one of the greatest wonders in all Thaiburley. Cunningly wrought tubes and vents draw air from beyond the wall and channel it through enormous horns and trumpets and flutes, built of wood and brass and cane in bewildering variety, each with its own specific pitch and tone. Still more wind is brought into play across curtains of bells and chimes. You never know what you're going to find when you visit the wind park. One minute all will be mellow wafts of sound and subdued tinkling, like some fairy orchestra at play, the next a great booming cacophony will break out, as if the fairies have been supplanted by giants.

"But go there on a concert night and the true wonder of the place is revealed. When one of the great pieces by a master composer such as Waschnet or Siebler is being performed, then you hear the wind park in all its glory. You see, each opening to the walls is controlled by vents and stops, the flow of air through them can be blocked and regulated, enabling all this vast barrage of sound to be shaped and directed into something remarkable. That, my friend is a wonder that everyone should hear at least once before they die.'"

Hal tried to picture the scene in his mind's eye, imagining himself sitting there listening to such magnificent music. "Sounds amazing; wish I could see it," was all he mumbled.

"Maybe you can some day."

Hal's attention snapped back to the man's face, to find him grinning conspiratorially. "I'm sure we can sort something out, if you really want this so badly."

Hal could hardly believe it and had to suppress a surge of hope. "Do you mean that?"

"I don't see why not." His new friend drained the last of his ale. "Come on, let's find a real alehouse."

The bargeman looked around, puzzled. The room was crowded, dimly lit, dingy but warm, and boasted perfectly acceptable ale. "This place seems all right to me."

"It's all right, granted," the other replied, before tapping the side of his nose knowingly with a single finger, "but trust me, it's not one of the best places." The man stood up and shuffled a little unsteadily towards the door. "You can stay here if you want, of course."

Stay here and let this fellow walk away after what he had just said so casually? Not a chance. "No, wait up, I'm coming." Hal scrambled to his feet and hurried after his new friend.

He was already a little hazy as to where they were in relation to the barge. Not far from the docks, obviously, and close to the shantytown known as the Runs, but it was a real warren of alleyways and tight streets around here, so beyond that he was thoroughly lost. Yet his friend led the way confidently enough, so he happily followed.

"It's breckin' dark here," he commented, as they moved out of reach of the nearest street lanterns.

"A short cut."

"Where are we going, anyway?"

"Just a little somewhere I know, a little way inside the Runs; someplace where the ale is as bitter as the girls are sweet."

"Sounds good to me." What did he have to lose after all? The barge wasn't due to leave until late the next day; plenty of time to sober up.

"You've had a taste of the girls here, I take it?"

"Oh, yes." Hal couldn't help but smile at recent memories. "There was this one last night. A real looker, with a mouth that could suck like a whirlpool swallowing a stick."

His friend laughed appreciatively. "If she's that good, I might have to look her up myself. Don't suppose you can remember her name?"

Hal frowned. What was her name? He could picture the girl easily enough: young though not too young, long auburn hair matched by even longer legs, a pretty enough face, though a little narrower than his ideal, and a peach of a bottom that just cried out to be slapped. He remembered the paleness of her naked back and shoulders as she knelt on all fours on the bed in front of him, the warmth of the skin beneath his finger tips as he raked his nails down from shoulders to ribs while taking her from behind. She'd cried out at that and twisted around, telling him to stop, the bitch.

He ended up having to slap her face a few times just to keep her quiet, but she'd asked for it. All of this he could recall, but her name continued to elude him.

"Maria," he said at length, trying the sound of it, but knew immediately it wasn't right. "No, Marta." That sounded better. "Yes, it was Marta, I'm sure."

From nowhere, pain exploded in his stomach. It took a split second to register his drinking companion's swift movement towards him which had preceded the pain. Instinctively, he brought his hands up to cover the hurt, feeling dampness and warmth, while the pain blossomed into agony. The strength seemed to have drained from his legs, which were suddenly unable to support him. His knees buckled and he slumped against a hard surface, a wall, which he commenced to slowly slide down.

Then a hand reached inside his tunic. He watched it emerge with his purse and other valuables before focusing on the face of his "friend", on eyes that were suddenly hard and bright and clear and focused.

"Martha," a voice said coldly. "Her name is Martha."

He felt a hand lifted, his ring removed. The face withdrew and the man turned away. Hal watched as the fellow sauntered off, a long shadow cast by the single flickering lantern. His vision seemed to be narrowing, as if shutters were slowly being drawn in from the sides. He continued to watch the man's back as it receded and his life continued to flow out from between his fingers, until the shutters closed entirely.

Dewar strode away from the dying bargeman. He had gone for the belly strike deliberately. The resultant wound was painful as well as fatal, and lacked the immediacy of a cut throat or a stab to the heart. The man would die more slowly, which suited the assassin just fine. He wanted the brecker to suffer.

That morning, once he had returned with Martha to the shack she both worked from and lived in, the girl had gingerly removed her clothes. Only then did he appreciate the full extent of the beating she'd received. There were vivid bruises to her throat, shoulders, arms, hip, thigh, back and to the ribcage, just below her right breast. There were cuts to both arms and severe scratching to her stomach, shoulders and back, where fingernails had raked blood. She suffered his expert fingers tracing the line of each rib, barely flinching as his touch brought obvious pain and refusing to break down, though a tear trickled from the corner of one eye and he felt her tremble more than once, as if struggling for control.

"Nothing broken," he concluded. "You were lucky."

She snorted. "You call this luck? He beat the shit out of me and then stole every penny I 'ad – my jewellery, everything. Some luck."

He doubted that. "You mean you hadn't stashed some coin somewhere safe?"

"Of course. I wasn't countin' that."

Silly him; naturally she wasn't counting that. Despite the circumstances, he smiled, though it was a shallow, surface-skimming expression. Beneath it a familiar emotion stirred; one that he welcomed like an old friend: rage. Dewar's rage was not of the scorching, incandescent variety, liable to flare magnificently and die away all too quickly. No, his formed rather an implacable, ice cold centre; cold enough to burn and very slow to disappear.

Martha was one of his people, one of those he depended on for information. True, he no longer lived in the City Below and his contact with the girl was sporadic at best these days, but how could he expect her to continue working for him and trusting him with secrets if he didn't look out for her during those times he was here? What would others think if they heard that he had seen her like this and done nothing? Professional pride was at stake.

His intention in escorting her home had been to have sex, to prove a point and remind her who was in control here, but, having seen the extent of the injuries, he changed his mind and so indicated that she should get dressed again.

"On, off – make yer breckin' mind up," the girl muttered. Yet he could tell she was relieved, and doubted she would be entertaining many clients for a day or two.

He made sure she understood that his need for information was urgent and told her that he would visit her again that night, stressing his expectation that she have something for him by then. After giving her some coins, he then left to see to various matters, one of which involved a guardsman and a spill dragon, and another the tracking down of a bargeman by the name of Hal.

That at least had been straightforward enough. There were few barges docked at the time and Hal was not an especially common name. Dewar chose his moment carefully, approaching only once the man was already in his cups, perhaps not deeply into them as yet, but far enough. Separating him from his friends proved easier than the assassin had dared hope, after which events ran like clockwork. He deliberately led the man into a near-abandoned area of the slums, an alley so out of the way that not even the locals had bothered to give it a name. A single lantern burned at its entrance, but other than that, darkness ruled. There was little chance of the body being discovered before morning. If then.

Dewar shivered and wrapped his arms around himself, rubbing them as he walked. It rarely got cold in the City Below, not really, but a chill wind sometimes blew in off the Thair and at night, with the sun globes dormant, the temperature could occasionally drop to less than warm, particularly this close to the walls and the river.

Local wisdom insisted that it was unwise to venture out alone at night down here. There were denizens of the City Below that no sane person would want to meet, creatures that preyed on the vulnerable and the

unwary. The lamplighters started their evening's duty
early and worked in pairs, while the razzers rarely ventured out at all after globes out. When they did it was
with considerable reluctance and invariably in force.
After dark, even the street-nicks went about their business in groups. Personally, Dewar had always enjoyed
the under-City at night and felt the dangers to be exaggerated. Besides, half the inhabitants lived in poorly
constructed hovels which were only one step away
from being on the streets anyway.

Of course, there was always the possibility that
somewhere along the line he himself had become part
of the problem and one of the reasons people stayed
indoors. The thought amused him.

Yet perhaps he was out of practice, or perhaps it was
simply the feeling of general unrest that had seeped
into his awareness via the myriad snippets of information and rumour that accumulated through the day,
but he felt less assured than he normally would. A
sense of wrongness gripped the City Below, permeating
each nook and cranny, oozing into every brick of every
building and even into the flimsy walls of the shanties.
Something was definitely out of kilter here, and for the
first time he could remember, Dewar no longer felt
completely safe being out on the streets at night.

He couldn't shake the feeling that he was being
watched, an almost electric tingling ran through his
body: a state of high alertness which had served him
well in the past. He kept walking but one hand hovered
close to the various weapons at his belt and his gaze
swept the shadows, trying to penetrate their darkness.

There was the suggestion of movement in one and
he froze. It was nothing overt, the merest hint of a

black form shifting in the depths of an equally black pool, but so attuned were his senses that he didn't doubt them for an instant. The only question concerned the degree of menace.

Dewar carefully removed his kairuken. An integral element of certain fighting disciplines in the far north, the kairuken was still virtually unknown in Thaiburley. Its business end was a razor-edged star-shaped disk, which was fired from a powerful spring-release catapult. Dewar considered it to be the best of both worlds – far more compact and easier to reload than a crossbow, it was also lethal over a considerably greater distance than any hand-thrown weapon.

One large, saucer-like eye stared out at him from the shadows as he raised the weapon. Small, whatever it was – and it certainly wasn't a rat or a spill dragon. He still kept half an eye focused on the peripheries, wary in case this was a distraction to mask the approach of some other threat.

Then the thing moved. It flowed from the shadow and along the wall. Slender, stretching, and so swift that even fully alert Dewar was almost too slow. The brief glimpse the assassin caught suggested a cross between a long, thin monkey and a spider. Instinct took over and he fired as it moved, the silver disk flashing across the intervening space and striking the wall a fraction behind the sinuous form. Or had it? There was a jerk as if the thing had been hit and then the creature was gone. Difficult to be certain, but it looked as if something other than just the disk might have fallen to the ground.

Dewar sprinted over, to scour the floor in search of whatever had dropped. He found it almost immediately:

a section of leg, no longer than his thumb, ending in a wickedly sharp clawed foot. Impossible to make out details in this dimness, but something felt wrong.

He retrieved his disk and, still clutching the severed section of limb, hurried towards more brightly lit environs.

Standing directly under a street lamp, he was able to see the thing more clearly. Fur, blood and wires, like something the dog master might come up with, but there had been nothing canine about this creature. Was the dog master branching out, or was somebody else moving in on his territory? And had the construct's presence been pure coincidence, or had it been watching Dewar?

The assassin frowned. He preferred to be asking the questions rather than puzzling over them. The sooner he could finish here and get back to the Heights the better. This return to his former home grew more disconcerting by the hour.

At least he could be confident that the Kite Guard's visit here was proving a frustrating one. Before waylaying the bargeman, he had met briefly with his new contact within the watch. Evidently Tylus had failed to gain the sort of support he might have hoped for and instead had been given the assistance of just a single officer, one of the newest and least competent in the department. The irony of that did not escape the assassin.

Dewar continued on his way, knowing that there was still much to do before he could allow himself to acknowledge his body's mounting weariness.

The first port of call was Martha's.

His initial knock was greeted with a yell of, "Go away. I ain't workin'."

He was not in the least surprised to find her alone, having left her that morning with a generous amount of coin so that she could afford to recover from her injuries without the need to see any punters for a day or two.

Her greeting of, "Oh, it's you," when she did recognise him was hardly the most heart-warming of welcomes, although he gained the impression that the girl was actually pleased to see him, probably because she found herself at something of a loose end without her usual level of company.

She was even more pleased when he presented the various items lifted from the dying bargeman.

Her gaze and then her hands fell immediately on a bracelet, a plain silver band, which had been cosseted with the man's purse. She ran her fingers along its inner surface, as if to make certain of a mark or engraving. "That's mine. Where did you...?"

She stopped, presumably her own imagination supplying the answer.

"I've just been having a drink or two with your old friend, Hal. He won't be needing these anymore."

She clasped the bracelet to her with both hands and he wondered what memories that simple trinket represented. Were those tears in her eyes? She looked up at him, a fragile smile ghosting across her lips. For a dreadful second he thought she was going to thank him and was grateful when she refrained, uncertain how he would have handled that.

"There's more here than he took from you, I'd guess," he said a little awkwardly into the silence. "Should see you all right until you feel up to working again."

The girl nodded. "It'll come in handy no doubt."

"Now, about this street-nick…"

"Don't worry, I found 'im for you. The Blue Claw made a deal with the Scorpions; passage both ways for one of theirs to use the Scorpions' steps. This wasn't no market trip – something special. The boy went up but never came back, least not by those stairs.

At last, the break he needed. "Good. You've done well."

"There's more. This ain't what I've heard, just what I can tell you."

"Go on."

"There's a lad runs with the Claw, name of Tom. Cute little fella and slippery as an eel. No one's better at hiding than Tom, 'e can slip in and out o' places you wouldn't believe. If the Blue Claw were gonna send anyone to do the impossible, it'd be him."

Dewar found he was smiling. He knew his faith in Martha had not been misplaced. "Thank you." It was rare for him to say those words to an informant. After all, their reward was the hard currency of solid coin exchanged for the far less tangible but often more valuable one of information, what need had they of thanks? But in this instance the girl deserved it.

Despite harbouring fears that his mind was too active, Tom dropped off to sleep almost immediately. His dreams were vivid ones, as his subconscious tried to process the images and experiences from the previous night's escapade, at the fore of his thoughts again after describing everything to Kat.

He saw once more the small, furred creature with wide hostile eyes, which arched its back and snarled at him, revealing sharp canines all too capable of leaving their mark on soft human flesh. He had no idea whether this was a wayward pet or some sort of verminous scavenger, but he opted to give it as wide a berth as possible. Instead of running away, the creature came to the top of the stairs and peered at him as he descended to the next Row, as if to make certain that he really was going.

Soon after, he found himself suspended above a scene of total wonder. Beneath him there opened up a vista that he could only think of as jungle. A kaleidoscope of plants and shrubs and trees stretched out as far as he could see. Everything was so bright – the world seemed depicted in tones of vivid greens, with more variety of shade and sheen and depth of colour than he could ever have imagined. Interspersed here and there with this bewildering verdancy were explosions of other colours, as blooms forced their way out of the shrubbery to claim a space and be seen – here a stand of tall stems topped with purple flowers, there a bush crowned with bright yellow sunbursts and beside it another that dripped with fronds of white, all rippled through with pink. Used to the blandness of the slums, this explosion of life was a revelation that went beyond anything he had imagined finding in the heart of the city.

No, not a jungle; he realised how wrong that initial impression had been. This was more a park, though far removed from the few wretched patches of open land which went by that name in the under-City. There was a pattern to all this apparent chaos – open areas of meadow interlinked by grassy paths which picked their way through the bushes and plants. The more he looked, the more obvious the hand of design became. The landscape was not the product of nature but of artifice.

Tom was doing his best at this point not to dwell on the most striking aspect of the situation, but soon arrived at a moment when he was left with little choice. Though solid in itself, the flight of stairs he was descending appeared to be unsupported, somehow suspended in mid-air, the bottom step ending a little distance above the canopy of the park's trees and leading onto apparently open sky.

Tom could feel the dizziness that assailed him on the city's walls stirring at the back of his mind and he fought to suppress it. This was no bottomless drop; there would be no terrifying plummet such as he'd been through before. This time the ground was clearly visible, and he could imagine himself surviving such a drop, provided the landing proved soft enough.

Perhaps that was it. Perhaps there was some mechanism at play to ensure that anyone stepping off the bottom step landed comfortably and unhurt, something which the people familiar with this Row took for granted but which he, a stranger, was unaware of. Maybe that was the whole point of the arrangement: to impress unsuspecting strangers.

So thinking, Tom was able to keep his fears at bay as he came to the end of the stairs and considered what to do next. He sat on the final step, intending to dangle his legs over the edge, but immediately encountered a problem. Where there looked to be open space, his heels struck an apparently solid surface, at a level with the stairs' foot, where by rights the floor ought to have been. Still not venturing from the step, he shifted onto his knees and began to feel all around with both hands. Sure enough, touch reported the presence of a solid floor, conflicting with what his eyes saw. They continued to insist that there was nothing there, not even glass.

Tom got to his feet, still on the bottom step, and looked around, searching for the next flight of stairs that would lead downwards. Finally he spotted them, a short distance to his left. Only then, with a goal located, did he risk placing one foot on the presumed floor. For long seconds he stood there, one foot on the step and one on solid space, experimentally transferring his weight between the two, testing and then testing again.

Not entirely convinced but realising that he had no other option, Tom took a deep breath and finally abandoned the stairs. Each step was a battle against his own misgivings; every forward foot was placed tentatively, with the expectation that at any moment he might find himself tumbling down towards the parkland below. Yet the floor proved firm. He had no idea how it worked, what this daunting surface was composed of; there was no reflection or minor distortion to suggest its presence, nothing whatsoever to alert sight – that most relied-upon of senses – to the existence of a floor at all. But it held.

He made a determined effort not to look down, keeping his gaze centred on the stairway he was making for. Not that this was exactly ideal either, since that particular flight promised to be an unnerving experience in its own right. Whereas the stairs he had just abandoned had been ordinary enough in their construction, these were anything but. Each individual

step hung suspended in the air, apparently uncon-
nected to its neighbours above and below.

After what seemed an age he reached the stairs and
started his descent. Whereas his walk to them had been
a tentative one, he now opted to throw caution to the
wind and ran down the steps, wanting to get them
over with, while being afraid that the invisible supports
might collapse at any moment.

In seconds it was done. For the first time in his life,
he stood on ground carpeted in grass, and marvelled
at the fact.

Tom surfaced from frail dreams, uncertain what had
roused him. The scent of grass was a memory which
drifted through his mind only to dissipate once his eyes
opened and focused on the present. His night-adjusted
vision interpreted the room in shades of grey and black
shadow. On looking for a darker shape which should
have been lying beside him and seeing none, he bolted
upright, gaze darting around the room; then he saw
her. Kat's hunched black shape sat by the opened door,
apparently staring out through the gap in the boards,
though he couldn't imagine what at.

"Is everything all right?"

"Fine. Can't sleep, that's all." She spoke as quietly as
he had; perhaps neither of them wanting to disturb the
night.

"What can you see out there?"

"Ghosts, mainly. Don't worry though, they're my
ghosts. Only I can see them and they'll never haunt
anyone but me."

He made an intuitive leap: "People you knew from
the Pits?"

She didn't answer immediately and he wondered whether the question had been too intrusive, but then she said, "Some. Among others."

He felt he ought to follow up with another comment but had no idea what and didn't want to risk offending her by saying the wrong thing.

While he struggled with this uncertainty, the girl asked, very quietly, "Do you believe in the Soul Thief?"

Tom would have laughed under any other circumstances. Did she still think him a kid, a credulous child? He remembered tales first learnt at the same age as the city's level verse, stories of a pale-faced woman in tattered black robes, who would creep into homes in the dead of night and suck out the souls from unsuspecting children while they slept, before disappearing.

"Of course not." Night-time in the City Below held enough very real mysteries and terrors without conjuring up imaginary ones as well.

"I do," she said in that same wistful voice. "I've seen her. She took my mother."

He stared at her back, trying to decide whether or not she was joking for all that she sounded serious, and wondering whether he dared ask. But he didn't. Partly for fear that she might then turn around and laugh, that she was teasing him, but mostly for the fear that she wasn't.

Suddenly Kat moved, whipping her head around, black against almost-black. "Did you hear something?"

He hadn't but now listened, straining to detect whatever she had. He heard it then; a fluttering, a faint whirring.

"There's something…"

The girl moved again, even as he started to speak. Not a hesitant rising to her feet, as if she were trying to locate something, but rather a savage spring from floor to standing in one explosion of movement, as if she knew exactly where it was.

"Aagh! Nearly had you," she said.

It was too dark for him to gain more than a vague sense of her movements, but he started at the abrupt bang, which must have been Kat's hand slamming against the wall, presumably carrying something with it, because the girl then proclaimed, "Got you!"

He then heard her grinding her heel against the floor.

"What was it, a bat?" Though he didn't really see how one of the blood suckers could have sneaked in unless it got past her as she sat with the door open.

"Nah, too small, and anyway, it felt made rather than natural. I'm sure there was metal in there."

"Something of the Maker's, then?"

"Probably. Won't be worrying us any more, in any case, whatever it was. Best we try and get some more sleep." She came and laid down beside him again.

"Good idea," he agreed, doubting that he would.

On the roof of the cavern, eleven small drones had gathered, swarming around a bulky protrusion like bees around honey. The object that drew them was a sun globe, one of the many synchronised light sources responsible for granting this subterranean world a semblance of nature's night and day cycle.

Not globes at all, the substitute suns had been named thus to strengthen the association with their celestial namesake. In fact, they were shaped like rounded humps, each one resembling a gigantic drop of water which had started to gather on a ceiling but not quite developed sufficient form or mass to drip down. Partial globes at the very most.

This particular one hung almost directly above the attic room where two weary street-nicks had taken refuge for the night. The sun globes were secured to the cavern roof by an array of deeply sunken rivets and bolts and cradled in thick cabling. The system's designers had gone for overkill. After all, nobody wanted one of these things falling onto the streets. Referring back to Insint, the drones had calculated that if the rivets and bolts were removed in a certain order, and if the cables were cut at exactly the right time, then this globe would fall a fraction off centre and could be persuaded to impact with the attic room in question.

This would be the work of many hours, particularly since there would now only be ten of the tiny droids available, one having gone to take over from its recently decommissioned fellow monitoring the two street-nicks. However, it was work that had already begun.

NINE

The doorbell's sonorous chime was the very last thing Magnus wanted to hear. Who could be calling at this hour? He toyed with the idea of ignoring it, but in the end sat forward, placed the bulb of warmed brandy on the table and rose to his feet. Unlikely perhaps, but this might prove to be important.

It was at times like this that he most missed Dewar. Finding a temporary replacement was always an option, someone to act as butler, cook and valet, but so far he had resisted the temptation. There were too many sensitive matters unfolding to risk having a stranger in the house. Magnus was not without enemies, some of whom would jump through hoops and dance on the tip of a needle to place an informant so close to him. Besides, he was hardly ever home – working all day and dining out of an evening – so only in the very early hours or the very late ones, such as this, did he miss being attended to.

Part of him regretted not setting up a means of communication with his agent, but it was too risky. Whatever method they employed would have been open to interception and he couldn't risk being implicated in any way. He knew he could trust Dewar to get the job done but he hated being uninformed. The man had only been gone a day and already Magnus was fretting, wondering what progress had been made.

As he left the comfort of his study and entered the comparative chill of the hallway, the bell rang again. Whoever this was, they clearly did not number patience among their virtues.

He arrived at the door and squinted through the spyhole. Though he had no preconceptions, what he saw still managed to surprise him. He didn't recognise the man's face as such but he certainly recognised the uniform: hooded tunic, white with purple trim, the most frequently seen semi-formal attire of the council guard. Magnus drew back from the door, horrified. Were they here to arrest him? A dozen possibilities chased each other through his thoughts. Had they somehow found out about Thomas – was there another witness only recently come forward? No, he would have sensed any such observer. Perhaps some other clandestine manoeuvring had been uncovered, though it seemed unlikely; he had been so, so careful. What then?

Taking a deep breath to compose himself, he adopted the winning smile that had served him so well through the years and reached towards the door. He would act the outraged innocent and brazen it out, whatever the accusation.

Two guards confronted him; big men who seemed to loom threateningly in the entranceway. He was aware of more guards behind them. Yet even as Magnus said, "Can I help you?" the pair parted, stepping aside to allow a further, slighter figure to step forward.

The smile slipped from the senior arkademic's face and all he could do was gape.

The man revealed by the respectful guards may have edged beyond the limits of middle age but his face still shone with vitality and his movements were smooth and assured. "Perfect!" the newcomer exclaimed, then laughed. "To see such a renowned politician as yourself at a loss for words is a rare treat, Magnus."

"Prime Master," the senior arkademic recovered quickly, bowing his head in respect. He felt he could be forgiven for a moment of less than perfect composure under the circumstances. After all, it was not every day that the ruler of the city council, in effect the ruler of all Thaiburley, came knocking at your door. "Please, come in." As if he had a choice.

Magnus stepped back and allowed the prime master to enter, preceded by one of the council guards and flanked by another. The balance, four as far as Magnus could see, remained outside, taking up station at the door.

"What happened to that charming manservant of yours?"

Magnus was instantly on his guard; the man was as observant as ever, nothing escaped the prime master's sharp eye. "Taking a leave of absence – a family bereavement, quite unexpected."

"How unfortunate."

"I've been meaning to sort out a replacement, but I haven't had the time. There's always so much to do."

They reached the study. The two guards remained outside while the senior arkademic and his guest entered.

"Your dedication does you credit, Magnus, but this will never do," the prime master said. "We can't have you neglecting yourself for the sake of the city. I'll send one of my own staff over to cover until your man returns."

Magnus was horrified. He could think of nothing he wanted less. "That's most kind, prime master, but really there's no need. I spend so little time here anyway."

Magnus lifted the carafe of fine brandy, with an enquiring glance towards his guest, who nodded.

"All the more reason you should be properly looked after when you are here. I'll brook no further discussion on the subject. My man will be at your door first thing in the morning."

What could he say? "Thank you, prime master, that's most generous." So much for keeping prying eyes away. He handed a bulb of freshly poured brandy to his guest, who was settling into the armchair opposite his own.

The prime master swirled the amber liquid in its bulbous glass and breathed in the warm, caramel vapours, smiling his appreciation. "Excellent! You always have had exquisite taste."

The pair saluted each other with their glasses, locking gazes for a second, before sipping the potent spirit.

"To what do I owe this unexpected honour?" Magnus asked.

"Oh, I merely wished to express my condolences on the death of Senior Arkademic Thomas. I know the two of you were close. Something of a protégé of yours, I believe."

"Indeed." Magnus stared down at his glass as if in melancholy reflection. Straight to the point. What did the man know? What did he suspect? "It was a terrible business. I felt so helpless."

"Yes, you were there, of course. A pity you couldn't have intervened and prevented this awful tragedy."

Magnus knew his part in this well, but it had never been more important that he play it to perfection. He placed his glass down, very deliberately, sighed and said, "I only wish I had arrived sooner, that I had been closer when the murderer struck. As it was, all I could do was watch as Thomas toppled over the wall, and the boy responsible was away before I could stop him. I conjured a spy-eye and sent it after him, then dashed to the wall, but Thomas had gone, of course. I was too late…" He paused, shaking his head for dramatic effect.

"Yes, I've seen the images from your spy-eye," the prime master said.

Had he now? That was interesting, and hardly reassuring. Magnus had no idea the most powerful man in Thaiburley was taking such a keen interest.

"Let us hope this Kite Guard you've assigned can find the lad and bring him to justice."

"Indeed," Magnus replied, offering a tight smile and trying hard to remain calm. His visitor seemed remarkably well informed.

"Well, thank you for the excellent brandy."

He placed the glass, still tinted with the amber of undrunk liquor in its bowl, on the table opposite Magnus's own. "The hour is late and I shan't detain you any further. I merely wished to express my sympathies and reassure you of my continued support and good wishes."

Continued? Magnus had never been aware of the man providing him with either. "Thank you for taking the trouble to do so, prime master."

His distinguished guest departed, collecting council guards in stages as he went. "And don't worry," he said on the way out, "my man will be here first thing to-morrow."

Magnus stared at the front door for long seconds after it had closed, wondering what that was all about. He turned and walked back to the study, deep in thought. A number of things were certain. The prime master had never gone to the trouble of visiting him at his home before. He knew altogether too much regard-ing the investigation into Thomas's death. He did not do anything without good reason.

No matter how Magnus added those facts up, the sum emerged as an uncomfortable question or two.

Was the prime master suspicious? Had the visit been meant as a warning? Was its intent purely to unsettle Magnus?

If the latter, it had succeeded admirably.

The night was an unusually quiet one. Lyle finished the few jobs that needed attending to in record time. The Blue Claw had embarked on just a single small outing in the early evening, which didn't require his presence, and there were no more planned for that night. He'd put Barton, his most reliable lieutenant, in charge of the job – a raid on a large warehouse which stood at the edge of the docks – some minor pilfering, nothing more. The importers turned a blind eye to such things – they knew the game – but even so a del-icate balance had to be struck. The street-nicks took enough to make it worth their while but not so much that it hurt the commercial interests to the point where business felt obliged to react. As with most everything in the City Below, it was all a matter of give and take, while being careful to never take too much.

Barton could be relied on to carry out the job efficiently, if only because it gave him one more thing to boast about. This was the lad's only major failing: attention seeking. He valued the good opinion of his fellows far too much. Otherwise, he was dependable and efficient. That combined with his popularity made him someone to keep an eye on. Lyle was no fool and knew that of all his lieutenants, Barton was the most likely to challenge him for leadership of the Claw at some point. As the lad grew bolder and more confident, the day when he would do so grew ever closer. But it hadn't arrived yet.

He waited to see the boys safely home, congratulating them on a job well done. The proceeds consisted of preserved food stuffs brought in by barge and waiting for transport to the City Above: pickled fish, dry cured meats, salted beef and other such, all of them easily shifted. Lyle inspected and stashed the goods with considerable satisfaction. All that remained was his usual late night inspection, checking to see that everything was secure and the lookouts were still awake and alert. The Claw were not especially at odds with any other gangs at present, but he still insisted that a proper watch was maintained. You could never be too careful.

Happy that all was in order, he headed for bed.

The day's only disappointment had been Tom's failure to return. It was getting to the point where he might have to accept that the boy had failed and been caught or, more likely, killed. It would be a shame to lose one of his more gifted thieves, but this had been a long shot at best, the chances of success remote. Besides, he had been well paid, which meant that the whole gang would benefit from one boy's sacrifice.

It also removed a potential rival for Jezmina's affections. Not that Tom was ever that much of a rival, of course. The girl had even been complicit in persuading him to accept the impossible challenge of raiding the Upper Heights in the first place; a clear enough indication of where her loyalties lay.

Perhaps now that Tom was out of the way it was time to admit how things really stood between the two of them, though perhaps not. Jezmina was so good at playing the wide-eyed innocent and Tom was by no means the only member of the gang she had wrapped around her little finger. It was good entertainment value if nothing else, so maybe he would leave things as they were for a little while yet.

One advantage of being in charge was having his own room, a place where the other gang members would only dare disturb him if something of genuine importance had cropped up. The one exception to that rule ought to be waiting for him at that very moment. The thought of her welcoming arms, her tender kisses and her soft, yielding body quickened his step.

This building had belonged to the Blue Claw for years, decades even. Nobody remembered or cared how it came to be in their possession. An old mansionesque building left over from more prosperous days when the docks had thrived, it was one of several such properties, mostly derelict, which clung to the corner of the docks; buildings which had, against all reason, avoided being swamped by the shantytown of the Runs.

Valuing his privacy in the brief moments allowed him, Lyle had chosen his quarters with care. A short corridor separated them from the communal areas. His hand reached the brass knob and pushed the door open. The room was in darkness, which was unusual. He whispered her name, "Jezmina?"

"Here." Yet her voice, even though barely above a whisper, sounded odd, strained.

"Is everything all right?" He reached for the wall lamp, familiarity guiding his hand to it almost at once.

"Fine."

His thumb pressed down on the switch, grating flint against flint. At the second attempt it sparked and he watched that tiny crumb of flame drop to ignite the oil.

In the lamp's wan glow he saw Jezmina sitting in a chair, eyes wide with fright, staring at him.

"Why are you sitting in the d…?"

No, she was not staring at him as such but rather past his shoulder.

As that realisation sank in, he felt the presence of the intruder behind him and the jab of cold steel at his throat. He stopped speaking, stopped moving.

"Because I wanted it that way," said a man's voice at his ear. "You must be Lyle," the voice continued. "We've been waiting for you."

Tom woke suddenly, with the feeling that something had disturbed him but no idea what. He sensed that morning was well on the way. It was still night but the darkness had thinned a little, to the point where he could see Kat crouching by the door in greater definition than the darker, featureless patch of blackness she had been when night held full sway. Had she been crouching there all this time? No, he clearly remembered her lying down again. And besides, the door was now closed.

Then he heard a sound from outside; just a faint scraping, but unmistakable. Someone or something was on the far side of the door.

He rolled to his feet, a move which earned him a glance from Kat, who immediately lifted a finger to her lips. Tom nodded, fully aware of the need for quiet. The lingering cobwebs of sleep still fuddled the edges of his thoughts, but they were quickly disappearing in the face of potential threat. He drew his knife and waited. One of Kat's long blades already rested across her knees as she squatted, still watching the door.

In the darkness, Tom didn't see the door handle turn, but he did see the door fly open and a figure shoot through; a man, who dived through the gap Kat had made in the boards, through the doorway and into the room. At least it was human rather than some monster, albeit the strangest man Tom had ever encountered. With the door open, more light was able to enter the room and by it, Tom could see that the intruder was bald and that his head, neck and arms were covered in an intricate pattern of tattoos. Not individual pictures, but rather what appeared to be a uniform design. Lines travelled in parallel up the man's neck, curling around one ear and continuing up to cross the dome of his head like a headband, before curling past the other ear and down again. That was just one set. There were others, and circles and crescent-moons and stars. Yet he gained the impression that each mark was integral to all the others, that they worked in concert to form a whole. He imagined that beneath the man's clothes, this net-work of tattoos came together, combining to produce a single arcane design. The only problem being that you would need to have the man's skin laid out flat to see it.

All this flashed through his thoughts in the split second it took the man to land, roll and come nimbly to his feet.

"Rayul!" Kat exclaimed.

The newcomer looked round at her and smiled. "Kat. We were wondering if it might be you."

The missing boards across the entrance would have given away the fact that someone was in here to anyone familiar with this place, Tom realised. At the same time, he noted that Kat still hadn't sheathed her knife despite the fact that she obviously knew the intruder. Others were coming in now. All were bald-headed and decorated in similar fashion to the first. A further board had to be taken down for the larger ones to enter.

There were marked similarities in their clothing, as well. All were dressed in tanned leather – short sleeved tunics which left their arms free and the extent of the tattoos exposed – and all seemed to be wearing skirts rather than trousers. Tom tried not to stare. None of them wore clothing identical to any other, but they were all similar enough to suggest some sort of uniform.

As the room filled up, Kat finally put her knife away, a little reluctantly or so it seemed to him. However, he now felt foolish holding his own small blade, so sheathed that too. As so often since returning to this unfamiliar part of the City Below, Tom found himself relying on Kat for guidance.

In total, there were five of the strangely similar men and the room felt suddenly cramped. Kat hardly looked pleased to see these new arrivals, which Tom found less than reassuring. These were no boys, not street-nicks in any sense he recognised and yet a memory stirred somewhere in the back of his mind: the Tattooed Men. Weren't there stories about such a gang?

He tried to remember but, beyond a vague sense that they were to be feared, failed to recall any specifics. One of the men was speaking, so the trawling of half-forgotten memories would have to wait.

"She's going to love this." Tom thought it was the first man to enter who spoke, the one Kat had called Rayul, but he couldn't be sure: they all looked alike.

"I doubt that, somehow," Kat replied.

"Who's your friend?"

"Name of Tom."

"What gang are you with, lad?"

"The Blue Claw." He answered that himself, not seeing any point in lying.

"A fair way from your own territory, aren't you? What's the story?"

"None of your business, I'd say," Kat cut in.

The man grunted, turning back to the girl. "As you wish. Doesn't make much difference. You know what comes next."

Kat might, but Tom had no idea. What did come next? There was nothing overtly hostile about the newcomers, yet their sheer physical presence had him feeling trapped, as if he was barely one step away from being cuffed and chained.

The girl's next words did nothing to dispel the impression. "It doesn't have to be like this," she said. "You could always let us carry on our way and just report that there was nothing here when you checked."

"You know we can't do that."

"Yeah, of course I do." She gave a wry smile. "But you can't blame me for trying."

"What are you doing here anyway, Kat?" one of the others asked. "You must have known there was a good chance we'd check this place."

The girl shrugged. "Didn't even know you were in the area. Besides, it seemed a safer bet than the big house." Tom tried to gauge what was going on but lacked the referents to do so. Kat was clearly ill at ease but at the same time chatted to these men as if they were old friends. Presumably that ought to be a good sign, yet the tension that was evident between them suggested otherwise.

"That's true enough. If you'd pitched up there last night we could have had a merry reunion all the sooner."

"She's there, then." Kat spoke as if this were a matter of passing interest at best, but she wasn't kidding Tom and he doubted she was fooling anyone else either. Whoever this "she" might be, she was clearly someone of importance to the girl.

"You can see for yourself in a few minutes. Ready?"

Kat shrugged. "As if I've got a choice. You don't need Tom, though, so let him go at least."

"I thought he was with you."

"I am," Tom said quickly. He appreciated Kat's concern but had no intention of leaving without her, even if that was an option.

They filed out of the room, two of the men staying back to replace the boards covering the door. Tom watched the girl for some sign, ready to run, to make a break for it if she did, though she gave no indication of doing so.

As they came out into the brighter environs of the under-City's breaking dawn, he was able to see their captors, if such they were, more clearly. The traceries of tattoos which marked each were in a uniform ochre colour, and they were astonishingly precise, resembling well-executed works of art. The combination of these flowing, arcane patterns and the men's hairless pates made them seem eerie, otherworldly even, and at the same time formidable.

Once they had come down to street level, Tom caught up with Kat and walked beside her, the pair of them bracketed by the taller men. "So, who are they?" he asked quietly.

"The Tattooed Men."

This time the words stirred fragments of memory: he had a vague sense that these were nomads, street-nicks without fixed territory, said to be fearsome fighters. "The wanderers," he said. "And they're friends of yours?"

"Not exactly."

"Enemies, then?"

"Not them so much as their Chavver."

"Chavver?"

"The Queen Bitch who rules their little gang."

"And it's this Chavver that we're now being taken to see?"

"Afraid so. Don't worry though, it's not you she's got a problem with, just me."

"Why, what happened?"

"Long story."

There were further questions he would have liked to ask but at that instant everything seemed to turn much darker, as if some vast object had passed between

them and the cavern's roof, cutting out the sun globes'
light. There was a distant, echoing sound of rending
metal. Somebody behind him shouted; a call that conveyed fear and urgency, a warning. Tom stared up, to
see an enormous object falling towards him. At first he
couldn't make sense of it, his mind unable to process
the image, then he realised it was one of the sun
globes, that it had somehow come loose from the ceiling and was plummeting downward. Only seconds
remained before it would impact with the ground, the
city.

Someone tugged at his arm and yelled at him,
though he didn't really hear the words: Kat. He was
slow to respond, mesmerised, unable to look away as
the globe grew larger and closer. He started to move
again, to run, allowing himself to be pulled along, but
he still could not resist looking back over his shoulder
in time to see the sun globe strike. It hit the low building adjoining the one they had slept in.

He watched in fascination as one edge of the mechanism began to buckle and fold, spreading out to crush
the loft room Kat had called a safe house. The process
seemed to occur in slow motion. The building caved
in, its roof and the top of the walls collapsing inward
even as the rest of the walls commenced to push outward.

Without warning, something deep within the globe
exploded.

A ball of fire blossomed forth, propelling stone and
metal fragments before it. Tom felt the heat, the wind
against his face and arms, and the trembling of the
ground through the soles of his feet. He ducked and
lifted a hand to protect his face, aware that debris was

flying in all directions. A chunk of something seemed to head straight towards him, as direct as a bullet. He barely had time to register its threat and certainly none to react, before the object struck him and he remembered no more.

The smell of burning hung in the air. Tylus stood just outside the station and gazed at a city which seemed in the process of bracing itself, as if expecting some awful catastrophe. No one awake could escape the knowledge that somewhere in the City Below a fierce fire had been raging. The very light was dimmed, the sun globes obscured by clouds of smoke which roiled around the cavern's ceiling. Every breath carried the acrid taint of it.

He headed inside to the squad room, where Richardson was already hard at work, catching up on the reports that his assignment to assist Tylus had prevented him from completing.

The young guard was a revelation. Since they returned with the three captured street-nicks, he had been a much altered person. The timid, apologetic demeanour had disappeared, to be replaced by a confident attitude that saw him hold his own in the squad room, answering back when put upon and taking the jokes of his fellows in his stride, as if they didn't matter to him anymore. He no longer acted like a victim.

The young officer's retelling of the mad chase through the backstreets sounded far more dangerous and exciting than Tylus's own memories painted it, and the Kite Guard's own part in events as seen through Richardson's eyes sounded a great deal more proficient than it actually had been.

Richardson's part in the capture of the three nicks, albeit that two of them effectively gave themselves up, had clearly given the young guardsman the required boost of confidence, and it was evident that his attitude to being assigned as Tylus's aid had also completely reversed. From being the superfluous officer given the task that nobody else wanted, he was now the one who had been honoured with the most prestigious job in the department. The more the lad acted that way, the more the other officers were going to believe it.

Looking at him, seeing the leap forward the young man had made, Tylus suddenly realised how much his own attitude had changed over the same period. Since coming to the City Below, he hadn't once questioned his own competence, his own right to wear the uniform of a Kite Guard. In the past couple of days he had acted and felt the part, without any sense of incongruity at all. It was a moment of true personal revelation for him. For the first time since being accepted, Tylus felt that he truly belonged in the ranks of the Kite Guard.

The three nicks' surrender and their desperation to be taken into custody were still something of a puzzle. What became immediately obvious was that the trio were terrified. What continued to be confusing was the source of their fear. According to the three nicks, it was the other Scorpions – their fellow gang members – that they were afraid of, but not in any manner which made sense. The three insisted there had been no falling out, that they had not transgressed within the gang's own particular code or crossed their fellow nicks in any way. Yet they were adamant that their own gang was after them.

When pressed for an explanation, all the kids could say was that the other gang members had changed, were no longer themselves, and that if the three didn't get somewhere beyond the reach of their former friends, they too would be changed. Apparently it was not just the Scorpions that were affected, and the three had no idea who could be trusted and who couldn't, which left prison as the only fully safe place they could think of.

Richardson seemed as bemused by these claims as he was, yet Tylus realised that he might have stumbled onto something important, that if this problem was occurring across several gangs it could be connected to the spate of street-nick related killings which were causing the watch such concern. He reported the matter immediately they returned to the station, and the three nicks were now being questioned by other officers. Hopefully, being more attuned to the streets and what went on here, they might be able to make more sense of the situation than the Kite Guard could.

As promised, the prisoners had provided him with the information he'd been after, and he now knew that a gang known as the Blue Claw had negotiated passage via the Scorpions' stairs for one of their members, and that the night before last, a boy called Tom had slipped up those stairs on a mission that clearly went beyond the norm. Word was that he was attempting to slip up-City, though not everyone believed that. What seemed certain was that the boy had yet to return.

Despite this last snippet of information, Tylus felt confident that he was closing in on the escaped street-nick. He felt the weight of destiny upon his shoulders and knew that he would soon bring the lad to justice and so be able to return to the Heights triumphant.

Not even Goss could question his fitness to belong to the Guard after this. More importantly, nor would he.

The key to all of this lay with the Blue Claw, he was certain. Only by questioning them could he discover why a street-nick had climbed so high into the city, what he had been after. Now all that remained was to convince the officers of the watch to mount a raid on the gang. As yet, no means of doing so had occurred to him, but he felt certain it soon would.

Opportunity arrived in the form of the station commander, Captain Johnson.

Tylus had met him after bringing the street-nicks in and still wasn't entirely sure what to make of the man. Younger than his duty sergeant, he wore the uniform of the watch with evident pride; neatly pressed trousers, creases straight and crisp, his fastidiousness a marked contrast to the sloppy, casual attitude the Kite Guard had noted in other members of the section. In fact, the good captain displayed all the qualities that had been drummed into Tylus as essential in an officer; and yet, down here, they made the man seem vaguely pompous and out of touch. It was another example of how his brief stay in the streets was already influencing Tylus, giving him a different perspective on many aspects of life. He was beginning to consider whether values were not entirely set in stone but were more flexible than he'd imagined, being affected by such factors as circumstance and environment.

Johnson even spoke differently from the officers under him, having a more cultured accent, leading Tylus to wonder whether he was a native of the under-City at all, or whether perhaps he had been assigned here from the City Above. What misdemeanour could warrant such a fate? Perhaps the captain was simply from a better district, though it was hard to believe that the City Below boasted any such.

Their initial meeting had been an awkward one, neither certain of status, one a captain, the other a Kite Guard on special assignment from a senior arkademic – who outranked whom? They settled the dilemma without ever acknowledging there was one, by treating each other as equals. Tylus was amazed by his own audacity; this was something he would never have dreamed of doing mere days previously.

This second meeting promised to be no less trying than the first. The captain came across to where Tylus sat next to Richardson, who disappeared as the senior officer approached. It was immediately apparent that the captain wanted something.

"You've heard about the incident in the early hours?"

"Yes, indeed," said Tylus. He assumed this was a reference to the sun globe falling and the subsequent fire, and had to wonder how anyone could have failed to hear about it.

"A terrible business."

"Terrible." It was the talk of the squad room. Officers had been called in from all across the under-City to fight the blaze, including their own station. A number of buildings had been gutted and the total of confirmed dead rose by the hour.

"Sun globes do not simply come crashing down of their own accord. Somebody must have brought this one down deliberately."

The captain stopped, clearly hoping for a reaction. Tylus refused to give him one. By approaching matters in this circumspect manner rather than coming straight out and asking a direct question, Johnson had placed himself at a disadvantage. Tylus rather enjoyed the fact that they were no longer quite equal. "Really?" was his only response.

Johnson fidgeted a little more, and cleared his throat: a nervous sound which almost caused Tylus to grin, though he fought hard to keep his face deadpan. "The thing is, you see, the globe itself has been pretty much blasted apart in the explosion. We're collecting the debris, of course, but it's proving to be a long and slow process. Goodness knows how much we'll be able to learn from whatever's left in any case…"

"Hmm. Very frustrating," Tylus said. He began to see what the captain was leading up to.

"What we really need to do is get up there and take a look at the roof, to examine where the globe fell from and hopefully learn something from that."

Tylus was tempted to agree and assure the captain that he thought this an excellent idea, but decided that the game had been played for long enough. So instead he looked at the man levelly and said, "Captain, are you asking me to fly up there and take a look at the scene on your behalf?"

"Well, yes. It would certainly be helpful. If you wouldn't mind."

Tylus frowned. "My problem, captain, is that I've been sent here for a very specific purpose, and what you're proposing isn't related to that purpose. Indeed, it would require me to take time out from my assigned duties."

"Of course, I wouldn't wish to interfere with your assignment unduly," Johnson said quickly, "but this wouldn't take long. I'd hoped, in the interests of inter-departmental co-operation, that you might consider assisting us."

"And I presume that I could count on your department to help me make up the time lost by providing me with assistance should I need it?"

"Certainly! Whatever you need; I guarantee it."

Tylus smiled. "In that case, captain, in the interests of inter-departmental co-operation, I'd be delighted to help."

"Excellent, excellent."

"One thing, before we go. Have you any idea where I could obtain some rock climbing equipment?"

Johnson stared at him, startled. "I'm sorry, did you say rock climbing equipment?"

TEN

Tom came to with his head thumping. Somebody was pulling him to his feet – a tattooed arm. He stared into a face that he thought might be Rayul's, though he still found it difficult to tell these tattooed men apart. Dust and small fragments of wood and stone fell from his body as he struggled upwards. More cuts and bruises but his head was the one that claimed his attention. He lifted a hand to his face, feeling his forehead, to be rewarded with a fresh lance of pain. His fingers found dampness, stickiness, and he stared at the red of his own glistening blood on taking them away.

Kat was there, agitated, anxious to move. "Come on," she urged, her voice sounding distorted and distant. "The fire's taken hold and it's going to be a monster."

He didn't need her to tell him that, he could feel the heat for himself. The building they had taken refuge in the previous night was gone, as were those next to it, consumed in raging flames. Dark smoke billowed upwards, plumes that dashed themselves against the high cavern ceiling. He felt himself pulled again and was running, staggering in the wake of the Tattooed Men and Kat, who kept pace with him.

"Weird gang alliances, demon hounds and now exploding sun globes falling on us; you're not the safest of people to be around, kid," the girl muttered.

Tom couldn't answer. It was as if the words were not intended for him at all but for somebody else. Nor would he have argued if he could, not even at her calling him kid again. Things were happening on all sides which he had no understanding of and no control over. He felt as if he were drowning, as if life was somehow racing ahead of him, dragging him along in its wake, buffeting him the whole while. Since he came back from the Heights everything had turned crazy. No, in fact before that – the murder and falling from the walls… Was there a connection? Was all that had happened to him since then a consequence of what he had witnessed on the walls? He didn't want to believe that, yet it offered an explanation – the only one he could currently think of. The question was, if true, what could he hope to do about it?

They passed guard units rushing towards the blaze. Other people started to appear at windows and doors, most of them bleary-eyed, curious to know what all the fuss was about, woken by the explosion but not yet able to grasp what was happening.

"Run," Kat yelled at them, and then, "Fire!"

The Tattooed Men joined in calling out warnings and soon they were not the only ones heading away, as people abandoned their homes and fled the spreading flames. A pair of fire carts trundled past, the strident peal of their bells all but drowning out the shouts of the attendant guardsmen who were frantically waving their arms and imploring folk to make way, while constantly sounding the carts' handbell. The carts were laden with pumps and vast coiled hoses capable of tapping into well-points and sewers. They were pulled by teams of great grey oxen. Trained for such tasks from birth, the animals were hooded, their noses, mouth and eyes covered, with scent parcels stuffed into the muzzle section to disguise the smell of smoke and prevent them from panicking at the proximity of fire. So the theory went. Tom had always doubted whether the system worked in practice, but he wouldn't be hanging around to find out on this occasion.

For once his curiosity lay dormant, buried beneath other concerns. His head continued to ache and he could still hear the explosion reverberating through his mind, as if the sound had slipped into his head through the ears and then been unable to find a way out again. He felt oddly detached and everything seemed a little surreal – a situation not helped by the stubbornness of his eyes, which refused to fully focus without the sort of extreme effort his headache hated. The fire carts' oxen looked fuzzy and distorted, as if they were alien creatures parodying oxen, and the accompanying guardsmen's shouts reached him as incoherent shrieks.

Tom followed behind Kat and the Tattooed Men as best he could, occasionally chivvied by the girl or by one of the men who might have been Rayul. Blue eyes, Tom noticed – not common here. They formed an anchor point, the girl and this tattooed man, something to concentrate on. He lost all clear sense of time and could not begin to guess at how long it took them to reach their destination, which proved to be a shop.

Afterwards, he would try to remember what the store sold, without ever being able to.

He shuffled into the shop behind Rayul, who nodded greeting to the gnarled man sitting hunched behind the counter. For some reason Tom saw the man with crystal clarity, or, at least, his perception of the man. He was gnarled in the manner of an old tree root from which fickle earth has been washed away by heavy rains, leaving it exposed to too much weather and too much sun. His leathery face showed the ravages of age and perhaps even pox, being severely marked by crevices of wrinkles. His scalp was only partially obscured by wispy strands of grey hair. He scowled at them from beneath long and wiry grey brows as they filed through.

Behind the shop front lay a single large room, an area which seemed to be filled with tattooed men.

"I'd better find Chavver," Rayul said, "warn her about the fire and tell her we've lost the small house."

"Oh, so you're not going to mention the fact that I'm here then?"

If Rayul replied to Kat's comment, Tom failed to catch it.

He was led to a bench, which he slumped down onto, head throbbing with renewed vigour. Activity surrounded him but meant nothing; he was aware of it only at the periphery of his thoughts, as something of no great relevance. He stared down at his hands, opened and closed them, then dug his nails into his palms, feeling the sting of pain as the nails bit, but nothing seemed to ease the throbbing in his head.

Soon after, he became aware of someone standing over him and looked up into the face of one of the

Tattooed Men – no, a Tattooed Woman, though she was as bald as any of the men and bore a similar tracery of ochre body etchings.

"It's all right, I'm just going to clean you up a little," a voice said.

She lifted something to his face – a cloth, damp and warm – and proceeded to rub at him gently, wiping away the blood. He didn't object, though he did wince when the cloth touched the wound, just above his hairline, sending fresh spasms of pain coursing through his head.

"Well?" Kat's voice, as if from a distance.

"It's the bang on the head."

"I know that much."

"What he needs is plenty of rest. Let him sleep it off."

"Right, so let him go to sleep while the fire burns the building down around us."

"Do you really think it'll reach this far?"

"No idea, but I don't fancy waiting around to find out, do you? Can you do anything to help him? Please."

"Maybe, although rest would still be the best remedy."

"Understood, but it's not an option."

"I'll see what I can do."

"Thanks, Shayna."

He felt hands on either side of his head, fingers pressing gently at his temples, and the woman's tattooed face loomed close. He tried to raise his own hand to ward hers off, but hesitated as a sense of warmth flowed through his mind and the woman's tracery of tattoos seemed to glow until they shone. He closed his eyes and concentrated on the warmth in his head. It wasn't unpleasant as such, just strange. Awareness slipped quietly away and he drifted into comforting sleep.

Tom woke up with a start, staring around, blinking away dreams that dissipated in an instant. He felt clear-headed and much more himself. His headache had virtually disappeared, leaving in its wake a vague sense of fragility and a tenderness around the wound itself when his questing fingers tentatively explored it. He felt so much better that he wondered, with a sudden jolt of concern, how much time had passed.

The room was a hive of activity. What most caught his attention as he looked about was the array of weapons, which seemed to be everywhere: long knives like Kat's predominated, along with full swords, but there were also crossbows, staves and other things less easy to identify. They all looked sleek, new and well cared for. These were no street-nicks, he realised, but a heavily-armed warrior band.

A short distance away Kat stood talking earnestly with Rayul. She glanced over as Tom stirred, made her excuses and came across to him, concern evident on her face. "You all right?"

"Think so. How long was I out?"

She shrugged. "Not sure; a few minutes at most."

Was that all? It had felt much longer. "There was a woman…"

"Yeah, Shayna. She's a healer – a damn good one too. Took away the pain and cleared your head – that's another one you owe me. She and I go way back."

"How do you know…?"

He was interrupted by the arrival of another woman, or rather a girl; it was difficult to judge her age. She had long black hair, which was currently tied in a ponytail. Her face and arms were tattoo-free, although she was dressed in much the same style as the others: leather sleeveless tunic and a skirt that was formed by layered strips of leather extending from the waist. Her attire was distinguished from the others' in being dyed much darker, virtually black.

She ignored Tom and stalked straight up to Kat, who stood her ground in the face of the newcomer's aggression and obvious anger. The two girls glared at each other.

"I was wondering how long it would take you to come over and say hello," Kat said.

The girl, presumably the Tattooed Men's leader, Chavver, took her time in answering, maintaining the glare as if that in itself might be her answer. Finally, she said, "If not for Rayul, I would've sliced you open as soon as you stepped through the door."

Chavver was larger than Kat; a little taller, with broader shoulders and muscular arms, bigger all round but, even so, Tom was struck by how similar these two seemed, both decked out in black as they were.

"You'd have tried to, you mean," Kat replied. "You're not good enough, you never were. The only reason you're in charge of this lot in the first place is because I didn't want to be."

The larger girl snarled and whipped out one of the oversized knives that Tom was growing used to seeing by now; Kat's twin blades were in her hand at the same instant.

"Enough!" Rayul stepped between them, pushing a hand out towards each girl. "For pity's sake, both of you, aren't you ever going to put all this behind you? What's done is done, now move on for all our sakes."

Activity in the room ceased, as everyone stared at the confrontation.

"You forget yourself, Rayul," Chavver said. Rage still burned in her eyes and for a moment Tom thought she might press ahead with an attack anyway, going straight through Rayul if necessary.

"Now is not the time," the tattooed man persisted, either oblivious or impervious to the threat. "The streets are on fire; it could reach here any minute. We must get organised and move out. You two can kill each other somewhere else, somewhen else, if you have to, but not right now and not right here."

"He's got a point," Kat said.

With a final glare, Chavver thrust her knife back into its sheath. Only once she had did Kat do likewise. Rayul relaxed and exchanged a quick glance with Kat.

"This isn't over," Chavver said, before turning to her men, none of whom, apart from Rayul, had moved a muscle since the face-off started. "What are you lot staring at? Come on, get your gear packed. We leave in two minutes."

Suddenly the room was filled with activity again as men scrambled around in final preparation, although, Tom had to admit, it certainly wasn't chaotic. Each individual moved with an unhurried efficiency that spoke of frequent practice and long familiarity with their part in the process. It was just the combined effect of so much movement from so many people which suggested otherwise.

In what seemed no time at all the Tattooed Men stood ready, weapons stowed and packs on their backs. With a nod, Chavver led the way out through a rear door, the Tattooed Men filing out behind her. Tom, Kat and Rayul hung back and were the last to leave. Tom glanced around as they did so. The room's walls were bordered with stacked boxes, presumably containing stock for the shop, but the place was otherwise empty. There was nothing at all to suggest that a large group of people had been staying there.

He remembered the weathered face of the elderly shopkeeper and wondered if anyone had told him they were leaving, and whether he would be able to make his own escape if the fire did come this way. Presumably so, since no one else seemed concerned.

Outside, the smell of smoke hung heavy in the air, but there was no immediate sign of the fire itself. They fell in at the back of the column, Kat chatting amiably with Rayul.

"Where are you headed?"

"The north corner."

She frowned. "Why, what's up there? And since when was the north corner part of the Tattooed Men's range?"

"It isn't, but it's as far away from everything as we can get without leaving the city itself."

"You're running from something."

"As fast as we can," he acknowledged, "and if you had any sense you'd be doing the same."

"What is it? What scares the Tattooed Men this much?"

He looked at her, as if weighing up the situation or his next words. "There are things going down, Kat; major things, deadly things. Watch the street-nicks, don't trust them. They may not always be what they seem, not anymore."

"What the breck does that mean? You've got to give me more than that."

"We'll be back once the dust has cleared, once we know how things stand. As for giving you more, I can promise you one thing: whatever comes out of this, the City Below will never be the same again."

"Oh come on, Rayul, that tells me frissin' nothing."

"It tells you more than you deserve." Chavver had joined them unnoticed and evidently caught the end of the conversation. "Rayul, take point." With that, she effectively ended their hope of learning any more.

The tattooed man nodded, gave Kat a slightly sour half-smile and headed towards the front of the column.

"You!" Chavver pointed at Kat, who smiled back. Had Tom been in the other girl's position, it would certainly have infuriated him. "You can make your own way from here!"

"With pleasure." She looked at Tom, who nodded. He would be glad to be away from the Tattooed Men, and particularly glad to put some distance between these two women.

"This isn't over, Katerina," Chavver said.

"Happy to finish it whenever you want to, Charveve. Just tell me the time and the place."

"The time will be as soon as this is all over, and as for the place, you know where."

Kat nodded. "I know."

"Make peace with your soul before you come there, *if* you come. Be ready to die, little sister." The last word was hissed in almost a whisper, but carried all the venom of a serpent's bite.

Tom stared at the pair as they separated. *Sister*?

Chavver turned to Tom, acknowledging his existence for the first time. "You should be careful who you travel with, kid." That even sounded like Kat. "She's not to be trusted." With that she swivelled on her heel and was gone.

"Bitch!" Kat muttered under her breath.

"Is she really your sister?"

"What's it to you?"

"Nothing, I just…" *Wondered? Found it hard to believe? Didn't understand where all the hate came from?* He had no idea what to add, so left the sentence hanging and let Kat respond to whatever she expected to hear.

"Yes, she's my sister, alright? It's not something I care to remember too often, but she is. Now leave it."

"And the Tattooed Men?"

"I said leave it." The sharpness of her tone left little doubt that she meant it.

They watched as the Tattooed Men walked away. One glanced back, not Rayul – Tom was at least able to distinguish him from the others now – and might have smiled briefly, but then turned forward again. Chavver was nowhere in sight, presumably having moved back towards the front of the column.

Even from the back they looked formidable, the last gang in the world anyone would want to mess with. So what had them so scared that they were heading for the most remote place they knew?

"Well, just you and me again, kid."

He nodded. "Are you still willing to come with me?"

"Guess so."

"Even after all we've seen and heard?"

"Look, I don't have to if you don't want me to. I

could just point you in the right direction and leave you here if you like."

"No, no, I..." *Want you here? Like having you around?* "I reckon we make a good team. Just don't want you to get caught up in whatever's going on for my sake, so if you want to head north or whatever, I understand."

"No, I said I'd see this through and so I will. If we get a move on, should have you back home by midday, I reckon. Then I can shoot back to the Jeradine quarter before nightfall. I'm sure Ty-gen will put me up until everything's blown over and the world has returned to what passes for normal down here, if it ever does.

"So, you ready to get going? The sooner we do, the sooner I can get off the streets myself."

"Fine." He tried to keep the relief out of his voice. "One thing, though: will you please stop calling me 'kid'?"

"Did I?" She shrugged. "I'll try."

Better than nothing, he supposed. "Do you know this area?"

"Some. You?"

"No."

She snorted. "Don't you know anywhere outside of the street your gang play in?"

"A few places, we just haven't found any of them yet."

"Be sure and let me know when we do. Come on."

And they were walking again, Tom keeping pace with the girl, lost in his own thoughts and trusting her to know the way. After a few minutes, he said, "Any idea what's got them so spooked?" He didn't need to explain who.

"None. Except that in the past day or two I've seen so many odd things down here that I'm well on the way to being spooked myself. The only difference is, I don't really know what I'm supposed to be afraid of, and I'm pretty sure they do."

Tom left it there. Having seen how sensitive Kat was when it came to the Tattooed Men he was wary of saying something to rile her again. He had a feeling they would be fresh in her mind and hoped that if he didn't push the subject, she might volunteer some information of her own accord. In the event, he didn't have to wait long before she did so.

"They're the survivors," the girl said. "From the Pits. The Tattooed Men are the ones who walked away."

Tom whistled. "No wonder they look so mean."

"Yeah." She smiled. "Not a gang you'd want to pick a fight with, that's for sure."

They walked on in silence for a few minutes, before she spoke again. "It gives you a real bond: fighting in the Pits, surviving. When we came out, after they closed the Pits down, it didn't seem right to just drift apart and join different gangs, we were too close, trusted each other above anyone else; so we became a gang. Only problem was there was no territory for us; everywhere was already staked out, so it was a case of move in and take over someone else's patch or wander, carve out our own way. After so much time cooped up in and around the Pits, we all had itchy feet in any case, none of us fancied staying too long in one place, so we became nomads within the city, finding our own places and own routes between the established street-nick territories. Course, we 'trespassed' on occasion and there was the odd fight in the early days, but few

gangs had the stomach to take us on twice, so bound-
aries adjusted."

"And you were part of this?"

"Yes."

"But you left."

"Yes."

The inevitable question hovered on the tip of his
tongue, but he could sense her bracing herself, ready
to snap at him if he asked, so instead he simply looked
at her expectantly.

After a few seconds she sighed. "There can only be
one queen, kid. It soon got to the point where either
Chavver had to leave or I did, otherwise we'd have
ended up killing each other. I chose to go. Simple as
that."

"And now?" Curiosity finally won out over sensitiv-
ity.

"Now it looks as if one of us will be killing the other
in any case. Soon as this is over. Whatever the breck
this is and always assuming I can tell when it's over.
Otherwise, she'll have a long wait."

She grinned and Tom joined her. "If I was you," he
said, "I wouldn't turn up either way. That'd really
make her mad."

"No, this has been getting under both our skins and
it's well past time things were settled, if only for the
sake of Rayul and the other men. She's going to lead
'em all into trouble otherwise."

He wondered what she'd learnt from Rayul while he
had been out of it. Enough to worry her, evidently,
though presumably nothing about what had sent the
Tattooed Men running for the remotest corner of the
under-City.

"Did you ever think of leaving the city altogether?" he asked.

"Yes, but I'm not going to. I've been out there once and didn't like it much."

"Really?"

"Yeah. Groups of us used to hire out as ship's guards now and again, to bring a little coin in. I went on one trip. Never again. There's a lot of open space out there and it's not for me. Guess I'm a street-nick at heart. This is where I belong."

"So, assuming you manage to survive whatever's wrong with the streets right now, you've got a fight to the death with your sister to look forward to."

"Yeah," she gave a wry smile. "Some future, huh?"

The fire had been brought under control. The smoke was sufficiently dissipated for Tylus to look things over, though it still hung over the scene in fragmented drifts and the smell would doubtless linger for several days yet.

Once in the air it was as if he stared down upon the rooftops through tattered layers of gauze. Even so, from up here near the cavern roof he was able to get a far clearer picture of the damage and was shocked at its extent. It had been impossible to get a true sense of just how many buildings lay in ruin from down on the ground. He was also amazed that the death toll was so light – initial reports had proved to be exaggerated and current estimates put the figure at around a dozen, which, bearing in mind the way the buildings here were crowded so closely together and the early hour of the incident, struck Tylus as remarkably few. Evidently those fleeing the fire had called out warnings to onlookers, and this was thought to have been a mitigating factor.

Having surveyed the destruction below, he now turned his attention to what lay above. The point from which the sun globe had fallen was easy enough to identify. Remnants of braces and metal fitments clustered around an unusually flat area of cavern ceiling, while the tattered fronds of severed cables hung down forlornly. Among all these, Tylus hoped to find a bracket strong enough to support him. He flew under the area once, twice, flipping onto his back as he sailed past so that he could search for a likely roost. Satisfied that he had located one, he came around again, this time heading straight for the chosen spot. In his right hand he held a spring-gated steel hook, from which a length of rope extended to encircle his waist. As he reached the roof, he clipped the hook deftly around a metal bracket and hoped it would prove to be as solid and strong as it looked. Thankfully, the hook remained firm and the bracket seemed able to support his weight. He now swung his knees up to strike the roof. Each knee was equipped with a suction cup. He had no great confidence in the things, having failed to get them to work properly even in training, and that had been against a smooth service rather than the irregularities of rock, no matter how much said rock had been levelled. Sure enough, the cups made only token gestures towards gripping, before pulling free to leave his legs dangling beneath him.

Unperturbed, Tylus half-swung, half-reached for another bracket, indistinguishable from the one he was tethered to. Finding it sound, he looped a second length of rope through it, which he secured with a slip knot.

The short rope ended in a stirrup, broad enough to accommodate both his legs. It took a little manoeuvring but he soon managed to get both legs through and so hung there, swaying gently to and fro like a man in the very skimpiest of hammocks. From this precarious vantage point he began to examine the scene, excited to have another opportunity to utilise what he considered to be his neglected investigative skills.

Tylus quickly found a number of revealing clues: screw holes in support plates, their threads still prominent, suggesting that the screws had been carefully removed. Had they been wrenched out by the weight of a falling object he would have expected to see the threads distorted or even sheared off. Then there were the cables. Those nearest him showed definite signs of having been neatly cut rather than torn. The evidence seemed irrefutable. This had been no accident but rather an act of deliberate sabotage, but to what purpose? What could anyone hope to gain by bringing down a sun globe?

It was then that he spotted something which seemed out of place: a small piece of mangled mechanism tangled up in one of the cables. At first Tylus couldn't work out why this innocuous looking piece of wreckage had caught his attention, after all, it wasn't surprising to find fragments of detached machinery in the wake of such a catastrophe. Then he had it: despite being tiny and severely damaged, this parcel of circuits and metal looked to be self-contained, a separate entity rather than a part of something. It was also, frustratingly, just beyond his reach.

He swung towards it, stretching but falling short. Another swing and he stretched further, almost making it this time. The secret, he decided, lay in building up a rhythm. He swung back and forth, back and forth, before pushing off with his left hand for added momentum at one end of the swing and straining with his right at the other. This time he touched it, but couldn't quite grasp the thing before he was carried away again. Next time! He gave a further, muscle-jarring push with his left and twisted around to stretch for all he was worth, snagging the cable that trapped the small mechanism with his right hand, pulling it towards him and finally taking hold of the tantalising object. Small enough to fit into the palm of his hand, it resembled a silver beetle, though lacking legs. Its central carapace had been dented and a seam on one side split open. Tylus imagined the cable, which he quickly freed it from, had whipped back when the sun globe fell, catching the mechanism and dashing it against something – perhaps the cavern ceiling. Yet for such an image to hold true, it meant this small thing would need to have been independently mobile, and surely, even if that were so, it would be impossible for such an insignificant device to bring a sun globe down on its own. He twisted in his makeshift harness, looking at the number of screw shafts, bolt holes and cables around him.

As he did so, something shifted. The plate supporting the bracket he was tied to had begun to pull away from the ceiling, presumably loosened by all the swinging he had just subjected it to. Tylus froze, staring at the exposed pins which were all that held him in place. He looked for something to hold on to, careful to turn only his neck and head, but he had let go of the cables when he freed the small mechanism and nothing else obvious lay within reach.

He tried moving, ever so slowly, but that proved to be enough. Suddenly there was nothing supporting his waist any more as the metal plate pulled completely free of the ceiling. He fell backwards, to hang upside down. The plate and bracket, still attached to him by the rope, shot past, narrowly missing his chin.

For a few seconds he dangled there like an incompetent trapeze artist, supported only by his crooked knees, then he felt himself over-balancing, his legs slipping out of the stirrup. He fell, the bracket and plate ahead of him, tugging him downward.

He brought his legs over, straining to hold them, to prevent them from going too far, desperate to get his body horizontal rather than being dragged into an uncontrolled cartwheel. In many ways this should be much easier than when he lost control on the walls. Then it had been a sudden change of wind direction that caused him to stall, followed by constant buffeting that made it all but impossible to control his spin. At least here there was next to no wind. However, the ground was also an awful lot closer, leaving very little time in which to recover from any mishap.

Perversely, the trailing rope with its metal deadweight helped. The pull on his waist acted as a centre, a focus, as he sought to straighten his legs and keep his upper body from shooting upwards as counterbalance to the rotation of legs and hips; all this in freefall, with nothing to steady himself against.

For an instant it seemed he would fail, that the sheer momentum of his legs would carry them beneath his body and on, but he tensed his muscles, thrust his stomach forward and dragged them back. Somehow, he did it, finding himself steady, with his body horizontal, paralleling the fast approaching ground. Tylus spread his arms, deploying the kitecape, feeling it bite the air and convert his plunge into a controlled swoop and then into a glide, arcing down toward the rooftops and then up again, gaining a little height before spiralling around to where Richardson, Captain Johnson and a knot of officers waited.

He chose his landing spot with care, close to the group of guardsmen. Unfortunately, they insisted on moving, hurrying towards him as he came down. The result was that he nearly took Johnson's eye out with the swinging bracket, which he was unable to do anything about until he had landed. Thankfully, the captain ducked at the last minute and the metal plate sailed harmlessly over his head. The Kite Guard felt solid ground beneath his feet once more and, much to his relief, still clutched the mysterious mechanism in his right hand.

Johnson recovered his composure quickly after nearly being decapitated and, even before Tylus had fully divested himself of rope and its attached weight, asked, "Well, did you discover anything?"

"Definitely sabotage," Tylus confirmed, and went on to relate his observations. He then showed Johnson the damaged device and explained his suspicions. Johnson examined the mechanism, frowning and evidently unconvinced, before handing it to an aide. "I'll pass this up the line and have it looked at."

A process that would likely take weeks and the results of which, always assuming there were any meaningful results, would be far too late to be of any help.

"Who did this?" Johnson muttered, "And what in the world were they trying to achieve?" Questions which echoed Tylus's own thoughts.

"Perhaps if we consider what they did achieve, it'll offer some clue as to their intentions," he suggested.

"Go on."

"As far as I can see, they've managed three things." He counted them off on his fingers. "One, brought down a sun globe; two, destroyed some buildings; and three, killed some people."

"The first two seem meaningless in themselves, which leaves–"

"Killing someone."

The captain stared at the Kite Guard. "You're suggesting this was an assassination?"

Tylus shrugged. "It's the best explanation I've come up with so far."

"Bit elaborate, don't you think?"

"Very, but if whoever is behind this wanted to make it look like an accident…"

"And they'd be unlikely to know we had a Kite Guard handy to make a quick appraisal." Johnson called out to one of his officers, "Sergeant, I want a full list of all the people who died in the fire as soon as possible: names, addresses where relevant and occupations likewise." He then turned back to Tylus, all smiles. "Thank you, Kite Guard Tylus, you've been most helpful."

"My pleasure; and when I need the department's help…?"

"Just ask."

Tylus watched the captain walk away. It made a great deal of sense to prioritise the identification of the victims. The more he thought about it, the more plausible his outrageous idea seemed. He decided, however, to leave his additional thoughts on the subject unspoken. Why worry the good captain unnecessarily? After all, he had no proof. But the thought refused to go away: if this had all been an extravagant ploy to kill somebody, who was to say that the attempt had succeeded? What if it hadn't? What came next?

Putting such concerns to one side for the moment, he hurried to catch up with Johnson. "Sir."

The captain turned round, all smiles. "Yes, Kite Officer?"

"You know you said that whenever I needed the department's help all I had to do was ask? Would now be a good time?"

ELEVEN

Dewar was faced with something of a dilemma. Once he learned from Lyle and an oh-so-willing-to-please Jezmina that the lad Tom really hadn't returned as yet and was now overdue, he had little choice but to wait. It was either that or start scouring the under-City for signs of the boy, and he simply wasn't in a position to undertake such a daunting task – too much ground to cover. Besides, the lad had to come back here eventually; there was nowhere else for him to go.

Breaking into the Blue Claws' headquarters in order to capture and torture their leader was not something he was likely to get away with twice. If he were to abandon the place now, it would mean relinquishing his current advantage: that of being on the inside, at the one place where his target was bound to turn up eventually. So he waited.

That left the question of the Blue Claw themselves. He thought long and hard about the best way to handle the gang, and eventually came up with a strategy. It wasn't a perfect strategy and would never be anything more than a temporary fix, but it should buy him the day or two he needed. If Tom hadn't shown up by then, he never would.

The key to the plan was Jezmina. Not many things frightened Dewar, but this girl did. He had no idea how young she was, she simply fell into the category of being far too young. Yet there was a sensual quality to her that belied her years.

Jezmina's complexion was slightly darker than most under-City dwellers, suggesting foreign ancestry somewhere in her past. This leant an exotic quality to her undoubted beauty, which he had originally overlooked as being nothing more than cute prettiness. She also knew how to play to her strengths; her dark hair was worn simply, with a centre parting which caused it to tumble down and frame her oval face. Most street-nick girls had a habit of doing outrageous things to their hair, presumably in order to stand out. Not her, she didn't need to. The hair, slightly arched eyebrows and drown-in-me eyes were virtually identical in shade, and the whole was completed by a full-lipped mouth ideal for pouting.

As soon as Jezmina realised Dewar had the upper hand over Lyle, her whole attitude towards him had changed. The way she transformed from snivelling victim into smouldering temptress was a wonder to behold. He had no doubt at all that she was trying to seduce him, and could well understand how someone like Lyle could end up completely at her mercy. This girl was dangerous, and she was exactly what he needed to secure his status within the Blue Claw.

Lyle would play along, partly thanks to Jezmina's persuasion, but mostly due to his fear of being hurt any further. Dewar had taken great care to inflict maximum hurt with minimum damage to the Blue Claw's leader, and the man's face was unmarked by anything other than pain. That, however, left him looking drawn and haggard when he appeared before the gathered street-nicks that morning and introduced Dewar to them. Which suited the assassin just fine.

Lyle sat in front of his puzzled followers, a robe pulled about his huddled form and obviously far from well. He explained how he had been struck down in the night by an aggressive ailment which was likely to see him incapacitated for a day or two. Only through the ministrations of Jezmina was he in a fit state to address them at all. By chance, his old friend Dewar had called by to see him and would be running things in Lyle's stead until he had recovered.

Dewar then took over, lambasting those who had been on watch for their inadequacies and explaining in detail how he had slipped past them with such ease.

In doing so, he hoped to keep the nicks off balance, to not give them the time to ask such awkward questions as why none of them had ever encountered Lyle's old friend before. Jezmina's support was invaluable. She backed him up and appeared suitably attentive to the obviously unwell Lyle.

Again the girl played a clever game, producing a faultless performance for the Blue Claw's benefit and doing all that he had asked of her, and yet she was probably whispering support to Lyle behind his back and would doubtless claim later that she had co-operated only because she had to. With those doe-eyes of hers, he felt certain she would get away with it too.

Being so ill, Lyle then retired to his quarters, though not before leaving strict instructions that he was not to be disturbed under any circumstances. Once back in the private room, Dewar injected his prisoner with a sedative before securely binding and gagging him.

This allowed him, in effect, to step into Lyle's shoes, directing the Blue Claw's activities, with the ever-present Jezmina to endorse his authority. The plans for that day, which Lyle had been only too happy to share with him, required just the slightest of amendments to ensure that he wouldn't need to leave the building at all.

During the time he spent with Lyle, the assassin had learnt all he could of the Blue Claw, its members and the gang's structure. He now put that knowledge to good use. The first thing he did was to organise the distribution of the previous night's spoils, putting Barton in charge of that job. He then systematically ensured that all the gang's lieutenants were occupied overseeing some task or other, even taking time out to show the nicks who had been on night watch exactly how he had slipped so easily past their defences, so that they could be on guard for similar intrusion in the future. It was no skin off his nose to do so. He had no intention of coming back here again.

Once he had every single member of the Claw organised doing something, he returned to Lyle's quarters, Jezmina beside him. He didn't yet trust the girl sufficiently to let her out of his sight.

He unlocked and opened the door, ushering her through in front of him before relocking the door once they were inside. As soon as he turned from doing so, Jezmina leapt on him, pressing her lips to his.

Again the girl managed something remarkable, catching him completely by surprise, which was a rarity. He took hold of her hair and pulled her off him, not stopping to be gentle, while his other hand shot up to grasp her throat.

"Try something like that again and you're dead!"

She stepped back, away from his grasp, and flicked her hair. A mischievous smile played at the corners of her mouth. "If you say so."

He went to say something, but thought better of it.

"It doesn't alter the fact that you kissed me back, just for an instant there, before you could stop yourself. Deny it, say what you want, but we'll both always know that you did."

She said this with such conviction that he almost believed it himself. She turned around and sashayed slowly away, every provocative step an invitation and a challenge.

Dewar stared after her in amazement, reminding himself that she was just a child, while wondering whether she had ever really been a child. He thought back to when he first surprised her in these rooms, to the timid, wide-eyed girl who had trembled and cried and submitted so meekly to being bound. Had any of that been genuine, even for an instant? Looking at her now, he very much doubted it.

The assassin was tired at a time when he couldn't afford to be, when keeping a clear head and sharp mind were vital. He had been up all night and knew that sleep could only be postponed for so long. Taking a nap now was a risk but a calculated one, and less dangerous than making a costly error later through lack of concentration.

Lyle was still completely out of it and ought to remain that way for most of the day, which just left

Jezmina to worry about. He led her to the bed, ignoring her inevitable comments, and tied both her hands to the series of stylised iron poles which formed the headboard.

"If this is how you like it, you should have said earlier." The girl maintained her flippant monologue.

This was hardly the most comfortable of positions for her, but it would have to do and in any case wouldn't be for long. He couldn't run the risk of anything beyond a brief nap and there was too much still to do in any case. He told the girl that if she kept her mouth shut and behaved herself, he might consider not tying her up the next time. It was a lie, but one which sounded plausible and seemed likely to hold her.

So he slumped into a chair, got comfortable and hoped that weariness would win out over his racing thoughts.

Dewar awoke refreshed and clear-headed, knowing that the nap had given him the energy he needed to keep going for now. He untied Jezmina, who appeared to have fallen asleep herself, and the pair of them headed back towards the main rooms.

As soon as they stepped into the common room he sensed that something had changed. Barton was there along with perhaps a dozen of the others, but their posture was too casual – they were trying overly hard to seem relaxed, the effort to do so undermining their intent.

Without any noticeable signal, street-nicks converged on Dewar from all sides. He wondered where he had slipped up, what error had given him away. Jezmina vanished immediately, ducking back out the door. There were several ways he could react to the situation, but decided to start by trying to brazen it out.

"What the breck is going on here?"

His challenge had no effect. The street-nicks continued to close in, not saying a word. So much for plan A.

Without any further preamble, four of the youths leapt towards him, coming in from all angles. He didn't wait for them to reach him but charged towards the one immediately in front, punching the lad, spinning and kicking at another. Hands reached for him. He twisted, punched, shoulder-charged, kicked and gouged. They outnumbered him but he had a few things going for him – experience, training and, over the majority of them, size. Also, there was the fact that no knives or other weapons had been drawn, which suggested they were intent on taking him alive. The fight was being conducted in virtual silence, which leant it an eerie, unnatural quality; the grunts of exertion and the creaks of disturbed furniture being the only sounds.

One of nicks hooked a leg around his and tripped him while another clung to his back, an arm around his throat. Knowing he was on the way down, Dewar threw himself backwards, carrying the kid behind him and landing on him as hard as he could. The lad let go. A kick flashed towards his face before he could do more than half turn away. His lip split and started to swell at once. He tasted blood, but still caught the foot, twisting it viciously, to hear and feel the crack of fractured bone. The resultant scream of agony was the loudest sound since the fight began.

Another kick came in to his side but he rode this one, using its momentum to help lift him back to his feet. One of the larger nicks threw a punch, but he ducked and bobbed, so that the fist flew over his shoulder, barely grazing an ear on the way through. He responded by shoulder-charging his assailant even as the punch went past, knocking him down, but there was another one in the way immediately. This one he dealt two short, sharp jabs to the kidneys with his right hand, while blocking a punch from somebody else with his left.

The nick he had knocked over tried to bear-hug his legs and pull him down again, but he kicked out once, twice and persuaded him to let go. Another kid was sent flying with a swipe of his left arm, demolishing a small table as he landed, only to come back at the assassin wielding one of the table's legs as a club.

Somewhere along the line Dewar had taken a blow to the forehead. Blood found its way into his left eye, stinging and raising tears which half-blinded him. Several blows rained in as he risked a quick wipe to prevent more blood trickling down while frantically blinking to clear the moisture. He took a blow from the table leg and felt a rib either crack or take a severe bruising.

He dared not draw his own weapons for fear of escalation: holding off a dozen nick's fists was one thing, dealing with as many knives was another matter altogether.

Four or five of the nicks were now out of the action, either unconscious or too injured to continue fighting, and Dewar felt confident he was winning when the door at the far side of the room burst open and a fresh batch of the Blue Claw came charging through, led by Bull, one of the gang's lieutenants, whose physique lived up to his name.

The assassin knew when he was beaten. Seeing these new arrivals eager to join the fray he turned, shrugged off the grappling hands of a couple of nicks, and ran for the door which led back to the hallway and eventually Lyle's quarters. He kicked off the most persistent nick, hurtled out of the room and pulled the door shut, clutching the handle to prevent it from being opened. It wouldn't hold for more than a handful of seconds, but he was already reviewing in his mind the easiest exit to reach from here. Escape route decided, he turned to run, only to see Jezmina already in the process of swinging something from above her head towards his. Before he had a chance to react, it connected.

Pain careened around his skull in jagged shards. He collapsed to his knees, fighting to stay conscious, and it was at that moment that the air reverberated with a piercing shriek. It shot right through him, the loudest sound he had ever heard, and evidently at the perfect pitch to cause maximum discomfort and pain. At first Dewar assumed the sound was inside his head, a bizarre consequence of the blow, but he saw Jezmina with her pretty face screwed up, hands pressed to her ears, almost doubling over in her attempts to escape the agonising noise. He was forced to cover his own ears, even as he toppled fully to the ground.

He lay there in a foetal curl, the palm of his right hand supporting his ear, cheek pressed to the floorboards. From this position he saw feet; a whole crowd of booted feet, razzers' feet, approaching on the run.

Only then did he finally concede that perhaps he was not going to escape after all.

Tom and Kat were making good progress and the girl still insisted she was confident of getting him home in plenty of time for her to return to the Jeradine quarter before nightfall when their journey was interrupted by a deep, mournful tolling from ahead of them. It was a sound immediately recognisable to any resident of the under-City: the body bell.

A death cart made its way slowly down the centre of the road, pulled by a pair of enormous oxen, their horns festooned with black ribbons and their backs draped with the traditional black cloth. This seemed to be their day for oxen, and bells. First the fire tenders and now the death cart. The beast on the right bore the bell, a great brass thing, suspended from its neck by a thick corded rope, ringing out its wail for the departed with every step; a far deeper and less strident clamour than the fire tenders' had produced. Clothed in black robes which extended from their high hoods to their ground-brushing skirts, two body boys accompanied the cart, one on either side, directing and keeping abreast with the oxen.

Quite why they were called boys was anyone's guess. They were clearly fully grown men beneath their concealing robes, these gatherers of the dead.

The combination of the two men standing either side of the oxen meant that the cart and its small entourage took up virtually the full width of the thoroughfare, all but forcing anyone else on the street to shuffle to one side and stand respectfully still until the cart had passed by, as tradition demanded.

It made little sense to Tom. See a body lying in a gutter and any resident of the under-City would either ignore it or rob it, yet when the same people encountered a cart filled with a whole load of similar bodies they were supposed to stand reverently with heads bowed while it trundled on its less than merry way. Why did one deserve any more respect than the other?

Such customs had always baffled Tom. Whether they were for religious or traditional purposes, elaborations of this sort tended to leave him cold.

Nonetheless, both he and Kat stood dutifully back against the wall as the oxen drew near. As ever, Tom tried to peer from under his eyebrows to catch a glimpse of the body boys' faces but, as always, he failed, the hoods revealing nothing but shadows. In theory, the body boys were supposed to remain completely anonymous, a custom designed to avoid the temptation of bribery. Body parts were valuable, though less so when the death carts were as well laden as this one appeared to be. In practice, the anonymity was a farce. Tom knew three personally, and all were more than happy to take a bribe. It was an accepted perk of the job.

"Looks like a full one," Kat muttered under her breath.

Tom could only agree. Not that either of them could actually see into the cart, of course, what with it being covered in sacking which was, inevitably, dyed black.

Once the cart had passed, normal activity resumed, with the entire street seeming to release a collectively held breath.

A Thaistess stood on the corner ahead of them, her dark green robe pulled closely about her, her hood up so that her face appeared only as a lighter shadow within shadow. For some reason it reminded Tom of the acolyte outside the temple yesterday, who had watched them so intently, just as, he felt certain, this priestess was watching them now, for all that he couldn't see her eyes.

"Have you ever had much to do with them?" He nodded towards the Thaistess.

Kat followed his gaze. "On occasion. Why?"

"Nothing." Tom didn't want to start an argument and had no idea of Kat's beliefs, but the priestess's appearance in the wake of the death cart struck him as distasteful somehow, as if the woman were working in concert with the body boys, collecting the spirits of the dead even as the cart collected their bodies.

"Do you believe in all that then?" he asked. The sect taught a complex doctrine, but at its heart was the belief that the goddess Thaiss sat at the source of the Thair, and that the river began with her own teardrops, cried upon the peaks of distant mountains at the very spot where her brother Thaimon had died. As the waters flowed down the valleys and gullies towards the lowlands, they were joined by the tears of all the people in all the world who had ever cried for a lost one, until the Thair grew into the mighty torrent which eventually flowed into Thaiburley. The city took its name from the river which meant, or so the sect's proponents claimed, that Thaiss was the goddess of the whole metropolis and all the people who dwelt within it. The doctrine taught that the citizen's spirits returned to the bosom of the goddess when they died.

"Listen, when you've been raised in the Pits like I was, it's hard to believe in any sort of gods or goddesses, at least in any kindly ones."

"So what's your connection to them then?"

She glared at him as if about to lose her temper, but then shook her head and smiled. "Do you ever stop asking questions?"

He grinned. "No."

"All right. When I first left the Tattooed Men, I managed to get into a bit of trouble. Ended up being hurt pretty badly, and for the first time there was no Shayna to turn to. Thought I was a goner, but then a Thaistess, Shella, took me in and looked after me, nursed me back to health. Think she may have had a bit of the healing power herself, because I was fighting fit again far quicker than I ought to have been. I looked out for her after that – ran a few errands and made sure no one hassled either her or the temple. In fact, she was the one who first introduced me to Ty-gen and his khy-bul sculptures."

Tom had been looking at Kat as she spoke. He now glanced back towards the corner, but the Thaistess was gone.

"Shella's all right. Never once tried to shove her beliefs down my throat, just took care of me when I needed it."

Tom grunted noncommittally.

Kat abruptly tensed.

"What?" Tom was glancing around, trying to spot whatever had disturbed her.

"Nothing," she relaxed again. "I thought I saw…"

Tom caught a flicker of movement above and behind the girl. "Kat!"

She spun around, following the direction of his gaze. A knife appeared in her hand as she moved, pulled from some concealed sheath; not one of her long blades but a smaller weapon: a throwing knife.

As she turned, her arm whipped around and cast towards the movement Tom had noted on the wall above, the thing which crept towards her with such apparent menace.

Her aim was true and the blade clattered against the wall, shearing through a spindly tentacular limb in the process. The impact was enough to dislodge the creature, which had been moving stealthily in Kat's direction. It fell to the ground alongside its severed limb. The thing looked similar to the creature they'd encountered the previous day, the one which Kat had thrown a stone at, but whereas the limbs in that instance had been hairy, this one's seemed more reptilian and snake-like. The single baleful eye remained the same, though.

"Breckin' Maker!" Kat stamped at the odd construct as it landed, but missed. The creature dodged her foot despite the missing limb, crowding against the wall to do so. Then, in a show of aggression that seemed to take even Kat by surprise, it stabbed down at her same foot with one of its own clawed appendages. Kat hopped back barely in time, turning the movement into an elegant swivel which led into a heel-first kick. This time she didn't miss, the full force of the blow pinning the thing against the wall, crushing the single eye.

Viscous fluid clung to her boot as she drew it away. She attempted to wipe it clean against the wall.

"I'm sure that thing was deliberately trying to creep up on you," Tom told her. He stepped forward to take a closer look at the ruined creature.

"Yeah, well, thanks," she said distractedly, lifting her foot to peer critically at the heel.

"I wasn't asking for thanks, I was just saying. Doesn't that seem odd to you?"

"I suppose so, but then the Maker is odd."

She stopped inspecting her foot, evidently satisfied, and looked across at him. As she did so, her eyes widened. At the same moment, he felt something land on his back, between the shoulders; not a particularly big or heavy something, and he reached an arm back to try and swat it off.

Then it stabbed him.

That first wound was to the back of his neck and was followed by three more to his back and shoulders. He felt each one go in; four shafts of agony following instantly one after the other. Nor did any of the blades withdraw.

Kat was beside him, then someone else as well, dimly sensed through the pain: the Thaistess.

"Don't try to pull it off," she seemed to say. "You might kill him."

He knew what it had to be: one of the Maker's creatures. So this was what the first one had intended for Kat, but what was the thing doing? The pain intensified and he might well have screamed.

It burned.

He could feel the clawed feet pressing into his body. The one attacking his neck and the other at the centre of his back were the worst, they seemed to be burrowing into his spine, but it was more than that. His mind burned.

He definitely screamed this time. "Get it off of me!"

"No, don't, whatever you do," that same voice said.

It felt as if the device was poisoning his thoughts. The very centre of his being was shifting, beliefs that were not his own attempted to assert themselves and he fought this invasion of everything he was with all his will. The result was searing agony.

He screamed again, and must have fallen over or collapsed, because his next awareness was of his cheek pressed against the ground, saliva drooling from his mouth. There were hands on his arms, trying to pull him upright. Then everything else was washed away as a wave of agony rose to engulf him once more.

While invasive and forceful on the surface, there was also a less obvious side to this attack. Beneath the bludgeon of force and pain, subtle alterations were being attempted, adjustments intended to curtail his free will, to channel and reshape his thoughts, prejudices and inclinations so that they conformed to a specific pattern and were remoulded to someone else's dictates rather than his own. Except that, if successful, they would become his own. But he wasn't having it. He refused to accept such an invasion of his very being.

Part of him suspected that the crippling pain was a consequence of his resistance, that, had he been less aware, the insidious influence would have slipped in and reshaped his mind almost unnoticed. But if pain was the price, so be it.

It was a peculiar experience. His whole focus had turned inward. His consciousness had withdrawn to a central core from where it could gauge the incursion in all its strivings, both subtle and overt. He had no idea why he was able to do this, how he even knew what was required to conduct such a defence, but conduct it he did. And, bit by stubborn bit, he was winning.

He remained completely oblivious to the goings on of the outside world, taking no notice of any sensory input. All that mattered was repulsing this insidious assault.

Bit by bit Tom reasserted his will; step by grudging step he purged the foreign influence from his mind. Once his eyes flickered open, once he felt able to look beyond himself again, he knew he had won.

He lay on his side, on a raised pallet in a small, plain room. His back throbbed, but it was a pain he welcomed, a sign that he had won the battle and returned to the world. With great care he reached behind to feel his back, finding fresh wounds with blood trickling from them. He sat up gingerly and then looked back at the pallet to see the Maker's creature on a sheet stained with blood. His blood.

He stared with morbid fascination at the instrument of his torment. It had segmented metallic legs but otherwise followed the same pattern as the others, with a small body dominated by a single eye. It lay on its back unmoving, with legs retracted and curled inward, and was clearly dead, if such a thing could ever have been considered alive.

He got to his feet slowly, careful not to touch the Maker's creature while trying not to stretch his back and so aggravate the wounds. Even as he did so, a woman entered the room. Her moss green cape marked her as a Thaistess, and he thought he recognised her from pain-clouded memories. Her hood was down and she looked far younger than he had ever imagined a priestess to be, with a fragile, sensitive face and long, dark-blonde hair. Kindly, that was the overall impression. Her almond eyes showed concern, but none of that stopped Tom from instinctively drawing back.

Kat followed immediately on the priestess's heels. "We heard you moving," the girl explained. Then, seeing his reaction to the Thaistess, she added, "This is Mildra. She helped you, brought you here when you collapsed, welcomed us both into her home and has been tending you since."

"How long?" he croaked.

The girl shrugged. "A couple of hours." Was that all? It felt like a lifetime.

The Thaistess moved fully into the room and tried to inspect his back. Suddenly conscious of having no shirt on, Tom turned to prevent her.

The woman looked at him. "May I?"

A little reluctantly, he complied. After all, had she meant him any harm she could presumably have done her worst while he was unconscious.

"I can help heal those." She didn't touch, apparently content with what her eyes reported. "But there could be worse. I'm going to touch your head, only for a few seconds. Will you let me?"

Tom took a deep breath and nodded. She moved her hands slowly, as if not to alarm him, and placed fingertips to his temples in much the same way as the Tattooed Men's healer had, but this time he felt no flow of warmth, in fact he felt nothing.

Then the touch withdrew and the woman stepped back. "Incredible. I would never have believed this. You defeated it!" She stared at him, her eyes full of wonder. "That must be why it clung to you for so long – normally they infect and move on, but you never fully succumbed and then overcame it somehow. The

Goddess has truly blessed you, Tom, whether you re-alise it or not."

Blessed? Tom didn't feel particularly blessed. Bruised, tired, aching and set upon, yes, thirsty even, but blessed hardly came into it.

The priestess produced a pair of finger cymbals, at-tached to her robe by a thin chord. Taking one in each hand, she brought them firmly together, to clash against each other and then slide apart. A single crys-tal-clear chime rang out, far louder than Tom had expected and evidently carrying further than he re-alised because a grey-robed acolyte entered scant seconds later, doubtless in response to the sound. A teenage girl of roughly his own age, she carried two jugs of water, one in each hand. Wisps of steam rose from the first, which had a cloth draped over half its mouth, while a small cup hung from the handle of the other.

The acolyte handed the second jug to the Thaistess, who filled the cup and handed it to Tom. Had she read his mind? He took the small metal vessel without say-ing a word and drank from it: chilled, clear water, which he finished thirstily. As he handed the cup back, he even found the grace to thank the woman.

Meanwhile the acolyte set about cleaning his wounds, washing them with the cloth and warm water. He winced at every touch but did his best to hold still.

"Heck of a mess back here," Kat commented, looking over the acolyte's shoulder.

"Where's my shirt?" he suddenly thought to ask.

"Got a bit ripped," Kat replied.

"How badly?"

"Terminally."

"We'll find you something to wear before you leave," the Thaistess assured him.

The acolyte completed her task and, after a nod from the priestess, left.

Kat stared down at the inert machine on the pallet, it's feet curled in as if to mimic a spider in death.

"What exactly is that thing?"

Tom noticed that she wasn't getting too close. Not that he could blame her.

"One of the Maker's creations," the priestess said, "although this one seems more machine than his usual half-way house. They're all over the under-City. How he's managed to create so many is a mystery. He must have been producing them for months, years even, in preparation."

"In preparation for what?" Tom asked.

"That's what we're trying to work out. As I say, they've spread throughout the City Below in recent days, and now they've begun to make their move, targeting street-nicks, latching onto them briefly and leaving something behind, taking control in some way."

Tom frowned. That wasn't how it had felt to him. "It wasn't all that 'brief' with me," was all he muttered.

"True," the Thaistess conceded. "You fought it. My best guess is that your resistance held it there, enabling you to kill it."

"What do they do, exactly?" Kat asked, still staring warily at the thing on the pallet.

"As far as we understand, they inject a seed which invades the victim's mind, crushes a person's will and finally takes over."

"No," Tom interrupted. "No, that's not quite right. It's not as straightforward as that." He paused, recalling the awful sensation and searching for the right words to express what he had endured. "It tries to change you, not take over," he said at length, realising how inadequate a description that was. "It's not like having someone force you to do something against your will, it's more as if they arrange things so that you really want to do what they're after, so that you run straight out and do it gladly. You're still you, but it's a different you, one who wants and believes in different things." The words petered to a stop and he looked up, helplessly. "I'm sorry, that's the best way I can describe it."

"No, that's excellent," Mildra assured him. "This is the first time anyone's broken the thrall, the first time we've been able to hear what the experience is actually like. You did more than that though, you managed to destroy whatever was put inside you and then killed the spider that left it there, which is astonishing."

Tom felt frustrated. "But I've no idea how!"

The Thaistess smiled kindly. "I know, but it still represents enormous progress. Before this all we've had to work with is observations, from which we assumed the process involved subjugation of will, but judging by what you're saying, it's more subtle than that: subversion rather than suppression. Tell me, do you think everyone who goes through this process is aware of what's being done to them?"

"Can't really say. I only know that I definitely was."

The woman nodded. "And you're hardly typical, so we would be unwise to use your reaction as a guide."

Tom had heard enough of this nonsense. "What do you mean 'not typical'? I'm just a street-nick, no different from any other." He hadn't intended to shout.

"Yeah, right." It was Kat rather than the priestess who responded. "Every breckin' street-nick I know can fool a demon hound into believing there's nothing there just by wishing it and then kill one of the Maker's creatures while he sleeps."

The girl blushed, presumably because of the swear word, having remembered where she was and in whose company. She offered a quick, "Excuse me, Thaistess," to the priestess.

"Kat's right, Tom," the woman said gently. "What you can do is extraordinary, and in your heart of hearts you know that better than anyone."

Tom shook his head, refusing to think of himself as being at all different from anyone else, but suddenly he couldn't meet the woman's eyes, so instead stared at the floor when mumbling, "I'm just a street-nick; that's all."

He looked up at Kat, who was biting her bottom lip in a way he remembered her doing once before when thinking about something. "Listen," she said to him, "I've been talking with Mildra and I'm not sure it's safe for you to go any further. If the Maker is targeting street-nicks with these things, perhaps you should stay here for now."

"No," he said quickly. Once he was back with the Blue Claw he could slip into the background again and simply be another member of the gang. Nobody there saw him as anything special.

Kat's smile struck Tom as a little patronising. "Keen to see that Jezmina of yours again, are you?"

Jezmina? He suddenly realised he hadn't spared her a thought all day. "No, that's not it, but I've got to get back to the Claw. It's where I belong."

The girl exchanged a look with the Thaistess and then shrugged. "All right, if that's what you want."

"You don't have to come, though." He suddenly resented Kat for talking about him behind his back. "I can make my own way from here and you can head straight for the Jeradine quarter."

"What, and pass up the opportunity to get my hands on the finest khybul sculpture I've ever seen? No chance. You're stuck with me, k– Tom." This time her smile seemed genuine and there was a familiar twinkle in her eye.

Despite himself, he smiled too.

"The offer to remain here was a genuine one," the Thaistess said. "Are you certain?"

He nodded.

"Very well." Another clash of cymbals brought the acolyte back and Mildra dispatched her to fetch some clothes. The Thaistess then examined Tom's back. "I have a little healing ability. I could help, if you will let me."

He'd come this far; though still not wholly convinced, he nodded.

Her hands were soft and gentle, with a warmth that seemed to radiate from them, gradually spreading throughout his back, touching and then engulfing each of the four wounds and sending a shiver of pleasure up his spine in the process. He closed his eyes and could easily have drifted back to sleep, it was so soothing. He was almost disappointed when he felt her palms lift away.

"Better?"

He flexed his shoulders gingerly and was surprised at how much the pain had lessened. "Yes, thank you. It now only hurts when I move."

The woman laughed, evidently surprised and perhaps even pleased that he had spoken to her in such a relaxed manner.

"Completely sealed up," Kat confirmed on giving the wounds a quick inspection.

The acolyte returned at that moment and Tom stared in horror at what she brought across to him.

"An acolyte's robe?"

"This is a temple of Thaiss, Tom, not a clothing store," Mildra said. "We don't exactly keep an extensive wardrobe here. It was this or a priestess's green, and I thought you'd prefer the grey."

Tom took the robe reluctantly and glared across at Kat, who was doing her best not to laugh.

"Don't you dare," he warned her darkly.

The Thaistess, Mildra, watched the two youths walk away, Kat with a nonchalant wave and even Tom looked back and smiled. There was a part of her that wanted to call them back, to persuade Tom to remain in the safety of the temple after all, but she didn't. Once they had disappeared around a corner she turned and walked back into the temple. As she did so, a man stepped from the shadows. "Well, that was certainly interesting."

The Thaistess nodded. "Wasn't it just? These abominations are even worse than we suspected."

"And considerably more subtle. It still intrigues me that the Maker is only going after the street-nicks."

"The gangs have their fingers in every pie worth talking about down here: import, export, retail, the black market, even passage between the Cities Below and Above. If you wanted to quietly seize control of all that goes on in the under-City, the street-nicks would not be a bad place to start."

"True."

"Do you think Tom and Kat were specifically targeted this time or just caught up in the general sweep of things?"

"No, I think on this occasion it was simply part of what we're seeing everywhere – the plan to subvert all the street-nicks. Tom's ability to resist has been a revelation."

"Could it be an indication that he's growing into himself, starting to realise his potential?"

"Possibly," the man conceded. "I just wish we'd known about him before all this began."

"How could we? Before this, his use of power had been minor; no more than that of a healer or any of the other limited practitioners scattered around the under-City."

"I realise that." He gave a wry smile, which brought unexpected warmth to his craggy, age-weary face. "Even I'm allowed to wish on occasion, aren't I?"

The woman smiled in turn and nodded in response.

"Thank you for calling me, Mildra. I was afraid we might never find this pair again after all the mischief the Maker's been causing. I regret my visit here has to be so brief, but I really must return up-City before I'm missed."

"Of course." She tried to keep the bitterness from her voice but was not entirely successful. Sharp as he was, the prime master caught it.

"What's the matter?"

She considered lying, passing it off as tiredness, but both her faith and her conscience demanded that she remain true to herself. "This just strikes me as wrong. You sitting up there in the Heights, safe, and me here in my temple, likewise, while death roams the streets and we send two innocent youths back out there, knowing what awaits them."

"I know, and I wish it could be otherwise, but Tom is the catalyst. I can't simply whisk him out of harm's way, not yet. We have to discover the full extent of what's going on here, and Tom is the only means we have of doing that."

"The only bait, you mean. And what of the girl, is she expendable? And the street-nicks who are getting killed hourly are acceptable losses, I take it."

"Don't judge me, Mildra. I do that often enough to myself. You know that if I could I would avoid every single death, but I have to look at the bigger picture."

The woman sighed. "Yes, I do understand. But why is it always the little people who seem to get hurt whenever anyone concentrates on the bigger picture?"

"This lad, Tom, is hardly one of the 'little people', Mildra, despite his diminutive size."

"I know, I know." She felt suddenly weary and the sense of guilt at letting Kat and Tom step back into the streets remained, despite the fact that she knew the reasons. "And yet, he's so innocent, so oblivious of his inheritance."

"Which is one of the things that makes him so valuable."

"But despite this value, you insist on sending him into danger."

"I have no choice. As you pointed out yourself, these things of the Maker's are more dangerous than ever suspected. There's more going on here than we know and we daren't make our move until we're certain of all our enemies. In the meantime, I know I can count on you and your sisters to keep an eye on this lad for me."

The woman nodded. "The goddess will watch over him."

"Thank you. And help will be on hand should it be needed." Dark shadows moved behind the man. Towering black forms which shone in the dull light.

The woman's eyes widened in shock and disbelief. "You've brought them here, to the goddess's temple?"

The prime master smiled. "Where else? They have to be kept out of sight for now. Can you imagine how quickly panic would spread through the streets were people to learn that the Blade have returned to the City Below?"

TWELVE

Tylus took stock of his restless troops – Richardson plus a dozen other officers of the watch, pulled away from their usual duties with no warning. A few of them had puncheons at the ready while others gripped thick, black iron chains; all of them had earplugs in place. They looked ready, despite the odd muttering of discontent.

The other units should be in place by now and there was no point in delaying things. He composed himself and gave Richardson the nod. The young officer scampered forward and attached the two devices to the wall, one either side of the door that was their designated entry point.

Now it was just a question of waiting; it shouldn't be long.

Tylus continued to feel a sense of destiny, that the gods were in some sense smiling on him and everything was going his way. Johnson had been immediately receptive to the idea of this raid, especially when the Kite Guard told him that it might have some bearing on the ongoing problems the watch were facing with the street-nicks and the inter-gang killings. In all honesty, he had no idea whether or not that was true, but he knew that raising the possibility wouldn't harm his cause. The sergeant who had first spoken to him upon his arrival at the station didn't offer so much as a word of protest when Captain Johnson strode up with Tylus by his side and asked him to assemble all available officers. The sergeant's name proved to be Able, which struck Tylus as wholly appropriate based upon what he had seen of the man to date.

Able was now around the other side of the building, with another squad of men, similar in size to Tylus's, while Richardson had taken the front with his own slightly larger group. The visiting Kite Guard had been trusted with the banshees, devices which the station's weapons master handed across with a respect that bordered on reverence.

"Freshly charged," he warned Tylus, "so be careful how you handle them."

Tylus took the oval, fist-sized devices gingerly. They were flat on one side and dome-shaped on the other, the dome being grooved to provide convenient finger holds. He had never encountered banshees before, though he was not about to admit as much and so immediately designated responsibility to Richardson. The young officer seemed to accept this as an honour, a misconception which Tylus was more than happy to encourage. One more boost to the young man's growing self-esteem.

Tylus fiddled with his own earplugs, making sure for the umpteenth time that they were firmly in place. Once deployed, these banshee devices were supposed to trigger fairly quickly.

Even with the earplugs and even though the devices were aimed into the building, there could be no missing the instant the banshees went off. A high pitched shriek filled the air. The Kite Guard and his men immediately leapt into action, rushing to the door. Six of the guards carried between them a thumper – a giant version of the puncheon. They positioned this unwieldy contraption level with the door's lock and catch and then fired. It acted as a battering ram, punching a hole in the door where the lock had been. No longer secured, the door was then easily kicked open, allowing the men of the watch to pour in.

Tylus felt confident that this raid on their headquarters would take the Blue Claw completely by surprise. It had been organised quickly and actioned immediately, leaving little opportunity for a warning to have reached the street-nicks, no matter how good their sources within the watch might be.

The sound from the banshees, which had been clearly audible outside, became deafening once they stepped into the building. And that was with earplugs. Tylus pitied anyone without them. He and his men moved forward swiftly, seeing Johnson's team off to their left, coming in through the front door.

Initially there were no nicks to be found at all, but as they moved further into the house they found their first group, including a girl – a pretty young thing – sunk to her knees with her hands clapped to her ears. Beside her an older nick lay curled up on the floor and a couple of others were slumped in the open doorway to an adjacent room. The hands-to-ears posture seemed universal, which was hardly a surprise.

Through the open doorway, Tylus caught a glimpse of total chaos. Street-nicks and furniture were strewn everywhere. He stepped into the room and made way for the watch officers, who streamed in behind him and started clamping leg irons on the incapacitated youths. There was a little blood in evidence, and surely the banshees could not be responsible for that, nor for the injuries apparent in many of the nicks – cuts, bruises, and at least one who appeared to have a broken leg. It looked as if their arrival might have interrupted a fight.

Was this further evidence of the gang violence the watch had been battling against of late? Had another gang attacked the Blue Claw here, in their very stronghold, or was it some internal dispute? As he looked around at the carnage, the banshees finally ran down, their grating screech trailing away to a whimper and then to merciful silence. With considerable relief, he removed his earplugs.

At last Tylus felt able to think clearly again, and it was time to start trying to make sense of all this. The oldest person he had seen so far was the man out in the hallway. He realised that maturity didn't necessarily equate to leadership, but why would anyone of that age stick around with a gang of street-nicks unless they had some level of authority? It seemed to Tylus as good a place to start as any. He stepped around fractured furniture, bemused guardsmen and dazed-looking youths, and made his way back into the hall.

The man had begun to sit up, if gingerly, feeling his ribs. Blood marked his face from a cut on the forehead. Altogether, he reminded Tylus of a boxer who had gone too many rounds with an opponent far better than him. Then the man looked up at the Kite Guard and Tylus felt the stirrings of recognition. Where had he seen that face before? He tried to see through the blood and the bruises, picture him unblemished and less dishevelled. Very ordinary looking and yet those eyes.

Then he had it.

"You're the senior arkademic's servant," he blurted out, hardly able to believe as much despite his own words. "What in Thaiss's name are you doing here?"

The man pointed to his ears, frowned and said, "Can't hear you."

Tylus repeated himself, upping the volume. This time the meaning seemed to get through, because the other responded, "Not servant, aide. My name's Dewar and the senior arkademic sent me down here to back you up." The man spoke over-loudly at first, presumably due to the ringing in his ears. Tylus sympathised. His own hearing was still troubled by the ghost of that screeching claxon and he could only imagine what it must be like for someone who hadn't benefitted from any protection. Dewar seemed to realise his error and moderated his tone when he continued. "I thought we might make better progress working independently, and came here following a tip-off. Captured the gang's leader and learned that the boy, Tom, hadn't returned yet, so decided to hang around." He was obviously having some difficulty speaking; quite apart from the problems he must still have been having with hearing, his top lip was split and swollen.

"You were involved in the fight here, I take it?"

"Yes. Things didn't quite go as planned and half the gang jumped me. I ended up fighting for my life and was in the process of trying to escape when you lot turned up and deafened us all."

Tylus felt an odd mix of anger, disappointment and wounded pride. The thought that the senior arkademic had sent someone else down here shook his newly acquired self-belief, leaching away the momentum of his perceived destiny. Didn't Magnus trust him to get the job done? Then he caught himself, refusing to be disheartened. He would use this to his advantage, more determined to succeed than ever, if only to prove to Magnus and everyone else that he could. There still remained the question of why this Dewar had failed to declare himself immediately on arriving in the under-City. This woolly nonsense about wanting to work independently struck him as a hastily concocted excuse rather than a sound reason.

Despite his doubts and his wounded pride, Tylus still waved away the guardsman who approached Dewar with the ubiquitous leg irons. After all, no matter what his presence implied, this was unquestionably the senior arkademic's man. Tylus had seen that much with his own eyes.

"Well, Kite Officer, and who have we here?" Captain Johnson had come across to join them. Tylus made the introductions and could see doubts similar to his own play across the captain's face.

Before he could frame any suitable response, he was interrupted by Sergeant Able. "Sir, there's something here you ought to see."

Whatever it was had clearly made the sergeant anxious and he didn't strike Tylus as the sort of man to disturb easily, so he decided to follow them as Able led the captain back into the main room. Dewar tagged along behind.

The room contained several clumps of disconsolate street-nicks, each group of four or five linked together by a chain attached to the manacles which all of them wore. There were twenty or more in total; only two girls among them, he noted. Whereas the boys tended to become street-nicks, cast-out or orphaned girls usually ended up working in washrooms or taverns in one capacity or another, or so Tylus understood.

Able went to the nearest nick and turned him around so that his back faced them, then pulled down the neck of his shirt. A long metallic limb, resembling some sort of steel serpent, appeared to be attached to the back of the kid's neck. Cutting away the shirt altogether revealed an outlandish and, to Tylus's mind, revolting semi-organic device. It had four of the long tentacular legs and a small body dominated by a single eye.

"What is that thing?"

"No idea, sir, but see this?" He revealed another boy's back. It bore four puncture wounds, fairly fresh by the look of them; one to the back of the neck, two to the shoulders and a fourth in the centre of the back, all in exactly the same positions as the hybrid mechanism was clinging to the first nick's back."

"They've all got them," Able said.

"All of them?"

"Yes, sir."

In fact, the only two free of such wounds were Dewar and the girl who had been with him in the hall-way. All the other members of the Blue Claw bore the ominous marks.

Closer examination revealed that the creature could not be removed by simply pulling or prising it off; the thing appeared to have burrowed into the street-nick's body with all four limbs.

Tylus stood and stared at it and felt a deep sense of outrage and revulsion. Neither Dewar nor the girl, Jezmina, could shed any light on the matter – both claimed never to have seen these things before – and the other street-nicks were refusing to talk at all.

A flushed Richardson hurried in to join them. "Sir, we've found this man Lyle, the Blue Claw's leader, exactly where we were told to look."

Dewar had supplied the information. The Kite Guard was still uneasy with the man's presence, but felt obliged to give him the benefit of the doubt.

"Did he have the wounds on his neck and back?" Able stepped in.

"No, sir, but…"

"Well bring him here then, lad."

"We can't, sir."

"What do you mean you can't?"

"We would, sir, but there doesn't seem much point. Someone's broken into the room he was held in and has stabbed him. He's dead, sir."

Dewar might have laughed if he weren't still half deaf from the buzzing in his ears, not to mention recovering from being beaten up by a score of youths and then hit over the head by a girl who had been intent on seducing him not long before. After all, here he was being rescued from almost certain death or an even worse fate by the bumbling fool he was supposed to be using as a smokescreen. He could just imagine what his good friend the senior arkademic would make of that.

He hadn't made up his mind what to do about Jezmina yet, although he was very interested to see that she didn't have the marks apparently left by this bizarre semi-organic device and so couldn't fall back on claiming that was the reason she had hit him. On the other hand, he understood Jezmina, perhaps better than he understood anyone else here. There was something comfortingly uncomplicated about the way she made a beeline for the main chance. Here was a beautiful young girl, sensual beyond her years, who knew full well the effect she had on men and adolescent boys alike and was fully prepared to use that influence whenever she could. Lyle led the Blue Claw, so she seduced him. Dewar seized control from Lyle so she adjusted her sights accordingly. Then, when it was clear that his influence had been broken and the gang had turned on him, so did she. Simple, straightforward and very direct self-interest; he admired her for that.

But, at the end of the day, she had hit him.

Jezmina could wait, though. It was the discovery of this abominable device that most occupied his attention. As soon as the watch sergeant revealed the thing he felt a shiver of recognition, remembering his experience in the back streets the previous night. There was no doubt in his mind that the creature he had clipped with his kairuken was related to this one. Had this been his intended fate? To have one of these grotesques straddling his back and burrowing into his neck and spine doing Thaiss knew what? He shuddered at the thought and stared at the thing with renewed distaste.

He sensed caution, even distrust, in the Kite Guard, and the watch captain didn't seem too enamoured of him either. Neither of which bothered Dewar much – popularity he had never been concerned with – but if he wanted to avoid the leg irons he was going to have to keep them convinced that his presence here was at least semi-official. He told them where to find Lyle, which was really telling them nothing at all, since they were bound to search the building thoroughly in any case, and, in the same vein, said, "This isn't all of the Blue Claw. There's still one group who haven't come back yet and possibly a few others."

"How many are we missing in total?" Johnson wanted to know.

"About a dozen, maybe a few less." Damn this split lip. It made his words sound like those of a semi-articulate simpleton. It also pulsed with dull heat, but that was nothing compared to the pain from his ribs.

Again, telling them the number of gang members still at large gave the guards little they wouldn't have discovered for themselves but it helped to build his credibility. So far, he hadn't encountered his new informant and hoped the man was not a part of the raid; seeing the person who had so recently tortured and broken him at such an obvious disadvantage might prove too great a test for such a newly-forged sense of loyalty.

He was as surprised as anyone when Richardson came back with news of Lyle's murder and wondered which of the Blue Claw was responsible for killing their own leader and why. Not that he'd miss the man, but he did fleetingly wonder whether the killing was down to whatever influence these devices were exerting or just a case of one of the gang's lieutenants taking advantage of unexpected opportunity.

Richardson joined the small group that had gathered to contemplate the disturbing device and had as much to add to the discussion as anyone; which was precious little.

"Looks like the sort of thing the dog master might cook up," the young guardsman observed.

"Not dog-like enough," Able replied. Dewar could only agree. The dog master had always focused exclusively on the canine form. It was an obsession with the man to an extent which the assassin had never felt inclined to explore.

"There is someone else across the city who dabbles in similar things." This from Johnson. "The Maker, I think he calls himself."

Really? Two warped minds playing with similar perversions? Dewar had never heard of this particular denizen of the under-City and had always thought the dog master to be unique, in both his delectations and his skills. Was this 'Maker' a recent arrival, perhaps? It was worth looking into, certainly.

The street-nicks were marched back to the station, Dewar having little choice but to return with Tylus and the guardsmen. They made a strange procession which earned stares and even a few jeers from those they passed, people who were doubtless used to seeing the unusual. Word of the Blue Claw's downfall would spread like wildfire through the streets.

Once back at the station, Dewar's injuries were inspected by the guards' medic, a portly, aging officer whose ruddy complexion suggested he might have been overly familiar with the medicinal spirit on occasion. The assassin was relieved to learn that his ribs had only suffered heavy bruising rather than any breakages, and stoically allowed them to be heavily strapped before rejoining the Kite Guard and his lackeys.

He arrived in time to witness the same medic attempting to remove the device from a decidedly reluctant street-nick, who kicked and screamed so much that it took three guardsmen to hold him face-down and bind him to the table. The lad fought as if his life depended on it, which indeed proved to be the case.

Evidently tiring of the nick's struggles, the medic held a cloth over his mouth, knocking him unconscious. The medic then made his first incision immediately below the point where the lowest of the device's legs connected with the boy's back.

"Interesting," he muttered as he continued, "it seems to have burrowed directly into the spine."

Whatever this medic's skills, they evidently did not extend to surgery. Dewar felt certain that he could have made a better job of this operation himself. Despite the efforts of the guardsman acting as nurse to swab it away, blood was soon everywhere. The nick died when the medic attempted to remove the spike from his spine, crying out immediately beforehand even through the anaesthetic.

All the operation left them with was a lot of blood and one dead street-nick, and they still had no clear idea what the devices were intended to do. Mind-control seemed to be everybody's favourite theory, and certainly there had been something unnatural about the way the street-nicks attacked him, Dewar recalled, particularly the silence. Yet he was far from convinced. To him the idea made little sense. How could anyone direct so many individuals effectively, even if such a level of control were possible? One or two at a time, maybe, but there were a score or so of the Blue Claw and probably dozens more infected street-nicks spread throughout the other gangs if suspicions were correct. It would be impossible to oversee so many individuals unless victims became programmed automata, which clearly these Blue Claw were not. He suspected they still had much to discover on the subject.

He knew there would have to be an interview, and the task of conducting it fell to Tylus and his young side-kick, Richardson.

"What puzzles me," the Kite Guard began, "is why Senior Arkademic Magnus would send his man servant to investigate anything, let alone a murder and its runaway suspect."

Dewar realised that in situations such as this, honesty was the best policy; up to a point. "I used to live in the City Below, so know the people and places down here, plus, I wasn't always a man servant and possess skills other than butlering. After you left the senior arkademic's home he got to thinking that perhaps I might have more success finding the lad through my old contacts than you would through official channels, so asked me to help. Knowing how close the senior arkademic had been to the victim, I naturally agreed to help."

"But that still doesn't explain why you didn't declare yourself once you were here."

"That was my decision. It seemed to me that if I was seen to be associating with the razzers, some of my sources might be less than forthcoming with what they knew. Better to work in total isolation."

"So, explain to us again how you came to be at the Blue Claw's headquarters."

The interview continued in that manner. Truth, half-truths and omission worked so much better than outright lies. By the end of it, the assassin felt confident that the Kite Guard was unlikely to find fault with any of his answers. He judged that he had laid many of the man's suspicions to rest, though perhaps not quite all of them. He was beginning to conclude that he had underestimated this Kite Guard. After all, this presumed buffoon had discovered enough to turn up at the Blue Claw's headquarters not long after he had done so himself, and managed to persuade an overstretched city watch to accompany him mob-handed. That was no mean feat and was certainly a great deal more than he would have expected from the callow youth who presented himself at Magnus's home. Perhaps the environment of the City Below suited him.

Jezmina continued to be a problem. Since she hadn't been infected by the mechanical creatures, it was decided that she should not be put in with the other Blue Claw, but with so many nicks being detained the station's cells were full to bursting, so for the moment the girl was manacled to the desk which the Kite Guard shared with Richardson.

As the three of them emerged from the interview room, two of the younger watch officers were chatting to the girl, broad grins on their faces, while Jezmina sat on a chair, hugging one knee – exposing virtually all of one shapely leg in the process, the one without the leg iron – her head cocked slightly to one side, as she smiled and batted her eyelids at the pair of them.

Able looked up at the same moment and spotted what was going on. "Hey, you two! Have you finished your reports yet?"

The two officers scuttled back to work.

Able frowned at Tylus as they passed in front of his desk and muttered, "We're going to have to do something about that young minx sooner rather than later or I'll never get any work out of this lot."

Richardson paused at the sergeant's desk and said a little hesitantly, almost as if he were afraid of speaking to Able, "My sister…"

"Done!" the sergeant said instantly. "Excellent suggestion, Richardson. Teaming you up with Kite Officer Tylus here has been the making of you. Take the girl straight round to your sister's now."

"But I haven't even told you what my sis–"

"No buts, officer. You're acting for the good of the department, and providing a poor unfortunate girl with a new start in life. Everyone's a winner I'd say, wouldn't you?"

Richardson looked anything but convinced. "I really think I should ask my sister first, sir."

"Of course you should," Able agreed. "Go round immediately and do so. In fact, take the girl with you to save time. And, Richardson…"

"Yes, sir?"

"Make sure your sister says yes."

"What does your sister do, anyway?" Tylus asked as they left the sergeant and threaded their way through a busy squad room towards where Jezmina sat.

"She's a seamstress; runs her own business making up dresses for a couple of the upmarket boutiques in the Shopping Rows. She's got a few girls working for her at the moment and I thought maybe she could use one more."

Dewar tried to picture Jezmina sitting demurely with a bolt of cloth in front of her and needle and thread in hand but completely failed to do so.

"So she's used to handling girls then, your sister?"

"Oh yes, raised two of her own, plus she's the oldest and brought all five of us up after my ma died, so she knows how to keep order. A bit of a dragon, to be honest; though don't tell her I said so."

Dewar smiled to himself. It sounded as if Richardson's sister might be exactly what Jezmina needed. The girl had all but ignored the assassin since they arrived at the station, presumably dismissing him as a potential target for her charms after trying to split his skull open. Tylus and Richardson, however, remained viable prospects, and the two of them were getting the full treatment: coy smiles, wistful gazes, flirtatious giggles, pouts, hair flicks and body stretches with arms above her head, chin thrusting up and pubescent chest forward. Bearing in mind she was chained to a desk, it was remarkable how inventive the girl still managed to be. Dewar shook his head, enjoying the opportunity to watch an artist at work.

Tylus seemed entirely immune to the girl's ploys, perhaps he had a girlfriend back in the Heights or perhaps he was simply too absorbed in being a Kite Guard to entertain such distractions. Richardson, on the other hand, was notably flustered in Jezmina's presence, almost tripping over himself to fetch her some water when she declared she was thirsty and visibly blushing when she rewarded him with a dazzling smile. Despite the girl's circumstances and her age, people, or rather men, continued to react to her as if she were anything but a young girl.

Dewar knew first-hand how powerful her allure could be, and he knew full well how the City Below could affect children – forcing them to become adult before their time in order to survive – but watching this girl, even while admiring her audacity and application, a part of him was saddened by the spectacle, he realised.

He was more than a little relieved when Richardson led her away, leg iron still in place despite her pleas. Dewar only hoped for the young guard's sake that his sister lived nearby. The less time Jezmina had to work on the lad's hormones, the better.

As she left, she finally looked directly at him; the first time she had done so since hitting him over the head. Her mouth formed a fragile, uncertain smile, which he thought might have been the first wholly genuine expression he had seen from her, and she said, "'Bye. It was fun."

Was it? Not from where he'd been standing.

On the face of it, everything was proceeding according to plan, yet Magnus couldn't shake the feeling that this appearance was deceptive. As threatened, the prime master had sent his man round first thing that morning. Magnus had responded to the doorbell's chime to find a tall, slender and impeccably presented individual standing there; a man whose manners promised to be as faultless as his appearance. Yet there was something in the fellow's attitude which made it clear that this was all a little beneath him and that taking care of a mere senior arkademic was his idea of slumming it. Despite this, Magnus welcomed him with as much grace as their respective positions required, and so ushered this undoubted spy into his home.

He left for the assembly hall a little earlier than usual, no longer entirely comfortable in his own home, feeling that his personal space had been invaded.

The morning proved a busy one. Magnus knew his remaining time in the assembly was short and wanted to be sure of his power base before moving on. Too many people had a tendency to forget how important the assembly was once they'd been elevated to the prestigious rank of master. Of course the council of masters was where the ultimate power rested, but the chief instrument of their authority was the assembly, and the degree of responsibility and decision making that devolved down to the lower body was considerable in its own right. Magnus had established himself as one of the major players in the city's secondary tier of power, and he had no intention of letting go of the reins here once he was promoted to the council.

So the morning had been spent cementing alliances and ensuring that things would continue to run smoothly in his absence. Once he had hoped that Thomas might be the man to deputise for him following his ascension, but that had been long ago and subsequently their paths had diverged. It still stung that Thomas should choose to stand with that harridan Syrena, the assembly's self-appointed moral conscience, and oppose him. After all he had done for the younger man, even nominating him for the assembly in the first place. No point in dwelling on that though, it was all wind past the walls now.

In theory, the assembly broke for lunch at the same time every day. In practice, the break was when much of the real work was done: the bargaining, the deals, the courting of the uncommitted. As things stood, Syrena and her allies lacked the credibility or support to seriously challenge his scheduled ascension, particularly without Thomas. He fully intended to ensure things stayed that way, so was wooing those neutrals who, over recent weeks, had displayed signs of sympathising with the harridan's position.

Somehow, Syrena had caught wind of an incident in his past – the proverbial skeleton in the closet. Quite how she had stumbled across the information was something he would dearly love to know. Not that it was important, since the accusations of his corruption lacked any firm proof. Thomas was the only person who might have leant them some validity – a conversation he had been a witness to some years ago suddenly taking on new significance – but, of course, Thomas was no longer available to corroborate anything.

Even so, this was a whiff of scandal that Magnus could well do without at present.

So he courted, befriended and offered support where appropriate, ensuring that Syrena and her allies remained insignificant voices crying in the wilderness.

It was this familiar dance of political manoeuvring that Magnus was fully absorbed by when he became aware of a disturbance, a rumbling of murmurs and exclamations that swirled around him. He looked up, a little annoyed at being interrupted but wondering what could cause such a commotion here, in the common room of the assembly. What he saw provided more than adequate explanation.

Moving steadily towards him, dispensing smiles and greetings as he passed, was the prime master of Thaiburley, flanked by four of the council guard. Magnus stopped speaking, forgot what he had been saying and so allowed the delicate web of silken words he had been so carefully spinning to disintegrate.

This was unprecedented. Never in living memory had council guards set foot in the assembly's commons. Despite the vastness of the room, Magnus felt hemmed in, as if the walls were closing inexorably towards him. He looked around quickly, seeking a means of escape, but knew that if he ran now, in front of so many of his contemporaries, all would be lost beyond any hope of redemption and he was not yet ready to throw everything away so wantonly. He waited, rising to his feet as the prime master's party arrived, with smile and greeting at the ready.

"Prime master, again you have managed to surprise me."

"Magnus, yes, I get to visit the assembly too infrequently these days – the pressure of time and responsibility, I'm afraid."

This sounded promising; no immediate sign of his being arrested yet at any rate.

The prime master took a seat, the four white-cloaked guards arraying themselves behind him. Once Magnus had also sat down again, he continued. "Look, apologies for the unorthodox entrance, but there have been developments in the Thomas investigation."

Magnus's heart skipped a beat. Surely the prime master was not about to discuss such sensitive issues here, where a hundred pairs of ears were straining to catch every nuance? The prime master could not possibly have reached his present eminence were he that naïve.

"Developments regarding you, actually."

Magnus tensed despite his best efforts. Was this it: arrest after all?

"I don't mean to alarm you, but a disturbing possibility has emerged." If this was intended not to alarm Magnus, it was doing a very poor job. "It seems that Thomas may not have been the intended victim of the murder."

Magnus blinked, wondering if he had heard correctly. "Pardon?"

"We now have reason to believe that you may have been the actual target, that the assassin killed the wrong man."

Magnus fought to control a very strong desire to laugh. "What?" was all he could manage.

"Think about it," the prime master continued, "a street-nick is assigned to kill you and is sent to a place where he expects to find you. On his arrival, he sees a man dressed in senior cleric's blue exactly where and when he was told you would be."

"Yes, but, I mean, who…?"

"Not for you to worry about, my friend; leave the answering of questions to the experts, who are working on them even as we speak. Our prime concern is for your safety. That's why the guards are here. Until this situation is resolved, I'm assigning two of the council's own guard to protect you. They'll be your constant companions until the monsters responsible for this appalling act are brought to justice, as they inevitably shall be." These last words boomed out sonorously, as if the prime master were delivering a stirring speech.

A ripple of spontaneous applause broke out among the onlookers, which quickly gathered pace until all those present were clapping enthusiastically. Of course the prime master wasn't naïve, Magnus realised; he was deliberately playing to an audience.

"I don't know what to say, prime–"

The man held up a hand, forestalling further comment. "No need to thank me, Magnus. It's just the council's way of letting you know that you have friends and you don't have to face this ordeal alone."

The prime master then excused himself and left, breezing out of the common room as he had breezed in. With him, he took two of the tall and solemn guards. Conspicuously, the other two remained.

In the wake of his departure, excited conversation bubbled throughout the room. Magnus sat and brooded, letting all the hubbub wash over him. How had this happened? Ostensibly, everything was being done for his benefit – the man servant, the guards – but in the process, he was being stifled bit by bit, his freedom of movement restricted. And, as yet, he could not think of a single thing to do about it.

The session bell called them back for the afternoon's proceedings, and Magnus filed out with his fellows towards the assembly hall, flanked by his newly-acquired white-cloaked shadows, who he hoped would wait at the doors. As he was about to enter the hall, a runner came up and handed him a slip of paper. He read the message as he walked but, on seeing its content, stumbled to a halt.

Magnus read the note again with growing disbelief. He clenched his fist in frustration, scrunching the sheet of paper up in the process.

"Bad news, Magnus?" asked a concerned voice.

He looked up to discover that his reaction had been witnessed by a fellow senior arkademic, one who wore her robe with unfailing elegance. As ever, her pure silver hair was pulled back severely and tied in a bun. Rumour had it that she maintained her faultless complexion courtesy of the judicious application of the arts, but the truth was that she had never looked any different. There were no specific moments when people could point to a sudden transformation, old to younger-looking; the wretched woman simply never seemed to age, so the rumours remained just that. Her grey-blue eyes now studied him closely, looking for any crack or weakness.

He smiled, with as little sincerity as she had expressed in her words. "Nothing of any importance, Syrena, though thank you for your concern."

The woman nodded and walked on.

Magnus smoothed out the paper and read the message for a third time, though he couldn't have explained why, since he knew perfectly well what it said. The message had originated from a Captain Johnson, a watch station commander in the City Below. It asked for confirmation that a man by the name of Dewar worked for him and requested a description of the individual if so.

What in the name of Thaiss was going on down there?

THIRTEEN

Tylus was relieved to see the girl, Jezmina, depart. He noted the affect she had on some of the men but couldn't understand it. To him she was just a child making a spectacle of herself and he found the sight both irritating and tiresome. The men who were taken in by her clumsy flaunting he could only pity. Richardson seemed far more charitably disposed to the girl, treating her as if she were some precious daughter, which made him the ideal person to escort her away. Once he did so, everyone was able to concentrate more effectively.

Looking back, once things calmed down a little and the thrill of new discovery palled, Tylus found he had mixed feelings about the raid. It had been a qualified success at best. Ironically, where it proved most worthwhile was in providing progress for the watch with regard to their ongoing situation with the street-nicks; the very carrot he had used to persuade Johnson to authorise the raid in the first place without any real expectation of success in that direction. It now seemed certain that these strange hybrid mechanisms were affecting the youths' behaviour to some extent and so were indeed connected to the problem. A happy circumstance which did his reputation no harm whatsoever.

Unfortunately, there was still no sign of the boy Tom, and general consensus seemed to be that if the lad had returned to the under-City early the previous morning as presumed, he should have found his way home by now. As he clearly hadn't, it was felt that he had probably fallen victim to one of the many dangers that lurked in the streets. This was all well and good, but it didn't help Tylus, who could hardly return to the senior arkademic with such vague and unsubstantiated conjecture. If the lad had perished he needed to establish exactly where and how. He was going to have to piece together the sequence of events that led up to whatever had become of the boy; only then could he stand in front of Magnus and report with confidence. That meant widening the area of search, with the most immediate priority being to establish exactly where Tom had returned to in the City Below. To discover this, he would have to check each and every stairwell until he chanced upon the right one. Which entailed dealing with the street-nicks. The problem being, of course, that the street-nicks were not fully themselves at present, so nothing he learnt from them could be relied upon.

All of which left Tylus with an awkward dilemma, one which was only likely to be resolved once he understood exactly what these devices were doing to the nicks and determined whether or not their effects could be countered. The latest developments had been reported through official channels and the watch was waiting for direction from up-City but, according to both Johnson and Able, instructions could be a while in coming.

"Nothing new in that," Able assured him. "We're well used to coping for ourselves down here. It's something you have to pick up quick in the watch if you want to survive."

From all that Tylus had heard, there was one place they could turn to for information while they waited for the wheels of command to turn: the dog master. If he dealt in similar mechanical-organic hybrids to these devices, as had been suggested, he might just be able to shed some light on the matter. Nobody had any better ideas, so Tylus set off to find this shadowy figure. Richardson and Dewar accompanied him, though neither seemed too thrilled at the prospect.

"You hear dark things about the dog master," Richardson muttered.

"The things you don't hear are even worse," Dewar assured him.

Interestingly, it was Dewar who led the way. Richardson admitted to having a vague idea of the areas the dog master haunted, but only Dewar seemed confident of the exact location, which added some credence to the man's claim of having lived down here in the past.

They took with them the deactivated device, which had been severed from the unfortunate street-nick's corpse. The mechanism had shown no sign of animation since being removed. Tylus, who carried it, was surprised at how light the thing was, and how small. Once they were cut away from the nick, the spindly legs had retracted, curling up on themselves to leave an irregular ball which fitted comfortably in the palm of his hand. This also had the effect of making the device seem even more organic, since it had curled up in much the same manner as a spider or other small creature might in death or when under threat.

Tylus held the thing in a cloth bag and was more than a little nervous about carrying it at all. He was doing so only by default. Richardson had made it clear that he was not about to touch the thing and Tylus had not even bothered offering the task to Dewar. For some reason, he was determined not to look weak in that man's eyes.

Dewar led them through a prosperous area close to the guard station. They walked on cobbles down Wood Street, where shop windows were filled with chairs and tables and cabinets and dressers, carved out of various woods in varied style, from utilitarian simplicity to extravagantly sculpted ornateness, though the former predominated. Many of these would have been produced by local craftsmen from wood brought in via the river, though some were undoubtedly imported already made.

Iron lamp posts stood silent sentry at intervals along the street's course, testament to the days before the war when electricity had been more widely available.

They headed down a side turning, past a tavern whose freshly painted sign declared it to be the Boot and Shoe Inn. Slatted iron-frame benches lined the tavern's wall, in front of which half a dozen ale barrels had been stood on end, each with a disc of wood nailed to its top to form a table. At one such, two bewhiskered men were sitting, their flagons of ale on the table before them. The pair glanced at the trio and wished them a good day as they strode past, though whether this was because of his and Richardson's uniforms or they were simply predisposed to politeness, Tylus would not have cared to guess.

The turning led into another broad avenue, again with its full complement of redundant street lamps. The houses here were two-storey and looked well maintained, but as they crossed this street and took another narrow turning, that soon changed. The buildings became noticeably more dilapidated while remaining substantial in size – faded reminders of better days.

In minutes they had moved from streets where people were plentiful to ones where they were almost entirely absent, though dogs remained numerous. Perhaps they always were down here and Tylus was simply more aware of them given who they were going to see. Most looked natural, which was not what Tylus would have expected from what he'd heard, but a particularly large and mangy-looking specimen, which padded away in front of them, looked to have a stilted, awkward gait.

One turning led to another and the state of the buildings in no way improved.

"He knows we're here," Dewar said quietly.

"How can you be sure?"

"Look behind us."

Tylus did so. Two hybrid hounds stood there, differing in size and underlying breed but unified by their shared patchwork of fur and metal. The larger of the two, which stood as high as the Kite Guard's thigh, boasted a pair of brown canine eyes; the smaller dog didn't. In their place it had two bulbous grills, unblinking bulges which looked to be built out of wire mesh.

The larger dog's jaw and, presumably, teeth were made from metal, while the smaller one's head looked completely natural apart from the meshed, insect-like eyes. Both had necks constructed of overlapping steel plates. Tylus was fascinated by the way these plates slid smoothly over each other as the dogs moved, a fact which became apparent as the larger hound padded forward, lowering its head on drawing nearer.

Dewar stepped towards the creature. "Dog master, we have business with you. And we bring you a gift."

He gestured towards Tylus, who reached gingerly into the cloth bag and pulled out the curled-up spiderish mechanism. He hated handling the thing, afraid that it was only playing dead and would spring to life at any moment, to dig its invasive claws into his body. Yet it remained inert as he held it out on his flat palm towards the hound, which sniffed at it suspiciously, as any wholly natural dog might.

The false-dog cocked its head, voicing an all-too convincing growl, which prompted him to lift his hand away slowly. It then trotted forward again, passing between them, until it stood in the direction they had been walking. A few paces ahead, it stopped, turned back to look at them and voiced a single, slightly tinny bark.

"I presume we're supposed to follow," Tylus said quietly.

"I would imagine so," Dewar replied.

As they set off after the lead dog, another hybrid hound arrived to join the smaller one behind them, with a fourth appearing almost immediately, this one the largest yet. Tylus tried to regard them as an honour guard. That way, it didn't feel quite so much as if he and his companions had just been relegated to the status of prisoners.

Their canine guide led them to a flight of old iron steps, black paint peeling from the handrail which was surrendering to rust. The lead dog didn't hesitate but trotted straight up the stairs. Slightly to Tylus's bemusement, the smallest of their four-strong escort disdained the steps altogether and instead scuttled straight up the wall, its limbs splayed out to either side like some disjointed crab. The lead dog pushed against the door at the top of the stairs, the bottom half of which instantly swung open, closing again once the dog had trotted through. Following at its heels, Dewar turned the appropriate handle and the door opened as one unit. When Tylus went to step in behind the arkademic's man, the wall-climbing dog skittered through the doorway above his shoulder, its back almost brushing his hair, causing him to cringe despite his best efforts not to.

He glared after the thing but soon forgot it as he stared at what waited on the other side of the door. He seemed to have stepped into a jungle, though one built by human hands rather than the dictates of nature. An undergrowth of clutter rose to his left: boxes, steel plates, coils of wire thread, circuit boards, pins, iron rods, small wheels, parts of goodness knew what machinery, all heaped together with no obvious rhyme or reason. Thick, bough-like pipes paralleled the floor and vines of steel cable looped from the ceiling in every direction, forcing Tylus to duck as he followed Dewar deeper into the room, while the whole place was oppressively hot.

"How creepy is this?" Richardson said from behind him.

Tylus grunted a noncommittal response. Bearing in mind the nature of the dog master's creations, he was just relieved that, as yet, there was no evidence of a pile of discarded organic parts to match the mechanical one by the door, particularly given the temperature in here. Then he saw the man himself, who stood before them with the lead dog at his side.

The dog master looked like some feral creature, as wild as any of the under-City's numerous unclaimed hounds. Not a tall man, yet his presence, outlandish appearance and sheer energy seemed to raise his stature beyond mere physical height. For clothes he wore a patchwork of what could only be dog pelts, which appeared to have been layered and stitched together in some mad artist's frenzy. Strips of tattered fur trailed from the arms like fronds and colour changes occurred apparently at random, with no thought to matching or blending: chocolate brown one minute, brindled grey the next, with a strip of creamy white here and a panel of sandy gold there. Tylus just hoped the skins had been properly cured.

The man's face matched his attire; unshaven, but not in the sense of possessing a beard, rather in the sense of someone who had simply forgotten to use a razor for several days, leading to a rash of peppercorn stubble in haphazard white and grey. The hair was unkempt, uncut in a fair while and whiter than the stubble. It fell in draggle-like strands over ears and neck and shoulders, hair which showed slight kinks and waves as it tumbled but would probably have been straight were it worn shorter.

Yet it was the eyes which dominated. Set above a prominent hooked nose, they burned like hot coals, with an energy that Tylus already thought of as manic even before this outlandish apparition spoke.

"What an interesting party it is that comes to visit me. An officer of the watch, a Kite Guard descended from the distant Heights and, last but not least, my old friend Dewar. How privileged I am."

Friend? Dewar had made no mention of actually knowing the man.

"Hello, dog master," Dewar said levelly and perhaps a little cagily. Tylus caught the hint of reservation and wondered exactly what the history was between these two. Should he be concerned about it? Had it been a mistake to let Dewar accompany them? A little late to worry about such things now.

"It must be, oh, I don't know, a long, long time since you were last here, Dewar; and how did you say good-bye on that occasion? By kicking one of my poor pets, as I recall."

"No offence or insult was intended to either you or your pet, dog master, but I was in something of a hurry and it would insist on trying to hump my leg."

"But it's a dog, and it liked you. What would you expect it to do?"

"Leave my leg in peace. All the other dogs down here seem to manage to."

"No matter, that's all behind us now, long forgotten." The dog master waved a hand with a casualness which didn't fool Tylus and he doubted whether it convinced Dewar either. "Now, I understand you have a gift for me?"

Tylus reached into the bag again. He had hoped that, having done this once already, grasping the device might be a little easier the second time. It wasn't. But he still held out the curled-up construct with a steady hand.

The dog master peered at it. "Hmm, vile things aren't they?" He then snatched the thing from the Kite Guard and casually tossed it up in the air and caught it again, as he might a ball.

"They're the Maker's," he supplied. "My pets have brought me one or two of late, but another one's always welcome."

"You know this Maker?" Dewar asked.

"By his deeds, certainly. As an individual? No. Nor would I wish to. I mean, look at this," he held the construct out to Dewar. "It's an abomination. The man needs locking up, which is what your two friends here should be doing rather than pestering an old man like me." He indicated Tylus and Richardson.

"We're working on it," Richardson growled, as if insulted by the implication that they weren't, although Tylus suspected the watch had suffered far worse insults.

"We were hoping you might help us discover what these devices are intended to do," Tylus said.

Dewar glared at him, as if he had spoken out of turn in some way, though he failed to see why.

"Help, you say? Why would I wish to do that?"

"Perhaps we could help each other," Dewar said quickly.

"Go on."

"You mention that your pets have bought some of these things back here, so you're aware that this Maker is encroaching on your territory."

"His horrors are everywhere," the dog master confirmed. "Mass-produced shoddy little tin cans with legs. They're crawling around all over the place, and for there to be so many he must be making them from a template and rolling them off a production line."

"Is that possible?"

"Anything's possible if you're willing to sacrifice quality. I am not. Look at Sirius here." He patted the hound beside him. "Pure craftsmanship and one of a kind. Whereas this thing," he tossed and caught the curled-up construct again, "is nothing more than inferior quality, assembly-cloned junk."

Dewar nodded his sympathy. "Yet the Maker's creatures trespass, they invade your domain."

"True, all too true. You are suggesting, I take it, that it would be in my best interests to assist you in your efforts since they are aimed at stopping the Maker and his invasive creations."

"Precisely."

The little man's head bobbed from side to side, as if he were inwardly debating the idea. "Your argument does have a certain merit."

"I'm glad you think so."

The dog master paced in front of them, as if considering the possibility. "So what exactly would you want of me?"

"Your expertise, your insight, your peerless knowledge," Dewar flattered, shamelessly. "Specifically, we need to find out exactly what these devices of the Maker's do and how they do it. Once we know that much, we can begin to work out a way of stopping them."

"And so you come to me." Abruptly, the dog master started to laugh; an edgy, hysterical sound. Tylus and Richardson exchanged anxious glances. "You must forgive me," he said as the laughter subsided, "but this is all just so wonderfully rich, bizarre even. As if the guard actually taking their responsibilities seriously is not astonishing enough, we now have you, Dewar, of all people, standing by their side. Despite what people may say, surely it is the world that has gone mad and not I."

Dewar's smile in response was a tight thing lacking any hint of amusement. "That's as may be, but you remain the one person best qualified to unravel the secrets of these devices. Will you help us and in doing so help yourself?"

"Oh, I'll help you alright; particularly since I already know the answers, so it won't require any real effort on my part. But there is a condition; something you must agree to do before I share my secrets with you."

"Namely?"

"When you go after this Maker, as I'm sure you will, you must take one of my pets with you." He patted the false-dog beside him. "I may not be able to accompany you in person, to witness his downfall with my own eyes, but at least I'll be able to see it by proxy."

All of which depended on their ability to find and defeat this Maker in the first place, of course. Tylus only wished he shared the dog master's apparent confidence on that score. Dewar looked enquiringly across at him. The Kite Guard could see no obvious objection to the man's demands, so nodded his agreement.

"Very well," Dewar replied, turning back to the dog master.

"Excellent!" The small man clapped his hands together and rubbed them with apparent glee. "Now, you want to know what these devices do. Tell me first what you think they do."

"Control people in some way…"

The dog master shook his head, "No, no, nothing like that; they don't control people, they infect them!" He spread his arms and hooked his fingers, looming forward like some villain from a pantomime intent on intimidating his audience.

"With what?" Dewar responded calmly.

"I'll show you!" The dog master's smile reminded Tylus of an excited child's, desperate to share a secret. He crooked a finger, summoning them to follow, then turned and walked across to a worksurface.

As he emerged from beneath a cluster of hanging cables and looped tubing, Tylus was amazed to discover that above this work station sat an array of screens fixed to the wall, three rows of them, the bottom two at least a dozen across, the top only a few less.

"My eyes," the dog master explained, gesturing towards the ranks of screens. Perhaps he noted Tylus's reaction, or perhaps he was merely showing off. "Everything my pets see, I see."

Each screen showed a different view of the under-City, each depicted in black and white but all with crystal clarity. With a start, Tylus realised that one of the images was of them, as seen from behind and from a low elevation. He looked over his shoulder to find the hound Sirius, which had led them here, staring back at him.

"Now, where is it?" The dog master was rummaging among a clutter of objects on one corner of the desk. "Ah yes." He picked something up, his back masking from the Kite Guard exactly what, and moved across to a bulky implement standing on another section; a microscope. He placed whatever he had found on the viewing stand, peered into the lens and gently rotated a large wheel, adjusting the focus. "There." He gestured for them to come forward.

Dewar looked first, then grunted and stood back to make way for Tylus. Closing one eye, the Kite Guard peered down, to see a transparent, segmented worm. As he watched, the thing wriggled, and a part of another, similar thing moved briefly in and out of view across the top left-hand corner. Tylus had encountered microscopes during training but had never felt entirely comfortable with these revealing glimpses into the micro-world. He stood up again quickly, allowing Richardson to step forward.

"What is it?" he asked the dog master bluntly.

"What indeed. It's a worm; an augmented, gene-spliced, tiny, tiny worm." Now the man's finger and thumb closed together before one squinting eye in dramatic illustration, leaving just the hint of a gap. "It's a cunningly designed and highly specific human parasite." He said the last as if revealing the secrets of the universe.

The dog master was quite mad, Tylus realised. Was he really the best they could look for as an ally?

The strange little man now came towards him, leering. "This unseen saboteur is carried dormant within these pathetic little constructs. When the spidery legs latch onto a victim, the two at the spine and neck each inject one of these tiny worms into the spinal column – two in case one should fail. The worms then make their way into the brain. Once there, the successful one targets specific areas, changing, changing, always changing, so that the infected person sees the world differently, thinks in new ways and wants new things.

He mistrusts his friends and schemes against them, wants them all to be infected just as he is. That's what drives him you see, that's what now shapes his desires. The parasite doesn't destroy a person, doesn't take them over, it simply moulds them into an altered form, into its vassal.

"While all this is happening, the spidery little device moves on to infect another victim and then another, with each victim joining a growing army of people colluding with the devices to produce even more victims.

"Very clever, these parasites, and very dangerous. They seem to be so specialised that the brain is only susceptible at a specific stage in its development, leaving them with a very narrow age range to target."

"Teens," Dewar said.

"Street-nicks," Tylus added. Something abruptly clicked into place. "And anyone who's outside that age range, who isn't vulnerable and gets in their way, the infected individuals will try to kill."

"Possibly," the dog master conceded dismissively. "As a defence mechanism, if someone threatens to prevent them following their new purpose; that would make sense."

Dewar grunted.

Doubtless he was realising that this was probably why the Blue Claw had attacked him en-masse for no apparent reason. Tylus's own thoughts were elsewhere. He was remembering his first encounter with Sergeant Able, and the guardsman who had rushed in to report two new street-nick corpses: "Older boys, lieutenants," the officer had described them as. Here at last was the explanation for the spate of street-nick deaths. He felt certain that, if anyone went to the trouble of checking, those killed would prove to be the older and younger boys, mainly the older ones, since they were most likely to be in authority.

"Yes, it's a very clever, very subtle little worm," the dog master said, almost gleefully.

"But I thought you said the devices were crude and lacked any real craft," Tylus blurted out, a little maliciously, because he thought he had caught the dog master out. The comment earned him another furious glare from Dewar. Not that their host seemed to take offence.

"Ah," said the little man, raising a finger dramatically, "and therein lies the true puzzle. How can someone inept enough to produce crude and offensive little constructs like that spidery device also manufacture such an insidious and brilliantly-crafted weapon as these parasites? The two simply don't go together, and yet clearly they do.

"If you ask me my friends, which of course no one will, that is the mystery you should really be trying to solve."

FOURTEEN

The closer they got to home, the more Tom began to fret about the sort of reception he could expect. What would Lyle say when he returned empty handed, what would he do to him? Tom had been so close to his goal, with the Upper Heights themselves only a few Rows away. Frustrating, but it was unlikely to cut any ice with Lyle. All he cared about was results, and "nearly" was never going to be near enough for the Blue Claw's leader. Then there was the question of Jezmina's reaction. Would he be a hero in her eyes for daring to take on such a reckless task in the first place, or a failure for coming back with nothing to show after doing so?

Tom felt that his luck, which had been so in evidence during the long climb through the Rows, had deserted him in the Residences the moment those two arka-demics stepped into view. Since then, things just seemed to have gone from bad to worse.

On top of all his other concerns, he wasn't sure what to do about Kat. In truth, he had begun to recognise the streets they now walked through some while ago, but hadn't said anything. To their left, just a short distance away, lay the edge of the Runs, and if they continued walking in their current direction they would soon stumble upon the market square, which was effectively the beginning of Blue Claw territory.

But he didn't want Kat to leave, not yet. He couldn't exactly explain why, even to himself, except that he liked her and trusted her. In the past couple of days he had enjoyed a closer sense of companionship with this renegade street-nick than he ever had with anyone else, even the other members of the Claw. And, despite all the troubles they'd been through and all the unrest that currently ran through the streets, he felt safe with her, knew that she could be relied on in a scrape.

He realised at some point she would leave him and he was prepared for that. Just not yet.

"You all right?" she asked, interrupting his thoughts.

"Hmm?"

"You looked deep in thought."

He grinned. "With all that's going on, can you blame me?"

"S'pose not." She looked around. "We can't be too far away now."

"No," he said quickly, suppressing a pang of guilt, "we can't be."

Despite him wanting Kat to stay around for as long as possible, he was also, at the same time, a little nervous about having her meet Jezmina. Quite what the sensitive and naïve Blue Claw girl and the maverick, worldly-wise street-nick would make of each other didn't bear thinking about. He suspected that neither would be impressed and that each would think a little less of him for associating with the other.

The nearer they came to the market, the more these worries grew. In fact, they took up so much of his thoughts that he completely overlooked the obvious until he and Kat arrived at the corner of a street he knew well: Thorp Street. Halfway along, on the left, was Thorp's Tap House, a dingy, grotty watering-hole, reputedly the oldest tavern in the City Below. Throughout much of its long history, the rooms above the tavern had acted as headquarters for the Sand Dragons, one of the gangs whose territory jostled uneasily alongside that of the Blue Claw.

He stopped dead in his tracks. Never, in all the many times he had walked past this particular corner, had he seen it free of street-nicks. It was one of the Dragons' permanent posts, yet today there was no sign of them. In fact, now that he came to think of it, they hadn't seen a nick all morning.

"Problem?" Kat asked, looking around, trying to see what had startled him.

"Yeah, something's wrong – there aren't any street-nicks."

She shrugged. "They've been rarer than an honest razzer all day."

"I mean here in particular."

"You finally know where we are?"

"I know that corner: that's Sand Dragon territory and they always have lookouts stationed there."

"About breckin' time you recognised somewhere."

Tom had been scanning the walls of buildings they passed ever since leaving the temple, yet when he glanced up now and saw what he had been afraid of seeing all along, it still made him start. One of the spider-limbed constructs was splayed against the wall behind and above Kat.

"Oh Thaiss, not again!"

The girl's knives were in her hands even before she spun around, following his gaze. "Persistent little breckers, aren't they?"

That first was joined by a second and then a third, sliding into view from the building's roof.

A passing man muttered something disapproving to his companion on seeing Kat's knives, loud enough for them to hear, but the words were spoken over his shoulder as he strode on down the street and Tom didn't really catch them. Like Kat, his attention was focused elsewhere. Instinctively, the pair of them edged away from the wall towards the centre of the street. Tom's gaze never left the three devices, which had become five, as the things crept down the wall, but presumably Kat's did. Either that or she had eyes in the back of her head, because the girl suddenly said, "Thaiss! More of them behind us."

Tom glanced over his shoulder, to see the wall of the building they were backing towards apparently alive with spidery limbs and unblinking eyes.

"How many of these frissing things are there?"

"Too many. Come on."

She tapped his arm and the pair of them started running, continuing down the street that led to the market. She had sheathed one of her blades, but still carried the other clenched in her right fist. Nor were they the only ones hurrying away from the swarm of strange devices. People changed direction and scurried away as quickly as possible, though it was doubtful whether any of them needed to have worried. There could be little doubt that the two teenagers were the quarry in this peculiar hunt; the spider-limbed bots scurried along roof edges and across walls and even skittered across roads, whatever was needed to keep pace with the fleeing youths.

"I seem to have done a lot of this since meeting you," the girl yelled across.

"What, run you mean?"

"Yeah."

He could hardly argue.

Not everyone was running away, Tom noticed. Ahead were a group who looked to be doing anything but. They were standing around as if waiting for the hunt to reach them.

"You know those missing street-nicks?" the girl called. "I think we just found 'em."

"I noticed," Tom replied between gasped breaths. His side was beginning to hurt, but he ignored it. A dozen or so nicks began to spread out, completely blocking the street. He and Kat were not simply being hunted, he realised, they were being herded. The nicks and the Maker's devices were working together in some unholy alliance.

They were trapped: street-nicks ahead and unnatural devices behind. The buildings were solid on both sides; no alleyways, no escape, unless… To his left a woman was just letting herself into her home, no doubt anxious to get inside and away from whatever was brewing out here.

"This way!" He grabbed Kat's hand and sprinted with renewed effort towards the woman, the pain in his side growing as a result but still manageable. The unfortunate homeowner saw them and screamed, but he pushed past her and into the house, charging down a hallway towards another door which gave way beneath his kick. Struck with all the force and fear that drove him, the door swung violently back on its hinges as he sprinted through, Kat at his heels.

"Woohoo! Well done, kid!" the girl called.

Was she actually enjoying this? And where in Thaiss's name did she get the breath to whoop from?

The now broken door led out into an alleyway, with the backs of more houses directly in front. Tom did not hesitate but headed right, still going in the direction of the market and Blue Claw territory. If they could just make it that far, he was sure that sanity would be restored. Barton or some of the others were bound to be hanging around the market and would come to their aid.

From somewhere behind came the snick of multiple metal claws on stone, telling him that at least some of the spider devices had found their way across the roofs. He resisted the temptation to look back and kept running. The street-nicks would have a harder time reaching the alley, or so he hoped. But the direction they'd been running in was pretty obvious and this alley only lasted until the next cross street, so the nicks could readily cut them off at the far end.

When another alleyway presented itself to their left, Tom instinctively lunged down it, trusting Kat to follow. The pain in his side was becoming burning agony; more than simply a stitch which he'd hoped it might be. His body ached from a dozen bruises and knocks sustained in the past couple of days and he wondered whether this was an injury picked up when the sun globe exploded; something which had been hidden among all the other minor hurts and was only making itself known now that he was forced to run.

The two-storey houses had been replaced by the familiar single level dwellings and he knew that they were close to the Runs. Yet he was stumbling, faltering, and didn't think he could go any further.

"Come on, Tom," Kat was there, grabbing his arm and urging him onward. "What's wrong?"

Despite her support, he sank to the ground. "Injured... side... You go on," he gasped between breaths that were now recurring shafts of pain.

But it was too late. The chittering sound of many claws had caught up with them. Kat drew her twin blades and stood over him like some cornered animal protecting its young.

There was no pause, no regrouping; the first of the devices to reach them simply flung itself from the low roof towards Kat, to be met by an edge of steel which struck it firmly in the eye. The thing went spinning away, trailing ichor in its wake. But this was just the first of many. The girl's blades span and twirled, becoming a blur of steel as they batted away and sliced into the rain of attacking devices. All the while, her feet performed an elaborate dance around Tom, who was recovering a little but could not see a way to stand up without tripping her or, at the very least, distracting her.

One of the things reached the ground intact. Whether it had been knocked there by Kat or had simply crawled down the wall, Tom wasn't certain. He picked up a large stone in his right hand but hesitated to throw it in case he missed. Instead he waited until the device scuttled within reach and then brought the stone down as hard and fast as he could onto that single malevolent eye. Moisture splattered his hand. The construct's long spider legs twitched and then lay still. Subconsciously, Tom had expected the thing to make some sound – a squeal or whimper – but it didn't. In fact the whole battle was taking place in an eerie silence, punctuated only by the sounds of sword meeting construct and the shifting of feet on dusty ground. He kicked the body away.

Now Tom found enough room to scrabble to his feet, drawing his knife as he did so. Perhaps his actions distracted Kat a fraction, or perhaps it was just the weight of numbers which swarmed around them, but as he came upright, Tom saw one of the constructs land on her back.

The thought of that thing burrowing into her – of it doing to her whatever it was they did – horrified him. Something welled-up from deep inside and when he screamed an anguished, "No!" he did so with all his voice and heart and mind, feeling his denial well up inside and tear out of him as if it were some physical thing.

Pain exploded in his head and he crashed down to his knees again.

The next thing he knew, Kat was gripping his shoulder. "Tom?"

He looked at her, trying to concentrate, but thoughts seemed disjointed, the process of stringing them together an insurmountable effort. "The devices…?" he managed.

"Gone," she said, shaking his shoulder, laughing. "When you screamed they just tumbled over. Dead as rusty daggers, all of them. Don't know what you did, kid, but just don't you go screamin' at me like that, all right?"

He tried to listen, tried to make sense of what she was saying, but he felt light-headed and in intense pain at the same time. The experience reminded him of when he had nearly died from the black island fever that had swept through the under-City a few years back. But, if anything, this was worse. Blinking up towards Kat, for an instant he thought he saw something behind her, not a device this time but an ethereal eye, the insubstantial ghost of one, at least. It reminded him of the Swarbs and the impression of an eye he had seen disappear in green light, except that this one seemed more, well, female.

The apparition was gone the instant he saw it, leaving an alarmed Kat peering over her shoulder, trying to see what he was staring at.

"What?" the girl asked.

"Nothing. My head…" He forgot about the ethereal eye and tried to think. He was in no shape to go much further; they needed to find somewhere to rest up quickly, but where was truly safe in the City Below?

"I know, but come on, we can't stay here. Those nicks are still about somewhere," Kat said, echoing his own thoughts

She helped him to his feet, half-lifting him from the ground.

"There's a temple of Thaiss…" he recalled suddenly.

"Where?"

"Not far."

"Can you make it there? Can you show me the way?"

"Think so." Once they found the Runs it should be simple; the temple was one used by the shantytown's residents – those who worshipped the goddess, at any rate. He decided to ignore the irony of a staunch non-believer such as himself seeking sanctuary from the Thaissians until later, once they were safe. Assuming they ever were.

They stumbled onwards in the direction of the Runs, Tom shrugging off Kat's support with a less than convincing, "I'm all right."

They had gone no more than thirty or forty paces when a shout sounded from behind them. Tom looked back to see a mob of street-nicks filling the alley and coming towards them.

"Breck!" Kat slipped her head and shoulders under his arm again, fortunately on the side that didn't hurt. "Now run!"

Tom tried to. He focused on doing nothing else, shutting out the hoots and cries of the pursuing nicks and forcing himself to think beyond the sharp edged pain clawing at the window of his thoughts, willing his feet and legs to move swiftly. Yet he knew this was never going to be enough, and pretty soon Kat realised as much as well.

She ducked out from under his arm and turned around, saying, "You go on, I'll hold 'em."

"No, I'm fighting with you."

"Don't be an idiot. In your current state you'd be as much of a danger to me as to them."

"I'm staying," he insisted.

"All right, no time to argue, but at least stand back and give me enough room to fight."

He did so, as the first nicks reached the girl. As before, all he could do was marvel at her speed, her elegance and her skill. She seemed to glide to the left, out of the first nick's path. A flash of steel and the youth fell, blood welling from his slashed throat. Steel clashed against steel, once, twice and a third time in rapid succession, before a second nick went down. But there were more, many more, forcing her onto the defensive and pushing her back.

Tom saw a blade catch her arm, droplets of blood flying from the wound as the knife tore free, but she didn't slow, didn't hesitate, and the nick responsible became the third to fall. Was he feeling a bit better, thinking a little more clearly? He would have to be. He couldn't simply stand back and watch, not any longer. Drawing his own knife, he trod forward, preparing to join the fray. But before he could do so, a voice called out from somewhere at the back of the attacking mob, a single word.

"Wait."

The attack paused, the relentless pressure eased and the nicks stepped back. Tom came up to stand beside Kat, who failed to acknowledge him. She was breathing hard, her face and arms splattered in blood, little of it her own, and there was a wild, dangerous look in her eyes unlike anything Tom had seen there before, even when they fought the demon hounds.

The street-nicks were moving again, shuffling to the side and making way for a figure who strode through their ranks to the front. The first thing Tom noted was the bald head, then other things began to fall into place. He stared in disbelief at the man who stood before them, a figure whose face and arms were covered in a web of ochre marks, but if he was shocked, then it was clear from Kat's stunned expression that she was doubly so.

"Hello again, Kat," a familiar voice said.

"Rayul?"

Tylus was still not entirely convinced this was the right decision, but it certainly seemed logical the way Dewar had put it to him.

"Do you really trust Richardson to report all of this accurately?" the senior arkademic's man had asked. "Even if you do and even if he surpasses himself, how much credence will the captain or the other guard officers give him? They won't, and we both know it. You're the only one of us who has sufficient authority and respect to explain what we've learned and ensure that they believe it."

"Yes, you might be right," Tylus agreed, "but I still don't see why we shouldn't all go back and report and then set out to tackle this Maker together."

"Because time is of the essence. The watch has to know about what's going on with the street-nicks as soon as possible and the Maker has to be stopped just as quickly, before he can cause any more mischief. You're the best man to deal with the first issue and I'm the best for the second, so we split our forces. Besides, I work better alone."

Tylus still had some reservations about Dewar and was curious about this new assertion that he was best equipped to deal with the Maker, but his arguments were very persuasive and in the end they carried the day. So the Kite Guard and his assistant returned to the station while the senior arkademic's aide went hunting.

The station was in even more of an uproar than when Tylus had first arrived from the Heights, but now it felt different. On that occasion the Kite Guard had found the frenetic activity daunting and disturbing, but now he felt excited by it. In just a few short days he had begun to feel a part of things down here.

"Welcome back to chaos, Tylus," Able said with a grin. "Are you willing to pitch in?"

"Pitch in with what?"

"We've got street-nicks on the rampage all across the under-City. According to reports, they're attacking people in the streets, breaking into homes, disrupting businesses and kidnapping apprentices." Apprentices? Teens again, which supported what the dog master had claimed. "We're about to go and kick their arses!"

Perhaps Tylus had done Dewar a disservice. By the sound of it, the sooner the Maker was stopped the better. "I can probably even explain why the street-nicks are behaving like this as well," he offered.

"Great, well, as soon as you see Captain Johnson, you be sure and tell him. Me, I'm not interested in the why, I just want to stop the breckers. Are you with us or not?"

Tylus sighed. Johnson was nowhere to be seen, presumably off duty or busy elsewhere. So much for rushing back to report what they had discovered. "Wouldn't miss it for the world," he replied.

"Good, because I'm short of decent commanders in the field."

Before he knew it, Tylus found himself assigned some men and then sent to see the station's weapons master.

What he was presented with when he did so astonished him. As the name suggested, the weapons master was responsible for the stockpile of weapons which

each guard station was equipped with, the special
items reserved for particular purpose, including the
banshees deployed against the Blue Claw, or for extreme situations such as this. Many of the weapons
were things which had been supplied by the arkademics up-City, generally single-use but potent pockets
of their art, just waiting to be deployed.

What Tylus expected was that he and his men would
march away from the room bristling with enough potent and exotic devices to brush aside battalions of
crudely armed street-nicks without breaking sweat. Instead, he was offered the meagre pickings which had
not already claimed by other units: one flechette gun,
a brace of dazzle bombs and two items which all but
defied description. At least there were enough protective helmets for everybody, but helmets were unlikely
to win a fight.

"Is this it?" he asked in disbelief.

The weapons master shrugged, "What can I say?
Cutbacks. There was a time I could have equipped
every man in the station with flechettes, dazzles and
stickies and even let 'em have the odd fire bomb, star-
burst and Phulxas on the side. Now, well, you can see
for yourself." He gestured towards the storeroom and
its predominantly empty shelves.

The two objects which Tylus failed to recognise were
identified by the weapons master as Phulxa plants.
These were essentially large and swollen, globe-like
buds attached to long, thick stems, standing as tall as a
man's chest. The bud was a vaguely disconcerting purple in colour, gradually metamorphosing to a dark
green as it approached the stem, which was stripped of
any leaves.

"And what the breck am I supposed to do with these?"

"Ah well, let me explain," the sweaty and swarthy weapons master replied, clearly delighted at the chance to show off his knowledge. "Essentially, the plant has been cut and frozen by the arkademics at the very instant of releasing its spore. The Phulxa plant's seed is a great delicacy, highly prised by all manner of creatures, so the plants have developed a cunning defence mechanism to protect their seed..."

Tylus listened with interest but was still far from convinced about these peculiar floral weapons, not least because of the awkwardness inherent in transporting them. Although not heavy as such they were certainly unwieldy, and the weapons master insisted they should not be carried together, for fear of triggering them prematurely, which meant that two of his officers would have their hands full carrying the wretched things like ceremonial totems. Tylus determined that these would be the very first weapons to see use as soon as they encountered the enemy, so freeing two more pairs of hands.

He returned to the squad room none too encouraged and found Richardson buckling on his sword, which reminded him that he hadn't even brought one with him to the City Below. They were hardly standard issue for the Kite Guard. He supposed under the circumstances it made perfect sense to be prepared, and so determined to claim one from the weapons master when he took the men to collect their paltry share of the station's field weapons, assuming there were any swords in stock.

In truth, he hoped they could avoid resorting to anything as inherently lethal as swords, particularly given the way the street-nicks were being manipulated into a cruelly twisted parody of their true selves. Sadly, hopes carried little weight in the real world and Tylus realised full well that circumstances might force his hand.

After gathering up their equipment and receiving a quick briefing from Sergeant Able, the Kite Guard led his men out. He had Richardson beside him and eight officers arrayed behind. They didn't exactly march; Tylus somehow doubted the guards ever truly marched. Besides, the two men carrying the Phulxas looked just as ridiculous as he had feared, but there was still a sense of steely determination about them, and the visored helmets that all now wore lent them added menace. The guards had been run ragged by the street-nicks in recent days, subverted or not, and the men's mood suggested they saw this as payback time.

The plan was to try and contain the rampaging nicks in certain areas of the city, and Tylus was given a specific position to defend. The maxim that news travels fast in the streets was fully supported as they moved through deserted avenues and across empty squares. Residents had either fled or, more likely, barricaded themselves in their homes.

The sound of distant violence reached them from somewhere – the smashing of glass and occasional shout – but there was no sign of smoke to indicate the nicks were setting any fires, from which Tylus took heart. They were clearly not yet that out of control.

They arrived at their allotted station. There was no cover and nothing obvious with which to construct any. Tylus deployed his men in a line across the street, waiting – though not for long.

They soon heard the sounds of a large, rowdy body of people moving towards them, growing ever closer. Beside him, Richardson shifted his feet nervously. Tylus looked across and tried to smile in reassurance, though in truth he felt far from confident himself, especially bearing in mind their paltry supply of decent weaponry.

"Hold steady," Tylus said to his men, pleased at how calm his voice sounded.

Finally the growing hubbub translated into something more physical, as the vanguard of what was obviously a sizeable mob rounded the corner at the far end of the street. At sight of the waiting guards, the nicks started to shout and holler in earnest.

And still they appeared. Including himself and Richardson, Tylus had a total of ten men at his disposal. At a quick count, he reckoned there were six or seven times as many youths coming towards them, with knives and clubs and chains in evidence. One kid, towards the front of the mob, kept smacking a length of chain against the walls of buildings as he strode forward. He seemed full of verve and bounce and hostile energy, as indeed they all seemed to be. The sound of chain against wall beating out an irregular rhythm only accentuated the menace.

"Phulxa bearers to the fore," Tylus instructed. "Fire when ready."

To his great relief, one of the men claimed to know something about these hideous plants, including such details as their typical range, and Tylus was more than happy to pass over responsibility.

A few tense seconds passed and then the man reached up to rub the stem of his Phulxa vigorously, just below the bulb, the other guard copying him. Though severed from its root, and some time ago at that, the plants suddenly reacted as if they were living things. The long stems curled back, over their holders' shoulders and then sprang forward again with astonishing speed. As they did so, the bulbous buds peeled open and each spat forth a single solid-seeming kernel, nearly as large as a man's head. These missiles sailed forward, one falling at the feet of the nearest nicks, the other going into the front rank of youths.

The way the weapons master had explained the process, the Phulxa produced hundreds of thousands of seeds each season, but only one would germinate. The remainder evolved along a quite different path, remaining tiny and developing a narcotic coating which had a potent soporific effect when ingested by mammals and other creatures. The Kite Guard watched in fascination as these two seed pods split open on impact, releasing what appeared to be a fine white mist which, stirred by so much movement, swirled around the feet of the advancing nicks and rose to engulf them.

Almost immediately, many at the front began to cough and stumble and then wilt to the floor. A dozen or more were out of action courtesy of these ungainly weapons.

Tylus now turned to his flechette gunner, who raised his weapon and took aim with his wide-mouthed blunderbuss of a weapon. The gun fired a cloud of tiny darts, each dipped in a sleep-inducing narcotic, derived, the weapon master had explained, from the Phulxa plant.

At his nod, the gunner fired, and the swarm of flechettes shot towards the advancing nicks, spreading out as they travelled. Where they struck, the youths reacted as if stung, slapping at their arms, legs and faces, before crumbling to the ground. A dent appeared in the advancing mass of nicks as the centre of the front row and many behind them went down. Tylus estimated that as many as fifteen had succumbed. Impressive, but still nowhere near enough.

Inevitably, many of the nicks would have been struck by more than one dart and the Kite Guard knew that multiple doses of the drug were potentially lethal, a fact which bothered him but which he deliberately ignored; there was no helping it.

A few crossbow bolts came back from the advancing youths. Tylus ducked as one flew narrowly past his left shoulder and a scream of pain to his right told of one hitting its mark. A guardsman collapsed, with a bolt through his chest.

The flechette gunner still needed time to reload. Reasoning that those nicks with crossbows had just fired their weapons and wouldn't as yet be any more ready to fire again than his own officer, he drew the net gun and decided to risk an aerial attack.

Turning to Richardson beside him, Tylus said, "Lead a baton charge when I fire, involving everyone but the flechette gunner."

Then he started to run. There wasn't much room, only enough for a few precious sprinted steps, before he spread his arms and took to the air, accompanied by jeers and catcalls from the nicks.

A few stones shot towards him, but none found their target, and then he was sailing over their heads, gaining height the whole while. With a dip of the shoulder he banked left, taking in as he did so another street not far away, where a thin line of brown and orange was struggling to contain a seething mass of youths. The fighting there had already degenerated to hand-to-hand and the heavily outnumbered guards looked to be in trouble. But Tylus had his own responsibilities. His banking manoeuvre brought him around in a tight circle and, seconds after taking off, he raced back over the heads of his own unit, firing the netting gun as he did so. The weighted corners shot out, deploying the net, which fell to engulf the front ranks of street-nicks.

On cue, the thin line of guards charged forward, unleashing their puncheons as they reached the entangled nicks, bringing them down swiftly. Having turned as rapidly as possible, Tylus came back over the scene, narrowly avoiding a crossbow quarrel which spat up towards him from the mass of nicks and grateful that it didn't catch his cape. He couldn't afford to be grounded now.

He landed beside the flechette gunner, calling out to Richardson and the others to withdraw, which they did, some a little more reluctantly than others, evidently enjoying the opportunity to administer a beating. One of the stragglers didn't make it back but was dropped by a crossbow bolt which skewered him through the side. The man fell to the ground still alive, and tried to drag himself forward.

Tylus watched in horror. He didn't want to order an advance and risk being overwhelmed by the street-nick's greater numbers, but at the same time couldn't just abandon the wounded officer.

Nicks from further back in the mob were already climbing over and around their fallen colleagues, and judging by the shouts and gesticulations, they weren't feeling in any way calmer.

The flechette gunner was finally ready again. He looked enquiringly at Tylus, who nodded immediately. The guardsman wasted no further time, raising his weapon and pulling the trigger in one swift movement.

The instant he fired, Tylus ran forward to the injured man, peeling him away from the red smear of blood which marked his efforts to crawl across the dusty ground, and helping him up, having to half-carry, half-support him as they staggered back towards the other guards. Richardson appeared on the man's far side to help but unfortunately their bravery proved to be in vain. Even as they reached the line of orange and brown, the Kite Guard felt the officer's body jerk. A second bolt had taken him through the back. Blood welled from the man's mouth and his eyes stared blankly. He was dead.

Tylus estimated there were still some two dozen nicks standing, which was still too many. He had the flechette gunner retreat twenty paces to reload, with instructions to cover their retreat when it came, which it inevitably would. With great reluctance, he gave the order he'd been dreading to his remaining men: "Sheath puncheons and draw swords. Advance in line."

They walked forward slowly, but the nicks came at them in a rush, preceded by a few large stones, too few to be much of a threat, then the nicks were upon them.

One officer, to the far right, went down almost immediately. Tylus parried a knife thrust with his sword, punched a nick in the face, and then barely knocked another knife aside as it came at his exposed side. In doing so, he stepped back and nearly tripped over the man beside him, Richardson.

The Kite Guard wasn't used to this type of a fight, he doubted whether any of them were. What he had envisaged as an orderly line of officers repelling a sea of hostile youths quickly degenerated into a melee which would suit the larger numbers of nicks for all that this was swords against knives. Besides, when the fighting got this close, knives were, if anything, an advantage, a fact he realised when barely jumping aside from another thrust aimed by a nick who had stepped inside his guard. The knife scraped the side of his belly, drawing blood. Tylus clumped the youth on the back of the head with the butt of his sword, just as an officer beside him went down with a knife in his belly.

This was achieving nothing. "Withdraw!" he bellowed, lifting and throwing the nick in front of him away with both hands, sending him sprawling into a pair behind, feeling his sword bite into the lad's torso as he did so.

A wonderful word, "withdraw", Tylus reflected as he sprinted back to where the flechette gunner waited. So much more dignified than "run".

As he ran, sword still clutched in one hand, he fumbled at his belt with the other, struggling to grasp one of their few remaining precious weapons: a dazzle bomb. Finally freeing it, he threw the fist-sized missile under-arm towards the ground behind him.

The result was spectacular, the street lighting up whitely, glaringly so, as if a miniature sun had just been born. Tylus saw his shadow and those of the other fleeing officers race ahead, reaching the flechette gunner in an instant and spearing beyond him. At the same time, the Kite Guard's vision dulled as the helmet visor darkened in response to the flaring light.

From behind came cries of dismay, consternation and fear, as the nicks were temporarily blinded by the glare. The light was short-lived, gone in less than a second, but the dazzle bomb had done its job. The guards slowed and, at a signal from Tylus, moved to the sides of the road, giving the gunner a clear shot. The man took his time before firing, but when he did so, the darts cut a swathe through the stumbling, disorientated nicks.

Tylus signalled to his men, sheathing his sword and drawing his puncheon again. Within seconds, Tylus, Richardson and the other three remaining guards were among the fumbling, ineffectual nicks, using their puncheons to good effect on those still standing. Only as they were doing so did Tylus realise that Richardson had suffered a deep wound to the upper arm. His left hand hung limp and useless, while the shirt above it was soaked in blood. Fortunately, this fight was over, the remaining nicks quickly neutralised.

All the officers carried reels of wide and strong sticky tape, which they used to bind the unconscious nicks' hands. Less reliable than iron, but a lot easier to carry. Four of the fallen guards were dead, but one still clung to life. Unable to take part in securing the street-nicks due to his own injury, Richardson tended the wounded guardsman.

Tylus looked at his tired and bloodied men, none of whom had escaped unscathed, and felt a swell of pride. The City Below guards might have a reputation for being corrupt and ineffectual, but no one could question the courage of these officers who had fought beside him today.

He was about to say as much to them, but was fore-stalled by a sudden commotion, a growing noise which seemed to emanate from the top of this street. He looked up with a growing sense of dread. Sure enough, a group of rampaging nicks appeared from around the corner. As soon as they took in the scene, with the few battered guards standing over the fallen nicks, they started to charge forward, yelling their defiance.

Tylus supposed he should feel grateful; after all, this was a much smaller mob – no more than thirty of them at most.

"Flechette gunner," he said, on a throat suddenly as dry as sawdust, "stand ready!"

FIFTEEN

As Tom stared at the tattooed man, he felt suddenly defeated, as if all that he and Kat had gone through in the past few days had been for nothing. There was no question in his mind that Rayul had fallen prey to one of the Maker's devices. It was only a few hours ago that they left him with good will and friendly words, yet now this formidable tattooed man faced them as an enemy. Tom barely knew Rayul but felt this was some-one he could have liked. The remaining energy seemed to drain from his limbs and Tom knew that there was no way he could stand against Rayul in a fight at that moment, which meant it was all down to Kat. How in the world was she supposed to oppose him, one of her closest friends?

"I'm not your enemy, Kat," Rayul said, his voice so reasonable, so normal, as if she were the one acting out of character. "Why are we fighting?" He took a slow step forward as he spoke.

"Stay back, Rayul!" Tom could hear the upset in her voice, though the knife remained steady in her hand as she held it out point-first towards her friend.

"This isn't what you think. Look at me, Kat." The tattooed man held his arms open. "This is still me standing here in front of you, but a better me, that's all. Everything is so much clearer now. It's a wonderful, liberating experience, not something to be afraid of. All that any of us want is for you to join us, so that you can feel what this is like for yourself."

The girl shook her head. Were those tears in her eyes? "Anything that's so insistent I should join isn't something I want to be a part of, thanks. Why do you think I left the Tattooed Men in the first place?"

"But this isn't the same. There's no Chavver to start with, and this is so much more." He sounded so certain, so enthused and, worst of all, so much like the same man who had discovered them in the attic room that very morning. This must be torture for Kat.

"Stay back, I said!" The girl shrieked as he edged another step forward.

"You can't win, Kat, you know that and I know that." His tone changed abruptly; the warmth and friendliness instantly replaced by a harder and totally confident edge as he presumably realised he was not going to win Kat over with persuasive words alone. "The boy's too tired or too scared to fight and we outnumber you fifteen to one."

Tom bridled but stayed quiet, not wanting to distract Kat. In truth, the more Rayul spoke, the angrier he was becoming and with the anger a little strength was starting to return to his limbs.

"But why bother?" Kat asked. "You know I'm going to take a few more of you with me. So what if you do succeed in 'converting' me? In the end, you'll still have lost more than you gain."

"You don't understand, do you? It doesn't work like that. This is our mission: to convert all those we can. If a few of us fall by the wayside, so be it."

"What then, Rayul? Once all the nicks in the City Below have joined you, what happens next?"

He laughed, casually, as if sharing some joke with a friend. "Then the real fun begins. Come on, Kat, be a part of the most exciting thing to happen down here in years."

"Not. A. Breckin'. Chance!" She pronounced each word slowly and precisely, emphasising the statement with a defiant glare which lifted Tom's spirits enormously.

His side still burned, his head still felt as if it didn't fully belong to his body, but a sense of calm settled over him, of resignation. He had no idea how he managed to destroy the Maker's devices when they attacked Kat but knew he wouldn't be able to do it again for a while, not with his head feeling as it did. He could produce no miracle to save them this time. It was quite possible that he would die here, and something deep inside him accepted that fact but, if that was to be the way of things, he had no intention of going down meekly.

"Fifteen to two," he said, coming up to stand fully beside Kat. "Those odds you mentioned, it's fifteen to two, not one."

Rayul laughed. "And you think you're going to make a difference, kid?" All attempts to cajole and persuade had disappeared from the tattooed man's voice now, to be replaced by an arrogance that Tom couldn't recall hearing from him before he was converted.

The rest of the nicks had begun shifting restlessly, as if restrained by Rayul's authority but only just. They wanted to pile into a fight and Tom wondered how long their patience would last. He recognised at least two familiar faces among them; Sand Dragons he had come into contact with at various times. One, Brent, a tall stringy lad with sandy hair and broken teeth, was someone he used to hang with sometimes when things were quiet for both gangs. The boy looked over, seeing Tom gaze at him, and nodded greeting, smiling his uneven smile. The gesture was so typical, so normal, that it disturbed Tom deeply.

Rayul sighed. "Very well, we'll do this your way."

In the blink of an eye he drew his short sword with his right hand while another weapon appeared in his left. At least, Tom assumed it was a weapon; he had never seen anything quite like it. The object resembled a section of netting, perhaps half a metre square, although clearly it was woven from interlinking loops of metal, and one end was weighted down with small silver metal balls. The tattooed man held it at the opposite end, so that the links were squashed together and the weighted balls hung downward. Then, as he and Kat faced each other, both crouching and shifting from foot to foot, he began to swing the peculiar weapon.

The other nicks continued to hang back, apparently willing to accept this as a personal duel for the moment, though he didn't doubt they would pounce on him in an instant once the confrontation ended; Kat too, assuming she survived. In fact, everybody shuffled back a few paces, to give the fighters a little more room.

The first aggressive move came from Rayul, who lashed out with the weighted mesh, attempting to snare one of Kat's blades. She flicked her knife out of the way with a twist of her wrist and then converted the evasion into an attacking move of her own, seeking to bring the blade down onto Rayul's exposed forearm. He in turn was too quick for her, withdrawing his hand and the weapon it held.

He laughed. "Fast as ever."

Kat made no response.

Next Rayul feinted as if again about to strike with the mesh but then he lunged forward with his knife. Kat spun to her left and out of the way, bringing one of her own blades around and down. They clashed, steel on steel. Kat's second blade came in behind the first and was likewise parried. The two moved apart and resumed their prowling, shifting from side to side in unison, always facing each other, like a pair of synchronised crabs. This time it was Kat who attacked, dancing forward, her arms and knives flowing through a sequence of lightning-quick moves which kept one blade or the other constantly striking towards her opponent. He had no choice but to back away, his own blade blocking hers and the mesh twirling a curtain of steel.

Kat's attack relented with no apparent result and the two faced each other again, The tattooed man now stood with his back to Tom, so close that he could have reached out and touched him. He had to shuffle to one side to see Kat at all.

Then Rayul did the unexpected, at least as far as Tom was concerned. With no warning, no apparent change of action at all, he released the weighted mesh. It flew the short distance to smack into Kat's hand, and wrist, wrapping around them. She cried out in surprise and pain as at least one of the steel balls struck her wrist, presumably numbing it, because the knife dropped from her hand. Rayul moved in swiftly, following up immediately behind the thrown weapon. Kat reacted, but a fraction too slowly. Tom watched in horror as the tattooed man's blade bit into her side even as she attempted to sway out of the way. Then the pair of them closed, grappling so tightly that it was impossible to see what was happening from where he stood. Both knives were hidden by Rayul's back as they struggled, wrestling and squirming, feet shuffling as each tried to trip the other while avoiding being tripped themselves. Tom's anguish grew – it seemed certain that the larger and presumably stronger man must win any contest fought at such close quarters. Suddenly, the two figures stopped. He knew instinctively that the fight was over and waited in dread to see Kat fall. He didn't want to look but was unable to turn away. Yet both of them stood there for an apparent age, before each took a shuffling step backwards, followed by another.

Tom saw clearly the moment when Rayul's legs buckled. The big man's knees seemed to give way and he simply wilted to the ground. Beyond him, Kat stood with tears streaming down her cheeks. Her long knife dangled in limp fingers by her side, red with her friend's blood, while her whole frame shook with the sobs that welled-up from deep within. Tom rushed forward, wanting to hold her, to comfort her, but his movement seemed to break the trance and suddenly all the other nicks were coming forward as well.

Tom thrust Kat behind him, standing between the girl and the nicks, menacing them with his woefully inadequate knife. This was it, he knew: the moment he was destined to die.

Instead, even as he braced himself for the fatal blow, the wall to one of the buildings behind the mob of nicks erupted – stone and brick flew out as if struck by an irresistible force. Almost immediately, the wall on the opposite side of the alley did the same. Time seemed to stand still as everyone stared, and through the still-collapsing walls, two figures out of nightmare emerged. Humanoid in shape, but impossibly tall, standing a full head and shoulders above the tallest man Tom had ever before seen. They were black from head to toe. Not dressed in black but apparently dipped in it; a seamless, gleaming jet which seemed to suck in all available light. They looked like somebody's idealised image of the human form, carved from burnished ebony and made real, but with the features still to be painted on.

Tom stared and knew terror beyond anything previously felt. All he could do was whisper, "the Blade!"

They moved almost too quickly for the eye to follow, crashing into the street-nicks, fists a blur. Perhaps half the youths had been felled before the others could react – some were sent flying through the air to crash into walls while others were simply swatted to the ground. No weapons, Tom noted, they only used their fists, but fists proved more than enough. To their credit, some of the street-nicks tried to rally, to defend themselves and fight back, but they were battered aside with contemptuous ease. The remaining lads, three of them, turned and ran for all they were worth. Even the goading of the Maker's devices had limits, it would seem. The towering black figures made no attempt to follow.

All he could think was *The Blade!*

A name feared by every denizen of the under-City, though none had been seen here in more than a generation. Inhuman warriors, the Blade had been stationed in these streets during the height of the war, and had terrorised them. Unflinching in their dedication and relentless in the prosecution of their duty, they had been charged with ferreting out spies and saboteurs and collaborators, dispensing their own brand of abrupt justice as they deemed fit. Hundreds, perhaps thousands had died, and word had it that the Blade were not overly careful to discriminate between friend and foe.

Tom stared at these apparitions, totally unmanned. He was aware of Kat beside him, though even she found nothing to say for once.

Were they going to be next to feel the Blade's form of justice?

One of the two dark creatures faced him and said in a surprisingly normal male voice, "You two, come with us."

Movement from the ground caught Tom's eye. He looked down to see Rayul's eyes flicker. He was still alive! Kat knelt down in an instant, holding his head.

"Rayul?" Her tears flowed freely.

The tattooed man raised a gentle hand to grasp hers. "Don't remember me like this, Kat, please… the good times, Kat… the good times."

Then the hand fell away and his eyes stared unseeing.

"Rayul!"

"Hurry, we must go," the Blade said.

"Where are you taking us?" Tom demanded.

"To the temple of Thaiss."

Tom knelt and, his hands on her shoulders, guided Kat to her feet. "We're going to have to do as they say, Kat."

"I know." She shrugged off his grasp, raised her hands to rub at her eyes, then bent down to scoop up her fallen blade, sheathing it. She looked across at him and simply nodded her readiness.

They set off, with one of the Blade in front and the other behind, forming as unlikely a company as Tom could ever have imagined, his growing conviction that the world had gone utterly mad confirmed.

Tylus realised exactly how much trouble they were in as soon as the flechette gunner fired. This group of nicks were clearly a lot cannier than the first lot, perhaps learning from previous skirmishes. Planks of wood, scraps of metal sheeting and even a section of broken door were raised as makeshift shields. Whereas previously the gun's discharge had cut a swathe through the recklessly advancing nicks, this time only four went down.

The Kite Guard knew his men had fought bravely, but he also knew they stood no chance of defeating this second mob and saw little point in throwing away lives to no purpose. Already there were a few crossbows being readied among the front ranks of nicks and several stones were lobbed, falling short, but that was enough to decide it for him. Reluctant as he was to withdraw and leave this section of the city open to the mob, there seemed little option. With a sinking heart, Tylus drew out their final weapon, the second flash bomb, and prepared to throw it.

"When this goes off," he said quietly to his men, "retreat."

"Do you mean run, sir?" the flechette gunner asked.

"Yes," he admitted, "that's exactly what I mean."

He looked across at Richardson, whose left arm hung limp, blood soaking through the length of the sleeve.

"I'll be fine," Richardson assured him.

A crossbow bolt fizzed through the air, narrowly missing Tylus's ear, and another struck the wall against which Richardson was leaning, spraying forth stony splinters. There was no more time to waste. Tylus raised his arm, preparatory to throwing the bomb, when something caused him to pause. The street-nicks were wavering, their bows lowered. They were pointing and shouting, edging backwards. Those at the back broke off and started to run away. Tylus's heart leapt: reinforcements!

He turned and looked over his shoulder, and could hardly credit what he saw there. Four towering ebony figures were trotting towards them, their loping stride eating up ground at an unlikely rate.

"Dear goddess," said a choked voice beside him, "the Blade!"

The guardsman touched his forehead with a middle finger and moved his hand down to his stomach, with fingers spread; the sign of the waterfall, of the goddess Thaiss.

"It's alright, officer," Tylus reassured him, "they're on our side."

The Kite Guard had seen the Blade only once before, at an official ceremony, but he was aware of their reputation and their history, and could guess the effect their appearance would have on denizens of the City Below.

"Are you sure, sir?" the officer asked.

"Yes, I'm sure," Tylus said, with more conviction than he actually felt as he watched the quartet of intimidating fighting machines approach, conceding that it was hard not to feel threatened.

The street-nicks were now in full rout, running to a man despite their numerical advantage, such was the terror inspired by these night-dark warriors.

One of the four paused to address Tylus in passing, towering above him and making him feel like a child summoned before a teacher. "Kite Guard, take your men back to their station. We'll handle it from here."

And then it was gone, loping after its fellows as they closed on the fleeing nicks.

Tylus turned to the wide-eyed flechette gunner and then to Richardson and the other stunned and weary faces.

"You heard the man," though he wondered even as he said it how appropriate that final word was, "let's get out of here."

Dewar was glad the Kite Guard had been dissuaded from accompanying him. The man seemed to assume they were now some sort of a team, which was a laughable concept, and Dewar certainly had no intention of setting foot in that guard station again. Not only did he feel distinctly uncomfortable in the place, but there was the added risk of being compromised by his own contact within the unit. Quite apart from which, Tylus's company had been wearing in the extreme and, having met the gormless Richardson, the assassin was finally able to understand how Tylus had managed to shine down here. The local guards had never exactly been the pride of the force but, if

Richardson was anything to go by, standards had slipped even further while he was away; the Kite Guard must have seemed a genius in comparison to the average officer.

He had another reason to be grateful as well. When the dog master stipulated that one of his pets must be a part of any attack on the Maker, the assassin feared that he would be lumbered with the large beast that had led them to the madman's lair. While doubtless strong and formidable in its own right, that particular false-hound had hardly been unobtrusive, and stealth rather than strength was the quality Dewar was relying on to reach the Maker. To his great relief, however, it was the small wall-climbing hound which the dog master assigned to him as guide and observer.

As far as Dewar could determine, the nick he was sent here to find had either been killed trying to cross the City Below or, more likely, had been subverted by one of the Maker's devices, like every other nick around here. Assuming the latter, the boy was not about to do anything predictable until the Maker and his influence were removed. Only once the Maker was dead was there any chance that the lad would start behaving normally again and return to the Blue Claw headquarters, where Dewar would be waiting for him. So, the sooner the Maker was taken care of, the sooner he could complete this assignment and return to the Heights.

Unfortunately, reaching the Maker's den was proving trickier than anticipated. Dewar found himself moving through a city in turmoil. Evidently the Maker had abandoned any pretence of subtlety and gangs of armed street-nicks now roamed openly through the under-City, looking for trouble. He skirted around one pitched battle as a large force of guards took on a mob of nicks, and avoided several other minor skirmishes. The whole place had the feel of somewhere under siege, which he supposed in a sense it was. People were cowering in their homes and battening down the hatches, hoping that trouble would simply pass them by. The real question now was how long before the powers upstairs reacted to the situation? React they would, he felt certain, but would the Maker be able to achieve his goal, whatever it might be, before that happened?

At least the nicks seemed to be avoiding the temptation to torch anywhere. So far. Fire was never welcome in the closed environment of the City Below and the youths seemed to retain enough common sense to know how dangerous it could be. However, he wouldn't bet on that common sense lasting forever, especially if things turned against them.

The mini-hound was leading him out of areas he was familiar with but, even so, Dewar knew enough of the city's layout to realise they weren't going the most direct route. At one point, he stopped and crouched down, staring directly into the dog's eyes in the knowledge that it's master would see all that the dog did.

"I'm giving you the benefit of the doubt for now," the assassin said slowly, trusting the dog master would understand his meaning even if the dog didn't relay sound. "I'm going to assume we're avoiding certain areas for specific reasons, but if I ever discover you've been sending me the long way round just for your own perverse titillation, I'll crush your little hound beneath my foot and then come back to see you for a chat regarding the wisdom of wasting my time."

The dog stared back, giving no indication as to whether the assassin's message had been understood or not. Its unblinking mesh-built eyes put him in mind of some giant insect. He straightened up and the small hound turned and continued to patter along in front exactly as before, as if he had never spoken.

The dog finally led him to an unassuming door in an ordinary looking building; green paint peeling from wooden planks, held together by a cross-plank which housed the latch and lock mechanism. If this was the Maker's lair, Dewar was surprised on a number of fronts – the first being the lack of any challenge. Alarm bells started ringing in the assassin's head but nowhere else. After all, this was supposed to be the headquarters of the man currently intent on overthrowing the accepted order in the City Below; so where was his security?

The little dog simply trotted up to the door, with no apparent worries at all. Dewar hung back, taking in every detail. Close by the door, something glinted on the ground. There was broken glass there and an object that might have been a small piece of metal. The ground itself immediately beneath these scraps seemed a shade darker, as if stained by something. If as he suspected this was blood, then it had not been spilled all that recently. This was a large building – a warehouse of some sort perhaps? Yet there was no sign of any windows. Moving away from the door, he slipped around to the building's side and then to the back. Just the one window – high up and small, impossible to reach from the ground.

Eventually, satisfied that it represented the only way in without resorting to the roof, he returned to the front and the door to find the dog patiently sitting in the middle of the street, waiting for him.

Still with strong misgivings, convinced this was some sort of a trap, Dewar drew both his short, broad sword and his kairuken and prepared to enter. Which was when he spotted the device above the door, its limbs splayed out and blending perfectly with the stonework. Only when it opened that single large eye did it become visible. The assassin felt like smiling. Hardly the most formidable guardian, but at least it was something.

He wasn't the only one to spot the creature. The tiny dog sprang into action, charging across the road and straight up the wall. The Maker's creature was quick but so was the dog. There followed a breakneck race across the building's front, with the device fleeing from and dodging the scampering mutt. Eventually, the spider-like construct made a break for the roof but the dog was too fast, leaping upon it. Both tumbled to the ground. The dog sprang to its feet and, while the device struggled to untangle its long legs, brought its tail over its head and stabbed down into that single eye. The action reminded Dewar of a striking scorpion. The tail's barbed tip penetrated the eye and kept going. The device shook and thrashed its limbs for a second and then lay still.

That was enough for Dewar. He faced the door, raised his foot and kicked it just behind the latch area. Wood splintered and the door swung open. Dewar span to one side and pressed against the wall. When no arrows or other missiles came flying out, he slipped through, weapons ready, still hugging the wall, to crouch just inside the doorway.

The first thing that struck him was the smell. The place stank, like a distillation of the stench that assailed you when you first stepped into the City Below. Similar but much worse. Something had died in here.

Then he saw the smashed creatures. Something which might once have been part machine and part monkey, another which looked like a mechanical lizard and several others less easily identifiable. They lay scattered at intervals along a wide corridor. The assassin pictured in his mind what must have happened here. A fight, an attack upon this place, with the Maker's creatures, for such he assumed them to be, fighting a rearguard action, a desperate defence which saw them falling one by one.

There was a sound, a buzzing hum which bubbled just above the threshold of awareness and seemed to emanate from somewhere ahead.

He edged forward, still clutching his weapons, and examined the nearest felled construct, the monkey. The device had been well and truly trashed, but what he found most interesting was the thin layer of dust covering the wreckage. He straightened and strode down the corridor with greater purpose, retracing the path of the imagined battle. The smell grew stronger and the buzzing grew louder with every step. He didn't pause to examine any further wreckage, confident it would reveal nothing new. What lay in the room at the far end of this hallway was all that mattered now.

He stepped into a space quite unlike the control room from which the dog master operated – there were no intrusive hanging cables and the room seemed less cramped as a result, despite the fact it was smaller. The mangled remains of various constructs littered the floor. There might have been no banks of screens but there was a large block of machinery with a desk beside it and a chair.

The sound and stench intensified further as he entered the room and the buzzing noise was finally explained. A black swarm of flies lifted into the air as if to greet him – a swirling cloud of insects which had been crawling over various organic scraps but which were concentrated around a slumped form stretched out on the floor: the source of the smell. A dead human body, and none too fresh either judging by its reek. Dewar had no doubt that this was the Maker, the man he had to come to kill. Somebody had obviously beaten him to it, and by some margin as well.

But if the Maker had been dead all this time…

Suddenly things fell into place. Dewar flung himself to one side, rolling through the dust, but he was barely fast enough. The small dog pounced, its clawed feet missing him by fractions. As he rolled again, the tail came smashing down, its barb striking the ground where his head had been an instant before.

Realising there was not enough time to get to his feet, Dewar pushed himself up into a sitting position, using the knuckles of his left hand, which still clasped the kairuken, to do so. The dog was quick. He had seen that for himself when it hunted down the device watching over the door, and he was given further proof now, as one of its feet, sharp enough to find purchase on a wall, pierced his supporting hand, skewering it to the kairuken. He cried out at the intense pain, but concentrated, knowing he had to react as quickly as the dog master's toy. The thing's tail was raised, ready to strike, and he had no idea what venom its sting might contain.

He brought his sword across, smashing into the device. Not a clean strike with the edge of the blade, but it was still enough to send the false-dog rolling away, freeing his hand in the process.

Dewar dropped his sword, snatched up the kairuken and, as the small dog struck a wall and so stopped rolling, fired. The razor-edged disc flew across the intervening space and struck the device, severing its over-sized head from the small body. The hound's body collapsed. Reclaiming his sword, Dewar got to his feet and walked across to the lifeless device – now the smallest pile of junk in the room. He picked up the dog's head and glared into the bulging mesh eyes.

"It was you all along, wasn't it, you bastard!" he said. There was no means of knowing whether the dog master was still receiving images through the severed head, but he continued to speak anyway. "You killed the Maker, took over the manufacture of these 'simple but effective' mechanisms yourself and then used them to carry this parasite of yours, all the while knowing that your deceased rival would take the blame. You all but told us as much when we were there, didn't you? Even taunting us by pointing out the discrepancy between the simple devices and the complex parasite, but we were too caught up in things to notice.

"Mark my words, dog master: you're a dead man. I'm coming for you, old friend."

It had been clever, having the dog kill one of the Maker's devices as they entered. Dewar could imagine the maniacal little man cackling away at that little sub-terfuge. He flung the false-canine's head to one side, stalked out of the room and walked with determined tread back down the corridor. As he neared the exit, the door swung violently open, and a figure stood there, framed by the daylight behind, so that he was forced to squint to make it out.

It was a girl, he realised; a black-clad, feral creature bearing twin short swords similar to his own, though not as broad in the blade. One of the infected nicks, he presumed, though her opening words to him, spoken as she slipped into the corridor, her movements as posed and graceful as a dancer, seemed to suggest otherwise.

"I hope you're ready, Maker, ready to pay for all you've done." The words were almost growled rather than spoken. "It's time for you to die."

SIXTEEN

Tom was dismayed when Kat announced she was leaving. "You're hurt," he pointed out. "At least wait until we get to the temple and let them see to your wound."

She glanced down at the cut in her side, from which blood still seeped. "This? This is nothing. I took far worse in the Pits."

"Yes, but–"

"Look, Tom, you don't need me anymore. I reckon the Blade can see you home safely enough from here, assuming there's still a home to go to, of course. The whole city's going to hell in a death cart, in case you hadn't noticed. And there's something I've got to do, something which won't wait."

He realised exactly what that meant: Rayul, and revenge. "I know, but…"

"See you, kid."

Before he knew what was happening, she leant forward and kissed him on the cheek, the corner of her mouth brushing the corner of his lips in the process, then she turned and was running, her side not seeming to restrict her at all.

He lifted a hand to where he could still feel the surprisingly cool touch of her lips on his face. He wanted desperately to follow but knew that if he was going to he should have gone immediately, that by hesitating those few seconds it was already too late. Kat was around a corner and out of sight. He would never be able to catch her. In desperation, he turned to the Blade, who had stood silently by and let her go.

"Shouldn't you have stopped her?" he asked.

One of the statuesque figures peered down at him. "No, we were sent to fetch you. The girl is irrelevant."

Not to him she wasn't. It was only then that Tom unfroze, running to the corner, to stand at the mouth of an otherwise deserted alley.

"Kat!" he yelled into the silence and the emptiness.

The Blade were beside him again. "We must go. There are people waiting."

What did Tom care who was waiting? Let them wait. Kat had gone, had left him. Nevertheless, he turned without a further word and went with the Blade, one of them in front and one behind as before, and he felt small and insignificant and, above all, entirely alone in the world.

"Sorry to disappoint you, kid, but I'm not the Maker."

The girl continued to eye him with malice and suspicion but at least she hadn't attacked yet. She moved like a trained fighter, and Dewar couldn't begin to imagine where someone as young as this had learned to do that. No ordinary street-nick, that much was certain.

"Someone's beaten you to it, beaten us both to it. That stench you can smell, that's the Maker, or what's left of him."

She didn't rise from her fighter's crouch, but reached out to touch a piece of nearby wreckage, wiping dust from her fingers afterwards even as he had.

"These?"

"His creations, destroyed in the attack, I'd imagine."

"Who?"

"The dog master." Why was he wasting time on this girl? Because she interested him, he realised. "He's the one who pointed me here when I knocked on his door and then had one of his creatures try to kill me when I found the Maker's body."

Her gaze flicked past him, down the corridor, taking in the other wrecked devices.

"Wait here!" and she slid past him.

He couldn't help but smile as he watched her jog down the hallway. She was slim but well-muscled – a lithe and wiry frame rather than merely slender – and she moved with a grace that was impossible not to admire: quite beautiful. Add to that her abundant confidence and the proficient way she handled her blades and the result was a highly intriguing individual.

She didn't go into the room, merely looked in from the doorway and then came back. "Not recent," she commented.

"No," he agreed, "a good few days ago."

"So this dog master…"

"Is behind everything and has seen to it that the Maker takes the blame," he finished for her.

She seemed to reach a decision and sheathed her knives. "Kat," she offered.

"Pleased to meet you, Kat, I'm–" As he spoke, he lunged, grabbing both her arms and slamming them against the wall. As he held her there, pinned, he re-membered Jezmina's ambush – the first one, which hadn't involved hitting him over the head – and on im-pulse he leant forward and kissed this enigmatic girl, clamping his lips to hers. Only for an instant, then he leapt back before she had a chance to react, to bite or to knee him.

Even as he landed, one of her knives appeared, its tip levelled at his chest, but his own was out just as quickly, levelled at hers.

They stood there at impasse, him grinning and her seething.

"Dewar," he finished. "And if you want to find the dog master, you're going to want me alive. I'm the man who can take you there."

With that, he very deliberately withdrew his blade and sheathed it. After a moment's hesitation, and with obvious lingering reluctance, she did the same. "If you try anything like that again you're a dead man, and I'll find the breckin' way myself."

He smiled. "Fair enough."

The palm of her hand struck him across the cheek, too quickly for him to react and too powerfully to be deemed a mere slap. His head was jerked sideways by the force and his cheek warmed instantly with tingling pain.

"That was just to prove that I meant it."

"I believe you," he said, gingerly rubbing his cheek.

"Now, are you gonna take me to this dog master or are we just going to stand here trying to score points off each other?"

"Follow me." He headed to the door and out into daylight, the girl directly behind him. At first he was on tenterhooks, conscious of her footfalls and wondering if she would seek any further retribution for the kiss, but the slap seemed to have satisfied her for now.

If he were ever going to team up with someone, he would take this girl over the Kite Guard any day. "Where did you learn to fight?"

"In the Pits."

He stopped and stared at her, tempted to ask if she meant it, but it was obvious from her face that she did. The Pits? And she was so young. No wonder she looked tough and competent. Normally, kids whose parents died, or who were thrown out because their families could no longer afford to keep them, ended up drifting into one of the street-nick gangs or into whoring, but there had been rumours that some found their way into the Pits. Anyone who fought in that place and was still around to talk about it would have to be able to handle themselves, but for a teenager, a mere kid, and a girl at that, to have emerged alive from the Pits was incredible.

"I thought the survivors from that little hellhole sported tattoos to show what they've been through."

"That's right. All except me and my sister."

She had managed to surprise him again. The two sisters who ruled the Tattooed Men were legendary, so much so that he never even believed they existed until now. The pair were said to be the greatest warriors ever to emerge from the Pits. "You're one of those two."

"Yeah, now can we forget the questions and get on with this?"

"Sure, kid, whatever you say."

"Don't call me that. I'm not a kid."

No, on reflection she certainly wasn't. In fact, Dewar wondered whether she ever had been.

This temple of Thaiss was identical to all the others scattered around the under-City, complete with water-fall and the familiar small pond. The water was crystal clear, Tom noted in passing. The Thaissians were the most popular and numerous of the cults and religions in the under-City, and not even the cockiest of street-nicks were likely to wash or urinate in the sacred waters, just in case.

The Blade led him into the building, where the Thaistess waited. Her hood was drawn back but her hands were hidden in the sleeves of her robe, meeting across her stomach. She was considerably older than the priestess met earlier in the day, deep wrinkles marking her face, though she still stood straight and proud. There was nothing soft or welcoming in her eyes, which held a harder edge than Mildra's had ever shown. She nodded to the Blade, noting Tom's pres-ence with a cursory glance, and then turned to lead them into an inner chamber, considerably larger than the one in which he had fought off the Maker's device and its influence earlier that day.

Two people waited there, both seated, one human and the other, against all expectation, a Jeradine. The latter stood up as the party entered and stepped to-wards them.

"Tom, what a pleasure and a relief to see you again," said a familiar flat and monotone voice.

"Ty-gen?"

Tom would never have believed he could be so

pleased to see a flathead. Even though he had only met him briefly, the Jeradine had been kind to him and it was a relief to see any familiar face at that particular moment. Not that Tom would have recognised him if he hadn't spoken.

Tom felt as if he might cry, from a combination of relief, despair, confusion and exhaustion, but he held the tears at bay, refusing to be the kid that Kat so often accused him of being.

"Where is Kat?" the Jeradine asked.

"She had something to do," Tom replied, the words coming with difficulty. "I think she's gone after the Maker."

"On her own? Let us hope she is careful." Ty-gen looked back towards the person he'd been sitting with, an elderly man with a kindly, smiling face, which was a marked contrast to the Thaistess' countenance. "Tom, I would like you to meet an old friend of mine. This is the prime master."

"We meet at last, Tom." The voice was as open and friendly as the face.

Tom stared. "The prime master?"

"Yes, for my sins." The twinkle in the man's eye broke through Tom's gloom and he smiled despite himself. He could hardly believe this, could hardly comprehend all that had happened in the past two days. Surely life had no further surprises to throw at him after this. *The prime master!*

"The boy is not well," the Thaistess said, her voice as frost-laden and severe as her appearance.

"Oh?" The prime master looked genuinely concerned. "Would you object to the Thaistess examining you, Tom? She's very skilled."

He nodded acceptance, too daunted to refuse. The woman deftly ran fingertips over his body, from the crown of his head to his knees. He stood stock still, as petrified as he had been at any time that day. While she conducted the examination, the prime master questioned him about his injuries.

"My side started hurting when I was running," he explained, "and my head…" How could he explain what he had done, when he didn't even understand it himself?

"When you destroyed the Maker's creatures?" the prime master supplied for him.

Tom nodded, surprised that the man knew about that. Then he remembered the insubstantial eye he had imagined seeing during the fight; perhaps it was real after all. Had they been watching him and Kat all along?

"He has a hairline fracture to a rib," the Thaistess said, ignoring Tom and addressing the prime master as if reporting on some damaged piece of furniture – exactly the sort of attitude that had caused Tom to mistrust religions and their priests for so long. "It might have been damaged earlier but only really made itself known when the boy was forced to run. As for the head, I can ease his pain but would not trust myself to tamper with its cause."

The prime master smiled. "I'm sure Tom will be grateful for whatever help you can give, won't you, Tom?"

He looked into the man's face, finding sincerity and encouragement there, and he nodded, if a little reluctantly.

"You'll have to lie on the divan and remove your shirt," the Thaistess said, addressing him directly for the first time.

Tom hesitated. He remembered the warmth and pleasure of Mildra's healing touch well enough, but this was not Mildra, and he didn't trust this sour-faced woman.

"Come on, boy, I won't bite."

Tom wasn't so sure,

"You can trust her, Tom," Ty-gen said.

Tom crossed to the long seat on which the prime master and the Jeradine had been sitting when he entered and, gritting his teeth, pulled off his shirt and lay down, wincing at the renewed pain that shot through his side as he did so. He looked up at the Thaistess as she approached, steeling himself against her touch.

"Kat was all right when she left you?" Ty-gen asked.

If they had been watching, surely they knew the answer already; unless they stopped watching once the Blade arrived. Perhaps he had imagined that eye after all, or perhaps Ty-gen was only asking in order to distract him, to try and put him more at ease.

"Fine," he replied. No she wasn't; she had been anything but fine, but the glib response came readily to his lips and, besides, it was easier than explaining.

This Thaistess' hands felt older than Mildra's – rougher-skinned and less gentle in their touch – but he still experienced the same sense of pleasant heat emanating from them as she pressed them to his body. The warmth enveloped the sharp, caustic pain, dulling its edges and slowly whittling the hurt away, until only the warmth remained. She lifted her hands and the comforting glow began to fade, but not all at once, the sense of well-being lingered, even as he felt the now familiar touch of fingertips at his temples. A new source of gentle heat spread through his skull, purging it of pain and leaving him wonderfully clearheaded for the first time since lashing out at the Maker's creatures.

"Thank you," he said to the Thaistess as she withdrew her hands.

She smiled – the first remotely kind expression he had seen cross those austere features.

The boy stood up and pulled on his shirt.

The prime master spoke to him again. "Now, Tom, I assume you're wondering what's been happening to you over the past few days." Tom nodded, since that was exactly what he had been wondering for much of the time. "I can explain it all to you, where your abilities come from and why they make you so special. But first, there's something I'd like you to do for me."

He might have guessed as much – no one ever did something for nothing, not even, it seemed, the prime master of all Thaiburley.

"Don't get me wrong," the man continued, as if reading his thoughts, "one doesn't depend on the other, I'm not attempting to make a deal here, but your help is needed urgently.

"You see, the attack on you and your friend by those street-nicks was not an isolated incident. All over the City Below the nicks, who seem to have fallen under the Maker's sway by the thousands, are on the rampage. The Blade can defeat them physically, but not mentally. Only you can do that. We need your help to save all those nicks, Tom, to purge them of the Maker's influence.

"Are you willing to do that, for the sake of your fellow street-nicks and for all the City Below?"

Tom stared in disbelief. For a moment there he thought this man understood, but clearly he didn't.

Tom would never be able to do something like this. He might have stopped a handful of the Maker's creatures at close quarters, but he had no idea what he'd done to achieve even that much, and the effort had left him with a crippling headache. How could he possibly do the same across the whole under-City? He simply couldn't, and it was unfair of anyone to expect him to.

"I don't think I can," he said. "I don't even know how."

"We can help you there, Ty-gen and myself, but only you can actually do it. Will you?"

Help? How could anyone possibly help him do something he didn't even understand himself?

Ty-gen reappeared – Tom had not even noticed him slip out. The Jeradine carried a complex piece of crystalline equipment which Tom recognised immediately as being made from khybul.

"This is a transmitter, Tom," the prime master explained.

"There are Jeradine with similar mechanisms in every temple of Thaiss throughout the City Below," Ty-gen added.

"The plan is, that if we can cause you to unleash the same sort of force you used to disable the Maker's devices," that settled it, they had definitely been watching, "Tygen's device will amplify and transmit that force; it will be picked up across the entire Row and sent forth, destroying the Maker's devices and their evil work in every street and corner of the under-City, thus freeing the street-nicks."

"And will that really work?" Tom wanted to know.

"So we believe, yes, although the only way to be certain is to try it. All you have to do is generate the same objection and repulsion of the Maker's creatures as you did before and we can take it from there. Will you try to do that, for all our sakes?"

Tom wasn't particularly looking forward to another headache, but hopefully the Thaistess could help with that. In any case, how could he possibly refuse? "Yes," he heard himself say. "I'll try. But I don't know how."

The prime master smiled. "Don't worry, we suspected this was an instinctive act and not a conscious one, that you hit out only when under extreme threat and wouldn't be able to reproduce the act at will, so we've made arrangements."

He looked across to the Thaistess. She raised finger cymbals and chimed them, an act which reminded Tom of Mildra, which again brought Kat to the forefront of his thoughts and emphasised her absence anew.

An acolyte walked in, bearing a glass tank in which sat one of the Maker's abominations, this one with limbs that resembled the jointed legs of a crab. The glass must have been reinforced in some way, because the thing kept striking against it with sharp claws, blows which brought no discernable effect.

Tom recoiled instinctively, even though he knew the thing was trapped.

"That's it, Tom," the prime master said. "I felt the stirrings of something then, but it has to be stronger."

His encouragement spurred Tom on and he strained for all he was worth, trying to recall exactly what he had done, how it felt when he lashed out as the things attacked Kat, but nothing happened.

The acolyte placed the glass tank down on the divan beside him, and the device's claws punched at the glass, seeming to come straight towards him until the sharp rap as they struck the sides of the container signalled their failure. He redoubled his efforts and again felt a stirring, but nothing more.

"Tom," the prime master said, "I can help with this. I can enable you to bring your power out, but it will mean an invasion of your privacy, of your mind, something I would never contemplate under normal circumstances. Would you allow me to reach into your head, to draw out the potential we need to save the City Below?"

Tom was taken aback. Someone reaching into his head? "Will it hurt?"

"My touch? No. But channelling the power may well do, as it did before, though I should be able to help shield you from some of that as well. The Thaistess will be here to ease your pain afterwards."

Again the woman smiled and Tom decided that he may have misjudged her.

He drew in a ragged breath, not at all certain about this, but even so, he nodded. "All right then."

The prime master didn't touch him, just seemed to stare towards him, and Tom felt nothing to indicate any intrusion or invasion as he'd feared. This time though, when the caged creature hammered against the glass, his reaction didn't stop at a simple stirring. It started that way but grew into a stream, a rush, an out-pouring. If the prime master was able to help deflect some of the pain, it didn't show. Again, Tom's skull felt as if it were ripping apart, and without any way of knowing whether or not his effort had been worthwhile, he crashed into blissful oblivion.

• • •

Despite being fascinated by this enigmatic and feisty girl, Dewar was, in truth, a little relieved when they went their separate ways. She made a prickly travelling companion at best. Their return to the dog master's lair was far swifter and more direct than Dewar's route from it. They loped through streets that had gone ominously silent, as if the tide of street-nick violence had swept through here already and left only emptiness in its wake.

Dewar found himself distracted by trying to guess Kat's age. The Pits had been closed for more than three years now, but that was little help, since he had no idea how old she was when she had fought there. In her teens, certainly, but whereabouts in her teens? He could always have asked, he supposed, before she disappeared towards the end of their journey, but he was reluctant to do so, both because he doubted the girl would have deigned to answer and because he didn't want her to think he was that interested.

He slowed as the streets became more familiar and he knew his goal was just a few turns away. The dog master must be aware that he was coming, so where were his creatures, the false hounds which were the man's trademark? As yet there had been no sign of them.

Dewar had always possessed excellent peripheral vision. The trick was to be aware at all times, to not get sucked into concentrating so intently on whatever demanded your attention – whatever was directly in front of you – that you ignored the small flutterings of movement which barely registered at the perimeter of vision. This was a skill he had taught himself through necessity, and it was one that proved of worth once more, when he rounded the corner to find himself confronted by two of the biggest false-hounds he had yet seen.

The two beasts started forward as soon as he came in sight, ears back, heads down and teeth bared. One looked to be almost entirely built of metal, with just the lower jaw bearing any visible fur. Each fall of its steel-forged claws resounded against the ground. The other, larger still than the first, was more wolf than any dog Dewar could think of, though this one too had its fair share of metal, notably around the chest and neck, while a steel frame supported the lower jaw. In addition, it sported a ridge of curved steel spikes running down the length of its spine. After a few leisurely steps the pair broke into a run, charging straight towards the assassin.

He readied himself, sword in one hand, kairuken in the other, focused and confident. It was just a hint of movement, easy to miss with two lethal constructs bearing down on you, which alerted him. It came from the opposite direction to the two attacking hounds and it was silent and low. A long, sinuous creature, more snake than hound, had attempted to creep up on him, its segmented body barely held off the ground by four stubby legs. Instinctively, Dewar leapt high, pulling his knees up to his chest in the process.

Teeth snapped shut where his ankles had been. As Dewar came down from his leap, he stamped hard, landing a foot on the device's neck, just behind the head. The body started to writhe, as if the hound was attempting to loop it around the restraining foot, but Dewar's other leg, the left, was already swinging forward. At the last instant, he rocked back on his right heel, freeing the dog just as his left foot connected, kicking the snake-dog into the air and sending it sailing towards the nearest of the oncoming brutes, the wolf.

The charging hound flicked its head up as if irritated by such a distraction. In doing so, it knocked the smaller hound further backward, to be impaled on its ridge of razor-like spikes. In doing this the wolf exposed its throat and Dewar unleashed the kairuken, far closer than he'd intended. Sparks flew all around as the snake-dog thrashed and died and the kairuken's disc ripped the larger beast's throat open, chewing circuits and cutting into internal mechanisms. The wolf collapsed, its front legs giving way first so that it nosedived into the ground. But the other dog was upon Dewar before he could bring his short sword to bear. It leapt, jaws open and aiming for his throat. Dropping the kairuken, he thrust his left wrist into the gaping maw. The thick metal guard he wore there was intended to deflect blades but would serve equally well to stop the bite of an ordinary dog. Unfortunately, this was no ordinary dog. The pressure on the guard and on his arm beneath was enormous and he could feel the metal start to distort, to buckle. At the same time, Dewar tried to arch his body to keep it away from those flailing claws as they inevitably came back to the ground, but he met with only limited success. One paw's worth of razors sliced through his trousers and into his leg.

The pain was abrupt and intense, but he knew how to cope with pain. Blocking it from his mind, he concentrated on bringing up his sword and applying it to the one apparent weak spot in this brute. He thrust the blade along the line of its jaw and into the construct's throat, pushing with all his strength. Still the unrelenting pressure continued and he was afraid the guard would buckle entirely, leaving his wrist to be crushed like some dry twig. He twisted the blade, working the tip deeper into the wound, and enlarging the area it could damage inside the thing's throat. Smoke started to rise from the dog's nostrils, so clearly his efforts were having some effect, but was it enough?

He gritted his teeth and leaned on the hilt of his sword, pushing it further home. The smoke increased and the dog started to convulse and twitch. Abruptly, it stopped; all movement ceasing as if somebody had flicked a switch. To all intents and purposes, the construct appeared dead, but it hadn't released the vice-like grip on his wrist. The inanimate body dragged his arm downward. Gingerly, Dewar withdrew his blade from its innards. There appeared to be fresh blood on it, and he wondered again what dark arts the dog master used to animate these hybrid creatures.

He eased the blade into the construct's mouth and twisted, to slowly prise the jaws apart. The pressure eased bit by bit, until he was finally able to pull his wrist free.

He reclaimed the discarded kairuken, reloaded and holstered it. Ideally, he would have liked to bind his injured leg as well, but the only things available to serve as bandages were his own clothes, and they were so filthy that tearing strips off of them would be just asking for an infection, so he let it be and walked on, limping slightly as the pain bit home.

A hound sprinted from a side alley, too quick to be stopped with the kairuken, so he used the sword. The encounter left him with a gashed arm to add to the bleeding leg. He did, however, have time to bring the weapon to bear and shoot down a small wall-climbing construct similar to the one which accompanied him to the Maker's lair. Another disc lost, leaving him with just three. He reloaded and continued.

Two more hounds charged towards him as he actually reached his destination. They approached in the strange, slightly disjointed fashion of these hybrid creatures – mimicking the gait of a true dog but not with total accuracy. Rather than fire and risk losing another disc, he sprinted for the door, praying that his leg would hold and taking the steps three at a time before pushing his way inside.

He wedged the door shut against the hounds' scrabbling claws, using items hastily grabbed from the heap of discarded junk which the dog master seemed to delight in keeping. No point in trying to be quiet or mask his presence; the man knew he was here. Despite his injured leg and gashed arm, this all seemed a little too easy. He had anticipated having to wade through an army of crazed dog-machine hybrids rather than simply fighting a few skirmishes. Surely the dog master had enough warning to summon greater protection than this. He added more pieces of metal and wood to his brace, recalling how the door split into two sections and therefore ensuring that both were obstructed.

The place was as oppressively hot as he remembered, and the draping tubes and pipes just as numerous and ludicrous. Were they a symptom of general sloppiness or simply an affectation? He suspected the latter. A loud thump came from behind him, a sound which reverberated, presumably as one of the hounds threw its weight against the door, but his makeshift brace held.

Ducking beneath trailing pipes, he made his way deeper into the room, treading warily even though he knew the dog master was alert to his presence. He was sweating – a reaction to coming into such a hot environment after his exertions – but his breathing was steady and the grip on his weapons sure.

It was unsettling, the lack of any challenge and he felt certain this had to be a trap. Nonetheless, he could see little choice but to keep going. The dog master sat at his workstation, back to Dewar, peering at his screens. The assassin did not hesitate, but raised his kairuken. Only to have something smash painfully into his hand and send the weapon spinning away before he could fire. He tried to raise his short sword but the object that had struck him, which seemed a solid ball of metal, was unfurling and wrapping itself around him. He looked to his left, to see the misshapen, wide-mouthed face of a dog hidden among all the discarded bric-a-brac, like some beast camouflaged in the undergrowth. The device had its mouth gaping open and from it stretched a long, flexible metal tongue, which was what had cannoned into his hand and now held him trapped, both arms pinned to his side.

The dog master spun around in his chair, laughing heartily. "Dewar!" he exclaimed. "How delightful to see you again. I knew that if I offered you a blatant opportunity you couldn't resist. You see, that's your problem, old friend. You might be devious, skilled and resourceful, but strip all that away and beneath lies the intellect of a lobotomised gnat."

The assassin tested his bonds, attempting to stretch his arms and pull them tighter to his body, to create the space to slip one free. But the effort was in vain.

The steel band tightened instantly to compensate, so that when he relaxed it cut painfully into his arms. "You set me up!"

"Of course. You shouldn't have kicked my pet."

Since he had just done a great deal more than simply kick one of the constructs, dismembering half a dozen of them, he wondered what this madman had in store for him now.

"It struck me as fitting to send you off on a pointless errand and then see you killed at the very instant of realisation, but I knew if that failed you'd come straight back to me; and here you are, caught like a fly in a spider's web." The dog master giggled, then sprang to his feet and stalked over to peer into Dewar's face at close quarters.

"It seems my little street-nicks might have failed. The Blade, you see." Dewar absorbed that: the Blade? "Who would have thought our lords and masters still take enough notice of what goes on down here to react so quickly, to commit the Blade once more? But no matter, order will be restored, the villain found dead, though sadly not with the body of a notorious assassin conveniently on hand, and I can continue on my merry way."

Dewar had to keep the dog master talking, had to make sure the man didn't glance back at his screens. "You think so? Even after they find the mangled remains of one of your little pets by the body?"

"Already removed. There's nothing to connect me to the awful events of recent days."

One of the screens showed somebody moving stealthily up behind the oblivious dog master. The view was from the device holding him, Dewar realised. The creature gave a bass grumble, presumably as much warning as it could manage without letting its captor go.

"What is it, my pet?" the dog master asked.

The dark figure moved swiftly but stealthily, while Dewar concentrated on keeping his eyes fixed unerringly on his captor, making sure he didn't focus beyond the man's shoulder even for an instant.

The rumbling growl came again, and this time the dog master looked set to turn around, but too late, the girl was upon him, clasping him from behind, a knife to his neck.

"This is for Rayul, you crazy brecker." Kat pressed the sharp edge of her blade home, drawing it swiftly and viciously across to open up the madman's throat.

Blood fountained as she pushed the corpse away from her. Now Dewar moved, turning swiftly so that more of the false-hound's tongue wrapped around him, which brought him closer to the squat, ugly beast. He then kicked it, aiming for the eye but narrowly missing. The thing started to retract its tongue, which gave the assassin enough leeway to free his sword arm. He instantly hacked at the length of steel band stretching between his body and the construct's mouth, the keen edge of his blade severing it, allowing him to shrug off the remaining bonds.

The hound instantly turned around and disappeared into the mass of junk and wires and cables behind it. Dewar saw no sense in pursuit, instead turning to the girl, who was busy wiping her blade clean of blood on the dead man's clothing.

"Nicely done," he said.

She looked up. "There's nothing nice about any of this. You were right though," the girl added. "I took to the roofs and he never saw me coming."

At Dewar's suggestion, Kat had approached separately, though the roofs had been her own embellishment. "Good," he said. "He was expecting me, and, seeing what he expected, didn't look any further."

"Lucky for you, seeing as how you got yourself all tied up."

"That was the general plan. It's called diversion."

"If you say so." She straightened, sheathed her sword and pushed past him.

"Where are you off to?"

"Anywhere that's cooler than this breckin' place."

The assassin looked around, recovered his kairuken, and followed her. The scrabbling at the door had stopped, he noted. Did that indicate the hounds outside somehow knew their master was dead, or...?

With Kat still several paces away from it, the door exploded – shards and splinters flying everywhere. Towering black shapes stepped swiftly through the resultant entranceway, stooping in order to do so.

"Oh, Thaiss!" Kat exclaimed. "Not again."

Consciousness brought with it a wonderful sense of well-being, though this evaporated almost immediately, as Tom opened his eyes. The Thaistess' face looming large brought everything back with a jolt.

She stepped back, allowing him to sit up. The prime master and Ty-gen were close at hand, the former smiling broadly.

"Did it work?"

"Yes, Tom, it worked. Spectacularly so. The Maker's devices have keeled over all across the City Below and the street-nicks have stopped rioting. Most of them at any rate; a few seem to have acquired a bit of a taste for it, but the guards can deal with them.

"Thank you, Tom, for all you've done."

He just shook his head, still feeling a fraud, that all this attention was undeserved.

Ty-gen came over and thanked him as well, which made him feel even more awkward.

Ty-gen then said, "Goodbye, Tom. I must go."

So soon? "If you see Kat…" Tom said, and then stopped, wondering what he could possibly ask the Jeradine to say for him.

"I'll remember you to her," Ty-gen assured him.

He nodded, realising that, inadequate though this might be, it was as much as he could hope for.

SEVENTEEN

Magnus was not worried, not yet. He knew that the process of elevation from the assembly to the council was a ponderous affair with no set timetable as such. It was just that he would have expected to have heard something by now. The preliminaries had been correctly adhered to: his formal nomination by the assembly, which he had accepted with suitable modesty, but that had all been more than a week ago. The next step had to come from the Masters, who were expected to formally ratify the assembly's recommendation and acknowledge him as official candidate. Once they had done so, he would be summoned for an initial interview to assess his suitability, with all the Masters in attendance, even the near-senile Crispus, whose imminent retirement left open the vacancy which Magnus was destined to fill.

So the ball was now firmly in the council's court. Of course, in theory they could refuse to accept his nomination and insist the assembly put forward an alternative candidate, but that had never happened, at least not in the past few hundred years. The only recorded instance of such a decision had become a dark and infamous period in the city's history. It had resulted in a schism within the assembly and even between the assembly and the Council of Masters, a situation which came perilously close to civil war.

That it could ever happen again was unthinkable. However, the longer the current silence continued, the more anxious Magnus became and the more likely people were to wonder. In truth, while the current delay was irritating it was hardly unprecedented, but if this were to go on much longer, whispered doubts would inevitably surface among his fellow assembly members. Magnus had already overheard one remark in the commons recalling that Crispus himself had been accepted by the council the day after he was nominated, though he was unable to identify who made the comment.

As a particularly tedious session of mundane business drew to a close, Magnus found that he could not even remember the subject discussed during the previous hour.

He recalled listening to an interminable dispute between two delegations of bakers, one claiming restriction of trade by the larger, more influential faction, and before that an agreement to send a group of arkademics to help with the repair of a section of wall damaged by a lightning strike during a recent severe storm, but after that: nothing. He had spent a fair while admiring the room's vaulted ceiling – the assembly hall extended for a whole four Rows – with its network of chiselled, inter-linking supports which resembled long bones and gave the impression that the entire place was situated in the belly of some skeletal leviathan. More time frittered away as he gazed out of the long, arched windows, making shapes from scudding clouds – the hall was built against the city's outer wall so benefited from natural light. Yet his mind kept returning to the Masters' silence, the prime master's cunning and the boy who had witnessed his guilt. What had a street-nick been doing in the Heights in the first place? Had he been placed there deliberately to spy on Magnus? If so, it seemed a strange choice; a street-nick in the Residences was hardly inconspicuous. And then there was the matter of the lad's successful resistance to his will. Perhaps, if he were the agent of another, an arkademic or a Master, that might explain how the lad defied him, but no; it hadn't felt like outside interference. The nick had broken free by his own efforts, Magnus was sure of it.

Dewar should have returned by now. The task was a simple one after all.

Something was wrong; he could feel it in his gut and had learned to trust such instincts. It was nothing specific, no clear signal that events had turned against him, yet somewhere in his head an alarm was ringing. The prime master was the consummate political animal, renowned as such, and Magnus knew that he had been deftly outmanoeuvred. With a smile and impeccable logic, the man had placed an agent inside his home and an armed guard upon his person, and all Magnus had been able to do was thank him for these restrictions each time. Intolerable. At least the guards were barred from the assembly hall itself and so stood vigil outside the door, awaiting his departure.

The final petitioner left, marking a welcome end to

this week's open session. Another day over and still no word from the council.

Just as the convener's gavel sounded three times, officially closing the day's business, the doors to the assembly hall burst open. A pair of council guards marched in. At first, absurdly, Magnus thought they must be two guards assigned to him, but behind the first pair came two more and after them, yet more. Twin columns of white and purple caped guards filed into the hall, splitting as they entered, one line turning left and the other right, so that they swiftly lined the back wall.

At first, a stunned silence fell over the assembly, but it lasted for only a few heartbeats. Some members remained in their seats even then, clearly shocked by such an intrusion, but an increasing majority leapt to their feet, demanding explanation and voicing their protest.

The presence of council guards in the commons had been highly irregular; for them to be here, in the assembly hall itself, was unprecedented. The place was in uproar. It seemed as if everyone was attempting to speak at once and above it all, the convener's gavel beat out a sombre rhythm as the man called ineffectually for order.

And still the guards marched in.

Nobody noticed a side door partially open and a single assembly member slip out. At least, Magnus hoped that nobody had seen him. There was nothing to suggest that the guards were there for him but coincidence was a fickle ally, and he somehow doubted that any of his colleagues would have done anything to merit such attention.

Only a fool failed to allow for disaster and Magnus was no fool. He had contingencies in place and, provided he acted swiftly enough, was confident that he could escape from the city altogether before anyone could stop him. Not an ideal end to his ambitions, but better this than a prison cell.

Then, as he hurried down deserted corridors, he sensed a presence ahead. Somebody was there, not yet in sight. Were they waiting for him, was this some sort of ambush? But no, there was just the one person and besides, how could anyone have known he would come this way?

Magnus prepared himself in any case, focusing his mind, marshalling lethal energies ready to do his bidding. He knew his capabilities and felt confident he could deal with whoever it might be in the unlikely event that the lurker ahead was anything to do with him. At his approach, the figure stepped out; a tall, athletically-built man who effectively blocked his path. Magnus slowed, trying to see the face, which was still in shadow. Despite this, there was something disturbingly familiar about the man, his body shape and posture.

Finally, just as recognition dawned, a familiar voice said, "Hello, Magnus."

"You!" Unable to believe his eyes, the arkademic could only stand and stare at the very last person he expected to see, and one of the few who knew him well enough to know what escape route he might choose.

Tom wondered where the prime master was taking him. After Ty-gen left, the man explained that it was time for them to depart as well, that there was something he wished to show him. This came as a surprise to Tom, who had imagined he would simply be allowed to go his own way again now that he'd done his bit, but the prime master clearly had other plans.

Tom couldn't even begin to understand how they left the temple. He walked with the prime master, listening to the man talk, and suddenly they were somewhere else. Somewhere warmer and darker, where the very air smelt different. Yet the prime master said nothing, just continued speaking in the same casual manner.

Tom had assumed they would be heading for the Heights, where the Masters lived, which were said to be the most beautiful and elegant Rows in all Thaiburley. But if so, the place was a disappointment – oppressively dark and dingy, not bright and airy as he'd imagined. In fact, this put him in mind of...

"Well, if it isn't our flying street-nick!" boomed a familiar voice.

"Red!" The big man loomed out of the shadows, a huge grin on his face. So he was back in the Swarbs' Row as he'd almost begun to suspect.

"Didn't expect to see you back 'ere so soon, little un."

That made two of them. Tom found himself smiling at the sight of someone whose generosity had made him an instant friend. He didn't even mind being called "little un", not by Red; after all, compared to him he was.

Tom's pleasure at seeing Red was tempered by a growing suspicion. He glanced from the swarb to the prime master, wondering at the connection between the two.

Not for the first time, Tom had reason to suspect that the prime master could read minds, as the older man said, "I have agents throughout the city, Tom. I have to, in order to know what people are saying and feeling, whether they're being treated properly or have fallen foul of some bureaucratic misfortune. Ty-gen is one such and Red here is another. But I didn't bring you here just to renew acquaintances. There's somebody I'd very much like you to meet."

A second figure stepped from the shadows behind Red, and all the boy could do was gape.

"Tom, of the Blue Claw, may I introduce you to Senior Arkademic Thomas, of the City Assembly."

"But… it can't be. I saw you…" He found himself unable to say the actual words, but the newcomer said them for him.

"Knifed, killed, pushed from the city's walls?"

Tom's mind was already filling in the gaps. "The Swarbs caught you, didn't they, just like they did me."

"Yes," and Tom realised what a winning smile this young arkademic had.

"And a sorry state he was in too," Red added. "Blood all over his front; didn't even think he was alive at first, but then we found the slightest tremor of a pulse and I called his primeness 'ere straight away."

"I came immediately but even then feared that I was too late," the prime master continued. "I'm no healer, but I was able to trickle a little energy into Thomas's system – not too much, I didn't want to overwhelm that tiny flicker of life, but I hoped it would be enough to sustain, to enable him to hang on until the experts arrived. Apparently it was, but even with the combined efforts of three of the city's finest healers, it was touch and go for a while."

The old man sighed. "I apologise, Tom, for all that I've put you through. At first it was in the hope of flushing Magnus out. I knew the man was a snake and his promotion to the rank of Master would be disastrous for the city, but without proof I couldn't block it, not without causing turmoil. We weren't certain Thomas would survive to bear witness, so I had to leave you vulnerable. When Magnus slipped his man Dewar into the City Below, I knew the plan was working, but then we lost you in all the confusion caused by the Maker. By the time we found you again, at the temple of Thaiss, it was becoming apparent just how big a threat the Maker was, and you seemed to be a focus for him as well."

"So you used me again."

"Yes. I'm sorry. I had no choice."

Tom could see what the prime master meant but still felt disappointed, victimised, as if he simply didn't matter to any of them.

"Until I regained consciousness," Thomas said gently, "you really were the only hope. I'm sorry for what you've been through as a result."

Tom nodded, still not happy at what he was hearing but keeping his resentment to himself.

"I only came round a couple of hours ago," the arkademic then added.

Tom stared at him in amazement. "What? But you look so healthy…"

He smiled again. "Blame the healers for that. Their talent truly is remarkable."

"Indeed," the prime master agreed. "I only wish we had more of them. Now, if you'll excuse us, Thomas and I must pay a visit to a certain senior arkademic and the assembly will be finishing for the day soon. Tom, may I leave you in Red's capable hands for a while?"

"Sure." The request struck Tom as ironic. He only wished that the prime master had asked his permission about some of the other situations he had left him in.

Before they left, Thomas took him to one side and said, "Don't be too harsh on the prime master, Tom, or on any of us. He's a good man, but he has the welfare of the whole city to think of, and that sometimes requires difficult choices."

"I understand," Tom replied, and found that, deep down, he did.

Magnus stared at the figure confronting him, at a loss for words. Finally he spluttered a disbelieving, "Thomas?"

But it couldn't be. He knew beyond any doubt that his former protégé was dead, had felt the life drain out of him before pushing him off the wall. This had to be a trick, some device of the prime master's to catch him off his guard.

They wouldn't catch him out that easily. He feigned a delighted smile and stepped towards him. "Thomas, how wonderful. They said you were dead."

The other arkademic took a step back and help out a warning hand. "No closer, Magnus, not after last time."

Thomas's outstretched hand crackled with silver blue energy. Despite all reason pointing to the contrary, Magnus felt increasingly certain that this was indeed

Thomas returned from the dead. "How? It's not possible."

"I know," the other assured him, "I can hardly believe it myself, but here we are." Thomas's mouth smiled but the gesture did not reach as high as his eyes, which burned with anger.

Magnus was not about to be thwarted, not now and certainly not by Thomas. He had no intention of facing a trial and submitting to justice. No knives were allowed within the assembly hall but he was a senior arkademic; he didn't need one. He struck without warning, thrusting his hand forward to release a bolt of searing energy.

Nothing happened.

He stood there for a second with fingers splayed, then stared at his palm, uncomprehending.

"The prime master has slapped a negation field on you," Thomas said casually, as if it were the most natural thing in the world. "Which, of course, leaves you unable to draw on your power. I, on the other hand," again the blue-tinged fire danced within a cupped palm, "am not so handicapped."

Thomas raised his hand. The blue energy it held intensified until it was almost blinding and suddenly Magnus realised that he would indeed avoid a trial, because a very direct brand of justice was about to be meted out here and now. In Thomas's situation, he would have done exactly the same.

"No, Thomas, please." It couldn't end like this, not after all he had achieved. "For the sake of the friendship we once shared, I'm begging you…"

"Enough, Magnus – I've heard enough! What mercy did you show me? What mercy have you ever shown anyone?" The blue fire continued to swell until it became all-consuming and the older man knew the ball of energy was about to be cast and that it would obliterate him. He cringed away, screwing his eyes tight against the glare and holding up his arms as ineffectual wards.

"You wouldn't, Thomas, not you, surely," he whimpered, all thought of dignity fled.

There was a pause and then a voice said, right by his ear, "No, you're right, Magnus, I wouldn't, and therein lies the difference between us."

Magnus risked opening his eyes. The fire was gone. Through a veil of azure stars he watched Thomas straighten up, turn his back and stride away. He walked across to join a group of figures who now stood blocking the corridor. Magnus recognised among them the white with purple trim of the council guard.

"Ah, Thomas, renewing acquaintances with an old friend, I see," said the foremost of the party.

"Yes, prime master; it seemed only fair."

"You can straighten up now, Magnus," the prime master said. "No one's going to hurt you. Are they, Thomas?"

"Indeed not, prime master, certainly not until after the trial at any rate; though I fear you might need to ask the assembly to nominate a new candidate for ascension." He smiled at Magnus, and this time the expression conveyed real mirth, even in his eyes.

Thankfully, the Blade were not the Kite Guard or even the Watch. They weren't concerned with the niceties of legal requirements and not exactly famous for their form-filling and meticulous adherence to rules and procedures. Once they were given a job they did it, in as effective and straightforward a manner as possible.

Clearly the group who burst in on Dewar and Kat had been sent specifically to deal with the dog master. This fact alone indicated that somebody with a little intelligence was on the case and had made the connection between the devices and the mad canine tinkerer. Once the Blade ascertained that the dog master was dead, they had no use for either him or Kat, so simply let them go.

Kat disappeared almost immediately, which struck the assassin as a very wise course of action. There was a deal of confusion in the wake of all that had happened, enough to keep everybody occupied in different ways. Nobody had the time to notice him as yet, or so he hoped, but Dewar was under no illusions; he knew that this wouldn't last. If somebody of perception was overseeing things down here, the assassin's roll in events would soon be discovered and that would lead to all sorts of awkward questions. He could have risked returning to Magnus but thought better of it. There was a pervading sense that things were starting to unravel and his going back to the Heights would leave a trail straight to the senior arkademic, which the man would hardly thank him for, even if he wasn't yet under suspicion himself. The Blade had been unleashed for goodness sake, what else might be going on in the city? He was not about to wait around until his collar was felt by the suddenly formidable hand of the law. It was true that for once he had fought on the side of the authorities and he could always hope that recent actions might count in his favour if it came to it, but they were unlikely to save him when held against the catalogue of less savoury acts he had performed for Magnus over the years, should those ever come to light.

Thaiburley was Dewar's home and he had no intention of abandoning it, but at the same time knew it was time to disappear. He decided to slip away before anyone realised, to lie low in one of the nearby towns and then, a few months from now, when everything had calmed down, he would ghost back into the city.

Many years ago a foreigner calling himself Dewar arrived in the City Below knowing little about this strange place, and he had built a life here. What he did once, he could do again. Armed with all that he now knew about the under-City, starting over should be comparatively easy. And who knew what the future might bring?

The stairwells were bound to be guarded, which meant his best route out was via the river. He made for the docks, already rehearsing in his head the way in which he would wheedle his way aboard whichever vessel was due to leave soonest. Of course, the script would need to be adjusted according to circumstances; a degree of improvisation was inevitable, but it never hurt to be prepared and a plausible back-story was essential though, at the end of the day, the contents of the heavy purse he carried with him was likely to prove the most persuasive factor in his escape.

"Dewar, isn't it – Senior Arkademic Magnus's man? Fancy meeting you here; are you going somewhere?" The words were spoken calmly, softly, yet they carried across the street with sufficient force to interrupt his train of thought and tear his plans to shreds.

He looked up to see a casually dressed elderly man sitting at a low table outside a tavern, the Twisted Fish. He recognised the name of the place and realised this was the same tavern where a certain bargeman had sipped his last ale the previous evening. He also recognised the speaker, though not his casual attire.

In all honesty, he was more than a little surprised that the man knew who he was. Their previous meetings had been infrequent and he had always been careful to stay in the background, somewhere behind Magnus. "Prime master, is that truly you? What a pleasant surprise." Half of which was true at any rate.

What in Thaiss's name was the man doing here? The City Below was in turmoil and goodness knew what was going on elsewhere, yet here was the most powerful man in all Thaiburley dressed like a pauper and drinking ale outside a lowly tavern. A tavern which just happened to lie in Dewar's path.

"Come, join me." The prime master gestured towards a seat.

How could he possibly refuse such an invite? "I'd be honoured."

The old man chuckled jovially. "I often wander around the City Below incognito, you know. Wonderful way to get a taste of what life's like down here. It's one of the benefits of Thaiburley being so vast, of course; hardly anybody actually knows what I look like, especially here, so far removed from the Heights."

Was the man trying to convince him that this meeting was pure chance? Did he honestly think so little of him? In fact, now that he had recovered from the shock of stumbling across Thaiburley's premier in such humble circumstances, he began to wonder whether the man was here at all. Dewar had seen first-hand what a senior arkademic could do, how much more was a master capable of? It struck him as increasingly likely that this was no more than an image, a conjuring of some sort, intended to delay him until someone more solid could catch up and arrest him.

If this was no more than an insubstantial likeness, there was nothing to prevent him getting up and walking away. And if this was not a projection but the man himself, was he, for all his vaunted abilities, faster than an expertly cast blade? Perhaps now was the time to find out.

Presumably, the prime master was an expert at reading body language, or perhaps even minds, because he said just then, "I do hope you're not going to make this awkward by attempting to leave when I'm so looking forward to our having a little chat."

The smile was as benign as ever, but the sideways glance caused Dewar to look in the same direction, towards where two towering black forms now stood. Dewar's blood ran cold. The Blade. He might take a chance on the prime master being unreal, but he was not about to risk taking any liberties with this pair of demons in human form.

"No need to worry," he assured the other man. "I'm not going anywhere."

"Good!" The prime master smiled anew. "I'm so glad. Now that we're both settled, I was hoping you might help me with a question, a dilemma really, that's troubling me. Specifically, what in the world am I going to do with you, Dewar?"

The assassin could have made one or two suggestions, but he suspected the question was largely rhetorical and, besides, he very much doubted his own ideas would match the prime master's, so chose to stay quiet.

"For years you've been Magnus's right-hand man, doing all the dirty, nasty things behind the scenes which have assisted his rise to power," the prime master said, which confirmed that Dewar's instinctive decision not to return to the Heights had been the right one, if nothing else. "And before that, I understand you were down here, killing and torturing citizens for money and perhaps for pleasure too. All this, and you're not even a native of Thaiburley, but an outsider who has latched onto the city's darker side like a leech and has been busily sucking out a living ever since. By rights I should lock you up and throw away the key. And yet…" Here the man paused and shook his head, still watching Dewar. "And yet in the past few days you have been instrumental in events that have helped to save the City Below from looming disaster; things which were entirely outside the remit that brought you here but you chose to do anyway. A cynic might even be tempted to wonder whether you saw which way the wind was blowing before anybody else and did these things in a last-ditch attempt to redeem yourself. But I don't see how that's possible. After all, when you left the Heights, your employer's star still appeared to be in the ascendant. Which suggests, unlikely though it may seem, that you actually chose to do the right thing when it mattered most."

Dewar listened intently, remaining silent even when the prime master paused, sensing that a wrong word now could do his cause irreparable harm. Besides, the old man had already stated his case for him.

"Some punishment does seem to be in order, of course, but what? You can't stay here in Thaiburley, not as a free man. I could never allow somebody of your talents and evident predilections to remain at liberty in the city, not unless you were actually working for me so that I could keep a close eye on you." Dewar came immediately alert. Was that an offer? "Unfortunately, for you, I don't operate in the same way the senior arkademic has been doing, so would have no need of the type of services you provide."

Evidently not. Unless…

Dewar drew a slow, deep breath. Now was the time to speak, and he knew full well that what he said here might just prove to be the most important words of his life.

Tylus was shocked and horrified to learn of Magnus's downfall and what he was guilty of. The news left him more than a little concerned about his own position. After all, he was only here at all on the senior arkademic's authority. A summons to meet the prime master did little to settle his nerves; quite the contrary, he felt entirely intimidated by the prospect of an audience with the man, not certain whether to anticipate congratulation or castigation. He remembered the disbelief he had felt when summoned to see the now disgraced senior arkademic, and this was even worse despite his newfound confidence.

The chosen setting for the interview, in a temple of Thaiss, would have struck him as bizarre at any other time, but its strangeness slipped away almost unnoticed under the circumstances.

He had seen the prime master from a distance several times before, at ceremonies and events, and his likeness was known throughout the Heights, but this was the first time Tylus had actually met him. His first impression was that the man was older and shorter than memory painted him, but this was quickly overshadowed by the sense of kindness and warmth which the man projected.

A temple acolyte served them chilled fruit juice and they sat with no table between them and almost facing each other, though the chairs were off-centre and slightly angled, as if to emphasise the informality of the occasion.

"You seem to like it here in the City Below, Kite Guard," the prime master said.

The observation surprised Tylus. He thought about it and was forced to admit, "Yes, I suppose I do."

"Certainly you've performed admirably since being assigned here, albeit the assignment was not all it seemed."

"Thank you, sir." He didn't know what else to say.

"Tell me something – and I should add that this little chat is strictly off the record – you've had a taste of life on the streets now. Looking at the Kite Guard, with the benefit of your experience here, do you think that perhaps the guard has grown a bit complacent, even a little soft, over the years?"

Caught off guard again, Tylus blinked, wondering how best to reply. "I think, sir," he said carefully, "that much of the training we undergo is of the highest order and that, as a result, today's guard is well prepared in many respects, but…" He hesitated, uncertain how best to continue.

"But you think that as individuals, the guard might benefit from spending a little time down here, in the streets? Learning about the harshness that life can bring to those less fortunate than themselves," the prime master said.

"Well, yes, sir, I do." As he said it, he realised this was exactly what he thought.

"It just so happens that I agree with you, Tylus, which is why I intend to see a training facility for the guard established here, in the City Below. Each and every officer will be required to serve a term here, giving them a taste of life away from their pampered existence in the Heights. Of course, the new facility will have to be overseen by an officer of the guard who has experience of the streets, and I can only think of one who fits the bill." He looked pointedly at Tylus.

"Me, sir?"

The prime master grinned, as if delighted by his re-action. "Yes, you, sir, if you're willing to take on the job."

Was he? Did he really want to give up the comfortable life and comparative luxury of the Heights to live and work down here? A few days ago, the thought would have appalled him and he would have considered anyone who even contemplated such a choice to be mad. But then he thought about how alive he had felt since arriving here, and about how effective he had been as an officer, and that led to him recalling how unfulfilled and inadequate he had felt before coming down here.

"Well, officer?"

Tylus took a deep breath. "Yes, sir, I'll do it."

"Excellent!" The prime master smiled broadly. "That's settled then. Of course, we can't have such an important operation run by a simple unranked Kite Guard, so it would mean promoting you to the rank of, say, captain. Does that sound acceptable?"

Captain? Now it was Tylus's turn to smile. "Entirely acceptable, sir, and thank you."

The other shook his head. "No thanks necessary. You've earned it, Captain Tylus."

For some reason, Tylus's thoughts turned to Sergeant Goss and he couldn't help but wonder. "Tell me, sir, you say every officer – would that include sergeants?"

"Most certainly."

Tylus grinned broadly. The more he heard about this proposed new position, the more he liked the sound of it.

As he left the prime master's chamber, still in a bit of a daze, he was surprised to bump into Dewar. He had assumed that, as an employee of the senior arkademic, the man would have been in disgrace and more than likely arrested by now. Perhaps he was less guilty than Tylus gave him credit for.

"Dewar," he said a little guardedly.

"Kite Guard," the man acknowledged.

"Are you here to see the prime master?"

"Already seen him." Judging by the man's expression, that audience had not gone as well as Tylus's own. "It seems I am to be exiled."

"Ah." No wonder he looked fed up. Suddenly words seemed inadequate, at least any that Tylus could think of. "Well, good luck," he finally managed.

Dewar grunted and with that the pair went their separate ways.

Exiled? Not that Tylus was surprised, on reflection. Circumstances might have briefly thrown the two of them together but he had never particularly liked the fellow or fully trusted him; those eyes, they were far too knowing.

EIGHTEEN

Tom found the Swarbs to be a sociable and likeable crowd. Some of the men Red introduced him to recognised him at once and had obviously been part of the crowd gathered on the walls the night he dropped into their nets. He learned it was not only people they trawled from the skies, but all manner of things.

"You'd be amazed at some of the stuff them up-City chuck away," one man confided. "Beautiful things, and worth a pretty penny too, often as not."

Tom was having so much fun he was almost disappointed when the prime master eventually returned to collect him, apologising for being away so long. When Tom heard where the man intended to take him next, he demurred, explaining, "I'm not very good with heights." The walls at night time had terrified him; the thought of something similar in the fullness of daylight froze him to the spot.

The prime master looked surprised, as if the idea of such a thing had never occurred to him, though his next words proved otherwise. "I suppose it's to be expected, given your background." A warm smile then lit his face, wrinkling his cheeks like folds of soft leather. "Fortunately, there are ways around such things."

"How do you mean?" Tom was instantly suspicious. He had no intention of going anywhere near the outer skin of the city at a high altitude, no matter what safeguards were promised.

"In some cultures, deep-rooted phobias are overcome by hypnotism, wherein the sufferer is placed into a state of trance, relaxing them and bringing their subconscious to the fore, which is then highly suggestible and so more accepting of instructions that quell the relevant fear." Tom shivered; this sounded all too similar to the Maker's devices tampering with the street-nicks' minds. "Effective much of the time, but crude. Here in Thaiburley, we can be a little more direct." The prime master's smile now seemed conspiratorial. "May I?"

The request brought to mind the Thaistess, Mildra, who had asked for Tom's permission in exactly the same manner before healing him. Swallowing on a dry throat, Tom nodded. After all, he had already let this man into his mind once.

He braced himself in preparation for some form of mental invasion and in the expectation that the prime master would reach towards him, perhaps place fingertips to his head, yet he didn't touch him, didn't move at all, and all Tom felt was the faintest of caresses, like a soft breeze ruffling the edges of thought.

"There," said the prime master, "all done."

Tom blinked. "Really? I hardly felt a thing."

"I should hope not," the old man said, feigning offence. He then sighed. "I only wish that all the city's ills could be cured so easily. If we had a hundred times as many arkademics, healers and Thaistesses, then maybe, but we don't, so must make do with what we have." He looked across at Tom and the infectious smile returned. "Are you ready now?"

"Yes," Tom replied and to his amazement discovered that he was.

"So this is it," he murmured. It would have felt wrong to speak loudly in such a place.

"Yes, Tom, this is the Upper Heights, the roof of the world, or of the city at any rate. Magnificent, isn't it?"

Magnificent was the right word, beyond any doubt. Around him rose a forest of turrets and spires and columns, some pointed, some sculpted, some oddly crenulated. All were carved from the faintly yellowish stone of the city, although many were discoloured with the passage of time, black sooty marks and other whiter deposits producing a mottled effect which enhanced rather than diminished the scene's appeal. Several were of uniform height and design, but even more were not. There appeared to be no overall pattern or plan, no symmetry to the arrangement at all, and yet the effect was beautiful, majestic beyond anything Tom had ever imagined. He turned this way and that, taking it all in.

For long moments neither of them spoke. Simply looking was enough.

"I never dreamt..." he began at length, but the words trailed away. What had he imagined? Something flat and featureless? Something solid at any rate, but there was nothing like that here. Walls rose and fell. The city's very highest Rows, where the Masters lived and held court, must be comprised of individual buildings he realised, even as in the City Below. A town built on the roof of the city itself; no, growing out of it, he corrected himself, since each building must presumably be accessible from below.

"Few people ever do," the prime master said softly. "Who could? And yet one man did; the architect of these levels, a man called Carley. He's barely remembered now, but in his day he was hailed as a genius while privately thought a madman. And the truth doubtless lies somewhere in between, that he was a little of both. Certainly no ordinary mind could have envisaged all this."

Tom shivered and pulled the cloak closer about him. The awe-inspiring nature of his surroundings didn't alter the fact that it was colder here than he remembered from the walls.

"Yes, it can get a little chilly up here at times," the older man commented. "Just be grateful this isn't winter. Come, walk with me."

A broad promenade extended around the inside of the city's outer wall, which they began to slowly stroll around.

"It goes all the way around, this walkway. If we had the time and the inclination, we could set out from this point and arrive back here several hours from now. It's a walk I've always intended to make one day, but have never yet managed to." He chuckled. "It would appear that I have the inclination but not the time, and, as I say, it's an undertaking which requires both."

Wisps of smoke seemed to rise from a nearby column. This was an example of one of the commoner styles: three tall thin columns rising in parallel to meet a bracket or cuff which held them together at the top.

Seeing the smoke, Tom suddenly realised what they were – chimneys, which had been cleverly incorporated into the overall design

"A remarkable man, Carley," the prime master continued. "He managed to combine aesthetics and practicality to conjure up this. The whole idea, you see, is that from wherever you stand on this walkway and in whichever direction you look, you're rewarded with a stunning panorama; something that's both interesting and beautiful. Carley was an artist, with the whole of Thaiburley's roof as his canvas, and he gave us a masterpiece. While others scurried around beneath him, carving out a mountain and spreading outward from its face, he was up here, levelling and reshaping the summit with peaks and valleys of his own." The prime master accompanied the comment with an expansive sweep of his arm, taking in the roof of the city. "Not so much a roof, as a crown."

Tom thought he caught a flicker of movement by a nearby turret. He peered but couldn't see anything there. However, as he peered at that spot, a shimmer in the corner of his eye again suggested that something had just taken refuge behind another more distant column.

"They're teasing you," the prime master said quietly. "Try to ignore it, or you'll only encourage them."

Tom stared at him, his mouth suddenly dry. "The demons, you mean?"

"Indeed, or so they're commonly called."

Tom's curiosity stirred. "What do you call them then?"

The man laughed. "I was told you were sharp. What do I call them? Many things, most of them far from complimentary, but on the whole, I refer to them as avatars."

Tom had heard the word and associated it in his mind with some of the religious sects in the City Below, but he had no clear idea what it meant.

"This is more than just a city, Tom. In many senses Thaiburley is alive. There's a force lying at the very centre of things here, which, in effect, is the heart of city, a force which gives Thaiburley its identity and integrity. This force is what arkademics are trained to utilise and shape, what the healers of the City Below can tap into in a very minor way, and what you are able to call upon to a far greater degree, despite never having been trained in such arts."

"You mean when I hide?"

"Yes, that and other things, such as when you destroyed the dog master's creatures. The demons are directly linked to this force, its purest manifestation."

The demons continued to flicker at the edge of the boy's vision, tantalising with movement but little form. He had given up trying to turn towards them, realising that in doing so he was playing their game and would never be quick enough. Instead, even while listening to the prime master, a part of his mind concentrated on trying to see them in the corners of his eyes.

"This 'force' is alive then?"

"Ah, there you hit upon the crux of a debate that has been ongoing for centuries. My own suspicion is that it all hinges on how you define life, but the truth is, we don't know. Nobody is entirely certain what our ancestors harnessed at the core of our city. Perhaps through you, we might find out."

"Me? How?"

"Those who built Thaiburley could interact with the core far more readily than we can today. The minor practitioners you're familiar with – the naturals with no formal training such as seers and healers – are all distant descendants of the city's founders. The core recognises their heritage, the trace of founders' blood which flows through their veins, and allows them to access its power in a very limited way; though few if any realise this is what they do. By some fluke of bloodlines and parentage, the founders' blood flows stronger through your veins than in any individual seen in centuries. The core recognises that and so grants you far greater access. That is the source of your unique abilities, which, when you fully realise them, will be the match of any wielded by the senior arkademics and masters who have studied and toiled for years to perfect the art of core-manipulation."

Tom stared in horror at the prime master. Was the man serious? Apparently so, judging by his expression. The news caused a peculiar twisting inside him. He did not feel excited or even intrigued by any of this, but rather horrified. All he wanted was to be a street-nick, no different from any other; unimportant to anyone except himself and those who knew him. Yet he seemed to have become noticed by all manner of people of late. He felt suddenly chilled, and not just by the gusting wind.

"I know this is a shock, Tom, but there's nothing to be afraid of, I promise you."

Easy for him to say. Tom felt giddy, a sensation that recalled the dread when he first looked over the city's walls a few nights ago but which was also akin to the feeling that had washed over him as he escaped the scene of the sun globe's crash: that of being completely overwhelmed by events. Suddenly, he didn't think he could walk any further, and stumbled to a halt.

"Time to turn back?"

"Please."

And they did so, with Tom no longer paying attention to the view or to the mischievous flickering of demons. It was strange; after he started trying to see them in the corner of his eyes he had caught glimpses. Nothing certain, just insubstantial impressions, but he thought he had seen humans with golden hair and sweeping white feathered wings.

The demons looked like angels.

Even that subject, though, was pushed to the back of his mind. He had more pressing things to ponder. Whether he liked it or not, it seemed Tom was going to have to get used to the idea that his life had changed for good. Being a street-nick was far from an easy existence, but it was what he was used to and what he could cope with. How would he survive doing anything else?

Kat had slipped away from everything without challenge. The Blade weren't interested in her. It seemed she was an irrelevance to most people these days, though not, unfortunately, to the one person to whom she might wish to be.

Rayul's death still haunted her, though it was no longer the aching, burning pain which had driven her to seek out first the Maker and then the dog master. It had cooled to become a solid dark lump of grief deep inside her; a twisted blackness which tore at her sense of being whenever she stopped to consider it.

On her way here she had seen street-nicks looking cowed and a little bewildered, and reasoned that the devices no longer influenced them, perhaps due to her killing the dog master. So things were returning to normal, which meant that for everyone else life could go back to being as it had been. She'd guided Tom clean across the City Below in extraordinary circumstances and was proud of that. But now the boy could return to the Blue Claw a hero, and doubtless to his precious Jezmina. While Ty-gen could find someone else to fence his khybul sculptures easily enough. No one was going to miss her.

It was funny, but after all she had been through in recent days, Ty-gen's intricate sculpture of the city no longer seemed important. What could she have done with it in any case? Nothing, except sell it. There was no room in her nomadic existence for an object of such delicate beauty.

As for Tom, she had grown close to the boy, no denying it, closer than with anybody since she had left the Tattooed Men, but so what? When she first met him all she saw was a kid, a slightly timid little street-nick with something to prove to himself and the world, and it was true that as they travelled together that had changed. In a remarkably short time she had come to see him as a person she might trust and like. Not that she had room in her life for boys or romance or anything like that. Besides, even if she had liked him in that way he was too young for her; and he had this Jezmina girl waiting for him.

As she slipped into the vast and imposing building before her, now derelict and showing the fact after a remarkably short time, she did so with a sense that this would be the last place she ever saw.

Not that she wanted to die, not that she had any intention of allowing such a thing to happen. No, she was going to go down kicking and screaming and fighting with every iota of her being, but she had a feeling that death was coming to claim her anyway.

Her footfalls were silent and light, barely disturbing the dust that coated the floor of the corridor. Emerging into the space beyond, she paused at the lip, gathering herself in preparation for walking out into this theatre of ghosts. This place recalled the worst times of her life, and the best. The smell of blood, of sweat, of animal fat and oil smeared on limbs so as not to allow opponents a firm grip, and overlaying it all, the smell of fear. With memories accepted and acknowledged, she stepped warily into this place where life and death had been decided on so many occasions. It was empty now of all but those memories, but she had plenty of them to keep her company.

Here for one last performance, her body responded to the occasion and her steps grew more confident, until she strode into the arena as she had so many times before, never knowing who would walk out alive again and who would be left dead in the dust behind.

The same then even as it was now.

She was amazed at how familiar this all felt. Somehow she had expected it to be different, a faded echo of the place she remembered in her nightmares, a place that might still look familiar but which felt entirely otherwise; yet the sheer presence of this large domed building still pulled at every hurt and fear and insecurity that shadowed her dreams to this day, as well as awakening the savage joy of combat, the blood lust and the heady elation of victory and survival, those twin sisters of destiny.

As she walked, she peered beneath the mist of memory to see the sorry state of dilapidation. Many of the benches where the crowd used to sit were now broken or ripped out. The griddled iron gates which used to be pulled aside to release terrors upon the Pit Knights – the mocking title given to those who fought here, whether man, woman or child – lay discarded in the dust. Yet this was still the place where it all began, where she first faced and meted out death. The place she had vowed never to set foot in again.

"Welcome home, little sister. Welcome back to the Pits," said a familiar voice.

She looked across to her left, to where a single figure sat hunched on the lowest row of benches, all but lost in the vastness and the dimness, hidden beneath the weight of recollection.

"Hello, Chavver." She wasn't surprised. She knew that her sister would have appeared soon had she not been here already. Their rift had been a rent in her soul, there since she left the Tattooed Men, a hole in her being which she had tried to live with but never really had.

Knowing her sister, things would have been much the same for Chavver as well. This was a situation that needed resolving one way or another, and the choice of location dictated how.

Chavver had already uncoiled from her seat and now sauntered out into the centre to join her. She stopped half a dozen paces away and smiled.

"Ready?"

"Always."

Kat's twin swords, the only physical things she still carried from her time here, were in her hands in the blink of an eye; at exactly the same instant Chavver drew her own blade. In her other hand, Chavver carried a small throwing knife – always a favoured weapon.

The two girls started circling, both moving nimbly on dancers' feet, neither breaking eye contact for an instant. Kat could hear the ghosts of voices, the insubstantial roar of the crowd. She knew that if she were to close her eyes it would all come flooding back, as if she had never been away.

"Just like old times," Chavver said.

"Except that then we stood at each other's backs and the steel pointed outward, not inward as now."

"Times change," said the older girl; and as she did so, she struck, lunging forward as quickly as a serpent.

Kat jumped back out of reach, but knew that the dance of death had now begun in earnest.

He walked down the street without ceremony, without guards or any of the accoutrements of office. Just a small, aging, but still sprightly man. There was little chance anyone would recognise him in any case, since etiquette demanded of those around him that they should be oblivious to his presence. For the next few hours he was simply a man visiting an old friend.

He stopped at the door and knocked.

Ty-gen opened it and invited him inside, showing his readiness for company by producing a bowl of chilled qixlav. This clear bitter-sweet drink, beloved by the Jeradine, was something the man was partial to, if in small doses. He only ever drank it during his rare visits here and suspected that if it were on tap in the Heights, he would soon tire of the novelty.

"So, all has ended well," Ty-gen said, once they were both seated.

"Apparently so," the prime master conceded. "The streets are no longer haunted by hybrid abominations, the Blade have withdrawn once more, but their reappearance will have reminded the citizenry here that they are not forgotten about by those of us in the Heights, Tylus is embracing the idea of a Kite Guard training school in the under-City – which I think will benefit the Kite Guard, the local watch and the citizens in general – and the street-nicks are suitably cowed. I've a feeling that the merchants will enjoy a comparatively untroubled time for a while."

"And you say that the assembly have nominated Thomas as their candidate for the Council of Masters in place of Magnus?"

"Indeed, and his candidacy has been accepted without delay." The prime master smiled, clearly delighted by this development. "What of the girl, Kat, has there been any news?"

"No," Ty-gen replied, "neither word nor sign."

"Don't fret. The girl survived the Pits; she can handle herself. I'm sure she'll appear when she's good and ready."

"I hope so. I have a gift for her; a reward and an apology for all that I involved her in."

"It was necessary, old friend."

"Was it? Sometimes I wonder." The Jeradine abruptly changed the subject. "What of the boy, Tom?"

"Ah yes, what a fascination he is. He's currently learning to accept his abilities and his heritage, both in terms of the potential and the responsibility that comes with it. I have a strong feeling that this lad represents the future of all Thaiburley, one way or another."

"So everything is resolved. And yet still you seem troubled."

The prime master nodded, his expression thoughtful. "Perceptive as ever, old friend. We're overlooking something, Ty-gen. There's a missing piece to this puzzle which continues to elude us. Consider: did the dog master really create this parasite himself? It's a remarkably sophisticated creation if so. And who brought down the sun globe which caused so much damage and came so close to killing Kat and Tom as they slept? Certainly not the Maker or the dog master. And finally, who arranged with the Blue Claw to send Tom all the way to the Heights for a demon's egg in the first place? Unfortunately, Lyle, the Blue Claw's deceased leader, carried that information with him to his death.

"When I can answer those questions, then I'll feel able to relax."

"Yet you have your suspicions?"

"Not as such, no. All I can conclude is that there's another player in this game, someone who has yet to fully show his hand. My worry is: what might he be planning to do next?"

Two grey and ivory plumed gulls hoisted themselves into the air on hastily spread wings, voicing their displeasure at being disturbed in harsh, scalding tones. They were the only witnesses to the large, ovoid shape which slipped from the substation's pipe and headed for the deeper reaches of the river.

Insint's carapace boasted a few less bubbled bulges now. There were two further indentations which would never be filled again, but that was acceptable. The drones had carried out their task adequately, even though it had failed to achieve Insint's goal.

One of the Thair's more fearsome denizens approached him, rising from the river's depths; a tigeel, an extraordinarily large fish, capable of swimming far quicker than he could. An eel-like body with shark-like jaws, the great predator circled around him, first above, then below, presumably in an effort to size him up. After a few minutes of this it came in for a swifter pass, jaws opening to nip at the edge of his carapace. Insint sent a pulse of energy along his body, so that the fish got a taste of electricity as well as unyielding metal as it nipped him. The jolt was evidently enough, because the tigeel swam off into the murky depths in search of less demanding prey.

Insint didn't mind that the sun globe had failed to kill the boy nearly as much as he did the failure of the parasite to bring the City Below to its knees. That had been one of his greatest weapons, hoarded for decades and then deployed with great forethought at what he deemed the right moment, and now it had been squandered. That, he regretted. At least the dog master hadn't lived long enough to betray him.

Nor was the parasite his only weapon. There were other ways of bringing Thaiburley toppling down. He just needed to be patient, which was something he was expert at.

Next time, he would plan more carefully. And there would be a next time; that much he vowed.

ABOUT THE AUTHOR

Ian Whates lives in a comfortable home down a quiet cul-de-sac in an idyllic Cambridgeshire village, which he shares with his partner Helen and their pets – Honey the golden cocker spaniel; Calvin the tailless black cat; and Inky the goldfish (sadly, Binky died a few years ago).

Ian's first published stories appeared in the late 1980s, but it was not until the early 2000s that he began to pursue writing with any seriousness. In 2006 Ian launched independent publisher NewCon Press. That same year he also resumed selling short stories,including two to the science journal *Nature*.

Ian is currently a director of the Science Fiction Writers of America, and chair of the British Science Fiction Association. He is currently hard at work on this book's sequel, *City of Hope & Despair*, and also an SF novel.

www.ianwates.com

*The second book of the City of a
Hundred Rows series*, City of Hope &
Despair, *is coming soon. Here are the
first two chapters.*

Extras...

ONE

The Four Spoke Inn failed to be all manner of things.
It wasn't the cheapest place around, nor was it the
warmest, the most welcoming, the largest, the busiest,
not even the most convenient. Yet it was a little of all
of these. The landlord, Seth Bryant, was well aware of
this. He had long since come to terms with the
hostelry's strengths and limitations, determining to
make the most of the former while learning to live
with the latter.

Seth knew his clientele and what to expect of them.
Many were regulars, but, the inn being situated where
it was, just as many weren't. This was one of the things
he loved most about the place – it offered constant variety to spice up the underlying sense of stability, as
comfortable as a well-worn chair, provided by familiar
faces who could be counted on to appear more nights
than not, picking up on conversations begun the previous evening or the one before that as if the world had
stood still in between. There was little opportunity for
boredom to set in, for life to grow stale, because new
faces were ever imminent if not already arrived. Every

time the door swung open and an unfamiliar figure strode through, the dynamics of the tap room would shift – sometimes by only a subtle degree, but by no means always.

This particular evening the bar was dominated by a group of bargemen who sat clustered around the long table by the window. They weren't yet deep in their cups but a few of them were well on their way, the volume of the conversation from that part of the room rising steadily as the ale continued to flow. Ol' Jake had taken to scowling in their direction at regular intervals from his accustomed perch on a stool at the right-hand corner of the bar.

"Don't know why you put up with them," he said to Seth as the latter drew him a pint of darkly sweet Dancastre ale.

"Yes you do," Matty said from beside him. "It's for the sake of their coin, eh, Seth?"

The landlord smiled. "What can I say, Mat? You've got me bang to rights. The old women'll be whispering in each other's ears and word will spread like wildfire through Crosston and all the villages beyond – the shock of it! Respected innkeeper caught accepting honest coin in return for ale!"

Matty laughed and slapped Jake on the back.

His friend's scowl only deepened. "All well and good, but do you have to accept it from them?"

"If you want the inn to still be here so you can keep coming in and moaning about every new face that wanders in then yes, Jake; I have to take coin from whoever's willing to part with it. Besides, they're not that bad."

"So you say," the old man muttered into his beer.

There were nine in total crammed around the long table – the crew of two barges, all male. Seth knew this lot; they'd stopped here before. Not all did. Some stayed close to their boats, sleeping on the great vessels as well as working them, irrespective of how prosperous a trip might have been, but not this lot. Their owner-captains were happy to let the crews enjoy an evening's relaxation from time to time when a trip had gone especially well.

As long as their tankards were frequently replenished and nobody riled them, there would be no trouble from this mob, while the inn's coffers would benefit considerably from their custom. Seth had ensured they were in good hands – he'd asked Molly to make a point of looking after them and she had plenty of experience with the like; knew how much cleavage to show as she leant across to collect the empties and how much of a wiggle to give her hips as she walked away again, while she wouldn't take offence at their coarse humour or ribald comments and coped admirably with wandering hands. Thank goodness Bethany wasn't on tonight. Younger, slimmer, less buxom, and by most estimates a good deal prettier than Molly, that one had a sharp tongue on her and a habit of not standing for any nonsense.

With no one waiting to be served at present, Seth left his station at the bar and wandered over to where the bargemen sat. "Everything all right, lads?" Contented murmurings rippled around the table. "Molly looking after you, is she?" At this the murmurings grew louder and more enthusiastic, with a few appreciative chuckles thrown in for good measure. "If you're hungry at all, we've a few of this morning's catch left

– good plump sandfish, only a few, mind, which we serve basted in butter and lemon juice on a bed of fresh river samph – or there's some mutton stew, steeped in a rich ale gravy, and we've a fully mature Cabrian cheese if you'd prefer. That comes with home-baked bread and I might even find you some really spicy Delian pickle if you've a fancy." He smacked his lips at this last. "Just let Molly know when you want to order anything."

They assured him that they would and, with a final smile, Seth sauntered back towards the bar. He stopped en-route to exchange a few pleasantries with Lal and Si, who occupied their usual table in front of the hearth and were deeply absorbed in a game of checkers. No need to have the fire lit at this season, thank goodness, but this would form a cosy focal point later in the year as winter began to bite. Seth just hoped that, when it did, this winter would be milder than the last, which had been especially bitter, with even the Thair threatening to freeze over – something Seth had yet to see in his lifetime – icy skirts forming on both banks, though they failed to spread out and meet by covering the truly deep waters in between. A little chill could be good for business, encouraging people to seek solace in front of a roaring hearth while warming their hands around a cup of mulled wine or cider, but when it was that cold they generally stayed at home and battened down the hatches.

With a rueful shake of his head, Seth banished memories of such lean times and headed back towards the bar, where Matty looked ready for a refill, only to be stopped by two merchants at another table, who had evidently been discussing the origins of the inn's peculiar name and were hoping for some enlightenment.

Seth smiled, trying to do so without any hint of indulgence; this was hardly the first time such a question had been asked of him.

"There's been much speculation over the years on that very subject," he told the two men – younglings both; the youngest sons of noble families most probably, who, seeing no opportunity for rapid advancement at home, set out flushed with dreams of making their fortunes by ferrying goods common in one area to places where they were not, little considering how many had already trod that path before them and how rare it was to find such undiscovered or unexploited commodities.

"Some would have it," he continued, "that a vintner travelling from far Kathay suffered an accident on the road and, unable to make proper repairs, had to continue with one of his precious wagon's wheels badly damaged and only partially mended, so that it boasted just four spokes rather than the original six. Yet that patched-up wheel carried him for many leagues, finally giving out here, where the great trade road meets the Thair. Taking this as an omen and judging it a likely spot, he set up shop where the wagon foundered and proceeded to sell his wines, doing very well in the process and establishing this inn as a result.

"Others claim the place was established by four strong-willed brothers who determined to go into business together but could agree on little else, arguing about every pernickety detail, until they found this spot. For the first time, all four agreed that this was where they should establish an inn, which they did, naming the place to reflect the four strands of their divergent personalities – all of which led away from each other in every instant but came together here and here alone."

"And do you favour either of these origin tales, sir?"

Seth smiled. "Truth to tell, no. Both have their appeal yet strike me as fanciful. I prefer the more pragmatic theory."

"Which is?"

"Well, you'll see that the inn is situated on the great trade route, that mighty road of commerce which stretches from distant Deliia in the east to the Atlean Sea in the west, bisecting the continent like the corded belt around some lanky cleric's waist. It also stands on the banks of the mighty Thair, the river that stretches from fabled Thaiburley, the City of Dreams, in the south to the distant northern mountains. I believe that these are your four spokes, gentlemen: the road stretching in two opposing directions on the one hand, the river doing likewise on the other. Four passages to distant lands, representing the greatest trade routes in the world, all four conspiring to meet here, at the hub."

One of the young merchants laughed. "Good fortune for you, then, Landlord."

Seth nodded. "Good fortune indeed. Now, if you'll excuse me...?" He looked towards the bar, where Matty still waited.

"Yes, of course."

There was a deal of truth in what Seth had told the merchants, though by no means the whole truth. Few people alive knew or even suspected that, and Seth certainly had no intention of enlightening anyone. Best to let sleeping dogs lie, as far as he was concerned.

Having reached the bar without any further interruptions, he took Matty's battered pewter goblet, which the man insisted was reserved especially for him though Seth couldn't imagine why – it was as worn and sorry a piece of tat as you could imagine. Even when new the cup could hardly have been remarkable, yet Matty would drink from nothing else. Presumably for sentimental reasons, though Seth had to wonder whether any self-respecting sentiment would truly wish to be associated with such an uninspired piece of metalwork.

As he placed the brimming tankard down on the counter in front of Matty, the door swung open. Seth glanced up in time to witness the most beautiful man he had ever seen step inside. This was not a description he had ever expected to make about any man – beauty being something he considered to be sole property of the fairer sex – but it was the one word that sprang instantly to mind. The newcomer was tall, with golden blonde hair which seemed to have captured a stray sunbeam or two as a net might snare and hold an insect. He had piercing blue eyes and the sort of face which a truly gifted artist might aspire to produce one day, were he perhaps to render the image of a god. Despite being muffled beneath a heavy dark cloak, his physique looked to be well-toned and muscular.

All conversation ceased; even the bargemen went quiet and simply stared as this golden youth crossed to the bar, where Seth stood gaping.

"What can I get you, sir?" Seth asked, remembering his manners.

The eyes flashed with what... amusement? "I have a fancy for some wine, please, landlord; white." His voice matched the appearance: clear, fully masculine, yet a little higher than some might expect and with a lilting, almost musical quality. "Do you by any chance have any Abissian white – a bottle of sundew, ideally?"

Seth swallowed on a suddenly dry throat. The stranger had just asked for one of the rarest wines in existence, a label prized by connoisseurs irrespective of vintage. The given year made a difference of degree alone, not to whether the bottle cost a fortune. Nobody would think to order such a highly prized drink at a mere roadside tavern.

Correction: one person would.

Seth was glad to note that conversation had started up again in the room around him. It gave proceedings a welcome sense of normality as he smiled at this new-comer, this individual who had just uttered words he had never expected to hear, and said, "If you'd care to step into the back room, sir, I'll see what I can find."

This earned him a few odd looks from Matty and Ol' Jake as he ushered the golden youth behind the bar, but there was no helping that.

Glancing over his shoulder as he led the unusual vis-itor through the dimly lit hallway that led to the back room, Seth couldn't help but note that the dimness seemed dispelled by the youth's passage, almost as if the lad glowed with light. Once they were away from prying eyes and inquisitive ears, Seth turned to the stranger. "You have something to show me, I believe."

"Indeed."

The youth dipped a hand inside his voluminous cloak and emerged holding something; a quite unre-markable length of wood, roughly as long as a man's forearm, perhaps a little more. It was slightly broader and squared at one end, more rounded at the other, but nothing special, one might think.

Seth stared at the crudely turned stick as if this were the holiest of all relics being presented to him. He licked his lips and said, a little hoarsely, "The fifth spoke."

"Just so," the golden boy said, and then smiled. He reached up to the clasp at his throat and, with a shrug of broad shoulders, sent his cloak drifting to the floor. The garment dropped languidly, as if in slow motion – a curtain drawn to one side at some major unveiling. Beneath, he was naked from the waist up, revealing the toned, bronzed torso of a young woman's dream, every muscle perfectly defined and not an ounce of fat in evidence.

And then he spread his wings.

White and pure, they filled the room and more, unable to fully extend yet still magnificent. The light was unmistakable now, shining forth from the visitor in a blaze of golden glory.

Seth found that he had fallen to his knees. "What do you want of me?" he asked in a voice full of reverence. And the other proceeded to tell him.

The room felt oddly smaller once the visitor had departed, as if the youth had taken something more than simply his presence with him. For long seconds the man who had been calling himself Seth Bryant for more years than he cared to remember stood as if frozen, his attention focused on a single simple word which burned deeply in his thoughts; two fateful syllables he hoped passionately would never need to be uttered while fearing that they inevitably would, or why else had he been told them? Drawing a deep breath, he picked up a glass from the side, polished it,

and then poured out a generous measure of brandy
from the accompanying decanter. His continued absence would no doubt set tongues wagging back in the
tap room, but what if it did? He needed a few additional moments to compose himself before facing the
customers again. No one could blame him for that,
surely?

After all, it wasn't every day that a man came face
to face with a demon.

TWO

From the Streets Below to the Market Row,
From taverns and stalls to the Shopping Halls,
From trinkets so cheap to exclusive boutique,
From the Cloth-Makers' Row and people who sew,
To haberdashers, tailors, and upward we go…

His name was M'gruth and he was on a mission. Yet these were unsettled times. Brief days ago gangs of subverted street-nicks had rampaged through the City Below, looting and killing, throwing themselves into pitched battles with the City Watch while strange spider-like mechanisms haunted the shadows. Nothing like it had been seen since the War. The Maker was dead, the Dog Master was dead, and the street-nicks were now a broken force; it would be years before they could hope to re-establish their grip on the under-City and its trade, if ever. In the aftermath, territories were shifting, unexpected alliances had been forged and new powers had begun to emerge and flex their muscles, keen to fill the vacuum left by the street-nicks' demise. Any journey undertaken at such a time promised to be a hazardous one, as the various pretenders scrambled to establish a position of prominence in the new order.

Most chilling of all, the Blade had once again returned to the streets of the City Below.

So M'gruth's movements were governed by two conflicting imperatives: haste and caution.

But M'gruth was a professional. He had lived with such pressures all his life. His progress was therefore swift, while every move was considered and every shadow scrutinised.

As a result, he was not the wisest choice of target for an ambush, as the three over-confident nicks were about to discover to their cost. Over-confident, because they must have known who he was; not by name, perhaps, but certainly by generic type. After all, it was written all over his body. Yet still they were lying in wait.

The terrain was a broken one; derelict buildings and shattered homes – the former pens and living quarters, guard stations, cook houses, weapons stores, practice yards – all part of the enclave that had sprung up around the Pits. Empty now, abandoned when that hellhole closed down; gone to wrack and ruin and left to the mercies of looters and scroungers, local folk who had undoubtedly dismantled the buildings piece by piece, wasting little time in taking what they needed for their own homes. Death by increment; no more than anywhere associated with the Pits deserved.

He ducked down behind a partially demolished wall, heading at a right angle to his original course. Crouching low and moving quickly, he circled and came up behind the first kid while the would-be ambushers must still have been wondering what had de-layed him, where he'd gone to. The lad had a crude sling in one hand and a pile of half a dozen oval stones beside him. The weapon was made from braided rope, even to the pocket in which the shot would sit. M'-gruth crept up unnoticed, tapped the kid on the shoulder and, as the wide-eyed boy turned quickly around, waggled an admonishing finger in the lad's face as he struck him hard across the forehead, using the pommel of his sword as a cudgel.

Transferring the blade to his left hand, M'gruth then took up the sling from where the unconscious nick had dropped it and fitted one of the stones into the vacant pocket. Peering beyond the small heap of rubble the kid had chosen to hide behind, he saw the second nick, now standing straight, craning his neck to try and spot the man the group were intending to ambush.

M'gruth whipped the sling round and around, only a couple of times, before letting fly. Perhaps the nick heard the sling slicing through the air as it spun or even the missile hurtling towards him, certainly he looked around just in time to meet the stone head-on. Two down.

The third, closer than the second and doubtless alerted by the collapse of his mate, raised his head and stared at M'gruth, who smiled and lifted his arm, hand still clutching the sling.

"Are you mad? See these?" and he rotated the arm, displaying the continuous pattern of ochre tattoos that ran up the limb before disappearing beneath his shirt to re-emerge at his neck and run on to adorn the bald pate of his head. "I'm a Tattooed Man for Thaiss' sake! Did you really think the three of you could take me?"

"S...sorry." The nick was backing away, fear obvious in every contour of his body.

"I don't have time to deal with you properly now, so breck off!" This last the Tattooed Man yelled.

The boy needed no further encouragement, but immediately turned and ran, almost tripping over his own feet in his haste to escape. M'gruth smiled. The irony of being attacked here of all places hadn't escaped him. He'd enjoyed this little diversion, for all that it had caused him a momentary delay. The thought brought his focus firmly back to the mission, and he hurried on.

If he were ever asked to name one place in the world he would least like to return to, this would be it; but needs must. He was now in the very shadow of that detested theatre of blood known as the Pits.

A moment later and he was passing under the arena's walls, something he had vowed never to do again.

He heard them before he saw them. Sounds that came rolling down the tunnel like echoes from a past he had tried so hard to forget. Sounds that sent cold shivers tingling down his spine, causing him to falter, to stumble to a halt for a second with his eyes closed. For a moment he was back there, sword clasped tightly in his hand, guts screwed up in a knot of terror and heart pumping with both fear and anticipation, as he wondered whether this was to be the day he died. It was the sound of combat that had halted him; the harsh clash of steel meeting steel, the gritty shuffle of feet manoeuvring for better balance, the grunt of expelled air from extreme exertion as muscles powered an attack or strained to repulse one. M'gruth gathered himself and ran on, reassured that he was not yet too late and afraid that if he delayed any longer he might be.

He burst from the tunnel into a large amphitheatre, flanked by curving banks of seats to all sides – crude wooden benches, many of which were now broken or absent entirely, presumably scavenged for material and fuel like the buildings outside since it wasn't that long ago the place had closed down. Other than that, this was much as he remembered it. The Pits, where people paid to see men die, and where friend was forced to slaughter friend simply to survive. M'gruth had always imagined that, if viewed from above, the arena and its seating would resemble some wide-opened mouth screaming obscenities to the heavens, those on the floor of the Pit a snack about to be swallowed by that unholy maw.

On this occasion the snack in question consisted of two women, girls really, though it was often hard to remember the fact, especially when you saw them like this, with knives drawn and battle joined. Both were dressed in black, even down to the leather boots, belts and accoutrements. Occasional flashes of silver studwork the only relief. The two girls wove an intricate dance of flowing limbs and flashing steel in the centre of the arena, strikes and counter strikes that challenged the eye to keep pace. M'gruth was a Tattooed Man – the fiercest warriors in the City Below, yet even he was dazzled by the speed of attack and riposte before him.

One of the girls was marginally larger than the other and perhaps a few years older, though the difference was slight and seemed to have had little impact on the fight as yet. Both were covered in a sheen of sweat and had suffered minor cuts, where blades had kissed against flesh and drawn blood, though presumably without causing any real damage, since neither seemed in any way hampered. Another thing that was impossible to ignore was how alike the pair looked.

M'gruth knew them both, respected and even perhaps feared them both, and at one time or other he had called each his friend.

The task that had been entrusted to him was a thankless one, though not impossible, or so he hoped. His job was to stop these two lethal girls from killing each other in a senseless fight. Each thought they couldn't carry on living while the other did; neither had yet stopped to consider how difficult it might be to live without their counterpart. Sisters. He was just glad he'd never had one.

"Stop it, both of you!" His shout sounded small and impotent even to his own ears, a mere whimper which was instantly swallowed by the vastness of this place, so he tried again, louder this time. "I said stop it!"

"Breck off!" Kat, the slighter of the two snarled without sparing him a glance, too intent upon her opponent.

"What are you doing here, M'gruth?" the other asked, without pausing in the fight.

"For Thaiss' sake, listen to me will you? She's back. The Soul Thief is back."

The two girls froze. For long seconds neither moved, though their gazes remained unflinchingly fastened on each other.

"You sure about this?" the older, larger girl said at length.

"Positive. Now will you both stop this madness?"

Slowly, ever so slowly, weapons were lowered, though neither girl stood straight, neither gave ground, and their eyes never wavered.

The older girl, Chavver, was the first to stand up, gradually abandoning her fighter's crouch. As her sister warily followed suit, Chavver looked at the Tattooed Man for the first time – if a glare infused with such fury could ever be considered a mere look – and said, "If this is some sort of trick to stop us from killing each other, M'gruth, you're a dead man."

He didn't doubt it for a minute.

Brace yourself for
CITY OF HOPE & DESPAIR
coming soon from Angry Robot.

angryrobotbooks.com

ANGRY
ROBOT

Teenage serial killers
Zombie detectives
The grim reaper in love
Howling axes **Vampire
hordes** Dead men's
clones The Black Hand
Death by cellphone
Gangster shamen
Steampunk swordfights
Sex-crazed bloodsuckers
Murderous gods
Riots **Quests** Discovery
Death

Prepare
to welcome
your new
Robot overlords.

angryrobotbooks.com